FRESH WATER FROM BEN GILE POND

EARL YORKE

Lucky Bat Books

A Lucky Bat Book

Fresh Water from Ben Gile Pond

Cover Design: Brandon Swann

ISBN: 978-1-943588-06-0

LuckyBatBooks.com

10 9 8 7 6 5 4 3 2 1

For Ryan

BLACK
CHRISTMAS

BAMPY HAD ALWAYS told Carl not to drink the rainwater, that whatever had infected it would eat him apart from the inside until he was violently defecating and vomiting blood. Bampy wasn't entirely right though. He had been too cautious because he could remember how things were in Maine before it all happened, before the water became unsafe for all living creatures except for the plants.

He had still been attached to a time when hope was a real thing, not something out of a fable long abandoned by people who didn't bother to learn how to read anymore.

Those who had been born after the change knew better. The rainwater was perfectly safe to drink, it just couldn't be allowed to touch the soil. If it was captured in a clean container, it was just fine. But people of Bampy's generation didn't trust it. In fact, they didn't trust *anything*.

So, in a way it was both poetic and tragic how Bampy's decision to show trust in a human being outside of their group for the first time in more than thirty years would ultimately lead to his death; that a single moment of compassion and caring in a world far removed from such odd and precarious behavior would see him gunned down, and the rest of them forced out of their home into the wilderness.

"Come along, Carl," Zoey urged.

Carl turned back toward the group, watching as his sister jiggled her overburdened backpack around on her shoulders. With an exasperated sigh, she reached under the pack and yanked down on her gray thermal, straightening the wrinkles he could see bunched up on her shoulders. His mother and father moved slowly up the trail, neither of them looking back.

He started after them, his steps slowing as he paused once again for another look back at the only home he had ever known. He gazed at the still water of Dodge Pond. At the far end stood the old Rangeley House. Their home.

Just one last look. That was all he wanted. The problem was that he had taken *several* last looks, and not a single one of them had brought about the feelings he sought. He wanted closure, some kind of overwhelming confirmation that what they were doing was the right thing.

"*Carl!*" Zoey growled. "We don't have *time* for this!"

With a frustrated sigh, he turned his back on Dodge Pond for the last time and hurried after his family. All he could do was hope that things might somehow sort themselves out in his mind as he and the others walked toward whatever awaited them in the backwoods of Maine.

"You're not even the smallest bit upset that we have to go?" he asked, catching up with his older sister. The trail, frequented by snowmobiles and various other all-terrain vehicles back in the days when gasoline was still obtainable, was just wide enough to accommodate two people walking side by side. Mom and Dad, as equally loaded up with gear as he and Zoey, walked some fifteen feet ahead with their black-and-white terrier/border collie mix, Tripp, taking the lead. The dog operated well enough off leash, sticking close by with frequent backward glances to make sure that his "pack" was still with him.

"Have you been drinking from the pond?" she said, using one of Bampy's favorite phrases, a phrase that loosely meant *are you nuts*? "We have no other choice."

"That doesn't mean you have to be okay with it."

"Carl, Zoey," Dad said, his voice low and firm, "keep it down." Ahead, Tripp stopped with one of his front paws curled up. He looked inquisitively back at them before trotting on down the trail.

That was the end of the conversation for a while, and Carl was perfectly okay with it. He had gotten the last word in, and judging by the look on Zoey's face, his point had stuck. At any other time this would have brought a smile to his face, but he was far too upset to bask in his victory. They lumbered along the overgrown trail, pushing aside branches from the ambitious evergreens that had retaken the pathway here and there.

It wasn't long before he was hit with the guilt of what he had just done. What, exactly, had he been looking to accomplish? He studied the look of despair on her face. Her brown eyes stayed on the ground as they walked through the yellow October grasses, their boots crackling through the autumn leaves carpeting the ground. The earthy, spiced scents of slow decay representative of the season rose up around them. Carl suddenly realized his sister had repressed all thoughts of the home they'd been forced at gunpoint to abandon, whereas he couldn't keep his mind off the place. Too much. Too soon.

And he had pushed her down into that hole.

"I'm sorry," he whispered, laying his arm over her shoulders as best he could. His fingers caught momentarily in her snarly, black ponytail before he managed to work his arm into the space between her neck and her backpack. As they walked he used his free hand to shove aside more branches. It was awkward to maintain the contact, but he was able to make it work long enough that she finally reached up and patted his forearm.

"Me, too," she said, blinking. A few tears trickled down her dirty cheeks.

Carl had no doubt the tears were for Bampy and not the house. He thought for a moment about helping her work through it, but quickly decided against it. He'd caused enough problems

already. Mom would probably put together some kind of me-
morial as soon as they stopped for the night (she was good with
those kinds of things), but for the time being it was important
that they keep their attention on getting out of Rangeley.

Tripp stopped dead in his tracks, prompting the rest of them
to do the same. As a family dog he had a lot of great uses when it
came to keeping morale high, but he was also a working dog, and
the thing he did best was let them know when danger was near.
Not that they had ever strayed very far from the Rangeley House.

It was incredibly rare to encounter anything wandering
about on hooves or paws anymore. The animals didn't seem to
understand that the water wasn't safe for consumption unless it
was first boiled. Add to that the fact that different water sources were affected in different ways, and you came to understand
why people fought so dearly to remain where they were once
roots were put down in places like Dodge Pond. As far as the
Richmond family knew, all major sources of water, regardless of
their levels of contamination, were fought over. There were even
stories in the early years of independent militias springing up
around major lakes and rivers, taking control, and limiting the
amount of water local residents could take home to boil.

Oddly enough, trees and other plants were not affected by
the tainted water. In fact, they seemed to have flourished since
Black Christmas when it all started.

Dad dropped to one knee, pulling his Remington .308 from
where he had it slung over his shoulder. Taking the rifle in hand,
he pulled back on the bolt, then slid a round into the chamber.
His gaze stayed on Tripp the entire time as the fur on the dog's
back lifted and his lips curled in a snarl.

Not one of them said a thing to the dog. No one wanted to
excite him to the point where he started barking.

The trail ahead curled up the side of a mountain. Carl studied
the pathway in the dull afternoon light that filtered through the
gray clouds, watching for the briefest flicker of movement. He

held his breath and listened, though not a single sound could be heard in the still forest. There wasn't even a light breeze to ruffle the leaves on the ground.

He glanced at Zoey, who had come out of her despair, at least for the moment. Though he was certain she noticed him looking at her, her gaze stayed fixed on Tripp.

Carl glanced back over his shoulder at the tiny bits of Dodge Pond that could still be seen through slits in the trees. With a deep breath he turned back to the trail, resting his attention on the dog. Tripp started to relax a bit, the hair settling down on his back and his body loosening up. Tripp yawned and turned to Dad, looking to see what was expected of him now that he was satisfied that whatever he had heard was gone—or more realisti-cally—had never existed at all.

Dad slowly unlocked the bolt on the rifle and slid it backward. He caught the shell as it was expelled from the chamber. Leaving the chamber open, he pocketed the shell, engaged the safety, and slung the rifle back over his shoulder. He moved slowly to his feet. Carl released his breath in a loud exhale as Tripp trotted on down the trail. Carl followed his family at a slower pace, his mind once again pondering the circumstances that had set their feet on this path . . .

. . . The Rangeley House had been Bampy's old camp, his vaca-tion cabin in the backwoods of Maine. When Black Christmas hit he packed up his family and took them there, figuring it was the most remote location he was familiar with. It didn't hurt that he owned the property, too. It was right on a body of water that would remain less contested than most of the more notable lakes and ponds around the state. Dad was Carl's age at the time. Though he rarely spoke of it, it wasn't entirely impossible for him to open up about Black Christmas.

For some reason, fate would have it that he'd been speaking of Black Christmas the very day their life in the Rangeley House came to an end.

They were arranged in their usual spots—Dad sitting in his corner chair beside the brick fireplace with a kettle of boiling water suspended on a spit over an open flame; Mom in the kitchen at the back in her tattered, white apron, putting some rice and Brussels sprouts together for supper; and Bampy sitting on the worn old couch with Carl and Zoey, stretched out and relaxed, his long, white hair untamed and wild. It had been a good year for their vegetable harvest. Most of the harvest had been pickled using the cider vinegar that Mom put up the previous fall. Given the camp's place in the woods, far off what remained of the highway, their gardens and small orchard remained relatively untouched. As a precaution they kept as much of the area enshrouded in camouflage netting as possible to avoid drawing the attention of any wandering vagrants. The gardens were their main source of food, producing an abundance of fruit and vegetables—much more so than gardens had produced prior to Black Christmas. The plants seemed to love the tainted water.

"Cold enough for a fire," Dad said, poking at the coals with the wrought iron poker. "Lucky it's such a dreary day or we'd be waiting for nightfall to get warm." He took a deep breath and stared into the open flames as a light frown came across his face. "The snow'll be flying soon."

"Time to dig in and get used to the taste of brine again," Bampy said, reaching over and tousling Carl's shoulder-length black hair.

Carl scowled and moved his head away from his grandfather's hand. He hated it when Bampy treated him like a little boy. He was almost sixteen, old enough to carry an adult share of the chores.

Bampy grinned and turned back to Dad. "Right about now your mother would be getting all her Christmas decorations out. Blast the warlords of this world who stole *that* holiday from you kids." He looked back and forth between Carl and Zoey as he scratched his chest through his black-and-red checkered flannel shirt.

"The kids are better off," Dad said. "Happy things like that would just confuse people now. Besides . . . I don't think I'd be able to look at a Christmas tree in the same way as we did back then."

Zoey sat up and rested her elbows on her knees. Her interest, like Carl's, was piqued. The fire cast flickering shadows along the knotty pine walls. The trace amounts of dull daylight that managed to get through the boarded-up windows did little to diminish the brilliance of the orange flames. Carl waited expectantly for either Dad or Bampy to speak.

"Because of Black Christmas?" Zoey asked. She looked surprised to have actually asked the question and Carl choked back a laugh. Zoey gave a nervous shrug and shrank back against the couch.

"That night," Dad said, shocking everyone in the room as he moved into his story. Generally, he had to be in a mood before he started talking about Black Christmas, a mood that often involved pulling out a bottle of the vodka Mom made from potatoes. "Every bit of my childhood was stolen in an instant. Neither of you kids could possibly know how big a deal Christmas was back then." His gaze shifted between them as Carl leaned forward. "You remember when I told you about what *money* was?"

Carl nodded.

"Well, this was a time of year when people would often spend all the money they had on presents for others," Dad said, looking at Bampy.

The old man nodded, and a few stray locks of his long, silver hair fell into his face. He pushed them back into place and remained silent.

"Like food?" Carl asked, not willing to divulge that he didn't really understand exactly what money was. He barely understood what a *present* was. Dad had said that a present was a gift, but as far as their family was concerned, gifts didn't translate into material possessions. Another day alive with a small amount of food in his belly was a gift, at least in this world, and it was not given by a single person. It was given by the world itself.

"In some cases, yes," Dad answered, shifting the coals around in preparation for adding another log to the fire. "But mostly things like . . ." Carl studied his father as he trailed off, then started again. "Like . . . clothes and tools, only brand-new—store-bought."

Carl nodded, though he still didn't fully understand. He knew both Dad and Bampy would get depressed if either of them went into detail about the times when they could simply slap a paper note down on a counter and walk out with bags full of food or new clothes made by people they would never meet.

"So, when everyone had their presents, they would wrap the gifts in pretty paper and put them underneath a fir tree in their house so that they could be opened on Christmas Day."

"They brought a tree inside the house?" Carl asked, confused but not truly surprised. People did a lot of strange things back then.

"Yes."

"Why?" Zoey asked.

Dad thought on this for a moment before turning away from the fire and looking at Bampy. Bampy shrugged.

"I suppose we never really thought about it," Dad finally said. "It was just our tradition . . . the normal thing to do at that time of year. Seems a little silly now, but we'd string lights and popcorn and cranberries on the tree, and we'd decorate the branches with various ornaments made of glass."

Carl frowned and Dad seemed to sense his confusion.

"Popcorn was a snack we used to eat. Corn kernels were first dried, then heated. They would pop open and . . . well, I'm not really sure how to describe it. I sure do miss it. Don't get me started on butter."

"What happened on the night of Black Christmas?" Zoey asked, obviously trying to refocus her father. Dad often needed such a push. It wasn't unusual for him to run off on tangents with regard to the various types of food they would eat in the old days. If Carl heard the word *hamburger* one more time, he'd probably throw a fit.

Dad leaned the poker against the brick hearth and placed another log in the dwindling flames. He rubbed at his face with calloused hands before smoothing down his long, black hair and continuing. "Bampy and Gram took me to my grandparents' house for Christmas Eve dinner and the family party we had each year. I remember being so excited. I'd wanted some kind of video game system, and it was all I could think about. There was no way for me to be sure that I was even going to get it, but I had a feeling." He chuckled. "I sure asked enough for it. Gram had started to shut me up every time I mentioned it. Funny . . . I can't for the life of me remember what it was called." He looked at Bampy, who shrugged again.

Zoey looked as confused as Carl felt. He had no idea what a video game was, but Dad moved on without explaining.

"On Christmas Eve it was always impossible to fall asleep," he continued with a quick smile that lit up his clean-shaven face. "The excitement of all the new stuff waiting for us the next day was too much. I could never stop thinking about it. I'd try to wake Bampy and Gram up at three a.m. sometimes."

"Yeah, and we sent you back to bed every time." Bampy chuckled.

"I suppose you did," Dad said, obviously finding it a bit more difficult to remember than Bampy. "Anyway, it was Bampy and Gram who woke *me* up that year. Along with the explosions at the shipyard."

"We were just far enough away to escape the blasts," Bampy added.

"It didn't *feel* like we were far away," Dad said. He shook his head and took a deep breath. "Imagine going to sleep, excited as you've ever been and expecting to wake up to a day of joy and celebration . . . and instead you're shaken awake by frantic parents as the world around you falls apart. Before you have a chance to get a handle on what's going on, you're thrown into a car and are speeding north as everything explodes around you . . ."

He trailed off, and Carl stared into the fire, trying to imagine what Dad was talking about. He wasn't old enough to have ever seen an operating car and neither was Zoey. They had seen the rusted-out heaps that were once functioning vehicles, but that was about as far as it went. If they were to see something like Dad was talking about, it would probably frighten them so badly that they'd die of a heart attack.

"All the way up to camp we saw more explosions," Bampy said, taking over. He scratched at the white stubble on his face. "We were so scared. The only stop we made was off of I-95—this was a major highway for cars back then—right outside of Portland. The city was already leveled, and what was left of it was in flames—"

"That's where they picked me up," Mom said from the kitchen. She walked over to the kettle of boiling water with a small cooking pot to fill.

"Hard not to stop and pick up a poor little girl sitting on her own on the shoulder of a major highway," Bampy said, smiling warmly at her. He looked back at Carl and Zoey. "It was your Gram who insisted we stop."

"It seems like forever ago," Mom sighed, dipping her pot into the large kettle and coming up with some water. Carl watched, his attention shifting briefly away from Bampy, as she brought the water to her face and inhaled deeply, making sure that the sour smell of rotted onions—a tell-tale sign of tainted water—was not present. All infected water shared this reek, which diminished and almost disappeared entirely if allowed to boil long enough.

"Seems like a different life," Dad added.

"What happened?" Carl asked, scratching at his faded, torn blue jeans and pulling down the sleeves of his red thermal shirt. "What caused the explosions, I mean?"

Bampy's answer was hardly the one Carl was looking for. Carl had asked this same question countless times in one way or another and the response had always been pretty much the same.

"Government," Bampy growled, his voice dripping with rancor. "Nothing more than a failed experiment that gave the impression that it was working for a couple of centuries, but was always destined to obliterate our race."

"I don't understand," Carl said. He looked at Zoey as if she might perhaps clue him in, but her attention remained on Bampy. Carl knew that she could feel his eyes on her, yet she chose to ignore him. It was reasonable to surmise that she also had no idea what the old man was talking about, but she wasn't willing to share this fact with him. This was typical Zoey, unwavering in her endeavors to avoid showing any kind of ignorance or vulnerability.

"And you're better off because of it," Bampy said, seemingly having no qualms about leaving Carl in the dark. He would go to great lengths to make sure that Carl and Zoey knew what a refrigerator and a smart phone had been, but he refused to elaborate on this topic.

"We came up over the Height of the Land lookout, overlooking Mooselookmeguntic Lake, just as the sun was throwing some color into the sky," Dad said. The fire popped, sending a burning coal toward his legs. He expertly swatted the coal back at the hearth, avoiding burning more holes in his already threadbare jeans. Clothing was so scarce that they had learned to be just as protective of their clothes as they were of their food. Dad scooped the coal up with the wrought iron ash shovel and tossed the smoldering ember back into the fire, continuing as if nothing had happened. "There hadn't been any more fires or explosions since we passed the burning paper mills in Mexico—that's the town in Maine, not the country down south. At that time the water was still safe to drink. Whatever contaminated our water didn't show up for another couple of months.

"I remember we came into Oquossoc—about two or three miles from here—and Bampy broke into the hardware and gun shop. He took the .308 and all the camo netting we now have strung around the place, and he probably took a few other things as well," Dad said, raising his eyebrows at his father.

"I've never stolen anything in my life," Bampy insisted. "I left four hundred dollars *cash* next to the register."

"That was money, right?" Zoey asked.

"That's right, girlie," Bampy replied.

"In any event," Dad said, "we loaded up the car and brought everything here. Aside from a few grocery trips in the months before the water turned, we've never left. After those first couple months . . . well, let's just say that as the world changed, people changed, too. People can turn into monsters when they're struggling to stay alive. It's a good thing the plants started growing so fast. Had our camp road not been swallowed up by the trees and ferns around it, I fear that we would have been spotted by now. We've been very lucky."

Bampy nodded. He gently patted Carl on the back. "Don't you ever forget, boy—the only way to stay alive in this world is to dig in and stay safe. I can only imagine what people have resorted to for food over these last thirty years, and I don't care to mention it here."

Pots clanged in the kitchen behind them. "Just a little longer on the rice and sprouts," Mom said, effectively ending their talk about Black Christmas. "James, you can take that water off the fire before too much of it evaporates."

Evaporate. That was an old-world word . . . like *grocery* or *phone.* Carl and Zoey had come to know a lot of those words, but their favorites were the old-world phrases like *hold your horses.* They understood that meant to slow down, but neither of them had ever seen a single horse, and based on how large the animals seemed when described by Dad or Bampy, it didn't sound as though Carl could easily pick one up and hold it like a rabbit.

"Yes, ma'am," Dad responded, pulling on his heavy gloves and lifting the kettle off the fire. He placed the steaming kettle next to the fireplace on a stone slab reserved just for this purpose. "Fit enough for the pope to drink."

Bampy laughed. *Pope* was a word Carl hadn't heard before and he made a mental note of it. He did not ask what the word meant, though he assumed it referred to someone important. Like a *king*, another commonly referenced item from the old world.

Among the plethora of old-world words and references that were constantly flung around in the camp between those over forty, there was one word that Carl vaguely remembered. A word that hadn't been used in a very long time.

That word was God . . .

TWO

CARL MARCHED FOR what felt like hours. The path wove through the woods, split into a fork, and continued on until it hit another fork. At each fork, Dad took the route that appeared least traveled. Like Bampy leading Dad, Gram, and Mom away from the horrors of Black Christmas, Dad did not allow any breaks until they were far enough into the woods to avoid making contact with another soul. At one point, the trail became two gravel ruts, running side by side through whatever vegetation happened to be the most dominant.

Dad gave no indication that he knew where they were going. As far as Carl knew, his father hadn't strayed more than a mile from the Rangeley House. Ever. It seemed obvious that he had made the decision to push deep into the woods to hopefully find a more isolated place for them to start over. This made sense on a certain level, but if Carl had learned anything from recent events, it was that no place was truly safe.

Carl watched with slowly mounting anxiety as Tripp lifted his nose in the air just as they emerged from a row of white pine and prickly spruce.

"Leash him," Dad snapped.

Carl removed a length of rope from the right breast pocket of his black-and-green checked flannel shirt. Untangling the rope, he called Tripp and waited for the dog to approach. The dog obeyed without protest, trotting over and allowing Carl to loop the rope around his neck.

Before them lay a grassy meadow, browning with the changing season. The rich, earthy smells of decaying leaves which had been so pervasive in the forest had been replaced with the scent of dry grass. A breeze cooled the sweat on Carl's brow and he studied the area, trying to figure out what had caught Tripp's attention. Overhead, the sky was darkening as the sun started its trip down toward the tips of the western mountains. The gravel ruts they'd been following were almost hidden beneath the knee-length grass.

Carl couldn't see anything that indicated there was water close by, the primary reason to put Tripp back on his leash. If the dog was left to his own impulses, he would almost certainly walk up to any standing source of water and drink freely and they couldn't allow that. Carl had heard the stories about how generation after generation of pups had found their way to the pond. Tripp was the last living dog in the line of Bampy and Gram's old house pets—Gambit, a wirehaired terrier and Sasha, a border collie. Considering how deeply inbred he was, it was a wonder he was so sharp.

"Can you smell it, Dad?" Zoey asked, lifting her nose into the air as Tripp had.

"No," Dad whispered, holding out his hand in a "keep your voices low" signal. Zoey nodded and Dad cupped a hand to his ear, gesturing for them to listen closely.

At first Carl could hear only the light breeze that had picked up a few hours into their march. It whispered through the trees behind him, rustling pine needles and amber-colored leaves both on the ground and still on the trees. The spicy scents of pitch, sap, and soil reached his nose.

He listened harder, shutting out the obvious sounds. After a minute or so, he was able to isolate the weak trickling of a brook. The water was too far away for anyone except Tripp to smell.

"A brook?" Carl asked, breaking the silence.

Dad shrugged. "Probably, but I can't really tell. Keep the dog leashed and stay sharp—where there's water there might be people."

Dad was generally what Bampy called "a cool-headed man," always taking plenty of time to think things through and often being overly cautious. Considering how far into the woods they were, odds were high that there weren't many people about.

Carl meticulously studied the meadow as Dad led them forward again. Tripp stayed at Carl's side as he walked, not pulling or making any kind of attempt to break free. The dog trotted happily along one of the gravel ruts, cutting through the tunnel of grass, staring occasionally up at Carl, his moustache of wiry black-and-white fur curling around the top of his muzzle.

The trail twisted through the meadow until it reached a slow-moving brook. Growing from the muddy shallows were a number of tightly grouped plants consisting of wispy, brown leaves that fluttered gently in the breeze. Interspersed among the leaves were dozens of yellowing reeds rising rigidly out of the water, thick, brown pods bursting with cottony white fluff at their tops. Carl immediately recognized the plants as cattails, and cattails meant one thing: food. His stomach growled at the very thought of eating, and suddenly he was aware of how hungry he was.

The family had cultivated cattails at the edge of Dodge Pond. Along with the multitude of vitamins that were found in the wild-growing plant, the plants were also an excellent source of starch and nutrition. Gram had taught Mom all about cattails and Mom had made sure both he and Zoey knew how to get the most out of them. The fact that the cattails before them were untouched was a good sign that they were alone.

"Long past the point of pollination," Mom said. "Too late in the season." She turned around and smiled. "But the roots should still be good."

Again, Carl's stomach growled.

Dad nodded and took a long glance around the field. Carl could tell he was still nervous. "Pull as many as you can, Kelly. Carl, Zoey, help your mother."

Carl handed Tripp off to his father and went about removing his boots and socks as his mom and sister did the same. As his bare feet touched down upon the sharp, stiff blades of grass at the edge of the water, he could almost hear Bampy grumbling and his heart sank.

On the list of Bampy's many baseless theories regarding the water was the idea that it was unsafe to expose your skin to any water that hadn't been boiled. A simple splash could mean sickness for days, but to outright submerge a body part spelled certain doom. The truth, however, was that it was perfectly okay to enter the water as long as you avoided getting any in your eyes, nose, ears, and especially your mouth. Mom had discovered this rather ironically while harvesting cattail pollen in her teens. Carl loved hearing the story about how poorly placed feet on the rocks around the pond had sent her sliding into the water, leaving her in a tizzy for days, certain she was going to die. When she didn't so much as develop a case of the snivels, she reevaluated Bampy's theory and put it to the test with another dip in Dodge Pond. She didn't get sick. Though Bampy insisted that it was a fluke, and that she should avoid such risks in the future (he even got Gram to harp on it), she stubbornly adhered to her own logic.

Carl struggled to push Bampy out of his mind as he rolled up the bottoms of his jeans and made his way into the brook with the women. A shiver ran through his body and his skin erupted in gooseflesh.

Judging by the chilly temperature of the water, they were probably into late October. Though Carl only loosely understood what Dad referred to as a *calendar* system, the family measured time in months. Since Gram hadn't started marking the days until well after they were established at Rangeley, the system relied mostly on the flux of the seasons for verification. When he associated the water temperature with the month of October it could easily have been November.

In any event, the water was cold and a little biting. More so the deeper his feet sank into the mud. Add to this the putrid stench of spoiled onions from the tainted water, and he had every reason to hurry with his harvest.

He carefully unbuttoned the sleeves of his flannel shirt, making sure not to put any extra pressure on the stitching. Rolling up his sleeves, he wasted no time wading over to the closest stalk and taking hold of its base. He wriggled the stalk back and forth while gently pulling upward so as not to break the plant before the root came clear of the muck. It was a slow process, but every botched extraction meant more time spent in the water.

Within a few minutes they had managed to toss more than twenty bulging, muddy roots into the grass at the edge of the brook. With each toss of his own, Carl looked at his father, whose attention shifted between the surrounding area and supervising the harvest. When they had collected about thirty or so roots, Dad instructed them to stop and get to work on cleaning and packing.

Carl sloshed his way through the cold murk back onto the stiff grass, happy to be out of the water. Turning about, he reached down to help his mother and sister. As Mom came out of the water she thanked him with a warm, loving smile before planting a kiss on his forehead. Her lips were notably chapped. Zoey was less affectionate, offering a nod with the left corner of her lips rising in a half smile. They went to work, splashing as much mud as possible off the harvested roots, each of which were long and twisted and brown with a number of smaller white roots extending from the sides like wire bristles.

A brief whine from Tripp interrupted their cleaning. Carl felt a pang of anxiety bubble up in his gut and immediately looked around. He scowled when he realized the dog merely wanted to get over to the stinky water for a drink. Dad gave Tripp a light slap in the spot where his tail met with his hindquarters, and that was the end of Tripp's outburst.

When the harvest was as clean as it was going to get, Carl unclipped the flap on his brown backpack and pushed things aside to make room for the roots. His mother and sister helped him load up, wrapping the roots in one of Carl's old sweatshirts, and within a number of minutes they were back on the trail again, marching north with the sun already behind the tall peaks to their left. It couldn't be too much longer before they stopped to make camp for the night, but Carl knew that Dad intended to put as much distance as he could between his family and the man who had taken everything from them, William Dewoh.

Once again, Carl's mind started to wander . . .

. . . With no natural predators around, Mom's flock of hens didn't require a rooster for protection. This was a good thing. Roosters were loud, and the family didn't need attention of any kind drawn to the Rangeley House. Because of this, with every new generation of chicks they raised, they would slaughter every male bird when they got to be three months' old—with the exception of those kept for breeding. If the birds started showing signs in their saddle feathers or comb before that time, they would naturally be dispatched, plucked, and eaten sooner. To maintain control, the breeding of their flock was very carefully orchestrated. A couple of roosters were placed with about ten hens. They were kept in an old, semi-detached garage that had been converted from a place to house vehicles into a place to house chickens. It was the perfect spot as it was indoors and helped to muffle the clucks, cackles, and bocks that they made. After these trysts ran their course, some thirty or forty chicks were hatched. The roosters used to breed them were promptly slaughtered.

The system was a good one, but like most things in this world, it wasn't perfect. While it was not common for a rooster to start crowing before four or five months, they got the occasional early bloomer and would find themselves startled awake by the sounds of a male bird greeting the sun. After that it was a mad scramble outside to reward the overachieving adolescent with a cleaver to the neck.

Though the odds, as Carl liked to say, were in their favor that nobody would be within earshot during such events (of which he'd been around for two), it just so happened that when it occurred this last time, someone outside of their family had been around, though they hadn't known it.

Carl heard the rooster through the walls of his bedroom. It started low, almost like a growl, before rising into a shrill cry. He flew out of bed, slipping out of the worn comforters like a snake shedding its skin and bolted toward his bedroom door. He staggered into the hallway that joined the camp proper with the two-car garage. Both his and Zoey's rooms were off this hallway.

The yellow light of the morning sun shone through the slits in the boards that covered the hallway windows. Carl didn't usually get up this early, but he was certainly up now. His mind set firmly on the rooster, he was barely conscious of his bare feet as he flew down the hallway toward the living room where either Dad or Bampy had already set out wood for that evening's fire. They were the first ones up every day, and judging by the absence of the cleaver in the kitchen, were probably outside looking for their target. He made his way out onto the gravel driveway and paused, rocks digging into the pads of his bare feet.

As if on cue the rooster cried out once more, though its voice was more panicked and erratic. Carl was once again on the move, followed by Zoey as she raced through the kitchen door and tailed him around the side of the camp. They rounded the garage and saw Dad and Bampy in the pen of chicken wire that contained the flock. The pen sprouted from the side of the garage like a bad blister and was nailed at various intervals to a circle of supporting pine trees. The men had already taken hold of the bird and had it pinned to the ground as it flapped its wings and squawked. Above them, Mom steadied herself, the cleaver held high in her right hand. Normally, they did not slaughter their birds this way; it was done using an orange cone that the elder Richmonds referred to as a *traffic* cone. Based on the look of it, the tip had once come to a finer point, but had been modified to allow a chicken's head to fit through. Using this method, they would lop the head off without having to worry about the bird fighting back.

This was a desperate moment, though, and Mom was struggling with it.

"I'm gonna hit your *hand*," Mom cried, lowering the cleaver a foot or so. She pushed a few errant locks of her waist-length, toasted brown hair out of her face.

"It's all right, girlie," Bampy assured her. "Just keep yourself steady."

"We don't have time for this," Dad growled, and flicked his wrist, snapping the bird's neck. It continued to flop around on the ground for a few minutes before going still. Carl and Zoey entered the pen and the five of them remained silent. Carl detested moments like this, moments when they all wondered whether or not someone outside the camp had heard the rooster crow. It made him feel vulnerable and exposed even though he'd known nothing but love and kindness during his short life.

The outside world was a different matter, unpredictable and often violent, at least as Bampy always described it. When something like this happened, Carl wondered if this would be the last moment of peace he would share with his family in their beloved home. It was fear of discovery by the outside world that caused Bampy to insist they avoid building fires during all but the dreariest of days, and even then they made sure that the wood was dry enough not to produce much smoke. It was the reason they barely spoke a word to each other when walking around outside.

Carl followed these rules, and countless others, obsessively.

Bampy didn't hesitate to remind everyone that while their family sat in the Rangeley House and tended their little farm, those less fortunate had learned to adapt to a different lifestyle. A more violent lifestyle. The kind of lifestyle that placed families like the Richmonds at the bottom of the food chain and left them vulnerable to the outside world.

Carl glanced up as Dad took the cleaver from Mom's hand. In one fluid motion, he brought the cleaver down, severing the rooster's head cleanly at the top of its breast. He handed the cleaver back to Mom before taking hold of the bird's head and inspecting its comb. "We should have spotted this one."

"Yep," Bampy agreed, picking up the carcass and holding his hand out for the head.

Without another word, Dad dropped the head into Bampy's hand. He looked down at his bloody hands for a moment before turning toward the pond and walking down to the camo netting at the water's edge. There he went about his usual routine, one Carl knew all too well—inspecting the shoreline to make sure that there weren't any visible signs of people. Carl studied his father's body language, waiting with a jittery impatience for Dad to be satisfied with what he saw (or didn't see). He breathed a relieved sigh as Dad reached forward, parted the camo netting, and stepped toward the edge of the water to wash up.

"Fool should know better than that," Bampy whispered to Carl. He growled like a cantankerous old dog as he watched Dad submerge his hands in the tainted water.

As Dad finished cleaning his hands, he inspected the camouflage netting that bridged the small gap between trees, a gap that used to be wide enough to offer a spectacular view of the pond and the surrounding mountains. Carl always thought it looked as though the trees were eating the netting as they grew. The netting blended nicely with the evergreens that lined the shore, regardless of the season.

Mom headed into her gardens and her "orchard" which consisted of four small apple trees and a beehive she expertly maintained. Bampy, still grumbling about Dad, took the remains of the rooster under the rotting deck that ran along the front of the camp, and cleaned the bird for that night's supper. The deck extended fifteen feet toward the water. Spanning the entire forty feet of the house's chipped and peeling brown facade, it stopped just shy of the garage. They no longer used the deck as it had decayed to the point where none of them, particularly Carl, had dared walk upon it for going on ten years. Not since Gram's accident.

Carl watched the others go back to their normal routines as if nothing had happened, still feeling a bit frazzled. He knew he should just tell himself that what was done was done and hope that the rooster's crowing had gone unnoticed. Zoey stood beside him in the coop, staring absent-mindedly at the ground, and he knew she was feeling the same. Carl reminded himself that they were far enough removed from the old highway that the sounds of the rooster could have been lost on the wind or muffled by the thick pine boughs around them. Still, there was no way to be certain.

He needed to do something to take his mind off of it all.

"Chores?" Carl asked.

She nodded, and they headed back into the house to dress and put on their boots. They exited the house together, Zoey jogging around the garage, presumably to join her mother in the garden.

Carl made his way toward the old camp road that had been used to access the cabin from the highway before the chaos of Black Christmas. The road was now little more than an overgrown forest trail, swallowed by birch and pine and spruce. Further along the road was an abandoned house labeled simply, The Firs. Bampy had waited for the folks who sometimes visited during the summertime to show up in the aftermath of Black Christmas, but they never did. When a few months had gone by and they still hadn't shown up, he and the others had broken in and stripped the place down. Bampy often spoke of this, making sure to place emphasis on how long he had waited. Carl suspected that, even though he was within his rights, Bampy carried a good amount of guilt.

Bampy and Gram had gathered the lumber they used to board up the windows from The Firs. They also found clothing tucked neatly away in rustic bureaus made of unfinished wood. The bureaus were broken down and used for more practical purposes, like fuel for their winter fires. The clothing found its way into the Richmond family's closets.

A couple hundred feet down the road toward The Firs sat the stump of an old maple, surrounded by varying lengths of drying wood. Most of Carl's days started off here at the chopping block.

He took one last look at the house before pulling up the folds of tarpaulin that concealed their axe. He took hold of the axe and pulled it free. The thing had seen many repair jobs over the years — the head had fallen off numerous times and its edge had dulled — but it still split wood as long as the person wielding it had a powerful enough swing. Bampy hadn't been able to swing the axe for more than ten years, leaving Dad the sole wood splitter until Carl was old enough and strong enough to help. Now they shared the chore, something that filled Carl with immense pride. It almost made him feel as though, in just that way, they were on the same level.

He stretched his arms, swinging the axe from one hand to the other as he prepared himself. Once he was warmed up, he pulled one of the green trees waiting to be split over to the chopping block and repositioned it until the tree was steady, the lower portion of the trunk resting on the block. He steadied the tree with one foot and began chopping. After three well-placed blows, the top portion separated from the rest of the tree, and he kicked the piece off the chopping block. He repeated the process until he had seven three-foot logs that he stacked along the edge of the camp road with the others that had been left to dry.

By the time he had moved on to the third tree, dewy beads of sweat had broken out on his back, prompting him to bury the tip of the axe in the chopping block and remove his checkered flannel shirt. He hung the shirt carefully on a nearby branch, then took a deep breath and turned back toward the camp. Anxiety flared like a bonfire at the sight of a man walking cautiously down the road, parallel to the house. The man eyed the camp as he grew closer to the short driveway that ran down toward the garage. Carl froze in place like a frightened animal, powerless to run or hide. He backed up a few steps, ready to grab the axe.

The man was short and stocky and had the most pronounced gut Carl had ever seen. He walked cautiously, shoulders elevated and head pushed forward as he took in everything around him. His salt-and-pepper hair extended down to his shoulders. It was parted in the middle, acting like bookends to the man's thick face and neck. He wore a thin, juniper-green jacket that zipped up the front, but was incapable of covering *everything* as the man's gut stuck out at the bottom. His pants were matching green wool, though faded and frayed after what must have been many years of use. On his feet were what appeared to be a pair of brand-new boots of the same type Dad wore: black rubber soles with simulated leather uppers and white wool that popped out of the top. Dad called them *bean boots*. A blue backpack hung from straps on the man's shoulders.

"It's a'ight," the man spoke in a curious accent that Carl had never before heard. The man's gaze was locked on Carl as he backed toward the axe. "I ain't gonna hurt'cha." The man's hands came up in front of him to show they were empty.

Carl knew better. Bampy had taught them all that the outside world was not to be trusted, that it had become so saturated in lawlessness that the breed of human it nurtured was nothing like those who occupied the Rangeley House.

He took hold of the axe, and the man stopped dead in his tracks. His lips curled slightly downward and his jaw began to tremble. His eyes narrowed and to Carl's amazement, tears rolled down his cheeks. Carl shifted his feet, feeling more awkward with each passing moment. He'd grown up with two very powerful and often *emotionless* men. This . . . display . . . was something very new to him.

Despite the man's apparent vulnerability, Carl was not about to lower the axe. Carl was bluffing, but the man didn't know this. The truth was that Carl had never even *thought* about taking the life of another person, and now that he was thrust into such a situation, he had learned something about himself: he couldn't do it.

Drawing in a deep breath, Carl sought out his father at the edge of his vision, looking for any signs of movement through the mess of evergreen trees between the camp road and the edge of the pond. Was Dad still looking over the netting, or had he slipped back into the house, or had he joined Mom in the garden? There was no way to be certain, leaving Carl with no option other than to stand where he was with his axe at the ready until the man either walked away or until someone from his family came looking for him.

That could take hours.

The man continued to blubber without speaking.

Carl thought for a moment about calling for somebody, but quickly forced the idea out of his head. Bampy would flay him alive if he drew further attention to their compound.

Another course of action would be to walk around the man and down the gravel driveway toward the Rangeley House to see if he might be able to get someone's attention. Aside from standing there and waiting, there really wasn't much else he could do.

Carl took hold of the handle with both hands and lifted the axe to his shoulder, ready to strike at the first sign of trouble. He kept his eyes on the stranger as he made his way down the narrow, overgrown road toward their garage and the spot where the visitor stood, tears still streaming down his cheeks. The closer he got, the more panicked the man seemed to become. The man was either out of his mind with fear, or he was an expert actor.

"Please don't hurt me," the man sobbed. "I didn't mean any hahm. Just heard the roostah and thought . . . I might actually eat dinnah tonight."

Carl's hands tightened on the axe as he circled around the man, keeping his distance and not breaking eye contact for even a second. He backed past the garage, heading toward the kitchen door. His body throbbed with the need to hurry, but he somehow forced himself to move slowly.

The man began to sob. A part of Carl wanted to feel bad for him, but the fear that came with seeing the first human being outside of their family was too strong to allow much in the way of sympathetic emotion.

"Carl? What the . . . ?" came Zoey's voice from somewhere behind him. "Oh, my!"

Carl heard something hit the front porch, followed by frantic footsteps and the opening of a door. Seconds later the door opened again, followed by the sound of Zoey's heavy boots clomping across the aging porch and then across the gravel of the driveway. A moment later, she came into sight to his right, Bampy's .308 pulled tightly to her right shoulder. The click of a round entering the chamber echoed in the still air.

"Oh, *no*! Please, I don't mean ya no hahm!" the man cried, loud enough to be heard throughout the compound.

"Shhhh, be quiet or I *shoot*!" Zoey said softly, yet with that tone Carl knew all too well. The man fell to his knees, his hands pressed together in a gesture that Carl didn't understand.

"You can put that down, Carl," Zoey whispered.

Carl looked at his hands on the axe handle, noting how white his knuckles had become. A part of him had forgotten that he still held the axe. Slowly, he lowered the tool-turned-weapon and rested it against the peeling brown siding of the garage, axe head on the ground. Mom, Dad, and Bampy rushed around the side of the garage and almost tripped over the basket of carrots and Brussels sprouts that Zoey had dropped before dashing inside for the rifle.

Mom gasped while Dad and Bampy remained silent. They didn't show much alarm, and why should they? Zoey had the situation under control. Carl's big sister was more of a man than he could ever hope to be.

Dad walked over to Zoey and stopped just beside her.

"Are you okay?" he whispered.

She nodded, eyes fixed on the man, staring him down through the rifle's scope. Her breathing was slow and steady.

"Do you want me to take the rifle?" Dad asked. He glanced at the stranger, then back at his daughter.

"I'm fine," Zoey said, her voice flat. "Do you want me to kill him?"

Dad looked at Bampy. The old man shrugged, obviously unsettled by Zoey's question. Dad studied the man without speaking. After a few seconds, he placed his hand on Zoey's shoulder and leaned in so close Carl could barely hear him.

"You stay on my left at all times. Don't get any closer than ten feet. If at any point it feels like the situation might grow out of our control, you pull the trigger. Do you understand me?"

She nodded.

"Follow me then," he said, walking slowly toward the man and looking him over. For a moment Carl wondered what Dad was looking for, then flushed as he realized the man might have a concealed weapon of some sort. Dad stopped just out of the man's reach with Zoey almost a perfect ten feet behind him.

"P-please, sir," the man wept, gazing pitifully up at Dad with blood-red eyes and swollen, tear-stained cheeks. "I didn't mean any hahm. I'm hungry. I heard the roostah and thought . . ." He sighed. "I'm hungry."

"Are there any more of you?" Dad asked, seeming to ignore what the man had said. His hand rested upon the hunting knife hanging from his belt in an old leather sheath. The man swallowed.

"No," the man replied. "I'm all alone. Gangs got my wife and kids when we was moving through Mexico. Learned the hahd way to avoid cities." His lips drooped downward once again and a fresh set of tears slid down his cheeks.

"Are you armed?"

The man looked past Dad at Zoey, who stood emotionless with the tip of the rifle pointed his way. She was still as a statue.

"I—I am, but you know I mean you no hahm. I could have used it on your boy, but I didn't," the man insisted.

"What is it?"

"A .45, tucked into the back of my pants. Take it, but please don't send me away unahmed."

"Zoey?"

"Yes, Dad."

"Any sudden movements and you pull that trigger, okay?"

"Yes, Dad," she responded without a second's hesitation.

Carl watched his sister with a strange mixture of pride and jealousy. He was startled as an arm fell gently across his shoulders. He glanced at his mother, standing beside him, her gaze fastened on Zoey and Dad. Bampy moved slowly away from the porch, toward Zoey.

"I'm going to take your weapon," Dad said, his voice carrying an unmistakable warning. "Stay just as you are."

The man nodded without a word.

Slowly, Dad approached, making sure to keep his distance and moving at an angle to avoid taking a bullet from the .308 if something were to set Zoey off. He bent and lifted the man's thin, green jacket along with the backpack he wore, then pulled out a pistol.

He walked back to Zoey and flicked the pistol's magazine catch, ejecting the clip, then pulled back the slide, ejecting the chambered round onto the grass. He tucked the gun into his waistband and placed the magazine in his left pocket.

Carl watched, his mouth partly open in amazement. As far as he knew, this was the first time Dad had handled this type of weapon.

"You said you passed through Mexico," Dad said. "Where are you from, and where are you headed?"

"We made it outta Woostah, Mass years ago. I needed to get my family out of militia territory. We were told that nawthen Maine was basically untouched, but yous got militias of your own. Caught us a few times, and . . ." he trailed off.

"You're in western Maine," Dad said, ignoring most of the man's story.

The man cocked his head and thought about this for a moment. "Well, it's not like we had a cah or a map to navigate wit. We was on foot."

"Anyone else know you were coming this way? You mentioned gangs in Mexico," Dad said, stepping a bit farther away and wrinkling his nose.

"No," the man said simply. "My family was hidin' out in a old Chinese restaurant while I was out lookin' for food. We should'a known it was ahready in use from how clean it was. When I got back . . . they . . . they was already dead and cookin'.'"

Carl had to think about this for a moment before he realized what the man meant. When it hit him, his heart sank. Judging by the tears in the man's eyes, it was obvious that this had happened not too long ago.

"I'm sorry," Dad said.

"Thank you." The man sniffed and used the sleeve of his jacket to wipe the tears from his eyes. Carl's heart skipped a beat as Zoey's finger tightened on the trigger. When the man's arm returned to his side, her grip loosened.

"Is it still your plan to head north?" Dad asked after a lengthy silence. "We don't have enough food to let you stay here."

"I will gladly be on my way. Does this mean you'ah gonnah let me live?" The stranger stared up at Dad with a glimmer of hope. A half smile began to materialize on his face.

Dad looked backward at Carl and Mom, a question on his face. Carl knew his dad was feeling uneasy. But they were not killers.

"I'm going to take you back to Route 4," Dad said. "From there I'm going to give you back your weapon and watch you go. If I see anything that makes me uneasy, it'll be a bullet in your head. You don't look back, and you don't *come* back. We've got guns and we mean to protect ourselves."

The man nodded vigorously. "I'll do anything you say. Thank you, oh, thank you!"

Dad nodded, backing up a few steps until he reached Zoey and took the rifle from her. "Go get the rooster."

Carl wondered if his sister was as confused as he was. Zoey hesitated briefly, then ran down around the garage and under the deck. Before long she was back, holding the headless rooster by its talons. She handed it to her father.

"You take this and you eat it," Dad said to the man as he walked over with the rifle balanced on his arm. He handed the man the plucked rooster.

"Ah you serious?" the man asked. He eyed the bird as if it were part of some trap.

"Think of it as a gesture of good will," Dad said. "You've been through the worst this world has to offer. I imagine you need a reminder that not everyone has turned in such a way."

The man's lip began to quiver again as he reached out and took the bird. "Thank you much."

"You're welcome," Dad said. "Now let's get you on your way." He turned and looked at Bampy. "Care to take a walk?"

"I s'pose," Bampy said with a nod. He walked over to Zoey and placed a hand on her shoulder. "Better be gettin' inside, girl." He nodded at Mom. "That goes for you, too." Bampy looked back to Dad, "Should we bring the boy?"

Dad thought on this for a moment, his eyes remaining on the man. Carl had been invited to take part in more "adult" activities since turning sixteen. It was as if they were grooming him for manhood. Bampy was mostly behind it, often making suggestions as he did now. Dad still tended to treat Carl like a child, as Bampy had the habit of doing sometimes with Dad.

"Okay," Dad said, flooding Carl with excitement.

Carl turned back to see Zoey's reaction. The exasperation that burned behind her eyes was enough to pierce momentarily through the nervousness that ravaged his body. For a moment he was warmed with the joy of victory. Her gaze stayed with him as Mom led her into the house and closed the door.

Bampy, Dad, and Carl led the man up the camp road to Route 4, which was about a mile and a half away.

Dad had reinserted the magazine and chambered a round before handing the pistol to Bampy. Not a word was exchanged. Not a word was needed. If they were to come across some kind of posse waiting for them at the end of the road, it would be best to have two firearms at the ready. Carl's nervousness returned once more as he realized he was the only one without a firearm. He was made to walk behind his father and grandfather. Neither one of them took their attention off of the man they were escorting.

When they reached Route 4 they found it completely deserted. As far as Carl knew, it had been almost two decades since Dad or Bampy had ventured out to the old highway. Carl had never been. The asphalt was gray as ash and cracked like a desert hardpan. Though there was still some semblance of the road Bampy and Dad had described running up Dodge Hill through the surrounding mountains, it was no longer the four-lane highway of old. The tall grass sprouting from between the chunks of cracked roadway left very little to see of the once heavily-traveled road.

"I thank you again, strain-jahs," the man said, lifting the rooster up before him and shaking it for emphasis. "There aren't many like us left in this world." Carl watched as his eyes fell down to his pistol, still held at the ready by Bampy. He didn't let his attention rest there for long. Carl assumed this was out of fear that it might be interpreted as a sign of aggression. He did, however, have the audacity to ask that it be returned to him.

Dad turned to Bampy, who nodded almost mournfully as he released the clip and ejected the round from the chamber. His eyes moved once more to the man as he prepared to hand the weapon over.

"You leave it like that until you're over the hill," Dad instructed. "If I see you loading it, I'll be taking that rooster right out of your cold, dead fingers."

"I understand," the man said, tucking the chicken beneath his right arm and reaching reluctantly forward for the pieces. He did as Dad had back in the compound, placing the clip and ejected round in one pocket and the pistol in the other. The next thing he did was one of the most peculiar and unexpected gestures Carl had ever seen.

"William Dewoh," the man said, extending his right hand.

Dad and Bampy simply stared at the hand as if it were some kind of venomous reptile. Manners, greetings, and farewells from the old world were so antiquated now that such behavior from a man—especially a stranger—inspired certain confusion and apprehension. Regardless, both men took Mr. Dewoh's hand, shook it, and bid him a safe journey. Neither of them bothered to introduce themselves. Dewoh's bloodshot eyes then settled upon Carl through the space between Dad and Bampy. He took a couple reluctant steps forward, his hand extended towards Carl as his eyes searched the two men for signs of disapproval. Dad and Bampy looked at each other before parting just enough for the hand to slip through. When Carl took it, feeling the grime upon the man's clammy flesh, he couldn't help shivering. Dewoh's grip tightened, and he shook Carl's hand up and down heartily before releasing it, drawing in a deep breath, and stepping onto what remained of the road.

With their awkward farewells made, they watched as William Dewoh walked up and over Dodge Hill, stopping a few times to catch his breath before disappearing from sight.

The rest of that day Carl's nerves refused to calm. He couldn't bring himself to believe that Dewoh would not return after everything Bampy had told him about the horrors of the outside world. He couldn't eat and he certainly couldn't sleep, though he quickly found this to be the case with his whole family. But when William Dewoh still hadn't returned after another day, he began to feel better about things. His fear diminished, replaced with pride at how generous and virtuous his family had been with the man.

After two days, things started getting back to normal, and life resumed its natural flow for the Richmonds.

On the third day William Dewoh returned.

THREE

C ARL HAD BEEN stretched out on the couch, still trying to visualize Dad and Bampy's retelling of Black Christmas. Zoey grunted as his arm got too close, no doubt interrupting her own reflections on the story. She grumbled and pushed his arm back.

"Now, now, you two," Bampy said. As Carl's gaze drifted over to the old man, he could see Bampy's eyes growing heavy. It was time for his afternoon nap, leading Carl to consider taking one of his own. It had been days since they'd sent William Dewoh on his way, and Carl was still trying to catch up from that first sleepless night.

Carl's thoughts turned away from Black Christmas and Zoey's bad mood as the image of William Dewoh standing at the edge of their driveway popped into his head. He couldn't get over the way that shabbily dressed stranger wept openly as Carl approached with the axe. Of all the bad luck, Dewoh had just happened to be passing by when that rooster crowed. They were just fortunate, Carl thought, that this man hadn't been one of those Bampy always spoke of—perverted and corrupted by the lawlessness of the new world.

The deafening crack of a rifle shot startled Carl out of his thoughts and onto his feet. Anxiety bloomed within his chest and cascaded through his gut.

Tripp barreled into the sitting room, barking furiously. As soon as he rounded the corner he was shushed by Bampy—now wide awake—and made to sit.

Dad leapt up and dashed across the room after the rifle hanging next to the kitchen door. Taking it in hand, with Bampy coming up right behind him, he pressed his back to the wall and slowly inched his way toward the boarded-up window that took up half of the door.

Dad took a deep breath and turned his head so that his temple touched one of the boards. From here he very cautiously rotated on his left shoulder so that he could peek through the cracks.

"I count twenty of them," Dad said, his voice falling. The more he elaborated, the more unbelievable and nightmarish it sounded to Carl. "A dozen men with weapons. Three women. Five children."

"We mean you no hahm!" came a familiar accented voice. The voice was stronger this time, carrying through the walls and boarded-up windows with a power greater than Carl remembered. Perhaps this was a voice reinvigorated by the energy it had garnered from a certain rooster. "We're taking the house and the land, but we'll let you go in peace."

Carl edged toward the door, Mom and Zoey close behind him.

"What are they packing?" Bampy asked, holding Carl back.

"A couple of 12 gauge pump-action shotguns, a mess of pistols, and three automatic rifles," Dad said, leaving Carl to form images of the weapons in his head. It wasn't long before he simply gave up and used the tone of Dad and Bampy's voices to judge just how serious the situation was. What he got from them was not comforting.

Bampy sighed. "There's no way we can take them—"

"I know you'ah in they'ah!" Dewoh's voice boomed. "Please don't make us come in aftah ya."

"What do we do?" Mom asked, her voice carrying an unmistakable fear. She pushed her way past Carl and stepped up behind Dad. Her hand fell gently upon Dad's arm, prompting him to back away from the door.

"We can't stand up to them, that's for sure." Dad looked at each family member, including Tripp. "I should never have trusted him. I should have killed him on the way back up the camp road."

"No, son," Bampy said. "That is not you. It's not *us*. We're better than them out there."

Dad shook his head slowly, at the same time lowering the .308 to the floor and resting it against the wall. Not a single word came out of his mouth.

There was nothing they could do to change their fate. It was what it was, and though it shook Carl to the core that his father was ready to surrender his home, he knew Dad wasn't about to compromise the safety of his family or their moral integrity by resorting to the same violence that those outside were almost certainly prepared to use. The same defeated resolution hung on Bampy's face.

Zoey was of a different opinion.

"There's only one way in," Zoey said in a whisper. "The kitchen door. We could pick them off one at a time as they try to come in for us."

"No," Dad said. "I'll not allow a single person in this house to put his or her life in danger."

"We can't just *give up* the Rangeley House!" Zoey exclaimed, moving in and reaching boldly for the rifle.

Dad pulled it out of her reach and shot her a stern look. She remained where she was for a moment before gradually stepping away from him. Carl joined her though he had not been part of the exchange.

A silence settled once more within the camp, one so deep and pervasive that even the crackling of the dying fire faded to nothing.

It was over. Their life in the Rangeley House had come to a close.

"You bettah talk ta me or we'ah gonna have ta come in!" Dewoh's voice blasted through the walls, shattering the silence and sending chills down Carl's spine.

Dad released a heavy sigh before turning back to the door. "How do I know you'll let us leave in peace?" he yelled, his voice booming powerfully through the kitchen and sitting room. Tripp stopped panting for a moment to regard him with his head tilted to one side.

"You have my word. You were good t'me, even though you should'a known bettah. I'm not gonna punish you for it, but I ain't lettin' you stay neithah."

"We could *all* stay," Dad offered, though even Carl knew it would never work out. The chickens and rabbits paired with the produce from the garden barely amounted to enough for the five of them to stay fed and healthy. The group outside would burn through what food there was in no time at all, though it was clear that such thoughts either hadn't occurred to them or were of no consequence.

"I'm 'fraid it doesn't work like that. I gotta look out for my own, and the less mouths we have to feed the bettah."

"Let us take some supplies then, something so that we can start over. Don't forget that we sent you on your way with something."

Dewoh didn't immediately respond, though the sound of their discussion found its way through the well-insulated walls.

"You'll take as much as you can fit into a backpack, but nothin' mo'ah," Dewoh finally said. "We'll let you leave ahm'd, but none of the food goes with you. You have ten minutes."

Dad turned and nodded to them. "Move. Get the backpacks out of the closet. Fill them with whatever you can."

Carl followed the others to the closet off of the kitchen where they stored the miscellaneous items not used in daily chores. In the far corner of the closet sat the book-bag style backpacks they used to gather apples in the fall. They filled the packs quickly and methodically. First clothing, then various items that were special to them. As he gathered his things, Carl listened to the clanking of pots and pans in the kitchen as Mom loaded up. From the neighboring room he could hear Zoey grumbling to herself. Dad was no doubt busy gathering his clothing as well as the various hunting and trapping items that they had stored in various places throughout the camp. As Carl stepped out of his room, his pack hastily filled with every scrap of clothing and every tiny trinket he owned, he watched the rest of the family moving about in the dying firelight, working against a hypothetical clock.

Carl headed through the sitting room toward the kitchen, pausing as Dad came rushing out of the bedroom. Dad skidded to a halt in front of Bampy, who continued to stand before the front door. The old man looked as though he hadn't moved an inch.

"Bamp?" Dad started, only to be silenced as Bampy's hand rose, palm out toward him. Carl watched the two men, his heart sinking as he tried to shake off the idea of what might be happening.

Bampy blinked and Carl felt sick as he watched tears run down the old man's cheeks. As Carl moved in closer he could read the horror and defeat in his grandfather's glistening eyes.

Dad used both hands to steady his pack. "Bamp, why haven't you packed?"

Bampy smiled through his tears. The men stared at each other, then Bampy lifted both hands and put them on Dad's cheeks. "I think I'll just stay here with your mother."

Dad's face dropped. "No. No, Dad, you have to come with us, the kids—"

"The kids'll be just fine with you and Kelly. I can barely walk across this room anymore. You think I'm gonna be able to walk up a *mountain*?" Bampy chuckled, though it was obviously forced.

Carl couldn't believe Dad was accepting Bampy decision. It was obvious in his body language, the drooping of his shoulders, the slight quiver of his chin.

"You can't . . ." Dad started, but Bampy shook his head.

"You go. Find a place to start over. You know how to live out there . . . you *all* do. You'll figure it out." He moved his hands to Dad's shoulders, then pulled him close. "Just stay away from anywhere settled."

Carl's heart sank. The weight of his backpack upon his shoulders suddenly felt like the weight of the entire world crushing down upon him. Neither man even acknowledged him and Carl understood that this was between father and son. A last goodbye between men.

Dad said nothing. His hands stopped fiddling with the straps of his backpack, the top of which hung low on his back. He wrapped his arms around Bampy's frail figure and rested his head on Bampy's shoulder, making Carl want to do the same, to bury his face into that wispy gray hair that always smelled so strongly of wood smoke. This was the man who had made their lives possible, who had carved out an existence that allowed Carl to enjoy sixteen years of peace in an otherwise savage world.

"I love you, boy," Bampy said.

"I love you, too." Dad's head didn't move from Bampy's shoulder.

"What is it?" came Mom's voice from the kitchen, followed by the muted clamor of pots and pans. Carl couldn't look away from the men in front of him.

Bampy attempted to push Dad gently away. Dad wasn't going.

"Find your center later, son. There is no time to waste. You need to get them out of here," Bampy said softly. An underlying tone that Carl knew all too well informed him that this was Dad's last warning before more direct orders were issued.

Slowly Dad lifted his head from Bampy's shoulder, looking the frail man over. Though a certain weakness had come to Bampy with age, he was still the only man in the world Dad dared not cross.

Working visibly to contain himself, Dad stepped away without a word, his gaze moving to Carl. Mom walked out of the kitchen, her heavy pack on her shoulders. She stopped and looked at them, a dark sadness sweeping across her face.

"Come here, girlie," Bampy urged, opening up his arms.

Mom did as she was told, unable to stop her tears. "You're not coming," she whispered, nuzzling her face into Bampy's red-and-black checkered jacket.

Carl looked over his shoulder as he sensed Zoey stepping into the living room behind him. The clicking of Tripp's claws upon the floor announced his entry as well. Carl's attention returned to Mom and Bampy.

"I can't," Bampy said. He looked at Carl and smiled.

"Bampy," Carl said, his jaw trembling. "You can't stay here, they won't let you." A quick look at Dad told Carl not to fight it, that he needed to keep himself together.

"I know that, Carl," Bampy responded. His hands moved up and down Mom's back as she remained in his arms. "I've lived a long and happy life here with you and your sister and your mom and dad. I'm ready to rest with your Gram."

"We can *fight*," Zoey said, stubbornly going against her father's wishes. She looked immediately at Dad, obviously expecting a harsh reprimand. Fortunately for her, he was in no mood to dispense punishment.

"Enough of that," Bampy said. "Come give your old Bamp a hug and get out of here before these people change their minds."

Mom detached herself from the old man and stepped aside, falling into Dad's arms.

Struggling to repress his grief, Carl staggered forward into the arms of his grandfather. Zoey came behind him, and they were both pulled into his chest. They stayed like this for as long as they could; until the moment when Dewoh told them that their time was up. Even then, they had to be pried away.

"Tripp, come," Dad ordered as he took hold of the kitchen door handle. As the dog rushed toward him, Bampy bent down and allowed his hand to run across the fur of Tripp's back. "Carl, pick him up and carry him until we're far enough away."

Carl obeyed, bending down and lifting the dog into his arms. He moved toward the door.

Dad reached down and took hold of the rifle with his free hand. Slinging it over his shoulder, he nodded to Bampy and pulled the door slowly open.

"James," Bampy said, backing slowly into the sitting room.

Carl stopped and turned with his father. Dad held the door cracked, allowing trace amounts of fading daylight to illuminate the kitchen. Looking at his grandfather, never more aware of how old and helpless he was, Carl held his breath and willed himself to stay strong.

Dad stepped in front of Carl, forcing Carl to move so that he could look at Bampy.

"Don't you *ever* regret the decision you made to let that man go. Not *ever*. And don't any of you forget who you are while you're out there," Bampy said. His voice was low and his tone grave. The expression on his face, even through the tears, conveyed the seriousness of his charge. With nothing more to say, the old man turned his back to them, walked slowly over to the couch, and took a seat.

Turning back to the door, Dad slowly pulled it the rest of the way open and led his family out to meet those who had come to evict them. As Carl stepped out onto the old porch, feeling its familiar give beneath him, he watched as Mom reached out and took Dad's hand. For a moment he thought about doing the same with Zoey.

The men were arranged in a line along the border of their property at the camp road. At the very center, holding his .45 at his side, stood William Dewoh. The expression on his face, though one of somewhat muted excitement, was not joyous.

Though he had proven himself to be quite the expert actor a few days earlier, he had no reason for subterfuge now.

Dewoh spoke up as Dad led the way down the stairs onto the gravel and overgrown grass of the camp's old driveway. "There ah people in this world who live fah this kinda stuff," he said, his head dropping a bit, though not quite hanging. He continued to make eye contact. "I'm not one of 'em. You was good ta me. I'm sorry that we need this place more'n you, but that's jus' how it is."

"There's not enough food here to keep you alive for very long," Dad said as they reached the group. He stopped, eyeing each of the mangy-looking critters who stood on his land. His gaze settled on Dewoh. "You know this to be true."

"Be that as it may," Dewoh responded. "There's food he'ah. You'll soon learn that every bit counts. A dinnah's a dinnah."

Dad shook his head and turned back to the Rangeley House for a moment before refocusing his attention on Dewoh. "I hope this one's worth the price."

"Wha d'you mean?" Dewoh asked, his body notably tensing. It was obvious that he imagined Dad might surprise them with some kind of last-stand attack.

"My father is too old to make it out there. If you want the house," Dad stopped briefly and swallowed hard. ". . . you'll have to clear him out first."

Dewoh looked at the still-open kitchen door. He closed his eyes and took a deep breath. When his eyes returned to Dad they showed cold and brutal understanding, yet for some reason he chose to offer an odd form of murderous compassion. "It'll be quick, I promise."

Dad shoved through the group of men and made his way down the camp road toward The Firs and the old trails beyond. Not one of the men made an effort to stop them.

Carl kept his eyes down, only once feeling bold enough to make eye contact with a few of the burly men as he pushed through the line behind his father and mother. Most of them sported ragged beards and moustaches that weren't even trimmed to the point where their lips could be seen.

Following Dad and Mom toward the second group, the women and children, Carl couldn't help slowing down to look them over. These were, after all, the ones who the men were fighting to feed and protect, right? The children were fragile-looking and emaciated. They were completely unkempt with dirt splotched all over their tiny faces and their hair hanging in strings and tangled locks down their backs and faces.

Not one of them made eye contact with Carl as he passed.

For a moment Carl found himself wondering if any of these children were William Dewoh's. He had obviously been lying about what had transpired in Mexico. Perhaps his group had been the ones to find an innocent family in the Chinese restaurant (whatever *that* was) and eat them. The man claimed that this was not how he was, but kicking a family out of their own home did very little to sell Carl on that assertion, regardless of how *accommodating* Dewoh was being about it.

As he made his way to the edge of the group with the dense wilderness spread out before him, Dad stopped and allowed Carl and Zoey to move ahead of him. All the while Carl kept waiting for the sound of gunfire.

It never came.

As Carl made his way into the woods down the overgrown camp road, he very stealthily bent down and removed the axe from the tarpaulin behind the stack of drying firewood.

Again, he waited for a gunshot, and again none came.

Pulling the axe to his chest to keep it concealed, Carl chanced a glance behind him. His mother's face was pale but without expression. His father's rugged face was the same. Somehow Dad was still holding himself together. Carl let his gaze drift back to their home. This was the last he'd ever see of it.

Carl struggled to draw a satisfying breath as his heart beat ferociously and his chest tightened further. He was relatively certain that he and his family were safe for the time being, but he could not stop his thoughts turning to Bampy, just sitting in there and waiting for his own demise.

Had Dewoh entered the house yet? Had the intruders forever tainted his beloved home? There was no way to be certain.

They'd gone a half mile or so around the edge of the pond, Dad once again in the lead, when they were stopped short by the crack of a single gunshot snapping across the pond and echoing out over the surrounding mountains.

Every part of his being told him to collapse upon the leaves that littered the ground and cry until his heart burst, but in the end, Carl was able to keep up with his father, mother, and sister without breaking pace . . .

THE
CEDAR SWAMP
INN

FOUR

CARL COULDN'T SHAKE the memories of their eviction. The event cast dark shadows over the back of his mind, sneaking up on him when he wasn't prepared. Finally, Dad led them off the trail and into the woods just as the last crimson ribbon of light faded from the sky. He didn't say a word to confirm they were stopping for the night, but Carl knew it to be so. Even Tripp noted the change and paused to look back. Upon realizing that they were leaving the trail, he doubled back and joined them moving through the thick cropping of pine.

The air carried the seasonal crispness of fall that almost always came in the early evening. Carl remembered the cool evenings generally started on or around the last harvest of summer vegetables from Mom's garden. He rubbed his arms and wondered if Dad would let them have a fire.

Images from the day still ran through Carl's mind, Bampy still at the forefront. Carl thought about his life in the Rangeley House; a life that he would never return to again. He thought about the fact they no longer had a roof above their heads.

No longer did they have beds to sleep in.

Carl felt a deep depression settle over him, and for some time he allowed it. What reason did he have to deny himself the right to a little self-pity? He didn't let the self-pity linger too long before deciding it was time to attempt lifting his spirits a bit. For Mom and Dad if not for himself.

Dad marched them deep into the woods, gathering chunks of dried wood and handfuls of dead leaves and needles as he walked. Carl copied him and noticed the others did the same. Soon, they were each carrying a full armload of fuel. Carl felt a spark of energy and excitement at the idea of sitting down before a fire. After all they'd been through, they certainly deserved it.

Moving through the overgrown woods was not an easy task. He didn't think it would have been any easier thirty years ago, when there were still animals to help trim the low hanging branches. Still, they managed just fine even with their arms full of wood. The pace slowed as they had to brace themselves against various branches, easing past slowly so the branch didn't snap back like a whip. All the while the sky grew darker, stars flickering through the pine needle canopy overhead. Finally, Dad stopped and looked back.

Carl had seen his father in this mode before, studying the natural markers. It was obviously more of a precaution than anything since Dad had deliberately led them west into the woods, toward the setting sun.

Dad dropped his wood and lowered his backpack, and Carl did the same. Wood rattled as Zoey let go of her load. Mom was last. Free of the burdens they'd been carrying, they voiced a collective sigh. As tired as he was, Carl knew better than to collapse on the carpet of needles. There was still much to do.

The area Dad had selected as their camp was *something* of a clearing. It was almost a perfect circle with a diameter of maybe ten feet. A number of juvenile evergreens had begun to grow toward the center, but for the most part it was clear.

"Carl," Dad said, his voice a cautious whisper even though they were clearly alone, "start digging." Dad measured out a circle of about two-and-a-half to three feet with his hands, a circle

Carl understood would be the fire pit they would use. Dropping to his knees, Carl went to work, grateful there was still barely enough light to see, while his father sorted through the wood and kindling.

The women began to process the cattail roots. They picked out a couple of roots each and dusted off the dried dirt with little brushes made from fistfuls of needles. Carl admired the efficiency of their "tools," though their pine-needle brushes were nothing compared to what they had back home . . .

Carl forced the thought away. The time would come for such talk, for a verbal purge of the horrors that dwelled within his mind, but this was not that time.

"How we doing, boy?" Dad asked, turning to Carl with a fist-ful of needles and twigs in one hand and an armful of the smaller tinder in the other.

Carl looked up from the hole he had managed to dig, feeling fortunate to have not run into any bothersome roots or rocks. He nodded at the small crater in the forest floor before raising both thumbs.

Dad nodded and walked over, eyeing the axe handle stick-ing out of Carl's backpack. The look of approval on Dad's face made Carl feel warm inside. He'd known the axe was vital to their survival in the deep woods. Without it they stood no chance of building a new home.

Dad dropped to his knees beside Carl and began to make a base of needles and twigs in the fire pit. On top of the twigs he arranged the medium-sized branches like a little log house.

"You brought the flint?" Carl asked. He had never known his father to make a mistake or forget something, and even the de-cisions surrounding Dewoh's release (of which Bampy had also been a part) did not count against him. In Carl's mind, James Richmond remained absolutely flawless.

Dad reached into his blue-and-green checkered jacket, a jacket identical to Carl's own with the exception of the color, and produced the stained wooden box that contained his fire starter. With expert care, he set the box down and removed the flint and magnesium sticks they had used for decades to start their fires.

With a smile at Carl, Dad took his hunting knife to the stick and flicked his wrist a few times, sending a few white-hot sparks into the tinder. The dry needles lit almost immediately, forcing him to lean in closer, working with both hands to feed more needles into the tiny blaze. Carl busied himself clearing the remaining needles from around the edges of the pit to avoid setting their entire campsite ablaze.

Within minutes they were warming themselves beside a fire large enough to give off a comfortable aura of heat, but still small enough to avoid drawing any attention. Carl was decidedly more confident that they were alone in the forest than his father appeared to be, but he wasn't about to question Dad's cautiousness after everything that had befallen them. He lifted his arms as Tripp nuzzled at him and plopped down in his lap.

"This is kind of like last summer," Mom said. She carefully placed cattail roots at the edge of the fiery coals. She handed a bunch to Dad and Carl. "You boys mind the ones on your side. Make sure to turn them as they brown so they cook evenly. When the outside's black, they're done, but make sure not to eat the cores."

Carl nodded, recalling the little cookout on the lawn back in mid-July, when they had done the same thing. There had been more food then, of course. It had been something of a summer celebration; something special put together for no real reason. He couldn't remember a more perfect night, sitting fireside with the stars shining brightly above.

"Remember how drunk Bamp got that night?" Dad chuckled, his gaze never once leaving the fire as if the scenario was somehow playing out in the dancing flames.

"Yeah," Zoey giggled. "Mom swore that she'd never distill another batch after that."

"He fell into the *fire!*" Mom exclaimed lightly enough to keep her voice from carrying. "Crazy old *coot* almost took me in with him!"

They all laughed quietly. "It was your idea to s—start dancing," Zoey managed to say.

Their laughter slowly faded, leaving behind the light crackling and popping of the fire. Dad sighed and moved to his feet, his eyes glistening. He turned toward the edge of the small clearing and placed his hands on his hips.

Carl watched as Dad left, understanding quite well that his father didn't want to show any vulnerability around his family. Especially around Zoey and Carl. He was a tough man, but those who knew him best also saw his tender side. Still, they would give him his space

Tears welled up in Carl's eyes, but before he could crawl inside himself, Mom spoke up.

"He was a good man. A *great* man," Mom said. "If it weren't for him and his quick thinking, not one of us would be here right now. Me least of all. I know it's easy to just let ourselves sink into despair, but he wouldn't have wanted that. Not one bit. I think that the best way we can honor him is to continue moving forward and living our lives by his example. I don't care what this world intends to do to us; we can't ever let it change who we are."

"And we won't," Dad said, his back still to them. "We'll find another place, and we'll build another home . . . only this time it'll be so far away from the roads of the old world that we'll stay hidden. We won't have to worry about building a fire during the daytime or walking more than a mile from the roof that shelters us. We'll—"

"James," Mom said, interrupting him, "we have plenty of time for that kind of talk. Come back to the fire and join us in remembering your father." She patted the ground beside her, though Dad's back was still turned.

He walked along the edge of their campsite, head downturned as if looking for something he had misplaced. Carl watched with curiosity as he reached down and picked up a branch about as thick as his thumb. Wiping his eyes with his free hand, Dad turned and headed back to his seat.

He immediately began to stir the coals. Once the flames had built themselves up again, he reached over, selected a few of the larger pieces of wood, and placed them upon the glowing structure. Flames began to lap at the new fuel.

Dad drew his legs up in front of him and folded his arms on his knees.

"What about the year the green beans didn't come in?" Carl asked, already chuckling in anticipation of his family's reaction.

The others erupted in laughter so loud Dad raised a hand to shush them. Tripp lifted his head from Carl's lap, trying to get a read on what was happening. As the laughter settled, Mom spoke up.

"You'd have thought it was the end of the world all over again!" she exclaimed, keeping her voice low. "Now there was a man incapable of shedding his grief. Every little thing that annoyed him stuck around like the stink of the water on your clothes. He didn't stop complaining until the first harvest that next year."

"I'll never forget *that* dinner," Zoey laughed, her hand absent-mindedly stroking Tripp's hindquarters. "We had a fresh kit slaughter and a rabbit dinner, but you gave him a plate full of beans!"

Once again, boisterous laughter filled the campsite. Even Dad laughed, and Tripp looked at them all as if he were annoyed with the constant interruptions to his sleep. The dog's attention fell on Dad for a few seconds before his heavy eyes drooped and his head returned to Carl's lap.

The banter continued back and forth as they tended to their cattail roots and eventually ate. It wasn't until the laughter and the tears had subsided and they were beginning to settle down with their backpacks as pillows beside the fire that Dad finally spoke up. His deep voice brought Carl out of a light sleep. He sat up, blinking sleep from his eyes, and listened.

Dad's eyes remained fixed on the flames of the freshly stoked fire, and his arms rested on his knees in the same manner he'd been sitting all evening. His voice was raspy at first, but as he spoke, his voice cleared and the crackling of the fire seemed muted against the power of his words.

"When I was a boy . . . back in the old world . . . Bampy wasn't around very much. He was a working man," Dad said. "He would go off to his job in the early morning, long before I was up, and would return in the late evening, long after I had returned from school." Dad stopped for a moment, looking at Carl to make sure that the word *school* resonated in some manner.

Carl nodded.

"Gram was always home—always there for me. Bampy . . . well, he wasn't. I would sometimes still be doing my homework when he got back." Again he looked at Carl. "*Homework* was an expansion of the lessons learned at school, meant to be completed at home to reinforce what you learned." Carl nodded once more, and he continued, "I'd sometimes ask Bamp for help with my work. He'd give it a quick look-over and tell me that it was easy stuff and that I should be able to do it without help. Then he would go off into the living room, crack a beer, and watch television for the rest of the night. Gram would finish preparing dinner, bring a plate out to the *working man*, and help me finish my homework."

Dad cleared his throat. "That was how it was in the old days with Bampy. He wasn't there for me in any way. Not for work, not for play, not for anything. He did what was expected of him: made the money that kept a roof over our heads and our fire stoked. He was a terrible father—"

"James," Mom said.

"A *terrible* father," Dad repeated. "Then Black Christmas hit . . . and he became a different person entirely. Suddenly life was no longer about working to bring home a paycheck. I think this helped to focus him on what really mattered. Once the water was confirmed to be tainted and we knew that we would spend the rest of our lives in the Rangeley House actually *providing* for ourselves, he changed." Dad cocked his head before shaking it gently back and forth. "No. He didn't change. He became the man he always was on the *inside*, just waiting for the system to collapse and free him from the prison of the working man.

"It's funny," he continued. A single tear trickled down his left cheek. The firelight glistened in its trail. "He always talked about how the new world changed people—and always for the worst—but I don't think he ever once realized how it changed him for the better." He blinked again, releasing more tears, which he made no effort to hide. As he continued, the sorrow and love in his voice caused a shift in his tone and inflection.

It was all Carl could do to keep his mouth from falling open in astonishment. This was a side of his father he had never seen.

"We spent thirty great years in the Rangeley House," Dad said. "All the things that you spoke of tonight are things that we will carry with us for the rest of our lives. If we're lucky, if it hasn't happened already, perhaps a small part of that wonderful man will rub off on us. I love you, Bamp—*Dad*. New world be damned for taking you from us. I—I . . ." he trailed off.

Carl scrambled to his feet, ditching Tripp, and moved to his father's side, wrapping his arms around him and feeling the others join them. Dad sobbed, and unfolded his arms, embracing them all. The family remained like this until Dad was able to bring himself back under control. Carl didn't know how long they stood there, and he didn't care. He would stay with his father for as long as needed and more.

Before long, Dad shooed them away and encouraged them to get some sleep, returning to his usual stolid self. Mom and Zoey planted a kiss on his head before moving back to their "beds," and Carl gave Dad one last hug before doing the same. Dad sat back down by the fire. He would probably stay up for a few hours to stoke the fire, a task that he would likely wake up to perform every couple of hours throughout the night.

As Carl drifted off, his mind returned to what his father had said earlier: *We'll find another place, and we'll build another home.*

CARL AWOKE TO the smell of burning pine and the crackling sounds of the fire beside him. At first he was disoriented, looking around the campsite and up at the deep, green canopy of ever-green needles above, but it didn't take long for the events of the previous day to wash over him like so much tainted water.

Black Christmas. Bampy's death. Being banished into the wilderness. Dad crying. It was difficult to imagine that he was capable of waking up after such a tragically eventful day with a mind so unburdened, yet here he was, feeling like he'd shed the entire ordeal like a hide stripped off of a rabbit. But he knew it wouldn't remain this way. Even now, as he began to relive it all in his head, his heart started to feel heavy, and his breathing became shallow, like a weight pressed down upon his chest, rendering him unable to take a full, satisfying breath.

Mom stirred on the far side of the smoldering fire. She stretched her arms slowly up above her body before bending her legs and taking hold of her knees to pull herself up. As she rose, the faux fur hood of her brown thermal jacket fell to her shoulders. A yawn stretched her face as she reached her gloved hands toward the fire.

The sky had begun to brighten, the sun painting the eastern horizon in brilliant shades of crimson and violet visible in splotches through the trees and behind the mountains. Zoey was the only one who had yet to greet the day. Dad and Tripp were nowhere to be found. There was no doubt in Carl's mind that his father was off on some kind of important business.

"Did you hear your father leave?" Mom asked, removing her rabbit skin gloves and holding her hands above the flames.

Carl shook his head. He studied the fire and the perfectly arranged pieces of wood. "He couldn't have left very long ago. The top layer of wood is still pretty fresh."

The morning was mild and unseasonably warm compared with the previous day. This did a lot to raise Carl's spirits and distract him from the anxiety already building in his gut. Before long he found himself backing away from the fire as the heat became too much. He watched with a certain mischievous interest as the heat began to interrupt his sister's slumber. At first she tried to roll away from the fire, but eventually the heat forced her to sit up. She scooted back as he had, beads of perspiration clinging to her cheeks and forehead.

"Did I sleep all winter?" Zoey asked, pulling her backpack around in front of her crossed legs with a soft grunt that seemed inspired more by irritation than actual difficulty. "When did spring get here?" She looked around the campsite. "And where's Dad?"

"He and Tripp had an errand in the forest it would seem," Mom replied.

"It's called *finding water*," Dad said.

Carl turned to see his father pass between two of the larger trees that lined their site, followed closely by Tripp, who gazed longingly up at the medium-sized metal pot in Dad's hands. Dad kept his gaze on the forest floor, carefully avoiding anything that might send him and the pot he carried crashing to the ground. Tripp's rope was coiled around Dad's left wrist and his checkered jacket was tied around his waist.

"I see Tripp's eager for a drink," Mom said, taking the words right out of Carl's mouth.

"He would have had a few gulps already if I were a decade older and no longer able to dive after the little mongrel." Dad laughed. He stepped over to the fire and placed the pot down beside it, making sure to push Tripp away a few times to prevent him from drinking out of the pot. Carl stepped over and took the dog into his arms with a groan. He was immediately hit with Tripp's own *good morning* as the dog's tongue lapped affectionately across his face.

"Okay," Carl said, laughing, "that's enough." He shifted the dog into his left arm and pushed Tripp's wiry, black-and-white muzzle away. Then he walked back over to where he had been seated and plopped back down on the ground.

Freed of the burden of watching out for an ignorantly suicidal dog, Dad went to work shifting the coals and still-burning lengths of wood around with his stirring stick. When he was satisfied with the arrangement, he took three large-sized logs from the dwindling pile and stacked them atop the burning embers. Once this base was properly arranged, he lifted the pot and placed it on top of the logs where the flames from below could lick its bottom and heat the tainted water within.

"I didn't wake you when I dug around in your pack, did I?" Dad slowly removed his hands from the pot, watching it closely for signs that it might topple beneath the degrading base it sat upon.

Mom shook her head. She pulled her pack up beside her and began to dig through it. The unmistakable *clink clank* of pots and pans left Carl assured that they would at least have items with which to cook. As her arms disappeared further into the backpack the clamor ceased. After a minute or so of careful searching, she removed a folded dish towel that Carl recognized as one they had used previously to dry their plates and bowls and cookware back at the Rangeley House.

"I had this packed away in the pantry along with the seeds we were drying," Mom said, slowly unfolding the towel.

"Did you get the seeds?" Dad asked.

Mom smiled. "I did. Along with something else I think you'll like."

"Good girl," Dad said, his face turning up into a smile that was so powerful Carl found himself smiling too. "Love you."

"And I you," she responded, uncovering eight six-inch strips of cured rabbit meat. Her eyes remained on Dad's. "How do you want it rationed?"

Ration. Now that was an old world word that had really come into its own in the new world. Carl had learned the word at a very early age, having heard his parents and grandparents use it several times daily. Everything was rationed in the new world, food and water especially.

"We still have some of the roots?" Dad asked, lifting his eyebrows.

She nodded. "Little more than a dozen."

"Half a strip each. Hopefully, we'll find more food before sundown."

"Doesn't look as though these trails have been used in some time," Zoey said, adding her own two cents. "We're bound to come across *something*." She opened her hand and took two halves of rabbit jerky, keeping one for herself and handing the other to Carl. Taking his ration in hand, Carl watched as his sister tore off a piece of her breakfast and chewed it.

"We can't depend on that," Dad said, reaching out and taking a strip of his own. He looked at it for a moment before breaking off a quarter and feeding it to the dog, who had stopped struggling to free himself from Carl's arms. Dad shoved the rest in his mouth and said, "We also can't be sure that there isn't anyone else out here. We can't afford to let our guard down for even a second, Zo."

"I know," Zoey responded, obviously wishing she could retract her statement. Carl couldn't help shaking his head, though he stopped as her eyes turned to him.

The conversation ended, and they proceeded to eat their breakfast in silence. Carl tried to take his time chewing, but he still finished before Zoey. Mom had an unnatural ability for really savoring her food and making it last at mealtimes. While the bellies of the others screamed to consume as much as they could in as quick a timeframe as they could manage, she seemed able to silence her impulses and really enjoy her food. Bampy used to tease her about it all the time, saying that her food would spoil long before the last bite entered her mouth.

Dad leaned over as a steady plume of steam began to rise from the pot. Carl rose to join him, looking inside and observing a steady rush of bubbles that told him the water had come to a boil. He stepped back as his father removed the pot from the fire.

"We'll be continuing north today," Dad said as he set the pot down to cool. "The plan is to get as far into the woods as possible before hopefully finding a source of water where we can build a new home. I don't intend to take more than another couple of days moving through the forest. We have to build ourselves a proper shelter before the snow starts flying."

Carl nodded in agreement, though with the weather as warm as it was he found it difficult to imagine wintertime was even approaching. Though he wished that the circumstances surrounding their current situation were different, it was a perfect day to be walking through the woods.

He quickly packed up the belongings he'd removed from his backpack and the rest of the family did the same as they waited for the water to cool. Gloves and jackets were shed and either stowed away or tied around their waists. The day was only going to grow warmer and more comfortable.

Before long they were ready to go, packs at their feet, waiting for the fire to die down and for Dad to give his okay on the water. Dad would simply allow the fire to burn itself out after they left the campsite behind. If he were to extinguish the fire using water or dirt, it would create extra smoke, and Carl knew how he felt about anything that might inadvertently draw the attention of any others wandering the forest.

Mom wore only her boots, denim pants, and her baby blue thermal shirt. Zoey wore her faded denims and blue thermal shirt. Carl was down to his red thermal and aging jeans, which matched Dad's outfit almost identically.

When Dad seemed certain that the water had cooled enough it wouldn't cause any burns, he lifted the pot and brought it to his face. Carl watched, licking his lips as he suddenly became aware of just how thirsty he was. Dad took a good whiff of the liquid, wrinkling his nose in a way that let Carl know the reek of rotten onions wasn't completely gone. Not enough to stop Dad from drinking though. He took a quick swig before slowly lowering the pot and swishing the liquid around in his mouth. His eyes moved thoughtfully back and forth across the canopy overhead in what Carl called Dad's "drinkability analysis."

"Is it okay?" Carl asked, absolutely *dying* for a drink. It had been more than a day after all. Even the smell of the water wouldn't be enough to turn him away at this point . . . or so he told himself.

Dad swallowed and passed the pot to his son. "Seems okay, but don't drink too much of it. You know how different sources hit the body in different ways."

Carl nodded before bringing the pot up to his lips. He quickly took a few glugs before his taste buds had a chance to object.

"That's enough, boy," Dad cautioned.

Unsatisfied, but obedient, Carl lowered the pot and passed it along to his sister. She also had to be stopped by Dad before drinking too much. Mom never seemed to have any trouble showing Carl and Zoey the discipline that they lacked. One mouthful was all she took before offering the pot to Tripp. The dog didn't hesitate, stuffing his face into the pot and lapping noisily.

Mom didn't seem willing to let Tripp drink too much. It wasn't long before she pulled the pot away, dumping the water on the ground away from the fire. She opened her backpack again and started to place the pot inside. Suddenly, she paused, a mischievous smile slowly spreading across her face. Carl watched with mounting curiosity as his mother walked toward him. She placed the pot upside-down on his head and turned.

"Remind you of Johnny Appleseed?" she chuckled.

"Who's Johnny Appleseed?" Zoey asked. She turned to Carl, gazing at the pot on his head until their eyes met. There Carl saw the same confusion that had washed over him.

Mom and Dad looked at each other for a moment. They shared a long look, smiles on both their faces. Then Mom took the pot off of Carl's head and packed it away.

Moments later, they were making their way back toward the trail.

FIVE

THEY HIT THE trail and resumed their northward course. Though Dad left the firewood behind, his poking stick came with them and he used it as a walking stick as they made their way up the trail, deeper into the woods and mountains of Northwestern Maine.

Carl kept glancing at the stick as they walked along. As far as he was concerned, it was a curious thing for his father to be using. Gram had been the only person Carl had ever known who required such a thing and she was weak and elderly.

"Is your leg bothering you, Dad?" he asked, alternating his gaze between his father's upper back (where a large sweat stain had already started to bloom between the man's shoulders, expanding out from what was assuredly a larger damp spot behind his backpack) and the poking-turned-walking stick.

"Nope," Dad replied. "Why do you ask?"

"Because you're using a stick . . ." he hesitated, then continued, "like Gram."

Dad chuckled a bit, but did not stop. He glanced back at Carl. "It's just a walking stick, son. It helps take some of the load off of your feet. You should try it."

Tripp stopped briefly about twenty feet ahead and looked at them as if wondering if he was missing something. After a brief pause, the dog continued down the overgrown trail.

Carl peered at the edge of the trail, searching through the leaves and branches littering the ground for a stick of his own as he thought about Gram and her walking stick and mulled over what his father had said.

Helps take some of the load off of your feet . . .

. . . Gram hobbled out onto the old front deck in the fading light of another beautiful summer day. The deck creaked and groaned as she slowly made her way along, even though she really didn't have much in the way of body weight to put a strain on it. She weighed 100 pounds soaking wet.

From where he stood at the door watching his grandmother, six-year-old Carl could hear Bampy talking to himself beneath the deck as he always did when working alone. By the sounds of it Bampy was plucking a chicken, which meant that another rooster had been found.

Carl scooted out the door, sneaking after Gram on all fours, trying to keep from being detected. She walked with her usual *clop, clop, clip*, a three-legged sound that had followed her every-where once she started using her cane to move about the camp. She wore the same boots she had worn fall to spring for as long as Carl could remember. They had even outlasted the rubber tip of her cane, which had worn off a year or so back.

Clop, clop, clip. Clop, clop, clip. She headed to the edge of the deck where she would typically lean against the railing and talk to Bampy. *Clop, clop, clip.*

"Is that the York High School Prom Queen I hear?" Bampy asked, his voice only slightly muffled by the old decking. Carl had suffered many a splinter from that wood, leading him to move with care, whether he was walking or playing his sneaking game.

Gram chuckled, then coughed. The *clop, clop, clip* ceased as she leaned heavily on her cane, trying to maintain her balance through the coughing fit. Before long Gram had herself under control. "Don't you start with that again, old man," she cackled, brushing her silver-white bangs out of her face. She smoothed down her blue-and-white dress and inspected it briefly. Gram always reminded Carl that the world may have mutated into a shadow of its former self, but that was no reason to stop caring about how she looked. Just because they had to live without things like showers and water-toilets didn't mean that they had to look like bums.

She clomped her way toward the edge of the deck. She could have kept talking to Bampy from where she was, halfway to the edge, but as Carl had come to understand, that was not their tradition. It was not their *thing*.

"You don't need to walk all the way," Bampy urged. "You aren't a spring chicken anymore."

"I can make do just as well as the rest of you," she argued. "Don't you forget it."

But Bampy worried about her. Even Carl could sense it. Plus Zoey kept him updated about everything that passed between the adults. That's how he knew Gram was older than Bampy, and in not nearly as good of shape. She had hurt her leg on the rocks by the pond years earlier and hadn't been able to walk right ever since.

"No, ma'am," Bampy said. Gram finished her journey to the porch railing without having to listen to what Mom referred to as Bampy's *sassiness*, which is what Mom called almost everything he said and did. Carl looked past Gram at Dodge Pond stretching out in front of them, partially hidden by the camo netting that surrounded the compound, the netting Dad and Bampy worked hard to maintain.

Carl moved after her, seeing how long he could follow before she noticed he was there. Making sure to maintain his slow, deliberate movements to avoid having to have Mom dig splinters from his fingers and palms, he veered off toward the other edge of the porch, reaching the railing the same time as Gram, though a good fifteen feet to the right.

"Jeremiah Richmond," Gram said, sounding like she was mad, though Carl knew she really wasn't, "you walk your old bones out here and talk to your *lady*."

Bampy chuckled. "As you wish, my dear," he said, stepping out and waving up to her with bloody hands. He bent forward in a dramatic half bow and winced. He tried to pretend his back didn't hurt, but both Carl and Gram were onto his tricks. "I beg your pardon for keeping you waiting. What is it I can do for you today?"

Gram laughed. "Cut it out." She leaned her cane against the railing and leaned alongside it. The railing moved just a bit. She looked down at Bampy and squinted, then smiled.

"What brings you out this way, my dear?" Bampy asked.

Gram looked at the pond, though Carl knew she couldn't really see much through the netting and the bushes and trees that had grown out of control. She took a deep breath. "Just wanted to let you know to bring an armful of wood into the camp when you come back up. We need to set another kettle boiling."

"You could have told me that when I came back in," Bampy said, smiling. "You sure you didn't come out for a quickie under the deck like old times?"

Carl wasn't sure what Bampy meant. There was nothing quick about plucking a rooster. For a moment he wondered if he should go back inside. Mom would be looking for him soon anyway. It was a wonder Zoey wasn't already after him.

"Ha!" she exclaimed, "you sure are a piece of work, old man."

"Indeed, I am," he said, raising his eyebrows.

She tossed her hands in the air. Carl knew Gram just wanted to get out of the house. Sending Bampy for wood was a pretty good reason as far as Carl was concerned.

"You remember our little cocktail cruises out on the pond?" she asked. Carl sat up and leaned on the rail. He looked out at the pond just like Gram was doing. The water caught the sun as it shimmered and reflected the glare through the waving trees and netting. Gram folded her arms on top of one another on the railing.

Excitement welled up in Carl's stomach. She hadn't caught him yet!

"What I wouldn't give for a margarita or a whiskey and ginger ale," Bampy said, turning and looking out at the water.

"The good days."

Gram sounded sad. It seemed like she was often sad these days. His excitement at not getting caught faded.

"These last years haven't been bad for us. We've made a very comfortable life for ourselves here," Bampy said.

Gram didn't say anything.

"I have a bottle of vodka stashed away if you want to join me in the shade for a drink," Bampy said.

"Where did you get a bottle of vodka?" Gram asked, eyeing him as she did whenever he was about to get in trouble, but Carl knew Gram was kidding. It was in her voice.

Bampy raised his hands defensively, a few feathers stuck to the tacky blood on his fingers and palms. He grinned again as he stared up at her. Gram gave him what Carl thought of as The Look, a look that both Mom and Dad described as *giving him the business*. The rest of the family made sure to keep their distance when Gram had The Look.

"Kelly might have slipped me an extra bottle with the last batch," Bampy said.

"Ah, so you're making shady deals with the hitchhiker, eh?" Gram laughed. Her expression relaxed as she leaned further over the railing.

"She's been a bad influence on me ever since we picked her up that night." Bampy ran a hand through his sweaty gray hair.

"Now, stop that!" she cried. "You just got blood and feathers in your hair!"

Bampy's lips curled down. He looked at his hands and shrugged. "Glad I can still get lost in a conversation with ya, Sarah. Completely forgot what I was doing down here."

"Guess I'm gonna have to give you a bath later," Gram said. "May as well prep the children if we're going to have hot water at the ready."

Carl froze, his teeth clenching. A bath. He hated baths.

Bampy frowned, "Great, now they'll be cross with me for a week."

"Good!" Gram cackled. "For once they won't be angry at their Gram!"

He shook his head and put his hands on his waist. "Are you going to join me for a drink or what?"

"Only if you clean those nasty hands of yours," she replied. "Go stick 'em in the pond."

Carl knew what was coming next and swallowed a giggle. Gram and Mom liked to push Bampy's buttons when it came to the pond water. Mom always said that the water was safe as long as it didn't get in your eyes, mouth, ears, nose, or . . . other body parts. Bampy disagreed.

Bampy cocked his head and raised an eyebrow. "Now you know better than that. No way I'm sticking a single finger in that cesspool."

"Yeah, yeah," she sighed. "Finish what you're doing down there while I grab a pot of water for ya to clean up in."

"You're the boss," he said with a smile before disappearing back under the deck.

As Gram slowly spun around, Carl froze in place. Their eyes met and his grandmother's lips lifted in a warm smile. She shook her head before bringing her finger to her lips.

She started *clop, clop, clipping* back to the door as Bampy went back to talking to himself about nothing. *Clop, clop, clip. Clop, clop, clip.* She made it about halfway across the massive deck before the wood began to tremble worse than Carl had ever felt it. The old deck was known by all to wobble slightly, but this was something different. This was scary.

Carl scooted backward toward the far end, wood splinters biting into the flesh of his hands and bare legs. A loud *crack!* filled the air followed by a loud *thump* from below.

"Sarah!" Bampy's voice turned Carl's stomach to ice. He scrambled forward to the gaping hole where his grandmother had just been.

He stopped himself as the boards shifted beneath him, staring down into a storm of dust and splinters swirling in the sunlight. He coughed as some of the dust swirled upward. The air cleared just enough for him to see Gram laying on her back, completely still. Her head rested on one of the large boulders that made up the edge of the foundation.

"No, no!" Bampy fell to his knees beside her and took her hand. "Sarah! Talk to me, please! Sarah!" He rubbed her hand between his. "C'mon, lady!" he said, his voice now an urgent whisper. Carl's breath caught in his throat as he saw blood trickling down the boulder's dusty surface. Bampy put his ear on Gram's chest, then sat up, rubbing her hand even harder.

"No, baby, no."

Carl stared at Gram's unmoving eyes as Bampy pushed himself to his feet. He scrubbed at his face and Carl could see new blood smeared across his cheeks.

"Gram?" Suddenly Carl couldn't breathe, as if Zoey were parked on his chest, something she liked to do when they were fighting. He sat up and saw Gram's cane laying at the edge of the ragged hole. He reached for the cane, but stopped himself as the boards creaked and shifted once more. His mouth went dry and he inched his way backward, keeping his eyes on the cane. For a minute he couldn't figure out why the cane kept blurring, then felt the tears burning down his cheeks. He watched as the last piece of his grandmother tottered forward and slid through the hole . . .

SIX

THE MIXTURE OF birch, evergreens, and underbrush thickened considerably as the day progressed, turning the old road into what might have once passed as a thin game trail. Were it not for the rocks that made up most of the trail, it was likely that the surrounding plant life would have reclaimed it by now. Instead of walking two-by-two with Tripp at the lead they were reduced to a single file progression through the thick woods.

Toward afternoon Carl came to fully embrace the concept of the *walking stick* as the trail turned mostly uphill. Well, it was actually *up-mountain*. The large, dried branch that Carl had chosen to help take the load off of his feet came in quite handy, though as enthusiastic as he was about it, he couldn't help shaking distant images of Gram from his mind every time he became consciously aware of using his new tool.

"Any chance we're going to stop for lunch?" Carl asked, immediately regretting the question. He had been so caught up paying attention to his footing as they climbed the rocky path that he didn't realize that he was speaking his thoughts aloud until it was too late.

He looked at Dad, who continued walking with no indication that he had heard at all. With a sigh of relief, Carl glanced over his left shoulder at Zoey. Over the years he had become quite adept at pinpointing when she was likely to tear into him proper. As his pace ebbed, she glanced up just in time to avoid crashing into him. Her lips pursed together and her eyes flashed. For a moment it seemed as though she was putting her words into the most efficiently hurtful sequence in her head before unloading them upon him. Fortunately, she was denied the opportunity.

"Tripp's onto something," Dad said. "Kelly, get the leash from Carl."

Carl grabbed the rope from where he had tucked it into the waistband of his jeans. He passed the rope to his mother who handed it along to Dad.

"Tripp!" Dad said. "Come here, boy."

The dog stood at attention some thirty feet up the trail, his nose lifted in the air. His head bobbed up and down ever so slightly as he processed the scents on the breeze. The white tip of his tail curled rigidly into the air.

The dog took a few additional sniffs, obsessively interested in whatever he was smelling, before he carefully made his way down the rocky path to Dad, glancing back repeatedly as he came.

Whatever was out there, it was inspiring behavior in the dog that they rarely witnessed. Anxiety gripped Carl's stomach and his mouth went dry.

As Tripp reached Dad and allowed the rope to be slipped around his neck, Carl could hear a slight rustling farther up the path. He swallowed hard, struggling to see through the overgrown brush. Judging by the growing noise, they would soon get a glimpse of the man or animal approaching.

Dad handed the end of the rope to Mom without looking back. He unslung the rifle from his shoulder and chambered a round. As his dad pulled the stock tight to his right shoulder, Carl heard the faint *click* of the safety disengaging. Very carefully, Carl shifted his weight onto his left foot and lifted his right onto a rock at the edge of the trail about the size of the old stump he'd used for a chopping block back home. He tested the rock's stability, then stepped up so he could see over the brush crowding both sides of the trail. The rock was large enough for him to stand with both feet quite comfortably, but the initial move put him briefly off balance. A momentary spike of panic exploded in his chest, but subsided as he recovered his equilibrium. The panic was replaced by a strange mixture of fear and curiosity as he gazed at the rocky trail ahead.

Carl could feel Zoey's eyes boring into the back of his head. He wasn't entirely sure if she was jealous for not having noticed the boulder first or if she was worried about him. Perhaps a bit of both. In any event, he was ready to jump back to the rocky trail at the first sign of danger.

Tripp let out a throaty growl as the sounds of snapping branches and tumbling rocks grew louder. Mom leaned down and stroked the dog's head.

"Shhhhh," she said softly as her left hand moved beneath the dog's muzzle and down his throat.

A high-pitched wheezing rose over the sounds of swishing pine and grinding rock.

Tripp growled again, then uttered a series of barks that actually sounded pitiful. Mom took hold of Tripp's muzzle with both hands.

Suddenly, a large animal broke through the brush. Rising from the left side of its head was a lone antler. The right side of its head had a barely noticeable stump where a second antler had probably been. The missing antler along with the fresh puncture wounds in its neck and chest suggested that it had recently been in a standoff with another horned creature. Its fur was filthy and mangy, and its left eye was swollen shut.

Exactly what had happened to the animal was unclear, but even as it struggled with its balance and blew out a hard gust of air, one thought registered in Carl's head: he was looking at a living, breathing *deer*! Its skinny legs and hooves scrambled frantically as it lost its footing on the rocks and came down hard on its side. It continued to struggle, legs scrambling in the air. The animal was so frightened it couldn't even get back on its feet.

Dad lowered the barrel of his rifle, but didn't sling it back over his shoulder. He carefully made his way toward the downed animal as Tripp tore his muzzle free from Mom's grip, barking furiously and straining against the rope.

When Dad was halfway to the deer, he glanced back at Tripp. "Tripp! Hush!" he quietly commanded. The dog quieted as the deer's wailing intensified. It struggled to regain its feet, but the feverish flailing only seemed to make things worse. Dad seemed to understand this, which explained why his approach was so unguarded, but it still wasn't clear just what he intended to do once he reached the animal.

Carl stepped off his rock back onto the trail. He began to make his way around his mother, intending to join his father. This was the first deer Carl and Zoey had ever seen. Both Dad and Mom had believed that the species had become extinct. Stories of the animals' power and grace had been shared over fires in the Rangeley House in great detail. Bampy had even kept a mounted head above his bed. This particular specimen hardly fit the mold, though, and Carl had a pretty good idea why. Based on the debilitating weakness of the creature and the way it wheezed—as if its lungs were full of liquid—he could tell it had consumed tainted water and was dying. Though its wounds were considerable, there was no mistaking that sound. He'd heard it from escaped rabbits and hens alike. It was always the same. Soon the deer would be coughing and defecating blood.

It was already dead and it didn't realize it.

He jerked to a stop as something—or someone—snagged his backpack. When he turned, he found Zoey close behind him, her face so twisted with frustration and disapproval that he dared not push her further.

Without a word he abandoned his intentions to join his father and turned to gaze back up the trail. Dad neared the animal and stopped just a few feet shy of its thrashing legs. After looking it over for a few seconds, he sidestepped off the rocky path, disappearing into the mess of brush and trees. For a while all Carl could see was the smaller saplings shaking as Dad moved through the dense foliage. After a minute or so he emerged back onto the trail above the deer and knelt down beside the animal, safe from the fury of its kicking legs.

The deer began to whip its head around, apparently trying to defend itself with its lone antler.

Where had the deer come from and how had it survived into adulthood? Based on the deer's wounds, it seemed as though it had been in a fight with another animal. Could there be others? If so, how had they survived?

Dad pulled his knife from the sheath on his belt. Taking hold of the deer's antler with his left hand, he pulled its head upward and drew the blade through the flesh of the animal's neck. Blood sprayed across the rocks and the deer gargled wetly for a moment. Then its thrashing legs calmed. A minute later it was still.

"It's . . . it's a *deer*, right?" Carl asked, equal parts curious and amazed.

Dad ejected the round he had chambered and slung the rifle back over his shoulder. He raised his right hand, indicating that Carl should lower his voice. It seemed to be a silly precaution— given how loud the deer had been—but Carl obeyed without question.

Dad motioned for them to come up the trail. "Keep the dog away," he whispered, his voice barely audible. "This guy's been drinking tainted water. That means it's in his blood."

Mom nodded and coiled the rope tighter around her right hand. Tripp pulled on the leash, intent on getting an up-close sniff of the deer as Mom moved carefully up the trail. A few rocks slipped from beneath her feet, rattling back down the path.

Behind her, Carl moved slowly, trying to stay patient and not rush his mother, though he could barely contain his excitement.

"Look at the size of that *tongue*," Zoey exclaimed softly, her voice coming from behind him as they reached the dead animal. The deer lay still upon the ground, its mouth open and its long tongue resting upon one of the larger rocks that made up the trail. Its glazed eyes, black as onyx, stared lifelessly down the mountain.

"Just don't touch it," Dad instructed as he wiped the blood off of his knife on the deer's hide. He tucked the knife back into its sheath and rose to his feet, his eyes remaining on the animal.

"How do you think he stayed alive for so long?" Mom asked, voicing the question in Carl's mind. She remained back a few paces, keeping Tripp away from the carcass.

Dad shook his head. "Can't say. It's possible he wasn't weaned from his mother until just recently, but no, that doesn't make sense—this is an adult deer. He had to drink water at some point early on. So did his mother." He sighed in obvious frustration.

"He's been fighting with other deer," Zoey said, pointing at the puncture wounds on the deer's chest and neck.

"Other deer, indeed," Dad said. "This means that somewhere out here the deer have found a way to stay alive and breed."

"A fresh water source?" Carl asked.

"Don't be a moron," Zoey said.

"That's enough of that," Mom said before Zoey could continue.

"Can't be," Dad said. He tightened the straps on his pack and turned to look up the trail. "Before Rangeley Town became too unsafe to visit, Bampy heard from almost everyone passing through that the water—all around the world—was completely tainted." His forehead creased. "There has to be some other explanation."

What other explanation could there be? Though Carl was not one to question his father's word, he found himself hard-pressed to find another explanation.

Dad reached out as Mom picked Tripp up and handed him over the carcass. Tripp twisted above the bled-out deer, his nose twitching feverishly.

With the dog safely in his arms, Dad took a few more steps up the rocky mountainside and waited as Carl, Zoey, and Mom made their way over the dead animal. Within minutes they were safely back on their way again, on the alert for other signs of life.

THEY FOLLOWED THE trail up and over the top of the mountain, arriving at its northern base by the time the sun touched the western peaks. Carl had figured they would have an easier, downward hike once they reached the summit, but it turned out to be nothing like what he expected. Though the trail was all downhill, the steep decline was no easier on his legs than climbing up. In fact, his muscles felt even more strained as he struggled to keep his balance on the rocks while competing against the force of gravity.

It seemed like it took them almost as much time to descend from the mountain as it did to make their way up, and with the majority of the day gone, Dad seemed hardly in a mood for talking once they reached the bottom. It was quite disheartening, especially since Carl was desperate to pick his dad's brain about the deer. After the trail leveled, Carl decided—against his own better judgment—to ask Dad the questions burning inside his head.

He stepped around his mom, making brief eye contact and smiling at the curious look on her face. To Carl's relief, she did not attempt to slow or stop him.

He came up behind his father.

"Not until we stop for the night, Carl," Dad said softly. He lifted a large pine bough out of the way and waited until Carl took hold of the branch. Ahead of them the trail connected with an old road before opening onto a vast clearing with waist-high, yellowing grass and another thick mess of pine at the opposite end. The road ran hundreds of feet straight through, and would have been barely noticeable beneath the gently waving grass if it weren't for its parallel gravel ruts. The grass had grown up around the edges and in the spaces between, but overall the road remained largely intact. A number of ancient stumps lined the edge. The cuts were so clean and flat that Carl wondered just what kind of axe had been used by the people who'd taken the trees down. Based on the large number of stumps, Carl suspected the grove of trees had been much larger, though the harder he looked, the more the grass concealed them.

"It's not about dinner," Carl said, handing the pine bough to his mother and watching as she handed it off to Zoey. It left him just enough time to see his sister shake her head at him.

They paired up at the edge of the meadow, walking together toward the far side, Dad and Carl in front and Mom and Zoey bringing up the rear. Tripp ranged ahead, the tip of his black tail waving above the grasses.

Finally, Carl raised the question he was dying to have answered, careful to maintain a degree of reservation to avoid making Dad angry.

"That was a male deer, right?" Carl asked, surprised to find his voice sounding weak and childish. It was almost as if he were trying to play the cute and innocent toddler who had no real understanding of when enough was enough with adults. Oddly, it seemed to work.

"A *buck*," Dad corrected him. "And, yes, it was."

Carl nodded, pleased at having drawn at least a few words from his father. He smiled. "That was a big buck, right?"

"About medium-sized," Dad said. Carl watched closely as his father studied the gently shifting blades of grass. As far as Carl could tell, the road hadn't been used by man or beast in years.

He thought about how an animal the size of the one they had come across could be turned into a winter-long feast and his mouth started to water. "Have you ever eaten buck meat?" he asked.

"Venison," Dad said, "or deer meat. Nobody calls it buck meat." He was silent for a moment. "Nobody *called* it buck meat."

"Have you ever eaten it?" Carl asked.

"I have," Dad said. "In the years before Black Christmas, Bampy used to bring me hunting up here."

"Is that how you know the trails so well?" Carl asked, shrugging his shoulders to adjust his backpack.

"We used to walk deep into the woods and sit around eating candy bars and drinking soda—that was what *hunting* amounted to back then. I can't say as I ever saw a live deer while I was out with him, but he always managed to find 'em on his own, mostly on the mornings when I was too lazy to get up before the sun and join him. It's ironic because when he hunted alone he was only one tier lower on the laziness scale—he'd load his rifle and a box of Butterfingers into the old plow truck and drive along clear cut roads just like this one until he either spotted a deer or set eyes on enough sign to pinpoint where they might be."

"What's a *sign*?" Zoey asked from behind them.

"What's a *Butterfinger*?" Carl asked at the same time.

"Butterfingers were candy," Dad answered. He had talked about candy in the past, but Carl had never tasted it and had no grasp of just what it was. Mom had given them honey from her beehives on special occasions, and would often liken it to candy, but something told Carl there was much, *much* more to it.

"And *sign*," Dad continued, "is any and all traces of an animal or a group of animals. Like piles of poop or places where the soil has been disturbed. Or places where tall grass is pressed down because an animal bedded down for the night."

Dad paused for a moment, his silence drawing Carl out of his thoughts about candy. He looked at his father, who was apparently waiting for more questions.

"Anyway," Dad said, "Bampy would pick the deer off from the truck or walk into the woods after them. Once he bagged his buck, he'd gut it right there on the spot and bring the animal back to town for weighing and butchering. We ate venison all winter. Steaks, ground meat, ribs. Ah, what I wouldn't give to see you kids with some real game meat in you." Dad frowned, then his face smoothed and he gazed at the forest on the far side of the meadow.

"That buck had to come from *somewhere*," Carl said with a smile. "Maybe we'll find more."

Dad didn't answer.

Carl slowed his pace a bit until he was walking beside his sister. Though he expected to get railed at over how much of a moron he was or something of the like, she said nothing.

Everyone seemed lost in their own thoughts. Tripp's head popped above the grass, looking back at them as if making sure everyone was still there. When his head lowered to the ground, his tail rose up to take its place. The tail drifted and swayed through the grass, Tripp's black and white contrasting with the brown and yellow of the meadow and making it easy to keep him in sight.

As they came within a hundred feet or so of the tree line, Carl halted as Dad stopped and called Tripp. Dad slipped the leash over the dog's head and handed the rope to Mom. There was no need for him to explain to any of them why he wanted the dog under control—the rotting, fetid stench of the swamp somewhere ahead spoke its own language.

Dad didn't hesitate to lead them into the dark woods. While the stench grew more and more robust with each step, the rotten egg smell of festering, bacteria-ridden mud and decaying wood overriding the scents of dirt and pine pitch, Carl knew his father wasn't about to turn back. The road was the only way forward— unless they wanted to backtrack over the mountain that they had spent the better part of the day crossing.

This part of the woods was the thickest they had yet walked through. White pines and spruce mingled with other trees Carl didn't recognize, creating a dense mass of vegetation that allowed very little sunlight to pass through the canopy above. Carl stared at the saplings struggling in the shadows of their elders. He marveled at the fact that the old road was intact and not completely overgrown. The gravel ruts that once were supposedly used by motorized vehicles seemed as if they could still be used, even after decades of neglect.

Carl's eyes adjusted to the dim light as the stench of the swamp grew more and more powerful. Tripp walked with his nose constantly lifted in the air, sniffing back and forth as he took in the scents. He didn't pull as he had when they encountered the deer on the mountain trail, but there was no denying his interest.

Carl moved to keep up as Dad adjusted the pack on his shoulders and quickened his pace a bit. Like the dog, Dad kept glancing back to make sure that everyone was with him. Carl stared for a moment at the sweaty black hair hanging limply against his father's neck, then glanced farther down the road and caught sight of a curious wooden structure in the distance. As they drew closer, he realized that the wood was in fact *metal*.

A weaving pattern of corroded steel waffled and arched its way up both sides of the road and Carl suddenly realized he was looking at what must be a bridge. The arches were supported at different intervals by matching rusted beams that ran at an angle up from the base where two wooden tire tracks traversed a series of thick, wooden planks. Beneath the bridge ran a modest-sized river that had been much larger at one time, judging by the small canyon cut into the landscape. The canyon snaked through the thick forest, though the small gap it created in the canopy above didn't allow much sunshine into the thick, evergreen tangle. The branches of the older pines that lined the river's edge had grown out of proportion under the influence of the tainted water, enshrouding the gap completely. It would seem that the tainted water was substantially more potent in swampy areas.

"Is that a . . . ?" Carl asked, suddenly uncertain he'd guessed right.

"A bridge," Dad said unenthusiastically. "Let me get a look before we cross it."

Nobody argued. Carl looked the structure over with interest. In all, the span was probably twenty feet in length, about half the length of their old front deck. This was the first time he'd laid eyes upon anything manmade outside of the Rangeley House. And a spoon or a kettle or a grandfather clock did not come close to being as impressive as this bridge—a testament to the long-forgotten powers of human ingenuity.

Dad reluctantly set his left foot on one of the wooden tire tracks, staring at the wood as though daring it to break. Though Carl could see what appeared to be rotted areas in the wood all over the bridge, the deck didn't give under his father's weight. A tiny flicker of anxiety sparked in his chest as images of Gram falling through the porch back home shot through his mind, images still as vivid and harrowing as the day the accident had occurred.

"If I make it across," Dad said, looking back at Mom, "each of you follows one at a time. Understood?"

As Carl watched his father begin to inch his way carefully across, he asked the first question that popped into his mind. "Why don't we just cross the river?"

He winced as someone slapped the back of his head. Turning around, he watched as Mom took hold of Zoey's hand and gave her The Look. Over the years Mom had honed The Look into a sharper weapon than it ever had been with Gram. Even Bampy had learned to mind it.

"The embankment is too high, son," Dad said, his tone emotionless and distant. Carl glanced back at the bridge as his father continued. "We'd get down there okay and cross the river in a

single leap, but getting up on the other side would be a chore."
Dad took another cautious step.

Carl studied the bridge and the water running beneath it and
saw what he had overlooked. The river itself was only four feet
across, but the banks along either side were close to twenty feet
high. Little reminders like this kept him thankful that Dad was
still around and in charge.

Once Dad reached the other side, he turned and motioned
for the next person to cross. Mom stepped forward with Tripp
in her arms.

"Send the dog on his own," Dad said. "No sense bringing any
extra weight with you."

She nodded and placed Tripp on the ground. Dad gave a low
whistle and Tripp set out across the bridge, his nose running
over every inch along the way. With only a brief stop near the
center to stick his head down between the thick beams that ran
beneath the deck, he made it across safely.

Dad picked the dog up in his arms and nodded at Mom, who
came to her feet and very daintily made her way down the same
track. Zoey decided to go next, keeping things slow, though her
stiff arms and awkward walk suggested a very obvious fear. As
she crossed the halfway point, it became obvious to Carl that
her fear was getting the better of her. Her pace quickened to a
jog, and she moved hastily toward Mom and Dad as they waved
their hands in an attempt to slow her down.

This was a great opportunity to show his sister up, and Carl
intended to exploit it to its fullest potential. He smoothed down
his thermal jacket and tightened the straps on his backpack before stepping up to the edge of the bridge. Without hesitation,
he began to walk very casually across the bridge, stopping every
now and then to look down through the beams or over the edges
of the metal railings.

Feeling quite impressed with himself, Carl continued his
walk, imagining that his family was watching from the other side

in captivated admiration. This delusion came crashing down as his father's irritated voice reached his ears.

"Carl," Dad said, "stop screwing around, and get your little rump over here. But, *slowly*."

With a frown and an acute spike of embarrassment, Carl automatically stepped forward without paying attention. His left foot slipped between the planks running beneath the tracks. His right foot slid out behind him in a half-split as his left leg was more or less *swallowed* by the bridge. With nothing to stop his momentum, he fell until his crotch met one of the cross planks. The pain in his penis and scrotum was worse than any blow he had ever taken from Zoey, worse than any fall he had ever taken in the yard. The world grew fuzzy around him and the voices of his family became muted and suddenly he felt like throwing up.

He shook his head vigorously as if it might somehow bring clarity to the world around him. He attempted to focus on his father at the end of the bridge. As Dad's blurry figure slowly sharpened, and the pain diminished enough that Carl was sure he wasn't going to pass out, he began to realize that something wasn't right.

It was the look of fear on Dad's face. Dad never showed fear.

The bridge moaned and Carl realized the wood around him was crackling and splintering. The aging metal squealed and suddenly all Carl could see was Gram's blood trickling down that dusty gray rock under the porch . . .

"Carl!" Zoey cried. Mom echoed the cry.

The world seemed like it was tinted red, the same red as Gram's blood. Carl watched numbly as his father went down on all fours and began to crawl out toward him. The bridge rumbled and shook. Panic welled up in his gut, adding to the pain in his pulverized crotch.

Carl used the pain to help him focus on the wooden tire tracks connected by the plank between his legs. Breathing deeply, he

placed his hands on each side, his fingers digging into the splintery wood, and attempted to push himself upward.

The pain intensified.

"Gah!" Carl cried He clenched his teeth and continued to
push himself up, using his right leg as leverage, but only managed to get halfway free before surrendering to the pain.

"Stop struggling," Dad gently commanded as the bridge
dropped a few inches. Bits of debris splashed into the water beneath them, sounding like the patter of rain upon Dodge Pond.
Carl focused on his father.

"Save your energy until I get there."

Somehow, Carl managed to relax though it seemed an eternity
before Dad reached him and stood.

He looked up as his father bent over him and reached beneath Carl's arms.

"When I say *push*," Dad whispered in his ear, "I want you to
do everything you can to move yourself out of that hole. As soon
as you're up, I want you to run to the other side, okay?"

". . . *kay.*" Carl clenched his eyes tightly against the anticipated
pain in his groin.

"Aaaaaand, *push!*" Dad cried, pulling up with what seemed
like boundless strength. Carl pushed upward as hard as he could
until he felt himself lifted free of the bridge. His stomach roiled
against the searing pain and again he felt as though he might
vomit, but he forced his eyes open as his feet touched down upon
shuddering wood. Still struggling through the pain, he felt the
bridge dip and bent his legs to keep himself balanced. A crackling *crunch* sounded from somewhere below them.

"Go!" Dad cried.

Though his testicles cried out at every step, Carl forced himself to run. Everything faded to a dull roar once more, including
Tripp's urgent barking. With each step the bridge seemed to fall
out from under him. He gave one final jump that carried him the

last four feet to the edge and fell face down on the gravel road. He lifted his head in time to see his father land beside him.

Cautiously, Carl looked back at the bridge. Though he expected the entire span to implode in on itself in a spectacular cloud of dust and debris, its final buckling was quite anti-climactic. The bridge groaned. At the center, where Carl had fallen through, the wood sagged before snapping in two and pulling the once-straight metal arches down along with it.

Dust and splintery debris rained down into the river.

Everything went still and Carl struggled to catch his breath, unable to part with the image of a single face in the aftermath of the bridge's collapse.

Gram's face.

SEVEN

ZOEY WAS GRACIOUS enough to refrain from administering her typical dosage of ridicule until they were a half mile or so away from the bridge. By this time they had entered the swamp, a festering stretch of damp, stinking earth that the old road meandered through, obviously laid in such an odd way to avoid the wet patches. The pungent stench of rot and decay seemed to overpower Carl's other senses as he moved along, relieved to feel the pain in his crotch diminishing to a light but persistent ache.

"You had us all really worried," Zoey said, her tone so syrupy Carl wondered when the bees would show up.

"Not now, Zo," he sighed, though a small part of him couldn't help admiring her ability to keep herself restrained until enough time had passed to ease his suspicions.

"I'm just saying that you could have been killed, and it didn't seem like that thought had even entered your mind until you slipped. Just think what it would have been like for Mom and Dad to deal with—"

"Stop it, Zo!" Carl growled. He looked at where Mom and Dad walked a dozen or so feet ahead, searching for some sign that they intended to step in, but for some reason they didn't seem to be paying attention.

"You little *idiot*," Zoey snapped. "Do you know what you could have done to this family? As if we haven't been through *enough* already! What was going on in that little brain of y—"

All at once the emotional turmoil building up inside him erupted. He grabbed Zoey by the shoulders and shoved. She landed on her backside with a hard *thud* that was accompanied by a loud clanking in her pack. She scowled up at him, her eyes burning.

"You *shit!*" she cried out.

"*Zoey Richmond!*" Mom yelled. Carl froze in place as if he were somehow the one who had uttered the word. The sounds of footfalls reached him as Mom closed the small gap between them and he turned around to face her.

Mom stopped above Zoey, her hands balled at her sides. Zoey remained where she was, staring up like a wounded animal too frightened to stand up and run away.

It took a lot to push Mom to the point where her kettle was on the whistle, but the use of swear words was always a reliable method. Bampy had, on a few occasions, attempted to remind her that in the old world it would have been a bit out of the ordinary to find a mother correcting her adult daughter for using such language, but he was always reminded that they weren't in the old world anymore.

And Mom's rules were hard as iron.

"Kel," Dad said calmly. He shifted his walking stick into his left hand and walked over, reaching out with his right to gently take Mom by the arm. She rolled his hand away with a flick of her shoulder, a tower of fury burning over Zoey.

Carl cringed. Instead of the arrogant sister, Zoey looked like a small child trapped in the shadow of her angry mother. He couldn't remember exactly when she had last been reprimanded. When they were small children such acts had been punished with a slap on the rear.

What, exactly, did Mom intend to do now?

"Please, Mom," Zoey pleaded, raising her hands in front of her. "I didn't mean it. It was a slip." She cringed, waiting for the axe to fall, eyes clinched shut. Carl almost did the same thing, but suddenly found himself gently laying a hand on his mother's shoulder and slowly stepping between her and Zoey.

"Mom," he said softly, watching as her eyes flickered. "We've been through a lot today." He paused for moment before reluctantly adding, "I shouldn't have pushed her down."

For a moment it looked as though Mom was going to push him out of the way. Then she slowly dropped her hand to her side, and took in a very deep breath, her fury visibly diminished.

"C'mon up, Zo," she said softly, sliding her hand around Carl's waist and pulling him close. The look of panic fled from his sister's face. She moved quickly to her feet and joined the group hug.

Mom's arms tightened and she planted a kiss on Carl's head. She turned her head, more than likely to give Zoey a kiss as well. "We need to find something for you two to put your energy into," she said, her voice reassuming its typical gentleness.

"You'd think walking through the woods all day would be enough," Dad said from behind them, sounding a lot like Bampy. His gaze was fixed on something farther down the road.

Carl followed his father's gaze. A few feet ahead of them the grassy hummocks and moldering puddles of swamp water came to an abrupt end. The road curved up a mild incline and around a corner, disappearing back into the trees. Tripp struggled against the rope, intent on moving down to the swampy water for a drink. Dad didn't seem to notice the dog's struggles.

Through a couple of tears in the thickening greenery above the sunlight had visibly begun to fade. Carl had been so obsessed with his slow recovery and inspection of the scenery around him that he hadn't been paying attention to the fleeting daylight. Looking back at his father, he realized that the man was anxious to get moving again. Probably wanted to put the swamp further behind them before making camp. There was little doubt in his mind that Dad was well aware of the time.

"We done with our little meltdown?" Dad asked, looking at each of them in turn. He coiled Tripp's leash around his right hand a few more times and gave the dog a quick yank to stop him from pulling.

"I'm sorry, Mom," Zoey said.

"I'm not the one you should be apologizing to," Mom said, releasing her hold on the two of them and stepping away. Without a word she began to make her way back up the trail toward Dad who was already on the move.

For a moment Carl and Zoey just stood there, studying each other. Carl was looking for signs of treachery while he was certain she was inspecting him for any cues that implied he intended to rub things in.

"I'm sorry I gave you grief," she said, rather begrudgingly.

Carl thought for a moment that he might call her out on the emptiness of the gesture, but he had learned from a very early age that such courses of action rarely ended in his favor. He nodded and clapped her on the back, eager to move on. It would be a lie for him to say that he wasn't somewhat hurt that she hadn't thanked him for saving her from the sting of Mom's hand, but Zoey was Zoey.

They walked for another mile or so as the road curled gradually up the low grade of a hill and the forest and brush began to thin out. The strong odor of the swamp stayed on the breeze and hung in the woods around them even though they were pretty far removed from the actual swamp. A few boggy areas showed up here and there, but became more and more infrequent. After they'd gone a quarter mile or so without any signs of water or mud, Carl watched with mild concern as Dad removed Tripp's lead and allowed the dog to roam freely.

That's when he saw the sign.

It couldn't have been more than two hundred feet ahead and was nothing more than an old piece of plywood nailed to a fir tree. The tree stood at what Carl thought might be the top of the hill. Faded words had been printed on the plywood in large, dark block letters, though at their current distance it was impossible to make the words out. Dad's pace quickened.

They covered the two hundred feet in no time at all, Carl marching close behind his father despite the building pain in his legs and the ache in his groin. They stopped just below the sign, and Carl could see that the wide board had once been painted white. It was attached to the tree about ten feet up.

The Cedar Swamp Inn

"What does it say, Dad?" Carl asked, looking the faded letters over. Time and weather had muted the paint to the point where it was now a cold gray against the browned wood, but they were still readable . . . for those who could read.

Bampy and Gram had expressed their regret on many occasions, as had Dad and Mom, that Carl and Zoey never learned how to read. Whenever the topic arose, it was usually Bampy who explained that reading materials had been used for fire and other survival needs long before Carl and Zoey came into the world. Had they known that their prolonged stay at the Rangeley House would end up being a permanent one as talk of the world collapsing and the water becoming tainted reached the mountain town . . . well, they would have planned better. As the years passed and Carl and Zoey grew into adulthood, the topic came up less and less. There was, after all, nothing to read around the camp.

"It says *The Cedar Swamp Inn*," Dad said, cocking his head at the sign like an animal trying to process something out of the ordinary.

Carl squinted up at the bottom of the sign, where additional lettering appeared. He stepped in closer and pointed. "What about this?"

Dad rose on his toes. "It says *No Vacancy*."

"What does all that mean?" Zoey asked. Carl turned as she and Mom came up behind them. Zoey's eyes nervously flicked between Dad and the sign, though Carl wasn't sure what had her so disturbed. "Is this someone's territory?"

Carl's stomach and chest tightened. He glanced back at the road with mounting paranoia. Who else had been here? Were they still around?

Dad shrugged. "It's some kind of hotel, obviously." The sarcasm in his voice was unmistakable and went a long way to calm Carl's nerves. Dad wouldn't be sarcastic if he thought they were in danger.

Though he wanted to ask his father exactly what a *hotel* was, Carl was still mildly frazzled and decided to keep his mouth shut and follow his father's lead. With one last look at his sister, who also seemed to relax, Carl followed his dad up to the breast of the hill. Dad stopped, looking down into the darkened wood of the forest, his thumbs hooked into his front pockets. Tripp trotted up and sat at Dad's feet.

Mom stopped beside Dad without looking at Carl or Zoey. Exactly why their parents weren't uncomfortable remained a mystery, but their easy manner helped Carl chase away his paranoia. Zoey walked slowly up the hill and joined them.

The road wound downward with the same thick cropping of fir and cedar along its edge. Darkness cast by the sprawling evergreen branches blocked out the dwindling light of day just as they had on the other side of the hill . . . on the other side of the sign.

"I've been here before," Dad said. His face lit up in an odd smile, making Dad look more like an excited child than a grown man. His eyes twinkled. "Back before Black Christmas. Bampy and Gram would pile everyone on snowmobiles and head this way. We'd usually pull off the trail at midday and roast hot dogs and drink hot chocolate. I was maybe ten at the time, but

I'm pretty sure the adults were drinking . . . something else." He turned to his right and parted the thick bushes lining the road, seeming to know exactly what he was looking for.

"It took me a second at first, but now it's clear as day." He shoved through the bushes, his voice fading. Tripp disappeared after him, his tail wagging enthusiastically.

Carl remained where he was, unsure if he should follow. Mom and Zoey also looked confused. They exchanged puzzled looks and then stared at the spot where Dad had vanished.

"Would you believe it?" Dad shouted, startling Carl. Of all the rules Dad had been a stickler about, staying quiet had been the most critical. "It's all still *here!*"

Carl shoved his way through the brush and branches. Based on the sounds of rustling needles behind him, Mom and Zoey were close behind. It wasn't long before he stumbled into a small clearing. He collided with his father's backpack, bouncing back as if he'd just hit a wall of solid brick.

Carl stepped back as his father stepped aside, revealing what remained of what must have been the Cedar Swamp Inn. A series of six boards, most of them rotted and drooping, were nailed to trees, parallel to the ground, like Carl imagined bunk beds would be. They were arranged in the center of a small clearing that had retained most of its space, with only a few struggling saplings popping up here and there. Directly in the center was the most impressive and elaborate piece of the fake hotel: what resembled a desk erected between two large cedars with a rusted-out metal grille just above it. It looked like a cage. Painted on the front of the desk in letters that had survived the elements much better than those on the sign at the road were more written words.

"What is it?" Carl asked, pointing at the grille.

"A check-in desk," Dad said. "This is a spoof on what we used to call *hotels* back in the old world. Think of it as a really bad version of a nice place where people would pay money for a room and a bed for the night. The desk is where you'd make the exchange."

Carl nodded, though he was a million miles away from really understanding. He pointed to the words beneath the check-in desk. "What does that say?"

"Cash and beer only," Dad chuckled.

"What *was* this place?" Zoey asked, stepping into the clearing and circling the check-in desk. "I mean, what was it *really*?"

"Just a drinking spot built by a bunch of good ole boys, I imagine," Dad said. He began to walk around and nearly tripped over something in the brown needles blanketing the ground. Hunkering down on his knees, he shrugged his backpack off and began to push the old needles aside, revealing a circular fire-pit built from rocks and cinder blocks. He looked up with a smile.

"Looks like we'll be checking in tonight," he said, his smile still beaming.

THE
OUTCASTS

EIGHT

B RYAR'S QUIVERING HAND moved slowly down from one flat, drooping breast as he suckled compulsively upon the other. His hand moved hesitantly across the aged and wrinkled abdomen to her cavernous navel and stopped. All of his fingers with the exception of his pointer folded back against his palm. The digit was boney and rigid, looking as if it might snap clean off with just the slightest amount of pressure. Beneath the overgrown fingernail was months' worth of filth, which turned the ends black as the night sky above.

The finger encircled her naval seductively for a few seconds, just as she liked it, gliding over her loose skin until slowly moving inward, toward the center like water circling a drain. Once his fingertip fell into the hole, he wriggled it around for a moment before setting it back on course to its main destination. The rest of his dirty fingers splayed out as they moved through the tangled jungle of pubic hair that rose like a thick triangle from between her legs.

She began to moan in anticipation.

This excited him, mostly because it meant she would probably be done quicker and he could get some sleep. He began to work her over with a greater amount of feigned passion and interest.

He pursed his lips tightly around her nipple and sucked hard, pulling it as far as he could into his mouth as his tongue circled around the pointy nub. Her moaning intensified, and he began to tap his fingers gently upon her lower belly as they made their way slowly through her little forest. Looping his left arm around her neck, he went to work on her other nipple with his free hand, both pulling and twisting harshly in the manner she preferred.

"Oh, Anthony," she moaned, calling him by his sex name. In the thirty plus years they had been up to this kind of business, not once had she ever broken character and called him by his real name. Just once, when she had first taken him into her bed as a child, he had asked if perhaps he might call *her* by a different name. That night he got a beating instead of a screw.

Molly Perkins went by one name and one name only: Ma' Lee. It was an interesting twist on her birth name and the fact that she had raised a litter of children. The locals back in South Berwick had given her the mantle back in the old days, thinking themselves mighty clever for it. She liked the nickname enough to not only keep it, but to ravage anyone who addressed her otherwise. Ma' Lee was the type who wouldn't think twice about sinking her nails into anyone who crossed her, members of her little brood not excluded.

"C'mon, Ma'," Bryar cooed, speaking out of the side of his mouth while he continued to stimulate her. He bit gently down on her nipple. "Purr for your Anthony, baby." His hand stopped just above the withering blossom between her legs where both of her hands were already hard at work. Slowly, his middle finger crept, alone, down through the oozing slit to where it settled on the tiny bulge of her clitoris. Her hands moved immediately away, settling on her bony thighs as she let his finger take over. It slid up and down and back and forth over the slippery surface, sending what he could only imagine to be bolts of lightning up into her gut with every pass.

Her moaning intensified to the point where her voice echoed throughout the empty building so loudly that Bryar worried it might wake the others. They had taken up temporary residence in an old shop right on the main strip in downtown Rangeley. Judging by the empty clothing racks and smashed glass display cases, which he could see quite well in the light of the full moon filtering through the surprisingly intact windows, he reasoned that it had once been a clothing store, though he knew very little about such things. He had only been eleven years old on the last Christmas Eve the world would ever see. Still, there were distant, foggy memories hiding in the dust and darkness at the back of his mind from the years before the water turned. They included visions of him walking through a mall with his mother. It was there he had seen similar racks and display cases, though often enough from the inside out as he used them to hide from her.

Regrettably, he'd always been found.

In an effort to keep himself from moving too quickly, he left his finger in its current task for another couple of minutes. If he did this too fast and the buildup wasn't proper, he would end up having to give her another. His eyes moved past her left breast to where his siblings huddled together at the opposite end of the abandoned store. They lay there, completely still, in spoon-type formation with their jackets draped over them for added warmth. At the very end of the group was Casey, the youngest of them and the only other female in the group. Her belly bulged, full of baby ready to pop out at any moment.

With a sudden hit of sick discomfort, he refocused on Ma' Lee. It was time to finish her off. He could tell by the way she shivered and breathed in a sputter that she was close. Clenching his eyes tightly closed, he set his tongue swirling like a tornado around her nipple and slid his middle and index finger into her.

Her climax was explosive, to the point where Bryar had to cringe away as she screamed directly into his ear. He quickly collected himself and moved back to her breast so as not to break the system that had delivered her so expertly to this moment.

Be finished, he thought as her body lurched upward and her legs clenched. His fingers and hand felt crushed between them. No matter how many times he had been through this with her, it almost always ended this way, and he never seemed to remember to expect it.

"Ooooh, waaaah," Ma' Lee cried out, "Yes, Anthony, *yes!*" Her hoarse, crackly voice—a memento from the old days where she would put away two-plus packs of Marb Reds a day—filled the room, causing those at the opposite end to stir.

Please don't wake up, Bryar thought, suddenly changing his plea to the universe around him. The only thing worse than Ma' Lee desiring more and forcing him into proper intercourse was what would occur if she detected anyone watching them. It would be brutal. It always was.

As Ma' Lee's arched back fell slowly down to the rough, carpeted floor of the old store, Bryar focused in on the group in the corner. To his horror, Casey's head slowly lifted from where it had been resting upon her curled bicep. She looked around the store in confusion, searching for the source of the noises that had woken her before quickly realizing what was going on and immediately dropping her head back down and feigning sleep.

Oh, thank you, Bryar thought. He gazed back at Ma' Lee, watching as she settled back down. Reluctantly, he removed his hand from between her legs and brought it up to rest on her wrinkled stomach.

Was it over?

She took a deep breath and sat up, pushing his hand off as if she were suddenly repulsed by the contact. She didn't even look at her son as she turned her back to him and went about putting her clothes on.

She was done.

~

Bryar woke to the rays of early morning sunlight coming in through the smudged windows of the store. He'd managed a few hours of sleep, but the fogginess of his mind and the soreness in his back and shoulders told him that it hadn't been enough. Typical for a morning after Ma' Lee got it in her head that she needed a little pleasing. It had been that way for over forty years, ever since he'd been a small child, innocent and defiled by his own mother, a woman whose elevator didn't quite make it to the top floor.

She was a very powerful woman. Not a single person who knew her would dispute this fact. Not even William Dewoh, who had dismissed them from his wandering posse after figuring them for the degenerates they were. He'd had to do it in the dead of night because he was legitimately fearful of how this 105-pound, sixty-two-year-old woman would react. Ma' Lee didn't look all that imposing, she was mostly skin and bone, but even a starving and emaciated cougar was dangerous. Dewoh knew this, which was why he'd snuck off while they'd slept.

That was two days ago, and Bryar and his siblings were still healing from the wounds their mother had inflicted upon them when she vented her frustration. Every time he sat up after waking from sleep, his stomach cried out in pain, almost forcing him back down again. Every accidental bump of either bicep was an agonizing reminder of how erratic and violent she was.

His younger brothers—Brett, Jackson, and Wade—had taken the brunt of her fury. They were all pretty close in age with Brett at thirty-seven, Jackson, or *Jack* as they called him, at thirty-six, and Wade at thirty-five. The bruises and cat scratches across their bellies and backs and necks had all been gifted to them by their *loving* mother on the day of Dewoh's abandonment. While their wounds were pretty harsh, though, Casey's were the worst.

Ma' Lee hated Casey. The twenty-four-year-old was always the first to feel her mother's wrath. Casey was a constant reminder of Ma' Lee's perverted sex. Though Bryar could count on one hand the number of times he found himself moved to a climax and subsequent ejaculation while inside her (every one of them while drunk), the cruel gods of fate had seen to it that fertilization took place. Ma' Lee had tried to terminate the pregnancy using a whole manner of diabolically clever methods, but Casey was a fighter from the outset and hung on until birth. When Ma' Lee attempted several times to abandon or outright murder the baby, Bryar had been there, fighting for her life, finding the willpower to refuse his mother's carnal desires if she attempted to harm the child. He took many beatings, even shed blood, but he eventually won.

The only thing he found himself unable to protect his daughter from was his younger brothers. The child growing in her stomach was a constant source of anxiety. Soon it would be time to fight for another tiny, innocent life born into a world full of ravenous wolves.

He lifted his head and looked at his mother through his tangled locks of shoulder-length, blond hair. She'd moved to the back of the store and now lay beside a wooden counter with a smashed-in display case. Though all he could see were her stained denim pants and her fuzzy bean boots with the odd steel toes, it was fairly safe to assume she was asleep. Still, he wouldn't put it past her to fake sleep while eavesdropping on her children, if only to find some flimsy excuse to unleash the fury that always teemed within her.

Sitting up slowly, Bryar moved quietly to his feet and walked over to his daughter, leaving a trail of footprints that crisscrossed with the others his family had left behind in the dust-encrusted carpet. Though the store had been looted long ago, there was very little debris aside from scattered coat hangers, shards of glass around the display case, and a few toppled clothing racks. He stood over Casey as she lay with his three siblings spooned up behind her. He gazed lovingly down at her. The bruises on her face had turned a deep purple the day before but were now starting to show signs of fading. It was a wonder the poor girl hadn't suffered a dislocated jaw or broken nose. The older scars that were generally a lighter shade of cream on her cheeks, jaw, and forehead had been blotted out by the new damage. Any other wounds were hidden from sight by Casey's long, blonde hair.

Her belly poked out from beneath her tattered pink sweat-shirt. Across the chest, letters spelling out *Ogunquit* had been very slowly losing their stitching and threatened to fall off at any time. The letters hung like leaves from a tree in the fall, clinging delicately to the branches that would eventually surrender them. Her free hand and arm rested on the exposed areas of skin at the bottom of the sweatshirt as if trying to hold in as much warmth as possible. They hadn't come across any maternity stores. They had to make do with what they had, and a very harsh and defeat-ing truth about their existence was the fact that everything they came across in the way of supplies was funneled down through Ma' Lee. She always got the first crack at caches of food and clothing. Though such events were very rare (Bryar could recall only three major finds in the nineteen years they had been roam-ing the state), they still occurred, and not a single scrap of food was permitted to touch their tongues until their mother's belly was full.

Bryar pulled his hooded sweatshirt off, bent down, and covered the exposed portion of his daughter's stomach. The sweatshirt was two sizes too large for him and had once been black but was now a sun-bleached gray. He reached down and pulled Casey's hole-ridden wool socks as high as he could over her skinny legs and pulled down on the cuffs of her faded blue jeans. The socks came down again with the pant cuffs but this couldn't be helped; they had lost their elasticity long ago.

Satisfied she was as comfortable as he could make her, he turned away and rubbed at his arms with his hands, not terribly cold, but made mildly uncomfortable by a small nip in the still morning air. He smoothed down the ratty blue t-shirt he wore. Having been a part of him for nearly a decade, the garment was delicate and full of holes just like everything else the group wore to cover themselves against the elements. It almost felt as if the material might crumble apart as he tugged at the bottom.

A minute or so passed, and he began to miss his sweatshirt, though he would not take it back now. The chill in the air was definitely hard to ignore. A part of him had hoped that the mild weather they had experienced the day before would last, though Bryar knew he was an idiot to hope for anything. It made him wish that they had set out the previous morning instead of hanging out a couple days in the store. There was no doubt in his mind that Ma' Lee would have them on their way soon given that there really wasn't anything in Rangeley for them. Besides, she had issues about staying in the same place for too long.

But when would Ma' Lee decide to move on? And where would they go?

Northbound travel made little sense given how much harsher the conditions grew in the wintertime, but southbound travel was also hazardous. While the temperature farther down the East Coast was more agreeable during the dark months of winter, the population was denser, and with a higher population of people, you inevitably came across the more massive, structured militias.

This was an acceptable tradeoff for a few months of cold, but they had already made their way a good fifty-plus miles north of the last militia-controlled territory without capture. There was no need to continue pushing toward what was once Canada, at least not in his mind. But he wasn't the one with the say. Not a single shred of democracy could be found in their little group. Ma' Lee had the first and last word on every issue or decision, something that she had butted heads with Dewoh about on more than one occasion. It wouldn't surprise Bryar at all to discover that this had been a large contributing factor to the man's decision to leave.

He turned away from Casey and walked to the windows at the front of the old store. They ran floor to ceiling and were about six feet wide. Four windows made up the front of the building, two on each side of a heavy entry door that showed signs of once being boarded up, perhaps against looters.

Gazing out onto the silent, empty street, he tried to imagine what the town had been like before the final Christmas. Many signs still remained above the various shops and restaurants that lined each side of the strip.

Rangeley was a curious place. One minute they'd been walking through thick forest overlooked by massive peaks and deep valleys, then all of a sudden they were in the middle of a medium-sized town complete with its own single-screen movie theater! Had people been inside watching movies that Christmas?

He'd been eleven years old and had loved going to movies. All he could remember of the last motion picture he had ever seen amounted to short blips of bright-colored animation accompanied by zany voices. Though he could remember how entertaining it was and how great it felt to have been away from his mother for a few hours, there was little else he could piece together in his head as far as details went. In fact, he didn't really remember any details at all.

Forcing the fuzzy haze of long, lost memories out of his mind, he refocused on Main Street Rangeley. He imagined the tall grass receding back into the earth and the cracked segments of roadway melding together. In his mind the yellow and white paint marking the lanes and parking spaces brightened once again, and polished cars that gleamed silver and gold in the sunlight raced back and forth. Little girls and boys dressed in pastel dresses and slacks skipped down the sidewalks without a care in their little heads while others laughed and munched on sweets in the shadows of the storefronts.

A smile spread across Bryar's face even though the dismal reality of life in the new world hung like a cloud over his fantasies. An odd sadness flushed through his body, diluting the tiny bit of joy he allowed himself. These visions were bittersweet. Enjoyable as they were, they represented a time and way of life that would never come back to this world. Smiling children trotting down the sidewalk without a care in the world? What kind of fable was this?

Gloom and despair returned to Main Street Rangeley as his daydream turned dark. The road cracked and the grass returned. The motor cars ceased to cruise the strip and were still as the rust that had consumed them returned. The children began to scream and run as if pursued by demons. The sweets in their hands turned to ash and they cried out—

"Where's your sweatshirt, boy?"

The screaming children disappeared as Bryar choked back a blood-curdling scream of his own. His body shivered uncontrollably at the feeling of warm breath on the back of his neck. Ma' Lee.

"I, uh," Bryar managed to say, "I was warm so I took it off." He took a deep breath and hoped beyond hope that she wasn't interested in a morning romp. Typically, she would come to him at night, but it wasn't *completely* unheard of for her to want him at the start of the day.

"It's freezing in here," she said as she walked around him.

He watched her out of the corner of his right eye as she stopped beside him and stood gazing at the town. For a minute or so she was silent.

"I said it's *freezing* in here. Where's your *sweatshirt*?" she yelled.

Behind them, someone groaned and she spun slowly around.

Bryar turned to his mother as her lips curled into a scornful frown. Her brow furrowed, pushing her light-tinted eyebrows down over her twitching eyes. Her nostrils flared as her drooping lips pursed together.

"Ma'," he said, reaching out to take her by the arm. He clenched his eyes tightly shut as his fingers failed to catch hold of her tan, hooded sweatshirt. Though he knew what was likely to follow, he dared not get in the way. If Ma' was in the mood for a fight, she would have it, no matter what anyone did.

A loud *slap!* was followed by an immediate howl of pain. Bryar's eyes opened, and he took a few steps toward Ma' Lee. She loomed over Casey who stared up, bleary eyed, from the floor. Bryar's gut clenched as he stopped where he was. Ma' Lee snatched his sweatshirt from Casey's stomach before delivering a furious series of slaps to the girl's face. Once again he closed his eyes, this time so tightly his eyeballs felt like they would explode out the back of his skull.

Footsteps thudded on the carpet as his brothers raced toward the front of the store and joined him. He could hear Wade panting like an excited dog, almost certainly enjoying the events as they played out. Wade was almost as warped as their mother, while the other two were no doubt just as fearful as Bryar, though he knew they could care less about what was happening to Casey. Ma' Lee might shift her attention to one of them when she was finished.

When at last Ma' Lee's hand was still and Casey's agonizing howls had diminished to a steady whimper, Bryar opened his eyes. Ma' Lee stood in front of him, his sweatshirt held out in her hand. Her hair hung in strings in her face and beads of sweat clung to her wrinkly skin.

He reached out, making only brief eye contact. He froze, his hand stopping inches from the garment. His mother's fully dilated pupils were large islands in a sea of white and red. They gazed right through him, seeming to enter his mind and his thoughts, searching for anything and everything she could use to break him down.

His jaw began to quiver. Beside him, Wade grinned goofily, his wiry hair sticking out of his all-but-bald head in odd places. Wade's only remaining teeth, four of them—all in his lower jaw, stuck up from his ashen gums like plateaus in a desert of filth and disease. When Ma' Lee's eyes briefly flickered over to her youngest, her lips pursed once more and she smacked him so hard that Wade fell to the floor. As his hand went instinctively up to his cheek, he looked back up at his mother. His smile intensified.

"What have I told you about—" She kicked him several times in the gut until he was a cringing ball.

Ma' Lee turned back toward Bryar and pushed the sweatshirt into his arms. He allowed himself a single look over her shoulder, just enough to see Casey struggle into an upright sitting position with her hands cradling her belly. He looked long enough to make sure that she was okay, not that he'd ever known her not to be.

Casey was a fighter.

"Get whatever gear you miserable wretches have together—on the double," Ma' Lee growled, her wild eyes darting around. "I've had enough of this place." As she walked back toward the rear of the store, she stopped briefly in front of Casey and slapped her again, sending the girl back to the floor.

NINE

NORTHBOUND IT WAS.

Bryar walked with Casey at the rear of the group, shouldering a backpack that he had filled with both of their belongings. Despite the pain that had jolted through his upper arms when he'd threaded them through the straps, his shoulders were appreciative of the couple days' reprieve they had been granted. As always, Casey made her way like a trooper, waddling along at a pace that kept up with the one set by Ma' Lee.

The buildings on either side of the road began to thin out as they made their way through the knee-high grass that had claimed the roadway. Bryar found himself somewhat disheartened to be leaving the town behind. Up until then they had traveled through a number of industrial cities, each built around the massive, smokeless stacks of paper mills, and each militia-controlled. Here they had found a quaint place nestled in the arms of auburn mountains without a single soul laying claim to it. Old store fronts with chipped and fading paint and windows that were still intact, boasted names like Mosquito Outfitters with barely legible slogans like "Mosquitos: The Maine State Bird!"

He tried to take a good mental picture of it all. For he knew he would never see it again.

At first they moved westward along the main strip as Ma' Lee searched for the route that would eventually carry them north. As the shops and stores grew less frequent, leaving only the birch and pine and grass that had grown up in between the buildings, they eventually came upon a roadway that jutted off to their right like a withered limb. Here the cracked pavement was visibly looser and almost bleached white from decades of unending sun. An old gas station sat on the corner, the station's rectangular, digital pumps torn apart long ago. The skeletal remains of old beverage coolers and the metal racks within tickled Bryar's memory, reminding him of the days when he was happy to get two sodas for $3, then the memory faded.

Casey had never known such things, nor had any of Bryar's younger siblings. They were all much too young—in Casey's case, not even born—to remember what it was like to crack open a fizzing bottle of pop and knock it back. Bryar envied them on a certain level: they couldn't miss what they'd never known.

Ma' Lee, on the other hand, was an obvious member of a small minority who preferred the struggle they endured on a daily basis. She was much more comfortable in this world. She was made for it.

"You okay?" Bryar asked Casey as they turned the grassy corner opposite the gas station where the sidewalk finally came to an end and began walking north. He kept his voice at a whisper to avoid drawing Ma' Lee's attention, and though he spoke to Casey, his eyes remained fixed on the long tangle of blonde-and-gray hair that extended down his mother's back.

"A little sore," Casey said, "but I've had worse."

"I know you have." He ran his right hand nervously through his hair. "How's the little guy?"

"Been still these last few days."

He took a deep breath and let it slowly escape his mouth. His mind was suddenly bursting with thoughts of the horrible things Ma' Lee might do to the child once it came. Second on his list of worries was Wade, whom he suspected to be the father. There was no telling what his youngest brother might do—or *try* to do—with something so little and innocent, but Bryar had seen what his brother had done with the various animals they had encountered. Though he didn't like to think about it, the only way Casey's baby would survive was to get it away from their little group. With Ma' Lee's obsessive attention, this was nearly impossible. Even if he and Casey were to somehow sneak away, Ma' Lee would have his younger brothers on their trail in no time.

"It's a good thing she prefers the face," he said, looking back at his mother. They had already pushed their luck.

Casey lifted her hands to her face and ran them down over her scars and disfigured nose, a nose that had been broken by her mother several times. Her hands drifted down to her belly. With a deep breath and a nod, she offered her silent agreement.

The group walked in silence as the sun made its way across the clear autumn sky. They carefully maneuvered among the shards of the old road, the smattering of birch and pine thickening considerably the further north they went. Occasionally, a rusted sign would come into view, giving the road designation. This told Bryar they were on an old single-lane highway connecting some of Maine's mountain towns.

Though the temperature wasn't as mild as the previous day, it was still bearable despite the coldness of the morning. Bryar pushed up his sleeves after an hour or so on the march, but he didn't break into a sweat. The farther north they went, the fewer manmade structures they saw, and most of those were old houses and camps, long abandoned, and in most cases demolished by the elements.

One place that caught his curiosity, mostly because of his fondness for the old culture, was an old logging museum. It was a large, two-story building perched at the top of a downward-sloping hill. A number of rusty antique tree-cutting instruments and tools sat in a sea of tall grass that used to be some kind of yard. Above the collection was an open-sided, wooden structure erected from crudely cut beams and capped with a decaying tin roof. Only a small portion of the roof still stood; the rest had collapsed upon the artifacts it had once protected. If it hadn't been for the sign out front, the exact purpose of the place would have been a mystery.

Bryar watched as Ma' Lee studied the sign swaying back and forth in the light wind. She stopped and turned around, wiry strands of hair hanging in her face.

"Brett, Bryar," she said, looking at each of them in turn before nodding at the museum. "Head on in, see if you can't find us something long and sharp since that *masshole* Dewoh made off with all the big knives." She pulled a small switchblade with a worn, wooden handle out of her front pocket. Even though it was a sharp, working knife—that fortunately she had never thought to use on any of her children—she stared at it as if she were sick of looking at the thing. Without a word, she returned the blade to her pocket and looked back at them.

Brett nodded and a lock of greasy blond hair flopped across his face. He pushed the hair back behind his ear and dropped the backpack he carried before straightening his black, woolen coat. Pulling on the belt that held up his jeans (which were a couple sizes too large despite the fact that he was easily a size forty-two), he began to walk slowly over to the building. Bryar hesitated. He didn't want to leave Casey alone with Ma' Lee and Wade. Jack wasn't much of a threat. He was quiet and kept to himself. Still, Bryar couldn't count on Jack to stand between his mother or younger brother if either of them were to make a move on the poor girl.

"Casey," Bryar started, "why don't you come take a seat on the porch over here and get some rest while we—"

"She'll do no such thing!" Ma' Lee hissed, stepping toward them. She stopped in front of Bryar. "You'll do as you're told, and the little cunt will stay right where she is. 'Less you *both* want a flaying." Bursts of spittle jumped from her chapped lips as she spoke, landing on his nose and forehead. One drop hit right in his eye.

Bryar rubbed at his face, turning slowly away with a frown. Casey knew better than to say anything, but he could tell that she understood how much he didn't want to leave her. They had been in this same position many times before. Though he had opted to stand against his mother on a few occasions in the past, his brothers had no problem holding him down if Ma' Lee decided to work him over.

Bryar sighed and made his way slowly through the tall grass toward his brother. Brett stood in front of the main building, looking more than ever like the stocky brute that he was, with his fingers pushed into his front pockets and his thumbs hanging out. He turned when Bryar joined him, and they headed toward the museum's front door.

"You really are a dumb shit," Brett said, shaking his head in what could have been frustration, though Bryar knew better than that. His brothers loved how defiant he sometimes was, regardless of how weak his resolve to act always seemed to be. It took the negative attention from Ma' Lee off of them and almost seemed to strengthen the bond that they shared with the woman. Though they would probably never find themselves the objects of her perverted lust as Bryar was, they were at least treated like true sons. That is, they were ordered around and occasionally rewarded.

"Let's see how much that mouth of yours starts flapping when Ma's beatings go too far one day," Bryar snapped. "There goes the body that keeps your belly warm at night. Not to mention the other uses you perverts get out of her."

"Yeah," Brett laughed, "at least I'm not her half-brother *and* her father."

They always liked to throw that at him when Ma' Lee wasn't around. They knew better than to speak openly of her lustful interests in her presence. That would earn them the beating of a lifetime.

"You just wait, Brett." Bryar sighed, taking the first step onto the dilapidated porch that ran up to the front door of the building. He felt the wood give a bit under his weight but quickly judged it stable enough to support him with only a slight bowing. "One day I'm either going to disappear or work up the nerve to finally end it all, and when I do you'll be next in line for her." The last part was a bluff for certain. He'd never kill himself and leave Casey alone, but he hoped that Brett, dull as he was, might overlook this fact. He took hold of the metal railing that ran up the right side of the porch and wasn't at all surprised to feel it come loose in his hands. With a gentle push, he sent the rail crashing to the ground in a heavy *foof* that sent a small cloud of dust drifting up through the grass.

As the dust was carried a few feet away by the light wind, Bryar felt his brother's hand come to rest on his shoulder. He turned toward Brett, fully expecting what came next, and the scumbag didn't disappoint. Brett's left fist hit him hard in the jaw, sending Bryar stumbling back off the step. It was just a few feet, though he managed to land on his back on top of the metal railing he'd shoved aside. Pain bolted through his shoulders. He tried to get his bearings as two suns spun erratically in the sky. The pain in his face didn't hit him with too much intensity at first, though the jolt to his brain left him severely disoriented and his ears rang. He squeezed his eyes shut as the pain in his lower jaw spread to just below his ears. For a moment he wondered if the jaw was broken and somehow found the nerve to move his mouth from side to side.

Not broken as far as he could tell. Opening his eyes, he watched as two Bretts stepped into his field of vision, both wearing massive smiles. Bryar blinked a few times and the two images came together into one solid. Brett fished around in his front pocket, no doubt looking for the four-inch folding knife he kept there, but if it was his intention to use the knife on Bryar, he quickly changed his mind. His hand came out of the pocket empty.

Just a gesture then. A gesture that said, *I could kill you if I wanted to.*

Both he and Bryar knew it to be an empty threat. Nobody touched Ma' Lee's sex puppet, at least not in any *serious* way.

The sound of Ma' Lee's cackling laughter reached his ears as the ringing from his brother's blow began to go away.

"Got anything left to say to me?" Brett asked, leaning down with his hands on his knees. His smile did not waver. Not even slightly.

Bryar tested his jaw again and looked up at his younger brother. "No." He wasn't about to risk another potentially bone-breaking blow from the psycho.

Brett turned around, shaking his head, and made his way back to the porch.

Bryar rolled onto his side and struggled up to his feet. Much to his relief, he was allowed to get up without Ma' Lee calling for more blood.

Still dizzy, he stumbled to the porch and up the steps where his brother was already kicking at the door. Bryar stayed back to avoid being hit as Brett used every bit of brute strength in his arsenal to bash his way into the old museum. After maybe a half-dozen powerful kicks, the door flew inward in a spray of splinters. They raised their arms protectively as the door crashed to the floor, sending a cloud of dust billowing into air that had apparently gone undisturbed for decades.

"Ladies first," Brett said after a quick look around the dark interior. He stepped aside and waved Bryar in.

Bryar glanced back at the roadway. Casey remained untouched. With a sigh, he walked obediently into the building, shoulders hunched against a kick from behind. Fortunately, the kick never came. Instead, he was allowed to walk all the way into the dark room with Brett a few paces behind him.

His eyes adjusted to the darkness, aided by the trace amount of light that managed to find its way in through the boarded-up windows. Dust drifted lazily through the air. Though the outside of the building looked more or less like a two-story house, the inside was unfinished and rustic, reminding him of a barn. The scents of wood and dust were strong in the air, a reprieve from the typical smells of death and decay they'd encountered in buildings elsewhere. This place was far enough into the woods to have been left alone for quite some time.

A set of stairs lay directly ahead of him, with a slotted box mounted upon a pedestal reading "Suggested Donation: $3.00/person. $5.00/family." The stairs led to an open loft that circled the four sides of the room. Five-foot-long saws that looked like they required two people to operate hung on the walls along with a number of chains with hooks on either end. Spikes secured to long, sturdy poles and a whole manner of metal cleats that attached to boots and were meant to aid in climbing trees were piled against the wall in several corners.

There were no axes or knives in plain sight.

To the immediate right of the entrance was what appeared to be an old kiosk or checkout counter. An old electric cash register rested beneath a thick layer of dust. Pinned to the front and top of the desk were a number of neon-colored t-shirts, proudly displaying the very to-the-point name of the museum: The Rangeley Lakes Logging Museum.

Brett yanked the garments from the wall, sending thumb tacks to the hardwood floor in a series of muted *pings*. He slung the shirts over his shoulder, placed both hands on the counter and vaulted over. Then he went to work looking through various cabinets and drawers.

Bryar worked his way deeper into the museum, shivering as the overall eeriness of the place hit him. There was something about being in an old, abandoned building, untouched for so long. It was like being in a haunted house, only it wasn't the ghosts of deceased people who roamed the halls; it was the ghost of another world, a world they would never know again.

Suddenly, any interest he'd had in the place abandoned him. He wanted to get out of there—now—but if he didn't make a proper inspection, he would almost certainly pay for it.

Walking the rest of the way toward the stairs, he placed his foot on the first step and tested its structural integrity by leaning his weight on his foot. Much to his surprise, it didn't offer so much as a single creak. He took hold of the unvarnished wooden railings and moved his other foot onto the step. Still no signs of giving. With a quick look back at Brett still rummaging through the junk behind the register, Bryar slowly began to climb.

Decades without use had apparently left the staircase physically sound. Bryar was able to make it all the way up to the loft without a single shriek or groan from the supporting lumber. The upper portion of the museum looked to contain a pictorial history of logging in Rangeley and the surrounding areas. Photographs of stern-looking men posing before large, mechanical devices and thick logs piled high were arranged in various groups with what looked like articles mounted nearby. It was too dark to read most of the text, not that it mattered much. He was certain that most of the words would be outside his understanding. The pictures spoke well enough for themselves, though the tale they told registered more as a myth about a structured world where food was plentiful and water was safe to drink than anything else.

Probably not the original intent of the exhibits, but it was the purpose they served now.

He made his way over to a glass display case, sniffing as the displaced dust tickled his nose. It felt warmer up here and the increase in temperature left him thinking for a moment what a nice shelter the place would make. It was obviously well-built and well-insulated to have lasted this long without any kind of upkeep.

Shards of glass were strewn across the floor, the first signs that the place had been looted. Bending down, he ran a finger across the largest shard before lifting the glass from the floor and tilting it toward the light coming in through the boarded windows. A thick film of dust was caked upon it, indicating the cabinet had been smashed many, many years ago. Looking back down at the shard, he noted how the sun caught in the glare upon the swath his finger had cut in the dust. The rest of it remained as dull and unreflective as dirt upon the ground. For a moment he thought about pocketing the shard, but quickly changed his mind. The last thing he needed was a gash in the leg as Brett threw him down again upon their exit.

He dropped the shard to the floor where it clattered against the others before going silent. Standing up with a groan, he looked the inside of the case over for a few seconds before letting out a long sigh and shaking his head. The interior was empty, though there had obviously been *something* useful within.

"Anything up there?" Brett's voice echoed up from below, startling him.

Bryar turned away from the case and walked slowly over to the banister that ran around the edge of the loft. He laid his hands on the dusty wood and gazed down at his brother. Aside from the shirts, which still lay over his shoulders, he clutched a silver roll of duct tape in one hand and a hammer in the other. Beneath each of his arms was a massive tin can. Despite the excitement that sparked like electricity in his empty stomach at discovering that Brett had found food, Bryar couldn't help feeling a bit anxious about what the *other* items in his brother's hands might be used for. Sure, they were useful tools when it came to

building and repairing, but Bryar was certain Brett hadn't selected the tools and the tape for their constructive uses. They spoke
one word, and one word alone, to Bryar Perkins.

Torture.

He glanced away, struggling to keep his imagination from
running wild. "There's a glass case, but it looks to have been
smashed in long ago. Not sure what was in it. Nothing else but a
bunch of pictures from the old days."

Brett shook his head. "Ma' won't be happy."

Of course she wouldn't be happy. When was she ever? Bryar
clenched his sore muscles in frustration and immediately regretted it. They could return with pounds and pounds of food, but
the fact that they were returning without new weapons rendered
the entire expedition a bust. "You wanna come up for a look of
your own?" he asked. A second set of eyes to corroborate his
findings (or lack thereof) might spare him his mother's hand.

Again, Brett shook his head. "Naw. No interest in helping
deliver the bad news." He smoothed down his jacket as best he
could with his arms full and walked out the door.

Not wishing to be left alone with the faces of the deceased
and the tools of their trade, Bryar turned and made his way back
toward the staircase. He kept his eyes on the floor and, as he
rounded the last corner and was about to take his first step down,
his eyes settled upon the worn, wooden handle of what looked
to be a knife resting on the floor behind a newel post a few feet
away.

He took a deep breath and held it as he slowly turned to
look back down at the first floor. There was no sign of Brett, and
judging from the sounds of voices outside, he was certain that
his younger brother was gone. Bryar shook his backpack off his
shoulders, letting it gently down to the floor. He closed the remaining four feet that separated him from the handle and took
hold of it.

It was a six-inch hunting knife, secured in a leather sheath. Probably dropped by a looter on his way out. Though the soft, wooden handle and metal front and rear quillons were marked with scratches from years of use, there was no corrosion. One of the men in Dewoh's party had carried a knife similar to this only more ornate. The man had been something of a sword-and-knife enthusiast, often going to great lengths to impress them with his knowledge and terminology.

Taking hold of the sheath with his other hand, he pulled gently, but the blade didn't come free. He studied the sheath, quickly finding a button clip that ran across the front quillon to keep the blade from slipping out. With a flick of his thumb and index fingers, he unfastened the strip of leather and removed the blade.

There wasn't a single blemish on the face of the polished steel. A quick test of its edge against the hair that grew on the back of his hand let him know that the blade was still sharp.

This was exactly what Ma' Lee had been looking for when she'd sent them into the building in the first place. He could never let her know about it.

TEN

THE NIGHT WAS clear and chilly, leaving Bryar fairly certain that Ma' Lee wouldn't be calling on him to play Anthony after the others were asleep. It was too cold for that. Above, the stars shone bright white, blue, and yellow, some pulsating as if the energy that fueled their glow was sputtering to an end far out in space. The full moon did a lot to light the spot they had chosen, just off of the road at the edge of the forest, leaving the glow of the fire to further illuminate their satisfied faces.

The bean cans, each about the size of Bryar's head, were found to contain enough baked beans to feed a small army. Naturally, Ma' Lee had the first crack at them, cutting and peeling back the lid before slurping up the contents. She didn't pass the can along until she was full and satisfied. She didn't even bother to heat the beans before eating.

After she'd finished, the can went around the crackling fire to each of her younger children, Casey excluded. The scent of fallen leaves slowly decaying upon the ground mixed with the deep smells of dried grass and burning wood as they sat uncomfortably on the gravel where they'd built the fire. The softer grassy area at the side of the road would have been a more agreeable option to their aching bodies, but they didn't want to risk the dry grass catching fire and surprising them in the night.

When the beans finally reached Bryar, there was perhaps a quarter of a can left, which he promptly passed along to his daughter without taking a single scoop for himself, much to the discontent of his growling stomach.

"Look at the noble man," Ma' Lee cackled. Bryar's brothers joined in her laughter. "Seems no one told him that the world of noble men came to an end thirty years ago."

Bryar looked up as her attention shifted to Casey. "How's it taste, whore? You enjoy taking food out of your brother's mouth to feed that little animal growing inside you?"

Casey didn't answer.

Fortunately, Ma' Lee was full and in reasonably high spirits. Had she not been, it was likely the can would have been snatched from Casey's hands before she was permitted a single bite.

Bryar continued to watch Ma' Lee for a minute or so. He knew his mother better than any of them, and the most predictable part of her personality was just how unpredictable her mood swings were. After some time had passed and Ma' Lee's attention settled almost reflectively upon the burning fire, he turned back to Casey, who ate staring at the ground. She shoveled beans into her mouth with her bare hands, looking like a ravenous dog who was unsure when its next meal might be found.

Across the fire, new chatter from Ma' Lee and his brothers diminished to whispers, which meant they were discussing something other than Bryar or Casey. For this he was appreciative. They didn't need a moment as special as one involving an actual meal to be tarnished by those filthy mouths.

He didn't really care if Casey passed the can back to him before scraping out the last bite. He could go a bit longer without food. Water, on the other hand, was something they needed to get into their systems as soon as possible. Since Dewoh's departure, all they had to boil water in was a small soup pan, so the discovery of the canned beans was vital for more than one reason. Once the beans had been eaten, the can could be used to store and then purify a greater amount of tainted water.

For a moment Bryar wondered why Ma' Lee hadn't opted to heat the beans, but quickly answered his own question. A mind as scattered and impulsive as hers never really thought things all the way through. Not the small things anyway.

Looking away from the can and its dwindling contents, he studied the flickering fire. He and Jack had collected the wood. Brett had used a bit of dry moss they had found growing on a cluster of white birch and the flint he'd stolen from Dewoh's group to start the blaze. Though their dysfunctional family was typically at odds with each other both physically and verbally, they always seemed to calm down and retreat into their own minds once they found themselves warmed by the hypnotic flames of a fire.

Bryar looked back at Casey as she wiped her mouth with a grimy hand. She smiled warmly at him, offering her silent thanks. Taking the can from her lap, she handed it back to him with a quiet burp, which caused her bruised cheeks to inflate briefly like those of a chipmunk. Not seeming the least bit embarrassed, she took a deep breath and leaned back, bracing her upper body with her arms. Her belly rose before the flames like a tiny mountain.

He couldn't help smiling back, especially after the burp. This was a sign that she had eaten her fill. The almost euphoric look on her face warmed his heart immensely. Not even her mother's taunting could diminish how great she felt.

He looked down at the can. Inside was a mush of beans, sugar, and molasses that looked better than any meal he had ever eaten, though most meals tended to strike him that way at first. He dove in without hesitation, bringing up handfuls of the mash and scraping them off of his fingers with his teeth. His taste buds were hit with a sumptuous blend of molasses and salt pork. As he ate, he couldn't help looking back at his daughter, still enjoying the look of euphoria on her face. It was the same look she had displayed as an infant the very first time he'd fed her. How she'd survived Ma' Lee's attempts to terminate the pregnancy was miraculous, but the fact that Bryar had been able to find enough formula to keep her fed . . . well that was beyond miraculous. Even more so considering he was able to keep the formula a secret from Ma' Lee, his brothers, and the southern militias.

It was a secret he had kept to that very day. One he had shed his own blood to keep from Ma' Lee . . .

. . . Exactly six years after the last Christmas they would ever celebrate, and five years before a fire set by Wade Perkins burned their house to the ground, condemning the family to a nomadic life, Casey Perkins slipped into the world in a pool of blood and whiskey on a late summer afternoon. The look of agonizing pain on Ma' Lee's face throughout the six-hour labor was something Bryar watched obsessively, committing as much as humanly possible to his memory so that he could revisit the event at later times in his life. For once, this woman who was both his mother and his unsolicited lover was in as much pain as she inflicted upon the rest of them.

The pounding of his brothers' fists on the basement door in the adjoining kitchen added another level of chaos to the birth. Because he couldn't have them interfering with the labor unfolding in their filthy living room, he had coaxed his younger siblings into the basement with talk of a stash of apples he had supposedly lifted from the Billingsley orchard down the street. The boys, who were all pre-teen with the exception of Brett, took the bait without a single thought about how well-guarded the orchard was and how impossible it would have been for Bryar to get in and out with a bushel. It wasn't until the door was slammed and locked that they figured it out. There was a beating in store for him once they were freed, but that was something he would worry about later.

There were more important things to focus on now. Like the blood that oozed out of Ma' Lee's heavily dilated vagina and the fact that the woman was hammered drunk and vomiting whiskey with every contraction. Bryar didn't know the finer points of child birth, or how it impacted the mother, but he did know one thing: his baby was coming.

Two days earlier, the local militia—the Berwick Brotherhood—had marched through and cleaned out most of their food. This was a monthly affair that typically involved around thirty men marching up to their doorstep and waiting outside while four of the Brotherhood's best and brightest ransacked the house. Depending on *who* was sent that particular month, certain items would be left behind, only to be taken by the next guy thirty days later.

The Brotherhood always had the audacity to thank the Perkins family for supporting the cause. Exactly *what* that cause was, Bryar had no idea.

Despite their best efforts, the Berwick Brotherhood had never discovered Ma' Lee's whiskey stash. There were a great many things for which Bryar could fault his mother, but her ingenuity and resourcefulness were not among them. She was as sharp as a tack, as the old timers used to say. In the basement was an old black-and-white television, the kind that rested right on the floor. It sat within its original, polished wooden cabinet with thin, stringy wires still poking out the back. The militia men would take a look at the relic and move on, never thinking to lift the unfastened top. If they had, they would have seen the dozens and dozens of bottles of amber liquid hidden inside.

Ma' Lee was as stingy with her whiskey as Ebenezer Scrooge was with his money. She would only take it out for a quick belt on rare occasions. This was usually followed by her summoning Bryar to her bedroom. On the day of Casey's birth, Bryar watched her finish an entire bottle during the first four hours of the ordeal. Immediately after she was finished, he was sent to the basement to fetch her another, and she made him promise that he would put the empty bottle away in the television cabinet to hide any evidence of the liquor. Even in her inebriated state, she was still sharp enough to make sure that her tracks were covered and that nothing was around to lead the militia men to the booze.

She worked on the second bottle, tipping her head up from the pillows that Bryar had placed beneath her and pouring a splash into her mouth every now and then. Sweat streamed down her face and through her hair until the pillow was completely soaked. The white shirt she wore seemed almost transparent, clinging to her chest and giving him full view of the breasts he had been forced to stimulate more times than he cared to remember. The dirt-caked, woven rug beneath her was drenched in a mix of sweat, bile, urine, blood, and whiskey. It would have to be burned when she was done.

"Let us out or I'm gonna drown your sorry ass in the river, Bryar!" Brett screamed from the other side of the basement door, just to the left of the living room. Directly ahead of Ma' Lee stood the stone fireplace that kept them warm in the winter. Pushed away from the chaos toward the edges of the bare gray room were the tattered couches and chipped wooden tables they ate upon on nights when there was food.

The bottle fell out of Ma' Lee's hand as a scream escaped her mouth. Bryar grabbed the bottle quickly to stop the whiskey from spilling out, knowing that he would be blamed for the loss at a later time when his mother was back to her usual, irrational self. Placing the bottle just out of her reach, he shuffled over to where he'd been squatting between her bent legs. There he watched as the baby's head began to show and his mother's screams grew louder.

"Aaaaaaaaargh, get this little bastard *out of me!*" she screamed. Her voice was so loud and so frightening that it silenced the threatening voices and pounding fists behind the cellar door. One of her hands pounded repeatedly against the floor while the other groped around, searching for something to take hold of and squeeze. Or perhaps she was just looking for the whiskey bottle.

"It's going to be all right, Ma'," Bryar found himself saying, immediately wondering why he bothered to comfort her. She had caused him nothing but pain for as far back as he could remember. He forced himself to focus on the coming child, reaching down as the hairless dome of the baby's head appeared to grow larger with each push. Ma' Lee's screams intensified until they were nothing but ringing white noise as he concentrated on the crowning head. He kept his hands low, ready to catch the baby as it emerged. Ma' Lee gave one last ear-piercing scream and Bryar's daughter slid into the light.

The baby started to cry immediately as if it were somehow aware of, and horrified by, the state of the world into which it had emerged. Life would be very difficult for this child, and Bryar knew this better than anyone. Not only did the baby have to survive in a world of tainted water, scarce food, and brutal militias, it also had to contend with the woman who had birthed it. Fortunately, it would not have to do this on its own.

Bryar took the baby—a girl—into his arms. He glanced briefly at Ma' Lee, who regarded the baby with a look of contemptuous hatred painted upon her face before passing out. The baby's cries seemed to keep his younger siblings at bay and Bryar had a wild picture of his brothers quietly plotting how they might exploit this new, weaker form of life.

He went to stand up to fetch a blanket, then remembered the umbilical cord was still attached. Before he could react, a dark red sac of blood-filled tissue oozed out of Ma' Lee. He grimaced at the sight and nearly vomited all over his mother. But he caught himself and went to work figuring out what he was going to do. He traced the cord to where it ended, right where the baby's belly button should have been. Suddenly he remembered seeing a dog giving birth, the memory so old he could barely hold onto it. He picked up the other end of the cord and the dripping sac. He carried it hurriedly, almost slipping out of his hand, into the kitchen as the equally slippery child cried in his arms. He slopped the bloody mass into the sink, then reached into the silverware drawer, and pulled out a carving knife. He studied the cord for a moment, then brought the blade down as close to the baby as he dared—about six inches away from her belly—conjured up the nerve and severed the cord.

There didn't seem to be any pain on the baby's part, but just as relief started to wash over him, a steady spurt of blood began to flow from the end of the cord still attached to the baby.

He dropped the knife in the sink, suddenly aware of how alien and dreamlike things had become. He needed to stop the bleeding. He scanned the kitchen in anxiety-ridden panic as he pinched the cord with his fingers and struggled to find something more permanent. But there was nothing in sight. Moving away from the sink, the baby's soft cries adding to his fevered urgency, he shuffled over to the old junk drawer beside the gas stove.

With blood oozing between his fingers, Bryar wondered if he had made a mistake in cutting the cord.

A mistake that could cost his daughter her life.

With both hands in use, one holding the infant and the other cutting off the flow of blood, he lowered himself carefully to his knees and took the handle of the drawer in his mouth. The foul taste of metal, not cleaned in decades, bit at his taste buds as he closed his lips over the oval handle. Biting down with his teeth, he struggled to pull the drawer open. The wood was swollen with disuse and resisted his efforts. He didn't care. The solution to his problem was either in this drawer or it didn't exist at all, and Bryar was willing to shed every tooth in his mouth to pull it open.

With a series of squeaks and squeals, the drawer eventually slid out. It was slow and difficult at first, but the farther it came, the easier the task became. He stopped as he found himself unable to bend backward anymore, leaving the drawer sticking out about a foot.

Bryar inched his way backward and moved carefully to his feet, making sure not to bump the baby's head on the protruding drawer. He peered at the mess of tape and paperclips and spent batteries until he found an old binder clip, one of the larger black ones used to keep a particularly thick document together. Before the world changed, the clip had been used to hold a folded bag of potato chips closed. Then it had been relegated to the junk drawer with no real purpose.

He let go of the umbilical cord just long enough to reach in and snatch up the clip. It took a couple tries, slipping out of his fingers once, but he was able to wipe his hand on his pants to get the job done. He carefully shifted the baby around in his arms so that he could use his other hand to straighten the severed cord before squeezing the clip open and closing it over the tip.

The bleeding stopped.

He spun around and dashed back through the living room, over his passed-out mother, and up the stairs to the second floor as the burden of the helpless creature in his arms collapsed upon him. He staggered into his room and placed the baby gently on his bed. In a dizzied fog, he wrapped the baby in his comforter, making several passes over the tiny body until all he could see was her teeny head.

He was the father of a baby girl.

Bryar left the baby where she was for a moment and all but collapsed upon the floor. As her weak crying faded in and out, he leaned his shoulder against the frame of his bed and shook his head like a drunk trying to keep himself from passing out. It was too much. All of it.

But this little baby was his responsibility. If he couldn't find the willpower and the nerve to care for her, no one would.

Shaking his head once more, he crawled on all fours toward his closet and drew open the folding doors. Hidden in the back was a loose wall panel, behind which lay a space between the studs. There he had stashed away dozens of cans of baby formula.

From the first time he had caught Ma' Lee in the bathroom with a clipped coat hanger Bryar had known that she would not care for the child if it actually survived. That was all up to him, so he'd prepared as best he could.

In towns and cities where people still lived together in loosely connected communities governed by their respective militias, there was always a dealer—someone who had stashed away various necessities and luxuries in the years leading up to the collapse of society. These people were known by many members of the community, and their services kept secret from the militias. If they were ever found out, the flow of goods like booze and cigarettes would run dry. These dealers didn't only cater to the vices of man, however. They also sold and bartered useful items like canned goods, hygiene products, and the ever-coveted bottled spring water.

Such a dealer lived in a shack in South Berwick, Maine, deep in the Vaughn Woods on the far side of the river. The locals called him Baker, though nobody was sure if this was his last name or his first name. Bryar had taken Ma' Lee's empties and refilled them with the untouched bottles, pouring about a quarter from each until he had a full bottle that he hid from Ma' Lee and his brothers. He then topped off Ma' Lee's bottles with boiled water and returned them to her stash. Meticulous as Ma' Lee seemed to be, she never seemed to notice her whiskey had been diluted.

Once a week Bryar would make a trip to see Baker in his shack. He had no idea where the man stashed his goods, but it was obviously not on his premises. Upon Bryar's arrival he would be given two cans of powdered formula for one bottle of Jameson. Baker always had the goods ready and waiting since he only made deals by appointment. He was a solid businessman and even threw in an occasional freebie to keep his customers coming back. In Bryar's case, this amounted to a plastic bottle and rubber nipple on a couple of occasions. On another trip Baker threw in a pacifier. Since Bryar was such a good customer and never traded watered-down whiskey, such offerings were consistent. In the months leading up to the baby's arrival, he had stocked up and hidden everything he needed to keep her alive for her first year. He'd hidden it all inside the wall.

Bryar pushed through a mess of old clothes and forgotten toys, using the fading sunlight filtering in through his window to find his way. When he made it to the back wall he pressed his palms against the cool surface and pushed up ever so slightly, feeling the thin sliver of wood lift free of the molding below. He ran his hands down the panel to the bottom, where he slipped his fingers around its base and pulled it loose from the panels on either side. The stale scent of old plaster and insulation hit his nose—a stench he had come to know quite well over the last year. As his eyes settled upon the collection of formula cans and other baby gear stashed between the shared wall of his room and his younger brothers' rooms, he wasted no time taking out one of the bottles. With his free hand he grabbed a can of formula. He'd never thought to check the expiration date, not that it would have mattered. Beggars couldn't be choosers.

Tucking both bottle and formula beneath one arm, he re-placed the panel and retreated hastily back to the bed. He pulled the rubber lid off the can and peeled back the metallic lining at the top. Inside was a little plastic scoop he used to shake a full serving of the powder into the bottle. He quickly replaced the lid and slid the can under his bed.

He paused, still quite overwhelmed but finding himself able to fight through the clouding murkiness of his nerves as wave after wave of mixed emotions ran through him. He gazed at the baby, still crying, though her cries were getting weaker. Her skin seemed caked in chalk now that she was dry. She would need to be cleaned and properly wrapped, but right now, she needed food.

Breathing heavily, he turned and ran quickly downstairs, past his still-sleeping mother and renewed threats from his siblings, into the kitchen. The junk drawer was still open beside the stove. Above it, a single-lane countertop littered with unwashed bowls and utensils ran across the far wall and beneath two windows. At the far end of the counter lay the stove. The ever-present smell of mold and decay permeated the air.

Using a ladle they always kept next to the purification stock pot on the stove, he filled the bottle with the lukewarm water they had treated that morning and screwed the rubber nipple onto its top. He gave it a quick inspection, the lactic, almost-spoiled smell of warm milk wafting around him, before taking a handful of water from the pot to cleanse the nipple of any pink fibers that might have come loose from the insulation in the walls. Then he turned around and dashed back upstairs, shaking the bottle vigorously as he ran.

The mewling cry of his newborn daughter grew slightly as he scooped her up into his arms, still buried deep in the blanket. He set the nipple to her lips and was amazed to see her latch immediately onto it. Her lips puckered as she began to drink, and all at once the tightness around her eyes and cheeks eased. She grunted and cooed as she drank, her tiny chest lifting up and down slowly as she breathed.

"You're going to need a bath, little girl," he whispered softly, studying the crusty lines creasing her face. He looked at his bed, trying to picture how he might keep her contained at night. From this thought his mind wandered to a whole manner of other obstacles that would certainly creep up as his daughter developed.

His mother and siblings were at the top of the list.

His anxiety bloomed, tightening his chest and restricting his breathing. He sat down on the bed, cradling the baby in his arms as he struggled to regulate his respiration and calm himself. Through the floorboards he could still hear, although faint and dull, the pounding fists and screaming voices of his brothers.

It would be difficult, but he needed to make it work. In a world seemingly devoid of meaning, he now had a job and a purpose . . .

. . . The bite of crisp night air on his cheeks drew Bryar's attention back to the dying fire. While he'd been lost in memories, his brothers had passed out on top of each other and Casey had curled up in front of him on the ground. Even Ma' Lee was out like a light, snoring away like a fog horn blasting over a blanketed sea.

Though he didn't want to disturb Casey, Bryar didn't want the heat from the fire to die off completely and wake the others. He inched away from her sleeping body and crept over to the pile of firewood.

He carefully stripped the bark from the wood, knowing the bark would burn quicker than the thicker logs. He laid the bark atop the still-burning coals, it ignited, and he carefully arranged a couple of logs in the flames, watching as the dried timber started to burn almost immediately. When the heat from the growing fire began to radiate once more, he spread his fingers, absorbing the welcome warmth. He studied his siblings and his mother, looking for signs that either his movements or the light from the fire had disturbed their dreams. Fortunately they seemed out cold.

It was the same with Casey. Though her bruised face was closest to the fire, she didn't stir. She lay completely still, one arm curled beneath her head and the other draped over her belly.

He watched her sleep for some time, unable to help the smile that came to his face at the sight of her so very much at peace. These were the only times when their minds could be truly at ease, and he was thankful for them.

Movement on the other side of the fire caught his attention. He watched with building apprehension as Wade's head lifted off Jack's chest and his arm began to move down to his waist. The hand continued to move as Wade rolled over onto his back, stopping at his crotch and fondling himself a bit before he was still once again.

Bryar thought about the knife he had found at the logging museum. He had taken care to stuff the blade into the very bottom of his backpack in order to avoid anyone stumbling across it during one of the frequent occasions where his brothers or mother would paw through his belongings. Though he wasn't yet sure if he had the nerve or willpower to use it against his family, he had it somewhat at the ready nonetheless, if only as an option in his mind. The time was rapidly approaching when he would need to make a decision to either take the lives of his mother and brothers during the night or escape with his daughter in hopes that they would never be found. His brothers had been younger and more easily dealt with when Casey was born. They were entirely different animals now, and he knew that he would be powerless to stop them from carrying out Ma' Lee's wishes for the baby.

But if they ran, they would be found. Ma' Lee and the others were so possessive of both Bryar and Casey that they would never give up searching. He doubted that even the idea of having two (and eventually three) fewer mouths to feed would ever enter his family's minds. They were like dogs, asserting their dominance over the weaker members of the pack. Still, that wasn't all of it. The truth that Bryar worked obsessively to keep out of his conscious thought was more basic and simple—he and Casey were sexual puppets. Given how primal such a need was in a human being, his family would keep searching feverishly until the two of them were found.

We could escape into the woods, he thought, his gaze suddenly wandering over to the row of pine and birch presiding over a dense tangle of underbrush at the edge of the old mountain highway. *They probably wouldn't expect us to leave the road. They'd probably backtrack to town, thinking that we'd gone looking for Dewoh and his people.*

It could work.

He looked up at the full moon. The light that reflected off of its pale surface would be enough to navigate the forest. They could start working their way into the woods as soon as Ma' Lee and the others went to sleep the following night.

But what if Brett or Wade decide to bed down with Casey?

No. With another can of beans at the ready and not a single shred of discipline when it came to rationing anything except liquor, he could safely bet on Ma' Lee cracking open the second can the following night. They would eat their fill and pass out beside the fire again. Once everyone was asleep, he and Casey could make their way into the woods and be rid of them forever.

Butterflies flew about in his stomach. The idea to flee had long been with him, but there was a reason why the other members of his family were so successful when it came to beating him down both physically and mentally: he was weak. Like the abused dog who stays loyal to its master, Bryar was somewhat dependent on his mother and brothers. The only time in the history of his existence that he had ever stood against them was to place himself between them and Casey. Especially when she was young and innocent and unable to defend herself.

Now there was another innocent on the way, one who could come at any moment. Just what he needed to cultivate the willpower to escape.

STUCK

Eleven

T HE CEDAR SWAMP INN was miles behind them, but Carl couldn't keep his mind from wandering back to the night they had spent there. As they continued north through the tall grass that grew between the gravel ruts of the road, birch and pine branches waving above them in the light breeze as the sun filtered through the foliage, he found himself both fascinated with and puzzled by the place, just as he had been during their time there. Talk of the old world and its relatively carefree way of life was something that he had taken at face value over the years but could never fully understand. Bampy had once told him about a place called Egypt, where thousands of years ago a primitive people had erected the most magnificent stone buildings, high as a mountain. According to Bampy, the stories of Egyptian life made sense to modern man on a certain level, but without *living* that way, the bulk of the significance was lost.

Well, now Carl had seen old world relics that fell into the mystical realm of . . . *partying*. According to Dad, men —and perhaps a few women—had transported the materials needed to build their little party spot miles into the woods, most likely on motorized all-terrain vehicles, and had pieced together the most random little campsite anyone from either generation could possibly imagine. While there was no doubt that Dad was thoroughly amused with the place, and in better spirits than any of them had seen since their eviction, Carl couldn't find a single practical application for the fake bunks and check-in counter. They didn't even provide any shelter. The items were purely ornamental, each a single, weak piece of particle board that would have collapsed had anyone even leaned against them.

Useless.

Carl had grown up in a world where *everything* around him had a practical function, where nothing went to waste. All items were used in a manner that benefitted the family as a whole. Having never really been exposed to alcohol, with the exception of an occasional snifter of homemade vodka, he had, according to Dad, missed out on a subset of old world culture that had produced such party spots. Drunken culture. The Cedar Swamp Inn was Carl's Great Pyramid. It was a remnant of a time from which he was far removed, and while the reason for its design and construction was very clearly spelled out, there was no way for him to truly grasp its underlying purpose.

Carl pushed the place out of his mind before he ended up with some kind of brain cramp. He smoothed down his red-and-green checkered jacket, his dry skin scratching against the coarse wool, and buttoned it at the top as the cool breeze that somehow found its way through the trees nipped at his chest and neck and tickled his nose with the familiar scents of grass, decomposing leaves, and pine pitch. With a quick adjustment of his pack, he was acceptably comfortable and continued along behind Zoey, who followed silently after their parents.

The previous day's warmth had been a very nice treat, but it did not return for a second day. Instead, they were back in the more seasonal fall chill and forced to bundle up as they pressed deeper into the forest. Not long after their departure from the Cedar Swamp Inn, they left the thick cedar woods and began to climb a small mountain, sparsely dotted with white birch trees. For the first time since leaving Rangeley, Carl was able to get a good look at the miles of forest around them—a vast expanse of trees and mountains with no visible signs of human habitation. Dad's pace quickened, leading them the rest of the way around the peak of the small elevation before the road wound back down to the mountain's base where they found a massive, mile-long meadow much like the ones through which they had previously traveled only larger. Long, waist-high grass swayed in the breeze. Farther out in the meadow, a rippling effect was produced as the wind swept more powerfully across smaller patches.

Carl caught up to Zoey and walked beside her. Although the distant, contemplative look on her face told him that she was deep in thought, he didn't think twice about interrupting her. If she was having as hard a time as he was trying to sort out what they'd seen at the Cedar Swamp Inn, he was doing her a big favor.

"How far do you think we've gone?" Carl asked.

"What?" she asked absent-mindedly. She shook her head in annoyance. "I don't know. Maybe fifteen or twenty miles."

"That's it?" he asked, flabbergasted.

"It's only been a couple of days since we left home," she responded, "and we're moving slowly so that *you* can keep up."

It was a cheap shot, but he let her have it. He let the conversation drop and watched Mom and Dad curiously as they walked along, chatting quietly between themselves. Farther ahead, Tripp's tail could be seen cutting through the grass as he followed the right-side rut. His tail would occasionally disappear, only to be immediately replaced by his little black-and-white face as Tripp glanced back to make sure that his family was still with him.

After what seemed like forever, the meadow eventually slimmed down to a point and the road wove back into the thick forest. Unlike the first leg of their journey, the diversity of plants around them began to expand, leaving them with more than evergreens and bushes for scenery. They were seeing more birch than they'd seen before. Dad looked the trees over as he passed, probably eyeing their paper-like bark as a potential fire-starter. When he didn't stop to collect any of the bark, Carl was mildly confused, but soon realized his father was simply waiting until they settled down for the night. Carl glanced in dismay at the sun still riding high in the sky. Looked like they wouldn't be making camp for some time.

The road dipped downhill for a bit and then meandered up and over several more hills. The grass crowding the road's twin ruts was bordered by a thick mess of trees and brush on either side.

"I don't believe it," Dad said, walking up to the tangle of tiny red branches growing at the edge of the road. Taking a few of them in his hand, he pulled them close and studied them.

"What's wrong, Dad?" Carl asked, moving toward him. He glanced at Tripp. The dog had noted the family had stopped and was heading back toward them, his tail swinging back and forth.

"There's game here," Dad said. "Big game." He held the branches so Carl could get a closer look.

Carl leaned in and stared at the tiny, red branches. He could sense Mom and Zoey peering over his shoulder. After what must have been twenty seconds of staring at what looked no different to him than every other plant they had passed while on the trail, he shrugged and stepped back.

"The tips of the branches," Dad said, "they've been bitten off."

Carl refocused and all of a sudden wondered how he had missed it. The ends of the branches were splintery and frayed with their white cores showing clearly. Not only had the ends been bitten off, it had happened fairly recently.

He glanced up at his father, excited to see a glimmer of hope in his eyes. As Dad turned to study the brush farther up the trail, Carl spun around to find the elation he was feeling mirrored in the faces of both his mother and his sister.

"We've gotta be near *fresh water*!" Carl exclaimed, almost jumping up and down. His hands shook.

"Not that again," Zoey growled. She shook her head dismissively.

"I think he might be right," Dad said. He'd stopped to look at another tangle of brush.

Carl watched with satisfaction as Zoey's mouth dropped open in disbelief. She quickly snapped it shut.

"Look—it isn't just that one bush," Dad said. He gestured with both hands at the brush lining both sides of the old road.

Now that Carl knew what he was looking for, it was as clear as day. The red brush had been grazed on up and down both sides of the road.

"Only a fresh source of water would be able to support this kind of life," Dad said, placing his hand on Carl's shoulder. He winked at Carl and smiled, lighting a fire of excitement in Carl's stomach. Tripp trotted up, seating himself at Dad's feet. With a yawn and a brief sniff of the man's boots, he took a deep breath and stared out at the road, eyes blinking almost sleepily.

"Wait, wait," Zoey said, edging her way between the two of them. A scowl briefly crossed her face, but disappeared quickly. "You said there isn't any fresh water anymore. The folks in Rangeley told you and Bampy that before you cut contact with the locals." Confusion wrinkled her face.

For a moment, Carl found himself so inspired by her tenacity that he began to question himself. The budding excitement within him suddenly began to wither as if crushed by his sister's own hands.

Dad shrugged. "There's no other explanation. There's obviously a lot of big game in this area, and whatever it is has been through here recently."

Zoey's lips puckered as if she were about to say something else, but she stopped. The confused expression on her face remained as she went back to studying the white tips of the bitten-off branches.

"So what do we do now?" Mom asked.

"Keep following the road," Dad said without a moment's hesitation. "We keep moving forward until we either come across a game trail or signs of clean water." He crouched, parting the grass between the gravel ruts.

Carl crouched down with him. "What are you looking for?"

"Tracks." Dad brushed off his hands and stood. "The gravel is too tightly packed. Whatever came through here wasn't moving through the grass." He took a deep breath and smiled. "No sense wasting any more time here. Everyone ready to move out?"

The fact that he had actually asked the question showed that Dad was truly in the best of spirits. His father's mood went a long way to renew Carl's excitement and push it to the point where he was almost giddy. Was it possible that they might find themselves roasting fresh meat over an open fire that evening? Perhaps even washing it down with fresh water?

Carl resisted letting out a shout of joy. There was life here—animal life—which almost certainly meant that there was also fresh water.

Now they just needed to find it.

Dad's pace quickened so much that Tripp had to trot in order to keep his usual distance out in front. Though they seemed to be rushing along, Carl knew better than to assume Dad was moving without purpose. He watched his father studying the roadside and kept his ears open, listening for the rushing or trickling of water.

Zoey maintained her typical sour attitude, lagging behind at the rear of the group. Carl had often wondered how his sister had become so cynical and pessimistic. Considering how satisfying their lives had been prior to William Dewoh, it made very little sense how she'd ended up such a wretch.

"You'll see, Zo," Carl said with a smile, his optimism rekindled despite the persuasive passion of Zoey's prior argument. He slowed and allowed her to come up beside him.

Zoey scowled.

"We're gonna be munching on *buck* tonight . . ." he paused for a minute, searching his mind for the other new word he had learned, "or *doe!*"

Zoey sighed and rolled her eyes. She stared up at the thickening canopy of birch and pine. "You do realize that you're going to be even sadder and *hungrier* than usual when we make camp for the night without your fresh water or your buck meat."

"Don't you think it might feel good to try looking on the bright side of things for once?"

Her hands balled into fists, but remained at her sides. "*What* bright side? When has there ever been a *bright side?*"

They both glanced at Dad, but he didn't seem to have noticed Zoey's raised voice.

"Gram's rabbit stew, summertime fires in the yard," Carl said. He lowered his voice. "Stealing sips from Bampy's vodka stash."

She shook her head angrily. "You don't get it."

Carl eyed her up and down, trying to get a read as to exactly how close she was to smacking him "Maybe it's *you* who doesn't get it." He took a few steps to his left, increasing the gap between them and nearly tripping over a rock.

Zoey shook her head and increased her pace. Carl decided it might be wise to give her the space she needed and hung back, watching as Mom moved close to Dad and took his hand.

JAMES STARTED AS his wife moved up beside him, took his hand, and planted a kiss on his stubbly cheek before pulling slowly away. Her face was framed by the faux fur of the hood that she wore, a remnant of the old world when people and animals had a decidedly different relationship for the most part. Stray locks of her light brown hair flowed across her cheeks, nose, and lips.

He reached up and caressed her cheek, losing himself in the memory of their first years together . . .

... Mud was always a spring staple in Rangeley. Each year when the temperature reached a comfortable level, the mountains of accumulated snow in and around the Rangeley House would thaw and release so much water into the ground that the tightly-packed gravel of the camp road would erode underneath and create little fissures and canyons. James had walked out there one particularly warm day with a bucket and a shovel and had put in close to an hour of work repairing the road before his father discovered what he was up to.

"What reason do we have to repair the road when we have no working cars and never leave the compound?" his father asked.

Though James had never been a particularly prideful young man, he had always struggled with letting go of certain things he could not change; things that perhaps he could have avoided had his mind been a bit sharper. When such revelations crossed him, obsession was almost certainly at their heels.

He found himself searching for ways to validate such a thoughtless waste of time. In the end he arrived at the conclusion that he was what his father had, on multiple occasions, referred to as a *workaholic*, and given the lack of chores at that time of year, his brain had justified the creation of some kind of work without really considering how practical it was. When he came back to his father with this explanation later that day, pushed by the need to explain himself, it was *then* that Dad let the ridicule fly.

"Oh, yeah," Dad laughed, "my boy the work-a-holic!"

"You stop it now!" came his mother's voice from the kitchen where she was already preparing her seeds for that year's garden. Kelly was with her, watching and learning at age fourteen just as she'd been doing for the past two years.

"Stop *what*?" Dad asked, his eyes sparkling. "I was just agreeing with him! He's the very *definition* of a workaholic—up at noon most days, half-assed job on his chores . . ."

James bit his lower lip and nonchalantly backed his way out onto the front porch as his father burst into a loud belly laugh.

He turned his back and made his way down the steps to the yard below.

"Now, don't take it like that, boy," Dad called after him. "I was just pullin' your leg!"

The words barely registered as James dashed into the woods, still not entirely sure how he had allowed his day to be so derailed.

It wasn't until he hurdled over the wood pile halfway between the Rangeley House and The Firs, the other camp that shared the road, that he realized it might be best at this point to simply force himself to move on and erase the events of the day from his mind. He had under-thought his decision to repair the road that morning and had over-thought his decision to stand up for himself. Yes, the best course of action at this point was to simply move on.

He ran the rest of the way to the abandoned, one-story camp, not stopping until he reached the back porch, which faced a pine forest that had begun to flourish in the couple of years following Black Christmas. The neglected cabin shed chips of brown paint as it slowly rotted away. Where once there had been a somewhat clear view of Dodge Pond through the trees, stood a prickly evergreen wall, dotted here and there with thin, white lengths of birch.

The boards beneath his feet creaked and gave a bit, but he paid no attention. The back of the porch was sheltered by a small overhang that had already lost most of its shingles, leaving bare, rotting plywood beneath. He sat beneath one of two small windows that faced the tree line. This particular window was still intact; the other had been busted in by his father when they ransacked the place for supplies after the owners—an older couple they had barely known—failed to return.

This was James' quiet place. This was where he could be alone and away from the others. While he knew that his father and mother were well aware that he came there, they seemed to understand that such trips were necessary and never bothered him.

"I'm not going to cry," he reassured himself as he leaned against the splintery siding. He hadn't cried since Black Christmas, and even then it had been for just a moment as the shock of being rudely torn from sleep and loaded into a car while the world exploded set in. In the days that followed that tragic night, it became rather clear that the world had changed. Stories from the locals downtown told of a country stripped of the governing men and women who had run it into the ground. All major cities had been destroyed. There was no doubt in James' mind, even back then at age sixteen, that things would never be the same again and that he needed to toughen up if he were to stay alive in this new world.

He had been working to that end ever since.

He drew in a deep breath and closed his eyes for a moment as his nerves began to calm. The light breeze that played about in the evergreen needles lapped softly at his face. It brought with it the scents of pine and pitch, along with the reek of tainted water. That sour onion smell that seemed to be everywhere.

He rubbed his face, feeling the patches of facial hair that had started growing in over the years. A shave with his father's straightedge was perhaps in order when he returned. Maybe even a bath.

A twig snapped off to the left and he whipped his head around so quickly a bolt of pain seared down his neck. The first thought that entered his mind was that his father had trailed him out there to apologize, which would have been a shocker worthy of committing to a diary if he kept one. However, it was not Dad who stepped around the corner, but the little hitchhiker herself, Miss Kelly.

She walked silently around the porch, wearing jeans Mom had modified to fit her (but still hung a bit loose and dragged on the ground) and a flannel jacket three sizes too large. Her arms were crossed over her chest, sleeves bunched up, and her head was down, watching her footing as she took each step. The porch didn't creak under her weight, which didn't surprise him. The girl was little more than a wisp of flesh and bone.

When Kelly reached the top of the stairs she glanced up at him, and though her lips remained in a perfectly straight line, her eyes were smiling. She took a few steps closer before asking, "Are you okay?"

"I'm fine," James replied, his voice shaky. He bit his lip and looked back out at the woods, studying the waving evergreen needles.

"I don't think he meant to make you feel so bad," she said, her voice soft and oddly comforting. She hunkered down on the balls of her feet before gently lowering herself to the porch and sitting cross-legged beside him.

For a minute or so he had nothing to say. Kind as her words were, they conveyed something he was already well aware of. With a start he realized how rude he was being. Kelly had come after him because she was concerned and wanted to help him out. He had already decided to push the day's events from his mind and move on, yet here he was dwelling upon them once more and being a jerk in the process.

"I know," he said at last, looking down at her. "Thank you."

A smile crept up to match the expression in her eyes. She reached out and patted him on the leg. "Does that make you feel any better?"

He returned the smile. "It does, Kelly. Thank you."

"Sarah told me to bring you back when she saw me going out, but we can stay here for as long as you like. Just make sure to take the dogs out before you go in," she said as she laid her hand back in her lap.

"I'm surprised Mom let you slip away during your *lesson time*," he said, holding up his hands and using air quotes, not that either of them really understood what exactly air quotes were. He let out a snort and dropped his hands back into his lap.

"She's already done for the day. The seeds are all wrapped in damp cloth, and I'm to keep wetting it every four hours," she said with a roll of her eyes that he knew to be more for show than anything else. Kelly hung on Sarah Richmond's every word.

"That's going to mess with your sleep pretty bad," James said, raising his eyebrows as if caring for seeds was the most daunting task he had ever contemplated. He let the serious look dissolve into a friendly half-smile to show that he was kidding.

"Yeah, well, your dad has to have his string beans!" she laughed, her voice as musical as the song birds that used to nest nearby.

When the laughter eventually subsided, not a single thought of the embarrassment he had suffered that day remained in his mind. All that was left was his appreciation for his friend—a girl they had found along the highway in Portland little more than two years earlier—who was now an integral part of their family. As he looked at her wrapped in that huge flannel coat, strings of untamed hair flying about her face, he couldn't help but smile.

"Thanks for coming after me, Kel," he said, reaching out and taking her hand. He gave it a squeeze before relaxing his fingers.

She looked down at his hand for a moment before looking back up at him with a beaming smile. "We gotta look out for each other, right?"

He nodded.

In the years that followed, The Firs came to be their spot. It was where they shared their first kiss two years later and where they explored each other's bodies in the years after that. It was where they first said *I love you*. Together, they grew stronger than they ever could have on their own. When hard times hit, they were there to build each other up, and when happy days were upon them, the joy was enhanced by one another's company. In no time at all, the prospects of the lives they might have once had in the old world no longer bothered them. Regardless of the state of the world they lived in, they were ready for a life together.

And so, on a particularly warm spring afternoon six years after his brilliant idea to repair the camp road, James found himself standing across from Kelly in their special spot on the porch of The Firs. He wore one of his father's old button-down shirts—the only one that had not been repurposed to some practical end. Kelly wore one of Mom's blue dresses. It fit well enough, cut off just below her knees on the bottom and just above her cleavage on top. A lacey tablecloth used on special occasions and kept immaculately clean over the years had been modified to serve as a veil.

They both wore Bean Boots.

Mom and Dad stood facing them, their arms wrapped around each other. Mom wore her white-and-blue checkered dress. Dad wore his black-and-red flannel shirt tucked into his blue jeans. He grinned at Mom for a minute, and James wondered if his father would tease her about looking like Dorothy, a character in a film James vaguely remembered.

"I've never been good with speeches," Dad said. "But since I'm the only one around here with the *authority* as elder to make you man and wife, I'll try to get through it as best I can."

James turned away from Kelly and shot his father a silent *cut-it-out* look, smiling as Mom gave his father's leg a good pinch. Like a good husband, the man with *authority* obeyed.

"Ah, just look at you kids," Dad said. "You know, I—I've never been one to put much stock in things like destiny and fate. I've always been the type who needs to keep as much control in my hands as possible. But if there's anything I learned from Black Christmas it's this: we aren't in control, at least not in the way we think. This world decides how our lives are lived. It always has. Even before Black Christmas, though we were all too blind to see it. I've never been more sure of this than right now as I look at the two of you."

James felt Kelly's hands tighten in his grip. He smiled down at her. Out of the corner of his eye, he saw his mother's arms circle tighter around his father's waist, her body drawing in closer.

"On the night that the old world burned and crumbled around us, Kelly was delivered into our family. After eight years we know exactly why—the two of you were made to complete one another," he said, Mom's head coming down upon his shoulder. "It is because of this that we're here today. You've made the decision to commit to one another for the rest of your lives and it is time to make it official. With that in mind, Mom and I have a gift for you."

James turned to gaze at his father, who reached into his left breast pocket.

"Open your hands, kids," he said with a grin.

James turned to Kelly. They opened their hands and two gold rings fell into them, the smaller gold ring into James' hand and the larger in hers. Startled, James glanced at Kelly. Her eyes sparkled with tears.

"Dad," James began, "this . . . this is too much."

Stubborn as ever, Dad shut him up with a brief wave of his hand. "I won't hear anything of it. You take these from us or this wedding stops right here and now." Though his father was smiling, James could see he was dead serious. A quick look at his mother confirmed that she was on the same page.

James met Kelly's gaze once more and they exchanged smiles. Their fingers closed over the wedding bands.

"Good," Dad said. "Now, let's wrap this up so we can go eat that rabbit I'm sure we're all thinking about." He chuckled. "Miss Hitchhiker, please repeat after me: I, Kelly Moulton, take you, James Richmond, as my husband, to love and cherish so long as I shall live."

Kelly repeated the words, her eyes locked with James'.

Dad smiled. "Hold out your hand, boy."

James complied.

"Put the ring on his finger, girlie."

Kelly complied.

Dad repeated the process with James making the vows to Kelly. As James finished speaking, he took his soul mate's hand and slipped his mother's ring on her finger.

A smile larger than life swept over Dad's face. It was so big and uncontrollable that he had obvious trouble speaking, but he managed. "With the authority vested in me as undisputed dictator of the Rangeley House—" he winced at another pinch from Mom "—erm, I proudly pronounce you man and wife. You may kiss—"

He stopped speaking as the two of them came together. In that moment there was only James and Kelly. No old world or new world. No ever-present threat from other survivors outside of their compound. No tainted water or constant struggle for sustenance.

Their shattered world was whole.

TWELVE

CARL WAS THE first one to spot the bridge ahead and was immediately hit with a sinking feeling, remembering what had happened with the last bridge they had crossed. Pain flickered in his groin, likely conjured up by his imagination since he had only felt mild soreness since waking that morning.

At first he wasn't really certain what he was looking at. Given that the telltale reek of tainted water had not yet reached them, when he first saw the aging structure, it didn't register as a possibility that there might be a water crossing ahead. As they drew nearer, Carl close behind his father with the women following behind, he watched with mounting concern as Tripp emerged from the grass in the middle of the road, made his way almost lazily out onto what Carl now realized was a bridge, and stopped upon the rusted metal span before one of four square holes at its corners. Sniffing with mild interest, he pushed his head down into the hole right up to his shoulders.

"Get him quick," Dad commanded.

Carl ran alongside his mother as she moved toward the dog. They both halted at the edge of the rusted platform. Unlike the bridge they had crossed the previous day, this one was simply a flat slab of rusted metal running between two crumbling concrete slabs. Mom looked just as apprehensive about setting foot on bridge as he was. Considering how completely exposed to the elements this particular bridge was compared with the one they had encountered near Cedar Swamp, it looked applicably unsafe, especially when taking note of the chunks of fallen concrete mingling with the rocks in the water below.

Carl's mind whirred, surprised that they hadn't smelled the flowing water before reaching it. *Tripp* hadn't even detected it. Even more curious was the fact that they were standing no more than ten feet up from the babbling, five-foot-wide stream, and he *still* couldn't smell it.

"Tripp, *come*," Dad ordered, sensing their reluctance to step onto the bridge. The fact that Dad also opted to stay back spoke volumes to Carl.

The dog pulled his head out of the hole with a dramatic sneeze then trotted back toward his humans, claws clicking against the metal. As Mom leashed the dog and began to pull him back away from the bridge, Carl glanced at the muddy edges of the stream. There, dotting the soft, black ground like a mess of triangular dimples, were a collection of animal tracks.

"Dad!" Carl cried. "Come look!"

His father stepped up beside him and studied the embankment below.

"There are herds of deer in this area," Dad said with the ghost of a smile. He turned and looked at each of them. Carl glanced at Zoey; she still looked skeptical.

His father began to make his way down the grassy hill. Carl started to follow, only to find himself stopped a few steps down by his father's voice.

"Not just yet," Dad said, "I want to test it first." He side-stepped the rest of the way down the hill, stopping at the edge of the stream.

"You aren't going to *drink* it!" Mom said. Tripp watched with growing curiosity, ears pricked and tail wagging furiously.

"Not just yet," he said, winking at her as he removed his gloves and tucked them into the waist of his pants. He turned back to the stream and squatted, his boots smudging the deer tracks. He cupped water in his hands, then brought the water close to his nose. For a moment Carl actually thought he was going to drink. A tickle of anxiety fuzzed like static electricity in his chest. He was relieved when Dad appeared to simply sniff the water up close.

"No scent," Dad said, dumping the water back into the flowing stream. "And animals are drinking here. A *lot* of them." Wiping his hands off on his pants, he looked up at Carl and the others. His smile returned. "I haven't smelled clean water since before . . . you know." He glanced under the bridge.

"C'mon down," he said. "*Carefully*. You know what a broken arm or leg means out here." He turned away, his gaze back on the ground. Probably trying to get a read on the direction the deer had traveled.

Carl scrambled down the bank, unable to keep from glancing back at the bridge a few times, relieved they weren't going to cross it. Mom and Zoey followed cautiously, their light footfalls barely registering as Carl joined his father.

The sun had started its slow descent, but it was just after midday if not just a tad later. They had plenty of daylight left to follow the stream to wherever it dumped out, assuming it did actually *dump out* somewhere.

"We'll follow these tracks along the stream," Dad said. "I want to catch something drinking from it so that we can be sure it's safe. We've made it far enough into the forest. If we happen to come across a larger body of water where we might build a new home, then so be it." He clapped Carl on the shoulder. "That sound good to you, son?"

Carl nodded, too excited to even speak. After everything they'd been through, losing both their home and Bampy in the same day, the fear and uncertainty of walking day after day through the wilderness with no destination . . . could it all really end in such a positive way? Could they actually end up settling into a better life than they had before?

"Kel," Dad said, "what say you?"

"Lead on," she replied with a warm smile.

He smiled back at her, and Carl smiled as well. Dad walked the three feet that separated them and planted a kiss on her forehead. As he turned back around he took hold of Tripp's rope and pulled him away from the water's edge. Mom coiled the lead around her hand a few more times.

Dad walked over to where Zoey stood gazing down at the flowing water. He brought his right hand up to her chin and tilted her dirty face up so that she was forced to make eye contact with him.

Carl watched with curiosity.

"And what about you, girl?" he asked, his voice barely loud enough for Carl to hear. Dad smiled again, a smile so large Zoey couldn't help returning it.

"Let's follow the stream," she said, immediately turning away. Carl was certain she didn't believe there could actually be fresh water and wild game, but he was confident they would soon find evidence even *she* couldn't refute.

Dad seemed satisfied. He turned away from the bridge and pushed aside the dry, leafless brush that grew at the edge of the stream. The brush was equally as nibbled upon as the growth along the side of the road.

Dad edged his way into the woods. Carl followed at a safe enough distance to avoid having branches snap back in his face. He looked from the tracks pressed into the mud to the mossy embankment that marked the water's edge. As they moved away from the road, the diversity of tracks grew. Paw prints of various sizes, some of which were large enough to make the hair raise on the back of his neck, joined what he now knew were deer tracks.

"Are those bear tracks?" Carl asked, his voice little more than a whisper. He glanced nervously around. This particular area was different than the areas they'd previously traveled through. Nearly everything was covered in a thick carpet of green spongy moss under which fallen trees and rocks of varying sizes were forever entombed. The moss created a bumpy, uneven surface where the only uniformity was the emerald growth dominating the area. The trees weren't as densely packed either, allowing for a greater amount of sunlight to filter down through the needles and leaves.

"Too small for bear," Dad replied, "maybe coyote or fisher cat." His voice was calm and went a long way to diminish Carl's nerves. Still, his worry wasn't completely alleviated.

"Are we in any danger?" Carl asked. He could almost feel Mom and Zoey listening for Dad's answer.

"We have the rifle." Dad adjusted the rifle strapped to his shoulder as if emphasizing his point. "We've also got Mr. Tripp."

Carl glanced back at the dog, his leash bouncing lightly about as his nose surveyed the mossy terrain around him. Was there some hidden savageness to Tripp that Carl had overlooked? The sappy look on the dog's face as he lifted his nose from the ground and let out a hacking cough, a result of the leash tightening too much around his neck, didn't help.

"What's Tripp going to do?" Carl asked, looking back at his footing in time to avoid slipping into a mossy depression. He shifted his balance, jumped over the hole, and hurried along after his father.

"He'll bark," Dad said. "Most animals aren't looking for a fight. If they're spooked by the sounds of another animal— especially a dog—they'll usually turn and run."

Carl thought about this, trying to picture a thousand-pound bear or full-sized coyote running away from a black-and-white oversized terrier. Still, he had never known his father to be wrong about anything before. The idea that Tripp might help keep them protected would have to be enough for now.

It wasn't long before they came across their first sighting of life. The group of rabbits they spooked made it cleanly away without losing any members of their modest warren. Carl estimated the group to include almost a dozen full-sized animals, all foraging in a patch of grass not yet encroached upon by the expansive moss.

Tripp began to bark, a bit late by border collie standards, as the last set of fluffy white tails disappeared over a mossy hummock. Mom dropped to her knees and took hold of the dog's nose, using her hand like a muzzle and staying firm though Tripp squirmed vigorously.

Dad stepped cautiously back around Carl before making his way to where Mom crouched with the dog. He squatted beside her and began to scratch Tripp behind the ears. This calmed the dog a bit, though he continued to stare after the rabbits, his eyes sparkling with excitement.

"Wild rabbits," Dad said to himself.

Carl's eyes met Zoey's. She quickly shook her head and turned away.

They continued along the stream, moments later coming across an animal Carl didn't recognize. It was small and chubby with what looked to be a soft gray coat. A fluffy tail almost the size and length of its body twitched above the ground as the animal drank openly from the stream.

Again Tripp began to bark, this time with such ferocity that Carl swore he and this creature were mortal enemies. As the animal disappeared, effortlessly dashing up a nearby tree, Mom struggled against the dog as his paws threw up clumps of moss in his attempt to follow. Dad stepped quickly in and pulled Tripp back, once again working his fingers through the dog's fur, massaging him.

"What was it?" Zoey asked.

"A gray squirrel," Mom answered. All eyes fell upon her. She smiled and winked.

"Go to the park a lot in Portland?" Dad asked, gazing up at Mom with his eyebrows lifted.

"Pfft." Mom shook her head. "You think my parents were the types—"

"It was drinking the water," Carl interrupted, no longer able to hold himself back. He glanced at his sister. She returned his gaze, emotionless.

"Yes, it was," Dad said, standing back up and gazing up the tree the squirrel had scaled. "But that's not enough for me. Not just yet."

He turned and led them further along the stream, stopping briefly to inspect a hole in the moss. Carl wondered if the hole could be the den of the rabbits they'd spotted. He made a mental note of the location so he could talk to Dad about it later and then they were on the move again, heading deeper into the woods.

THE TREES BEGAN to thin and ahead Carl could see another open area. At first it looked to be another meadow or perhaps a marsh. The sun was almost at the end of its slide toward the evergreen mountains in the west, and the sky was tinted an orange and purple that grew more visible as they approached the opening.

Carl suspected that they had traveled for close to two or three hours after leaving the road, and the sun's position in the sky confirmed his suspicions. He gave himself a mental pat on the back, pleased to find his skill in calculating the passage of time still intact. Back at the Rangeley House they had kept Bampy's old grandfather clock in good working order. Carl had always used that clock to test his calculations. Dad hated the thing. It would wake him up at night on the quarter hour with its boisterous dings and dongs. He even threatened to chuck it in the pond on one occasion. But he never did. It was the only device they had for telling time that didn't require electricity, and he would have been flayed alive if he'd actually disposed of what Bampy considered his favorite piece of décor.

That clock had been the *only* remaining piece of décor not repurposed to some more practical end. Gram used to lament about the knotted pine tables and chairs that had long ago been relegated to reinforcing the camp's structure.

He forced the images of their old home out of his head, not wishing to bring back the despair he had worked so hard to banish. He focused on his father and the break in the trees ahead. The opening was barely a hundred feet or so in the distance, and judging by the diminishing moss and the presence of knee-high, yellow grass, he figured they were probably coming to another meadow. When they finally broke out of the trees, he found that he was slightly off.

The stream they'd been following carved its way through a small patch of tall grass dotted with the desiccated stumps of fallen trees before dumping into a small, squarish pond no longer than four hundred feet across in any direction. It was surrounded by three mountains just tall enough to block out the rest of the world. A small peninsula jutted into the water at the far end, with what looked to be the southern extension of the stream feeding out just to the peninsula's left.

Trees of varying types circled the pond, all stripped of their low-hanging branches. Carl recognized maple, oak, and birch along with a whole host of evergreen varieties, including some he didn't recognize. Orange, yellow, and red fall leaves decorated the shores of the still, clear water. Carl's gaze was caught by a single auburn leaf as it floated on the breeze before delicately touching down upon the glassy surface. It was in this moment that he spotted the animal on the opposite shore.

"Look!" Carl cried, stepping up beside his father and pointing at the edge of the pond just to the right of the small peninsula. A massive brown creature that looked to him like an oversized buck was drinking from the pond. Its enormous antlers curled upward from its head, each side like a large, curving basin ending in rounded points. As the animal raised its head, a torrent of water fell from its mouth and a little nub of hide beneath its neck flopped back and forth.

"I can't believe this," Dad said. "I haven't seen a moose since I was probably twelve." His eyes were fixed on the majestic animal as it lowered its head once again and resumed drinking.

"Over there!" Mom exclaimed. Carl spun halfway around. Along the left edge of the pond a herd of more than twenty deer walked out of the forest. Among them were several large bucks and at least five young. The rest were all female. Carl held his breath as several of the does looked their way. Black ears twirled, and for a moment the herd was still.

Carl jumped as a chittering screech pierced the silence. He glanced up into one of the pines behind him and saw a tiny, red-furred creature clinging to a bobbing branch. The animal glared down at them, its wispy tail flicking irritably.

"And that's a red squirrel," Mom said. Quite the squirrel expert.

"Why's it so angry?" Zoey asked.

"I imagine it doesn't like us being in its territory," Dad said.

Carl turned back to the deer.

"I—I don't believe it," Dad whispered.

One by one the deer slowly began to move toward the pond. Some walked directly into the water, took one last look at the Richmond family, then lowered their heads to drink.

Fascinated, Carl waded through the grass, intending to cross the stream and make his way over to the bank the deer were on. He stopped about ten feet from the slowly moving water and looked back. "Should we kill one?" he asked. He nodded at the .308 on his father's back.

His gaze locked with his father's, and suddenly Carl understood how hard his father had been working to get a hold on his emotions.

"No. Not yet," Dad said. "We need to wait until we can properly preserve the meat. A kill like that will feed us for weeks if we save it right."

"Okay," Carl said with a nod. He turned back to the stream, which shrank to a more manageable three feet just before opening into the pond. Reaching the stream's edge, he bent his legs, feeling the spongy earth beneath his feet give a bit as his weight settled, and leapt across.

He cleared the gap easily, but was shocked to find himself sinking. He gasped as he teetered back and forth, trying to keep himself balanced. Before he realized what was happening, he'd sunk up to his waist in thin, watery mud. A deeply robust scent surrounded him, reminding Carl of the outhouse at the camp. Somehow he managed to stifle the curse that wanted to break free of his lips. The only thing cursing would do right now was set off his mother.

He wiggled his feet and legs. When he felt his boots start to slip off, he stopped moving and turned to look back at the others. He tried not to sound panicked as the cold water seeped through his pants.

"I'm stuck!" he cried. He placed his hands on top of the grass to either side of him and tried to push upward. His hands immediately sank.

Mom spun around. Tripp's leash fell from her hand as she started toward him, though she made it only a few steps before Dad caught her arm.

"Wait, Kel," Dad said in a calm voice. "It's a bog. You can't go out there. You'll just get stuck, too."

Carl tried not to panic and worked to keep himself frozen in place as he quickly discovered that every movement seemed to make him sink deeper.

"What are we going to *do*?" Mom demanded. She stopped struggling but kept looking at Carl as if afraid he'd disappear any minute.

"You're going to have to trust me," Dad said.

"Dad!" Zoey cried suddenly.

Carl's stomach tied into a knot as his sister dashed frantically across the grass toward the water's edge. "No, Zoey!"

"Tripp!" Zoey shouted.

The knot in Carl's stomach tightened as Zoey took hold of the dog's leash and dragged him away from the pond. The wiry fur that grew from his nose was wet and dripping, and he licked his chops as if he had just finished the most satisfying meal of his life. A grunt escaped Tripp's mouth and his head bobbed up and down a bit as Zoey took him into her arms and began to inspect him, but Carl knew what had happened.

Tripp had been drinking from the pond.

"Everyone follow me," Dad said, walking back toward the forest. He glanced at Carl. "Don't worry, boy. We're coming back to get you out of there. You just stay where you are." He gave Carl a playful wink.

If that was his father's way of telling him not to panic, it didn't help at all.

"What about *Tripp*?" Zoey asked, almost tripping over something Carl couldn't see as she followed her parents back into the trees.

"We'll deal with that later," Dad said.

"But—"

"*Later*!" he growled.

Zoey walked silently behind her mother. She did, however, throw a few scathing looks back at Carl as they headed away from the pond.

Carl took a deep breath. The cold water seeping into his pants and boots was uncomfortable to say the least, but not as chilly as he would have expected given the low temperatures they'd been experiencing. When they had first emerged from the forest, he hadn't really noticed the cold breeze that blew across the open water, but he sure was noticing it now.

First the bridge, now this, he thought. *Zo is going to have some fun with me tonight. Assuming there is a tonight.*

He might be stuck in the mud for the rest of his life, Carl realized. Would Mom and Dad try to keep him fed somehow? Even if they could get food to him, he didn't have any blankets and would freeze during the night. The muck around him would freeze and then it would snow. What would *that* feel like? Would his legs be frozen solid beneath him for days or possibly even *weeks* before the frigid temperatures turned him to ice?

Would Mom and Dad and Zoey have to sit there and watch animals pick his carcass apart until all that remained was his sun-bleached skeleton sticking out of the muck like some demented grave marker?

He shook his head so forcefully he felt like Tripp after his yearly bath. When he stopped and the swirling images had settled, he focused on his father's blue-and-black jacket moving in and out of the trees. He appeared to be leading Mom and Zoey toward the bank where the deer were drinking, though the larger members of the herd were less interested in quenching their thirsts at this point and more interested in the approaching newcomers.

Water made its way into his right boot, soaking his wool sock and making him shiver. He wriggled his feet around a bit, hoping that perhaps the movement might help to keep his toes warm.

He needed to do something, but what? Carl thought long and hard. Bampy would have said that he was thinking so hard something smelled like it was burning. Carl grinned at the memory, then frowned as an idea popped into his head. Reaching over with his left hand, he took hold of the right strap of his backpack and carefully pulled his arm out of the strap. Once that arm was free, he repeated the process, freeing his other arm, then pulling the pack in front of him.

He focused intently on the backpack, pulling it as close to his body as he could and turning it lengthwise. He draped his arms over the pack and leaned against it, seeing how much of his lower half he could lift out of the muck. An explosive burst of energy released within him as he felt his feet rise a few inches.

Let's not get too excited yet, he thought, allowing his backside to slip back into the mud so that he could get a good look at the pack. Muck had oozed into his boots along with more water. He wriggled his toes uncomfortably and carefully flipped the backpack over, trying to minimize his movement. Though a good deal of water had been pressed out of the mud and grass beneath the pack, there was no serious indentation left behind. Maybe he could use the pack to help disperse his weight.

He glanced at the far shore as the deer suddenly spun, lifted their tails, and bounded into the trees in the most elegant retreat he had ever witnessed. Every leap was fluid, every landing perfect. Carl couldn't help being mesmerized by the immaculate brightness of the white fur beneath their tails.

Dad burst onto the shore and dropped his backpack. Pulling the rifle carefully off of his shoulder, he moved over to a nearby pine tree and leaned the rifle, barrel up, against the trunk. Mom and Zoey emerged from the woods behind him, immediately dropping their gear as well.

Thirteen

"GATHER AS MANY sticks and branches as you can load in your arms," James instructed, holding his hands apart before them in a measurement of about four feet. "No smaller than this."

Kelly and Zoey nodded.

He took Tripp out of Zoey's arms and tied the leash, now caked with water and mud, around the nearest tree. He carried the dog out as far as the lead would allow, making sure that he would not be able to reach the water, and set him down in the grass. Then he joined the others collecting the materials he would use to create a path of sorts out to his boy.

He glanced around and realized that they were on an old access path. While the path had been understandably neglected by humans, the fact that it was still noticeable as a pathway told him that it had become a fully functioning game trail. When their current crisis was over, he intended to see if the path eventually connected with the road they had been following.

The path was littered with fallen, dried-out trees and the limbs that had broken free over the years. The wood was now an ashy gray color, but not everything was rotten, which came as something of a surprise considering their close proximity to the water. A quick integrity test reassured James that the limbs would not break under his weight when spread across the mire.

While the women busied themselves collecting sticks and branches that had already broken free and fallen to the ground, James focused on snapping larger branches off of the fallen trees that lay across the game trail. He worked with a determination that wouldn't allow fatigue to slow him as he gritted his teeth and broke off limb after limb, chucking each one into a pile. It wasn't long before the smells of his own perspiration began to waft up, mingling with the scents of dried wood, mud, and pine.

As he finished snapping the last remaining limb off of a long, skeletal tree, he took hold of its ten-foot-long trunk and dragged it to where the spongy surface of the bog transitioned to the firmer soil of the shore. He dropped the tree at the border of the grassy muck and positioned it so the thin end was pointing back toward the trees. He lifted the tip and walked forward along the trunk's length, shoving the tip into the air as he went. With a throaty growl he thrust the tip upward, tipping it over its center of gravity. The trunk fell forward with a hollow thud and James eyed it critically. This would be the first piece of his pathway into the bog.

Movement caught his attention and he glanced out toward the pond. Carl had somehow freed himself from the muck and was crawling toward the shore with his backpack out in front of him.

"Wait!" James yelled. While he was absolutely delighted to see the boy freed from the mud, it was the absence of boots on Carl's feet that drew most of his concern. With winter coming on, there was no way the boy could go without his boots. "We have to get your *boots*!"

CARL STOPPED AND wiped away the beads of sweat trickling down his brow. With a nod to his father, he relaxed his arms and allowed his upper body weight to rest on the backpack. He glanced back over his shoulder, noting that he had made it perhaps five feet and had left a sloppy trail of flattened grass and pooled water behind him. He looked back at the shore where his father was walking across the trunk he had dropped, balancing effortlessly while carrying an armful of dried branches. It was difficult not to be impressed with how easy Dad made it look, walking along a thin trunk with such a large load in his arms.

Would *he* would ever become such an intelligent, coordinated and resourceful man, Carl wondered.

As Dad reached the end of the tree, he very slowly squatted down, shifting the wood into one arm, then carefully laying the branches, one by one, lengthwise across the grass. Behind him, Mom and Zoey dropped more branches before returning to the forest.

Fortunately, the bog took up only the back end of the pond, and from the point on the shore where Dad was back gathering another armful of branches, it was only perhaps seventy-five feet to Carl. The wooden path that was currently in the process of being laid had already covered about twenty feet by Carl's estimation. He watched his father make his way back across the trunk, this time with a heavier load. It was a very careful and decidedly precarious process, but Dad handled it masterfully, reaching the end and once again carefully arranging another seven feet worth of wood path.

Carl remembered his boots, and began to scoot around with the backpack still in front of him. After making a complete reversal, he started to inch his way back to the hole he'd made. The hole was now an oval puddle surrounded by yellow grass. Pulling his backpack over to his left so that he could hold onto it, he bit down on the cuff of his right sleeve and pulled his arm out of his jacket. With the jacket out of the way, he repeated the process with the thermal shirt he wore beneath, only this time pulling the sleeve up as high on his arm as it would go. Bracing himself against the almost-intolerable cold, he stretched out on his stomach and lowered his hand into the hole, fishing around for his boots in the muddy water.

His hand came into contact with icy sludge sooner than he expected and he let out a groan. This wasn't going to be as easy as it first had seemed.

He pushed his hand down farther, feeling around with his fingers and frowning a bit as the water came up to his shoulder and began to soak his chest. He kept feeling around, but after a minute or so, still didn't find anything remotely boot-like.

Carl sighed. He had been waist-deep in the hole. He was really going to have to get in there if he wanted his boots back.

Pulling his arm back out, he released another irritated sigh before glancing back at his father. The path was now perhaps twenty feet away and still growing steadily. Taking inspiration from his father's determination, Carl turned back to the muddy hole and pushed his arm in deeper. He stared at the water just below his face and swallowed back the fear. Years and years of being told not to allow unpurified water to get into his mouth, nose, ears, or eyes made him freeze in panic.

After another couple of minutes spent swiping his hand back and forth, the tips of his splayed fingers finally brushed across something solid—just out of reach. He would have to submerge his face. There was no other option.

You won't survive the winter without boots. And it was the truth. There was no way around it.

Gathering up every bit of faith he had that the pond water *had* to be fresh, he drew in a deep breath. Creating as much pressure as he could to keep water from running into his nose, he pursed his lips together, and squeezed his eyelids shut. Then he pushed his hand deeper into the muck until half of his face was submerged.

He quickly found the object, grabbed tight, and with his left arm tightening around the backpack, pulled the boot up out of the water and placed it on the watery grass next to his pack.

One down.

He shook water from his face, pulled himself back onto the pack as much as he could, and wiped his face with his left sleeve. Satisfied that none of the water had entered his body, he glanced at the boot. It was from his left foot. Given that he was now facing away from the direction he had originally jumped, he adjusted his search, took another deep breath and shoved his arm and face back into the water.

JAMES STEPPED BACK onto the trunk and repeated his balancing act. As he reached the end and stepped onto the smaller pieces that he had arranged like the crossties on a train track, spaced unevenly a foot or so apart on average, he slowed down a bit. He didn't want to miss and step between the branches. The farther out he managed to get, the slower the process had become, but he was determined to do this right and avoid any other accidents.

Reaching the end of the path, he squatted carefully for what seemed like the thousandth time, keeping his eyes on the branches beneath him. Once again shifting the weight of the wood into his left arm, he placed the mixture of logs and branches one at a time, stopping only to move carefully forward before laying another group.

As he set the final piece from his current bundle, he realized Tripp was barking. Turning back, he was shocked to see the little dog jerking his head to and fro against the rope with such force that he worried Tripp might snap his own neck.

Something else was wrong.

Tripp lunged forward, launching into another series of aggressive barks and growls, his attention apparently focused at something on the shore behind Carl. James turned around, paying careful consideration to his footing before looking at Carl, who emerged from the mire just ten feet away from him and tossed his second boot into the grass. For a moment James thought maybe Tripp was overreacting, then a pack of coyotes emerged from the woods. They stalked along the shoreline, their heads lowered and tails sticking straight out behind them. In all, he counted seven. Seven sets of yellow eyes, all ravenously fixed upon his son.

"Get *away*!" James cried, waving his hands and nearly losing his footing. He dropped his arms to his sides and recovered his balance.

"Carl," he said, struggling to keep his voice calm. "You're going to have to crawl over to me. Now!"

CARL QUICKLY WIPED the water off of his face and looked around to see what all the commotion was about. He caught sight of the approaching animals, and the feelings of accomplishment that came from fishing his boots out of the mire were replaced with panic. Unlike the deer and moose and squirrels he'd encountered so far, these dog-like creatures did not seem afraid of him. They stalked toward him with purpose, and something in their body language told him it wasn't for a friendly sniff hello.

He grabbed his boots in one hand and awkwardly began to push himself toward his father, using the backpack to keep from sinking.

He moved forward, inch by torturous inch, keeping his eyes on his father's face. He fought the urge to look back over his shoulder. That would cost him time that he might not have. One question tumbled through his mind as he moved: wouldn't the animals have the same trouble he'd had in the water and mud? In any event, the farther away he got, the better.

His father's eyes flicked back and forth between Carl and the pack and Carl knew he didn't have much time.

His knees dug into the mud as he quickened his pace, no longer able to keep his movements slow and deliberate. His heart thudded in his chest as anxiety spiked through his body like expanding cracks across a sheet of glass. With his weight more or less evenly distributed, he was able to move without sinking too far down with each push, but it felt like he would never make it to the wooden platform and his father.

JAMES TOOK A quick look behind him. Kelly and Zoey were nowhere in sight. Tripp was still fighting his leash, and suddenly he wriggled out of the rope and dashed out into the grassy marsh. The little mutt moved with a swiftness and grace that he'd never shown before. A tinge of concern welled up in his gut, but James forced it away and turned back to Carl.

If Tripp sacrificed himself in order to save Carl's life, so be it.

"Give me your hand!" James said, bending his knees and stabilizing himself before stretching out his right hand. Carl was perhaps three feet away and completely covered in muck and grime.

The boy reached out and took hold of James' hand just as Tripp splashed past them like a black-and-white bullet. A very soggy, very wet, bullet. James shifted his grip and took a tight hold of his son's wrist before bending his knees and pulling. Carl's lips pressed tight as he rose to his knees, then stepped on the backpack before moving carefully onto the branches that were not already holding James' weight, abandoning both backpack and boots.

They both turned to watch Tripp rush fearlessly toward the pack. The coyotes stopped and lowered their heads even farther. The hair on their backs rose, and their lips curled back, exposing sets of sharp, yellow teeth.

"Dad!" Carl cried, "we have to—"

He was silenced by deafening crack of the rifle. The sound echoed and reverberated across the pond and off of the surrounding mountains like a blast of thunder, nearly causing both of them to fall backward. James grabbed his son, and after a momentary wobble, they looked back across the stream in time to see the last of the coyotes flee into the woods. Tripp, who had never before heard a gunshot, spun around, his tail tucked between his legs.

His ears pressed flat to his head and his gaze darted around the pond, looking for the source of the terrifying sound.

"Tripp!" James yelled, looking to regain control over the dog before he decided to chase the coyotes. "Come here!"

The dog obeyed, hesitating a moment when he reached the stream, then wriggling his haunches and jumping across. He splashed easily across the bog, only sinking awkwardly in the muck a few times. As soon as Tripp reached them, James reached down and scooped the dog into his arms, his balance faltering for a moment.

He looked back at the shore. Zoey stood at the grassy edge, rifle in her hands. Kelly stood beside her.

FOURTEEN

ONCE A FIRE was built and Carl's clothing was hung up to dry, Dad filled his arms with one final load of branches and walked slowly out on the wooden pathway. He moved carefully to where the logs and branches came to end and arranged the additional logs across the grass and mud.

Carl watched him work and rubbed his arms briskly in an effort to chase away the cold. The fire danced and popped as the sun slowly disappeared below the horizon, stripping the sky of its interlacing mesh of orange and purple light. Dad would have to work quickly if he wanted to have enough light to make it back to shore.

You should be out there helping him. Carl was fairly shocked that Zoey hadn't mentioned it yet. Though he understood that he deserved something of a beat down after what had happened, a very large part of him understood that it wasn't realistic to be getting after himself for such things. He was, after all, sitting half-naked beside a fire, wearing nothing but a pair of Dad's tattered boxer briefs.

A sudden gust of chilly air set his teeth chattering as the breeze picked up, ruffling across the water and up through the grass at the edge of the bank. He inched closer to the flames, holding his hands out and allowing his palms and fingers to absorb as much heat as they could before rubbing his arms again. As the breeze subsided, he caught sight of his father moving back across the wood path with Carl's backpack strapped to his back and Carl's boots in his right hand.

"Here you go, baby." Mom's soothing voice reached him just before a heavy, quilted blanket draped over his shoulders. He wasted no time grabbing the edges of the quilt and pulling it tight across his chest.

"Thank you, Mom." His heart warmed, and he couldn't help smiling as she placed her hands on his shoulders and kissed him on the top of the head.

She patted his shoulder and gently scratched his upper back before moving away. Dad was heading back along the trail that followed the edge of the pond when Mom headed down to the water, metal pot in hand. She walked to the water's edge and collected some of the assumedly fresh water before turning back around and making her way back up to the fire.

"Deer, moose, rabbits, squirrels, and coyotes," Dad said, shaking his head and smiling as he shrugged the backpack off his shoulders and hunkered down on the other side of the fire. Planting the mud-caked boots on the ground, he removed their cloth liners and stood back up. "Makes you wonder what else has managed to survive around here."

He didn't seem the least bit angry at what had transpired that afternoon. Quite the opposite, actually. He was in the best mood Carl had seen him in since, well . . . *ever*. Even Mom eyed him with what appeared to be a mix of curiosity and suspicion as Dad made his way down to the edge of the pond and began to wash the mud out of the boot liners. When he began to whistle, Carl wondered if perhaps he *had* accidentally consumed tainted water and was having hallucinations.

Dad's whistling suddenly stopped. "Look!" he cried. "Did you see that *fish* jump?"

Carl caught sight of a thick ripple pulsing its way through the water, barely visible in the twilight.

Fish?

"Are you *sure*?" Mom asked, looking equally as excited. She set her pot down at the edge of the fire and ran down to the water.

Carl watched his parents as the warmth of the fire collected in the blanket. Combined with his body heat, he felt almost comfortable. Had he been in any other position he would have rushed down and stood with them.

Bampy's tales of their first weeks and months at Dodge Pond following Black Christmas had almost always included fish. Just as the tainted water was poisonous to animals who drank from it, it was equally lethal to aquatic denizens. Even before the water was confirmed to be tainted, Bampy was smart enough to boil any water taken from the pond. Bacteria and parasites were at the top of his list of worries. But it wasn't until he began to notice large amounts of dead fish washing up on the shore, their eyes clouded and lifeless, that the nature of the contamination became somewhat clear. Similar reports came from those living at the edge of Rangeley and Mooselookmeguntic Lakes. There were even rumors that massive marine animals had washed ashore along the coast of the Atlantic.

A large splash sent another series of ripples running across the pond. Dad whooped and Mom squealed like a little girl. Carl stared at the water, hoping to get a sight of the next jumping fish. He watched as Dad placed the boot liners on the grassy shore and wrapped his arm around Mom's waist. They both slowly fell backward into the grass.

It wasn't long before another fish leapt out of the water, its large body wriggling as if it were trying to swim through the air before falling back in. Mom and Dad exclaimed again and Carl found himself clapping beneath his blanket. The only person who apparently didn't share the enthusiasm was Zoey.

Carl turned and looked at his sister, sitting five feet behind him. Tripp slept in her arms, exhausted after the excitement of the afternoon. Her hand stroked gently across his cheek and down his neck.

Their eyes met, and Carl wondered if she had been staring at him the whole time. He took a deep breath and sighed.

"Let's have it, Zo," he said, scooting himself around so that he could face her properly. The warmth of the fire on his back felt marvelous and left him somewhat annoyed with himself for not turning around sooner.

"Have what?" she asked, her voice low and distant as if she was talking in her sleep. Her face was painted in flickering orange light. The dark woods rose behind her like a giant black wall. She continued to stroke Tripp's wiry coat, not once breaking rhythm.

"Oh, c'mon," Carl said, not believing for a second that his sister wasn't trying to pull something. She was obviously working some kind of angle in order to make his eventual drilling all the more brutal. "Just let me have it. I know you're angry with me for what happened today. You're *always* angry with me. I could *fart* too loudly and you'd give me a punch in the gut."

She shook her head. "I'm not angry with you." Her voice was still quiet and dreamy as she continued to stroke the dog.

"Then what's with the *look*?" he asked, scowling as he studied her.

"What?" she asked, shaking her head as if she were just waking up and trying to get a handle on her surroundings. Her hand ceased its rhythmic caressing, and Tripp looked up in a silent showing of disapproval. Rubbing at her face, Zoey took a deep breath and her eyes met Carl's, her expression dispassionate and neutral. "I'm not angry with you," she repeated. "I'm angry with myself."

Carl stared at his sister in disbelief. "Why would you be angry with yourself?"

"Because I've been in denial this whole time. Just *look* at this place, Carl. It's perfect. I never thought I'd see a living animal—other than the rabbits and chickens and Tripp. In just *one day* I've seen moose, rabbits, deer, squirrels, coyotes, and *fish*." She looked down at Tripp, whose nose shifted ever so slightly from side to side. His black eyes stared up at her, catching flashes of firelight.

"There's fresh water here," she said, scratching beneath Tripp's chin. "After spending my entire life hearing stories about how perfect the old world was and how the rest of our days would be spent struggling to stay alive in a world no longer made for living creatures . . . we stumble across *this* place."

A blast of emotional lightning splintered deep in Carl's chest as he watched a smile unlike any he had ever seen slowly spread across his sister's face.

He was speechless.

"Look at them," Zoey said, her voice deep and full of passion. She nodded at their parents.

Carl scooted slowly back around, his gaze settling on Mom and Dad as Zoey walked over and planted herself down beside him. Light from a few early stars cast brilliant dots in the calm waters, mirroring the heavens above. Mom and Dad sat side by side, their silhouettes sharp against the vibrant mirror. Mom's head rested upon Dad's shoulder.

Zoey rubbed Carl's back, and she lowered her head to his shoulder. The fire danced merrily as she whispered, "We're home."

INTO THE
NIGHT

FIFTEEN

G O SLOWLY," BRYAR whispered as they moved carefully
through the trees using the moonlight filtering through the
swaying branches. This created an alternating pattern of milky
light upon the forest floor as if a million tiny fingers flittered about
above. It was easy enough moving through the open patches of
grass where no underbrush grew, but as they navigated through
tangles of vines and brush, it became decidedly more difficult.

The first fifteen minutes in the woods had been the hardest as
their eyes worked to adjust to the low light, but after that things
became a bit easier. Travel was by no means easy, but they were
doing better than he had originally expected, which left him reasonably optimistic that his plan would work and that they would
be far enough away from Ma' Lee and the others by morning to
ensure that they were never found.

It was necessary to make their escape in a way that made it
difficult for Ma' Lee to track them. Bryar had led Casey to the
edge of the forest across the road from their camp and then directly into the trees. There was no path to follow, and he was mildly
nervous that he might end up leading them in circles as he did
his best to approximate a westward course, but this was the best
plan of action. With any luck, Ma' Lee and the others would head

back toward the town as he and Casey went farther and farther away.

Casey had yet to voice a single complaint as she waddled along, Bryar assisting her over fallen trees, large rocks, and other natural obstacles that cluttered their path.

After what he estimated to be at least three hours of pushing through the trees and brush, he decided it was time for a break. As if it were somehow meant to be, they broke through the thick greenery of pine needles and thin, leafy branches and into a fifteen-foot-wide, moonlit clearing with a fallen moss-covered tree laid across a bed of grass. Helping Casey over to the tree, he eased her down into the grass and helped her lean back against the trunk. The scents of dry grass and decaying leaves was particularly strong here, overpowering the smells of pitch and soil prevalent elsewhere in the forest.

"How are you doing?" he asked, looking her over for any serious signs of fatigue. Her stringy blond hair hung in her face and was pushed back and forth as she breathed. It hung in snarls over her pink sweatshirt. She had been too focused on keeping herself from falling over in the woods to push the stray locks away, though now that she had a chance to sit down she immediately shoved her hair behind her ears.

"I'm okay," she said between breaths. Her hands moved down to her belly as she worked to regulate her breathing.

"We can't stay for long," he said, his tone soft and apologetic. "We need to put as much distance between us and them as possible before someone realizes we're gone."

"I know," she said. "I didn't ask to stop." She gave him a playful wink and a half-smile.

"Yeah, yeah," he said, returning the smile, "you're a tough one all right. But it's the little one that I'm worried about. I don't want your baby coming tonight."

Her hands worked their way gently over her belly as she seemed to process his words. "I think we've got some time yet on that one." She began to scoot herself back up when Bryar's hands came gently down upon her shoulders and settled her back on the ground.

"Wait," he said, "just a little longer."

She gave him a begrudging nod and returned her hands to her belly.

Bryar sidestepped around her and sat down against the tree. He thought about removing his backpack, but decided to leave it on. As he allowed himself a moment of relaxation, he thought about what things would almost certainly be like when the others woke the next morning. Hopefully, Wade would be the one to discover his and Casey's absence—that discovery would likely fetch a harsh beating from Ma' Lee. And if anyone deserved a beating, it was Wade. Next came Brett. Bryar really didn't have any bitter feelings toward Jack, who only did as he was told and didn't seem to take much delight in the violent actions that Ma' Lee sometimes expected of him. He was just an innocent, mindless pawn. The only thing that had kept Bryar from bringing the poor fool with them was Jack's loyalty to Ma' Lee, which was indisputable.

"We should get moving, Bryar," Casey said. "We can't be wasting any time. You know what's going to happen to me if she finds us. We've never tried to leave her before. She'll kill me for sure."

He already knew this, of course. His threats to stop *playing Anthony* were not likely to hold up should they be brought back into the fold. Not even the need to keep Casey around as a means of subduing their brothers' sexual urges would be enough to spare her the beating that Ma' Lee would unleash should they be found.

Bryar's stomach clenched as he suddenly felt very naïve. Of course, Casey would have already considered this. He had taken it upon himself to shoulder all of the responsibility and worry that came with the decision to finally break away from the group. She was not a child, nor had she really ever been one. She had been forced to grow up the day she was born, and he had been in a sorry state of denial about it.

Moving slowly to his feet, he readjusted his backpack and wished that he had taken it off after all. Reaching down, he took her hands in his and helped her up. "Let's get back on the move."

He led her by the hand around the fallen tree and out of the small clearing. As they moved back into the trees, he hoped that his sense of direction would keep them on a straight path away from the others.

He felt ridiculous having told Casey that they couldn't stop for long and then having her push to get them back on the trail. Yet another example of how weak he was in a leadership role. It just didn't suit him. His strengths lay elsewhere, like in his ability to withstand the most graphic and brutal abuse. Even there he couldn't give himself all the credit. Had it not been for Casey, he wouldn't have had a reason to keep fighting all this time. It was even quite possible that he would have taken his own life by now had she not been a part of it.

Suddenly he wondered if he had made the right decision. Was he the right person to be leading Casey away? Would he be able to keep her alive out here in the wilderness?

There was still time to turn around and backtrack to the camp. They could be fireside before the sun was up and nobody would be the wiser about their attempt to escape.

But what about the baby? Ma' Lee and the others would have absolutely no use for it once it was born. They'd likely leave the newborn by the side of the road with its cord still attached . . . or worse.

No, as unqualified as he was to be leading a pregnant woman through the woods, Bryar Perkins was making the right decision. The *only* decision.

He gasped as the ground beneath his right foot slid out from under him. He grabbed wildly and caught hold of a nearby tree, steadying himself as loose dirt and gravel cascaded off the steep edge of a drop-off. The rocks pattered into a ten-foot deep by twenty-foot wide ravine, lined on either side with large trees and a number of younger saplings struggling to grow up and out from the bottom. Beyond the ravine the land appeared to slope away as if they were either descending a mountain or making their way down into some kind of basin.

Casey stopped behind him. She reached out and wrapped an arm around his waist, presumably in preparation to pull him backward should he lose his balance. As he took a few steps backward, she released her grip and stepped back as well.

"You okay?" she asked.

"Yes, I think so," he breathed. For a moment he thought about explaining himself—that he had been absorbed in thought concerning his incompetence as a forest guide and complete lack of leadership skills—but there was no reason. He had nearly demonstrated his insecurities by taking a dive into a hole in the ground.

"Are we going to try to climb down?"

Bryar thought this over. Quick glances to the left and right showed the cut in the ground continued as far as he could see in either direction. Gnarly tree roots stuck out of the eroded ground at irregular intervals along the edge. He looked back at Casey, his gaze settling on her stomach.

"It's too dangerous," he said. "We'll have to follow the edge until it ends or until we can find a safer way across. Even if we could get down there without killing ourselves, it's going to be a lot harder to get up the opposite side."

She nodded, and he felt his shoulders sag in relief. Had she questioned him, he would have started to question himself, and that was something neither of them needed.

Bryar pushed a few errant strands of hair out of his face and led her along the edge of the ravine. He tried not to let himself dwell on the idea that the entire endeavor would have been so much easier in the light of day. All that did was beat him down further, and he was already quite low.

They walked for perhaps twenty minutes or so before the ravine began to taper. In no time the twenty-foot gap was ten, and shortly after that the swath ended in a downward-sloping point. The time lost amounted to no more than thirty minutes, leaving them to resume their westward course once again.

The terrain was definitely sloping downward. It was only a slight decline, but they were certainly moving downhill. Even with the bright glow of the full moon, there was no way for them to get a truly decent picture of what lay in the distance.

"You doing okay back there?" he asked, keeping an eye on his feet and what he could see of the leaf-littered ground.

"I'm fine," Casey replied.

As they walked he could feel by the wavering tenseness in her grip that she was having some trouble. The muscles in her arm occasionally tightened as she struggled to keep her balance and composure.

There was nothing that could be done at this point. They couldn't alter their route, and backtracking uphill after spending a good forty-five minutes moving down was also not an option. Instead, he slowed his pace dramatically, forcing her to do the same. Though he wasn't sure if she had noticed, she didn't protest, and he turned his attention to getting them safely to the bottom of the hill.

IT TOOK ROUGHLY two hours, but they carefully picked their way down the hill, arriving at the bottom without incident. Once the terrain leveled off, Bryar asked Casey if she needed to take another break. She immediately declined and pushed him to continue moving forward. He silently agreed but he would only allow another couple hours of travel before finding a safe place for them to bunk down and sleep out the rest of the night. As far as he was concerned they were far enough away. He clung fiercely to his original theory that Ma' Lee would suspect they had backtracked and force his brothers to return to Rangeley in search of them. After all, there was no reason for Ma' Lee to suspect that they had stolen off into the woods.

SIXTEEN

IT WASN'T THE sparse amount of dull sunlight radiating over the eastern mountains that interrupted Wade's slumber. The fire had died completely, leaving nothing to warm his chest and belly. He raised his head and squinted through eyes that weren't yet ready to commit to opening for the day, searching for Casey as his pants began to bulge at his crotch.

The morning was chilly, and the air filled with the scent of decomposing leaves. This mingled with the light scents of chalky gravel and grass growing at the edge of the crumbling road.

Brett was still asleep on his back, his mouth wide open, though he wasn't snoring. The burly man's right arm loosely encircled the last can of baked beans, which the family had easily finished off the night before after Ma' Lee had had her way with it. It was amazing how she could eat so much, yet remain so emaciated. Then again, it also made little sense how Brett managed to stay so big and robust.

But Wade didn't really dwell on those things. In fact, he didn't really think about much at all. He was a creature of impulse, relying mostly on his instincts and never really giving much consideration to the consequences of his actions. He just did what felt right, and his target in such an event was typically his younger sister, who he was too mentally inept to also identify as his niece. Not that it would have mattered.

When his visual scan of their ramshackle camp left him unable to locate Casey, he thought about calling out for her, but a look at Ma' Lee, who was still asleep, told him that might be a bad idea. He always watched for cues from his mother—like the faithful dog he was—and he knew very well not to disturb her in the morning.

He slowly sat up and turned around, looking back at Jack asleep behind him. His older brother was a curious sight. For one thing, he looked so different from the rest of them. Though there were finer, more subtle aspects of Jack's build and personality that were decidedly un-Perkins, the only real difference as far as Wade was concerned was Jack's hair. It was brown, not blond like the rest. The brown strands extended down Jack's chest and constantly shed dandruff like a cloud spitting snow.

His brothers had some theories as to why he looked so different. Wade was his typical clueless self on the matter.

He looked Jack up and down. Casey was not behind his brother, either. He noticed a series of scabs on Jack's left hand, and for a moment Wade thought about crawling over to pick at them. Reaching up and rubbing at his sleepy eyes, he decided, in a rare showing of self-control, not to follow this impulse.

So where was Casey? The only other person she could be bedding down with was Bryar, and Bryar was nowhere to be found.

He shuddered a bit as a thought exploded in his head like a bomb. He studied the smoldering ashes, which Bryar should have tended during the night. It was his job. Very rarely did they ever wake up to anything less than a pile of still-warm coals and even then a beating from Ma' Lee would often follow, starting with Bryar and following its natural course to the rest of them. All that remained this morning was chalky, gray ash.

He rubbed at his eyes once again. Then he ran his hands over the bald dome of his head, pushing back what little hair he had left. He heaved himself to his feet—struggling a bit to keep his balance as his right foot snagged a large rock at the edge of the road—and surveyed the larger area around them.

All he could see was a bare stretch of grass concealing the crumbled remains of the old mountain highway. A light breeze worked a crisp chill across his skin. The chill amplified the fear and anxiety that ravaged through his body like an aggressive virus.

Casey and Bryar were gone.

"Mmm . . . mmm . . . Ma'." His voice refused to come out as anything more than a quiet whisper. His instincts wouldn't allow him to wake his mother.

This was different though. She would beat him even harder if he *didn't* wake her up.

"Mmm—*Ma'*!" he stuttered, his voice loud enough to draw a series of groans and stretches from his brothers.

Ma' Lee remained curled up like a sleeping cat.

Wade stomped his feet up and down in frustration and scratched nervously at his head. A frustrated whimper emerged from his throat as he danced around, trying to figure out what to do.

Drawing on every bit of strength and determination he could find, he lowered his hands from his head and walked slowly over to Ma' Lee. "Mmm . . . mmm . . . *mmm—Ma' Lee!*" he sobbed, tears of panicked frustration rendering his vision a blurry mess. He blinked, clearing his eyes for a moment as he came within a few feet of his mother.

It wasn't that he was afraid of the beating he was certain to receive. If anything, a part of him *wanted* it. No, what had him so tweaked was the idea of disturbing this woman for whom he had so much respect and adoration. In his little mind this was a terrible sin. Still, even he understood when it was necessary to disturb Ma' Lee. This was beyond any doubt one of those moments.

He squatted down, and reached toward her shoulder with a slow, shaky hand. Behind him, he heard rustling as his brothers started to sit up and look around.

"Mmm—Ma' L—"

Ma' Lee's hand came swiftly up as his hand touched her shoulder. She smacked him hard across the cheek.

Wade fell to the ground, the sting in his cheek momentarily alleviating his panic. He grinned up at the brightening sky, as pain rocketed through his skull.

"Where do you get the *nerve*?" Ma' Lee yelled in a venomous tone. She wasted no time rolling over him and straddling his belly with her legs. Balling her hands into fists, she let her fury rain down on his smiling face until a steady stream of blood trickled out of his nose down through the creases at the edge of his mouth. Jack and Brett remained where they were.

"Fuckin' *retard*," she hissed, finally shoving up to her feet. She gave Wade a kick in the gut for good measure before turning to the others. As he rolled over onto his side, excited energy swirled above the pain that had him immobilized. As his gaze fell upon his brothers, he found himself overwhelmed with anticipation.

Both Brett and Jack closed their eyes and rolled over, playing like they were asleep.

"Why's this fire out?" Ma' Lee asked, her hands once again balling up. Eyes squinted in anger, she took a brief look around the camp. "Where've Bryar and Casey gone off to?" She turned back to Wade and gazed down at him like a cat eyeing a maimed mouse. Taking a few steps toward his head, she squatted down.

"Is this why you woke me?" she asked. "Were you trying to tell me that they are gone?"

Wade sniffled a bit, his nose no longer registering the scents of wood smoke and decaying leaves, and after a brief and uncontrollable gargle of blood, he turned his head and coughed crimson liquid upon the yellowing grass and cracked pavement. Looking back at his mother, he slowly nodded his head, putting as much feigned sorrow as he could muster behind the gesture. From the back of his fragmented, chaotic mind, a voice questioned his actions, asking with genuine shock and dismay why he didn't try to push her for more pain.

Ma' Lee's face quickly contorted into a livid scowl. A white-hot fire seemed to burn in her eyes as she sprang to her feet and began to kick him repeatedly in the crotch. When he tried to close his legs instinctively against her brutal assault, she delivered a few kicks to the sides of his gut before stepping back and turning on the others.

MA' LEE SCREAMED IN rage as she covered the few steps to her other boys. She went to work on Jack first. The steel toes of her furry boots made contact with his gut, narrowly missing his bottom ribs. She avoided breaking bones when she could, even in her wildest rage, in order to keep her boys useful to her.

Jack lurched forward, greasy locks of hair falling into his face as he wheezed and struggled to take in a lungful of air. The attack was so swift and brutal that he didn't even have time to cry out.

Beside Jack, Brett's eyes cracked open and met hers. A look of horror spread across his face as she turned on him, still screaming ferociously. He lifted his hands as she dove, her sharp nails biting into the flesh of his arms. As she worked, Ma' Lee began to feel his arms weaken but only after she'd left a collection of deep, bloody scratch marks behind. She paused, hoping he would assume the attack was over. When their eyes met again she shoved his arms aside and went to work slapping him in the face. She rained down blow after blow on his right cheek, growing fiercer as the skin turned bright red. She knew from experience that the more tender and raw the skin was, the more responsive it was to pain.

"Arrrgh!" Ma' Lee cried, delivering a final blow to Brett's dark red cheek. She drew in a deep breath and tossed her head back, looking at the sky as she exhaled. She remained completely still and oblivious to the fact that she still sat on her son's chest.

"Brett," she said, looking down at him after a minute of silence.

"Y—yes, Ma'?" Brett stuttered beneath her, his voice a quivering whisper.

She casually pushed herself to her feet, and solemnly looked at each of her three remaining boys. "Get your shit together. I'll bet you anything those brainless cunts went back toward Rangeley, maybe even that museum. If they think I'm just gonna let 'em go, they'd better think again."

The boys sprang immediately to their feet and collected their gear. She watched with satisfaction as they moved quickly in spite of any lingering pain. They knew that if they weren't speedy enough, she'd beat them all again.

Within minutes, all of their belongings were together and strapped to their backs. Ma' Lee moved over to the fire and took hold of the small soup pan they used to purify their water. The black plastic handle had long disappeared, leaving a metal stub poking out from the filthy, charred bottom. Inside remained a small amount of water.

She tipped the pan and finished the water, rolling her eyes at the pathetic looks on the boys' faces. Tossing the pan to Brett, she grabbed the can of beans and ran her fingers along its bottom, scooping up a slimy finger full of dark mush and shoving it in her mouth. She looked the can over for a moment before tossing it to Brett.

Though his face showed confusion, she knew he dared not ask any questions. He simply shook his backpack off of his shoulders and forced the can into the main pouch with the soup pan. He pulled the pack onto his shoulders once again and waited for orders.

"I hope you little fuckers are ready for a long walk," she growled, circling around them like a drill instructor. "'Cause we aren't stopping 'til we find them."

Not a single response from the boys.

Ma' Lee pursed her lips together, took a deep breath, and with one last disappointed look began to walk back toward Rangeley. She stopped to blow a snot rocket into the ditch that ran along the right side of the road and noticed a white "O" hanging in the red brush at the forest's edge. The frayed pink stitching around it was unmistakable.

"Sneaky . . ." she growled before pinching her left nostril shut and blowing a blast of mucus into the grass.

SEVENTEEN

JAMES ENDED UP keeping watch all night, unsure what he might expect to see in the way of other animal life. Coyotes were his chief concern. These animals hadn't seen humans in who knew how long, and in a world where coyotes were likely to be the chief predator, he was worried how bold they might be when it came to going after new prey.

While the moon was hiding behind a few bulges of ash-gray cloud, he caught sight of a number of yellow dots on the far side of the pond. More than likely some kind of animal eyes reflected in the light of the fire. In all he counted nine sets. It was probable that they were coyotes, but he couldn't be absolutely certain. If they were the same coyotes they'd seen earlier, there were two extra with them. Their prevalence seemed to indicate that they were the main predators in the area. This left him mildly unsettled, though his anxiety was quickly nullified by relief as he thought back to Zoey's impromptu test of their thirty-year-old ammunition.

Good thing Bampy had been so obsessive about where they had stored it.

With his rifle draped over his left forearm and his finger resting on the side of the trigger, he watched the eyes as they moved about like flickering, earthly stars in the darkness. A cold wind swept down from the mountain behind him, carrying the scent of dried pine needles and decomposing leaves. The wind ran across the water, and he could almost picture the coyotes sniffing at the smell of smoke and whatever odors he and his family gave off. He wasn't sure if it was the gunshot from earlier or the blazing fire, but the animals didn't seem interested in approaching. This pleased him. Another couple of nights like this and perhaps he might allow himself some sleep.

As daylight began to crest the eastern slope, he caught sight of a moose emerging from the forest with her adolescent calf. The animals lumbered slowly through the boughs of deep green pine and warm-colored leaves before wading into the water and dipping their noses for a drink.

A thrill of excitement made the hair on his arms stand on end. That made three moose he'd seen since arriving at the pond. Just one of the creatures would provide enough meat for them to survive the entire winter. Given the chill of the season and the welcomed absence of insects at the pond, it wouldn't be very difficult to smoke the excess meat for storage. The only question was: where would they store it?

He'd thought about how best to build a proper shelter off and on during the night as he considered how their new life at the pond would take shape. It was a given that they would build some sort of cabin, most likely on the small peninsula that jutted out where the southern end of the pond narrowed back into a stream, but since he had never before attempted such a thing, it was certain to be a struggle.

They would do it, though. They had to. Fate had not delivered them to such a sanctuary only to have them die within months of finding the place.

Satisfied any threats were long gone, he ejected the round he had chambered hours earlier and released the magazine. He snapped the shell back into the clip and placed it in his pocket. Slinging the rifle over his shoulder, he got to his feet, walked around the fire, and knelt down beside Carl. The boy was curled on his side, his back to the dying fire. James rested his hand on his son's shoulder before gently nudging him awake.

Carl looked dazedly around. A smile appeared on his face when he glanced over his shoulder. "Morning, Dad."

"Good morning, son," James said with a smile of his own. He nodded at the cow and calf. "Ever seen a young moose before?"

It was a ridiculous question. Until the previous day neither of the kids had ever seen a moose period. Carl rose on his knees for a better look.

James watched with a warming joy as Carl peered across the still water. He followed his son's gaze, his attention coming to rest on the large, brown creatures. The moose didn't seem the slightest bit concerned with the family of humans on the opposite bank. Both cow and calf went about their business, sinking their long noses into the pond and drinking in long gulps. Their heads would occasionally come back up, releasing a shower of excess water.

"Is that a doe?" Carl asked.

"A cow," James corrected, watching his son's smile droop into a brief frown.

"What's the baby called?"

"A calf."

Talk of cows and other farmyard animals had come up occasionally over the years, but not enough for Carl or Zoey to form any kind of tight understanding of what an actual milk cow was. James watched as his son repeated the alien words—out loud at first, then silently forming them with his lips as he committed them to memory.

"I was thinking about taking a walk," James said. He moved to his feet, not expecting any kind of argument.

"Sure," Carl said, pushing aside the quilt. With the exception of his boots, he was fully dressed again, having donned his clothes the previous night once they'd finally dried. The liners for his boots hung over the fire on sticks James had buried in the ground. When he reached over and took hold of the liners intending to hand them to his boy, he found the wool-type inserts were not only dry, they were also quite warm and toasty.

Carl quickly reinserted the liners in his boots and pulled the boots on, probably trying to capture as much of the warmth as he could. He stood tall and looked at James. "Where are we going?"

James gazed down the trail that ran along the eastern edge of the pond. The various game animals had left the grass parted like the hair of a gentleman ready for a night on the town. Though the trees thickened the farther the trail ran into the forest, it was still a recognizable path.

"I want to see where this trail leads," James said, walking around the quietly sleeping women, both curled toward the still-warm embers of the fire. He quickly untied Tripp's lead from the tree. The dog stood with a long, drawn-out yawn, stretching out his front paws. "If it ends at that road we were following, I want to make sure that no one else is going to spot it."

An image of William Dewoh standing outside of the Rangeley House with his posse of armed men flashed through his mind. He focused on Carl and took a deep breath. A fearful look crossed Carl's face and James wondered if the same thought had occurred to his son.

Carl shook his head as if clearing it and went to his backpack. Unfastening the top clips, he worked the protruding handle of the axe free and rested it over his shoulder.

"Good idea," James whispered with a wink. He glanced down at the dog and decided to remove the leash altogether. Might as well let Tripp run free. There was obviously no problem with him drinking the water, and if any aggressive animals happened to stumble across their path, there was always the rifle to scare them off.

James took the loaded magazine from his pocket and snapped it into the rifle, leaving the chamber open. Satisfied that they were as prepared as they could be, he headed up the trail with Tripp moving into the lead. Carl walked beside him until the thick cropping of evergreen needles and red-and-orange leaves became too thick, at which point he dropped back. The high-pitched chitter of a red squirrel followed their progress. James' pace slowed a bit as he took a quick look at the canopy above. The little animal had himself well hidden, though, and finally James turned his attention back to the trail.

The slope of the eastern mountain rose somewhat sharply on their right, a mess of trees clinging stubbornly to its face. The view of the mountain disappeared the farther they walked. The birch, maple, cedar, and fir they passed through had the first of their branches jutting out approximately six feet above where their trunks met with the earth. The lower branches had probably been stripped and consumed by deer and moose during the winter when food was scarce.

After about a hundred feet the trail opened into a roundish, twenty-foot-wide clearing. Knee-high grass, yellowed with the season, grew up from the ground, though not so thick as to block from view the thin scattering of shale stones that lay in patches, preventing the grass from completely dominating the area. An earthy, hay-like smell hung strong in the air, undiminished by the light breeze that made its way through the trees. The only other break in the grass was an old stone fire pit built along the right side of the clearing. Above the pit hung an old metal sign, the paint upon which had faded away.

"Another drinking spot?" Carl asked, stepping over to the fire pit and kneeling down to inspect it. It looked like most of the rocks were still there, along with a few pieces of rotted wood piled beside them. The wood would crumble into pulp in his hands if he tried to pick it up. The interior of the stone circle had been reclaimed by tall grass.

"Possibly," James said. In truth, he wasn't entirely sure what the place had been used for.

Carl stared at the fire pit as James walked around the edge of the clearing, looking for the other side of the trail. His foot caught something buried in a patch of loose dirt and discarded pine needles. He bent down and took hold of the object, pulling it up for inspection.

It was an aluminum can. The portion that had stuck up out of the dirt was nearly eaten away by rust, but the upper part had been preserved from the elements. He turned the can over, eyeing the tiny slit in its top curiously before turning it back around so that he could inspect the writing on its face.

With a smile he carried it over to Carl. As he closed the gap between them, he glanced at Tripp, who had, in one of his rare, impressive moments, found where the trail picked back up at the northern edge of the clearing. Reaching his son, James handed him the can. "Drinking spot, indeed. This was a beer. Old Milwaukee."

"Is that some kind of alcohol?" Carl asked.

James laughed. "I suppose, though Bampy always referred to it as donkey piss." He nudged his son playfully with his elbow before taking the can and tossing it into the fire pit. He shot a paranoid glance over his shoulder to make sure Kelly hadn't somehow followed them in and heard him say the word "piss." But the edge of the clearing was empty.

He clapped Carl on the back, and headed toward Tripp.

The trail led them a few hundred feet further before emerging from a dense wall of pine and brush onto what appeared to be the road they had initially been following. It had to be the same road. The gravel ruts through the tall grass were identical, and unless there was a fork somewhere along the way, it was highly unlikely that another road had been cut this deep into the wilderness.

Stepping out onto the road, James noticed Tripp's tail heading east through the knee-high grass and called him back. The dog's head stuck curiously up above the yellow blades before disappearing again. The tail headed back toward them.

"You think this is the same road?" Carl asked, rotating the axe handle in his hands.

"I'm pretty sure it is," James said, studying the fall-colored leaves, red brush, and dark green needles that made an unofficial barrier to their trail. He tried to place himself in the shoes of any-one who might happen to walk past. Would they be able to see the path and identify it as a viable route?

"Well, *that's* going to have to come down," Carl said, point-ing up at a wooden sign just to the left of the trail. The sign was attached to a large tree some seven feet off the ground. It was so well hidden in the yellow, orange, and red leaves that James hadn't even noticed it. Come winter, when there weren't any leaves left to conceal it, the sign would have been impossible to miss.

It was probably two feet by two feet and, though it was now a sullen gray, had at one time been painted white, judging by the flakes of paint still clinging to the wood. Written upon it, spelled out in small strips of wood that were nailed to the face of the sign, was a name.

"What does it say?" Carl asked.

"Ben Gile Pond," James said.

"Ben Gile Pond," Carl repeated, a thoughtful look on his face. "How do you think this place has been here all this time—with a sign and all—and never been claimed by anyone?"

That certainly was a mystery. The only answer that came to James was that the pond was just too deep in the woods and no-body in their right mind would set off into the wilderness of the new world unless they were suicidal. Without all-terrain vehicles, the back woods had become something of a new frontier.

"I don't know," James said, studying the letters on the sign over and over. "I guess this place is just too isolated."

"What does that mean?"

James tore his attention away from the sign and thought about the question for a moment. "It means far removed from settled areas. I guess this place was just waiting for us." He glanced back up at the sign as Tripp trotted up and sat on his haunches.

Carl nodded, leaving James wondering if that had truly been enough of an answer. Without a word the boy walked toward the sign, still twirling the axe. Inching his hands down the wooden handle until they were almost to the bottom, he turned to look back.

James nodded, keeping his eyes on the sign, tracing over the hand-cut letters spelling out the pond's name. He read the words over and over again several more times as Carl raised the axe over his head and struck the small piece of wood. Most of the letters fell free after the initial hit. On the second strike, the wood snapped in two and fell to the ground.

Ben Gile Pond, he thought, walking over to collect the pieces.

EIGHTEEN

BRYAR AND CASEY stepped out of the woods onto what must have been an old logging road judging by the relatively intact gravel ruts. Lining the ruts both inside and out was the tall, yellow grass that had been prevalent for as long as they'd been walking.

Bryar saw the discovery of the road as a very good sign considering the difficulty Casey was having making her way through the forest. She was taking it like a champ, but he was almost certain that sooner or later there would be an accident. A backwoods road was safe, regardless of how much it raised the odds that they might come into contact with other wanderers.

"Left or right?" Bryar asked with a smile. He tried as best he could to hide the weariness in his voice. Though his body had fought an impressive battle, he hadn't allowed himself to fall asleep when they'd stopped in the early hours of the morning. Nothing would have been so terrible as to be woken by Ma' Lee's fists just when they believed they might have finally escaped her tyrannical clutches. When it had been time to go, just as the light of the sun was poking up over the mountains, he'd gently woken her, and they'd resumed their course. They'd been walking about an hour when they'd come across the road.

"Left," Casey responded, "definitely left."

"What has you so bent on going in that direction?" he asked curiously.

"Because left is west," she said, looking back at him. "East would just take us back to the highway we were following before we made camp, right? Back to them."

He glanced at the sun slowly rising to his right. With a shrug, he said, "I'm not really sure. All old roads like this have to dump out somewhere." He said this with the confidence of someone who actually knew such things to be true, and the plain truth of the matter was he did not. Still, he was desperate to keep her faith in him as high as could be, if only for morale. He smiled. "Left sounds good enough to me."

His right hand rested on the hunting knife he had taken from the logging museum. He'd attached the sheath to his old, cracked leather belt so it rested on his right hip. He watched as her eyes fell on the blade. It didn't take long for her to look back up at him, approval written all over her face.

She cradled her stomach in her hands and waddled her way over to him, resting her left hand on his shoulder as she struggled to keep her balance. Her right remained on her stomach.

"What is it?" Bryar asked.

A smile spread over her face. "He's kicking. Been a while since I've felt the baby kicking."

The wave of relief that suddenly washed over him was unlike anything he had ever felt before. Yes, he'd felt relief many times, usually after Ma' Lee was done beating him or had rolled off of him. Still, he couldn't believe how good it made him feel to know that both Casey and the baby were all right. At least as all right as they could possibly be at this point.

"It's been a while, huh?" he asked.

She nodded. Drawing in a deep breath, she tilted her head back, lifting her face to the sun. After a moment spent basking in the light, she turned to Bryar and patted his back, then pushed herself away and glanced back at the forest.

"What's wrong?" Bryar asked.

"I was just thinking about what will happen if she catches us," Casey said. She looked down at her belly.

"No more talk of that," he said firmly. Just going by the way she had said it, he knew there was more, but he wouldn't hear it. Not a word. His hand curled around the worn, wooden handle of his knife.

Casey studied the knife, then looked up at him.

"I promise you that if any of them ever gets close to you again, I'll—I'll . . ." he trailed off. Oddly enough, he knew exactly what he wanted to say, that he'd kill them, but for some reason he wasn't able to get the words out. It was important that he do so. Judging by the concerned look on Casey's face, he knew she needed some kind of reassurance.

"I promise," Bryar said again. "I promise I won't let any harm come to you or the baby."

That would have to do.

He studied her eyes, looking for signs of release from the pressure building up behind them. She looked back, maintaining the eye contact. Bryar could only hope she could see the sincerity he was trying to convey, regardless of how vague his statement had been and how flimsy his resolve might eventually turn out to be. His promise to protect her would be honored somehow.

"We need to get moving," he said, wishing that there was more time, but the fact of the matter was, the more distance they put between themselves and Ma' Lee the better off they were. This part of the promise he could keep.

"I know," Casey said, leaning in and kissing him on the cheek.

"Left?" he asked, forcing a smile.

She nodded. "Left."

~

ZOEY AND MOM were up stoking the fire, a fresh pot of water already boiling, by the time Dad and Carl returned. Looking over the pond as the trees began to thin around them, Carl could see the two women seated at opposite sides of the fire. The closer they got to the little campsite, the stronger the scent of wood smoke grew, intermingling with the autumn scents of the forest. The slight nip that had been in the air when he and Dad first set out was slowly being chased away by the rising sun.

Tripp flew down the trail toward the women before slowing and trotting proudly along, nose lifted as if checking the newest addition to his territory for unwanted intruders. Carl followed his father over to their temporary camp. He carried the axe while Dad held the scraps of broken wood, all that remained of the sign.

"Where've you two been?" Zoey asked, doing a very poor job of hiding her disappointment at having been left out. She poked at the fire.

"Just took a little walk," Dad said. "Wanted to see if the trail that runs out of here connects to the road we were following before."

"Does it?" Mom asked.

Dad nodded, sitting down by the fire beside Zoey and taking the stick out of her hand. "Yes." He laid the broken pieces of the sign down beside the fire, leaving Carl to wonder if he planned to cast them in for fuel. A sense of relief spread over him as Dad pressed down a patch of grass with his hands and began to reassemble the sign, putting each piece together like a puzzle. It didn't take long. After a few minutes he had a reasonable recreation of what he and Carl had seen when the sign was still attached to the tree.

"What does it say?" Zoey asked.

"Ben Gile Pond," Carl answered. Zoey looked unimpressed, her eyebrows raised and lips pulled into a tight, straight line as she stared at him. Carl broke eye contact, feeling like a submissive dog.

"Ben Gile Pond," Dad repeated, gently patting Carl on the back. Carl felt slightly better.

Dad gazed at the patched sign as if trying to commit it to memory. Then he looked at Mom over the crackling flames. "What do we have left for meat? I'm thinking a proper breakfast is in order. Then we'll see about making some snares to catch our dinner. I want to get the snares done early so that we can spend the afternoon getting some kind of shelter up."

Smiling, Mom pulled the remaining strips of cured rabbit meat out of her backpack and distributed them, one for each person. It wasn't until his first salty bite that Carl realized how hungry he was. All the action the previous day coupled with the long walk with his father had left him running on empty. As he chewed, thoughts of his family enjoying a well-earned feast flooded his mind. They were going to set snares, which meant they would have more meat, and with the seeming abundance of wild game, they didn't necessarily have to be conservative about their rationing anymore. In fact, the days of rationing might just be over.

The herd of deer eventually emerged from the forest, though they approached the water from the right side of the small peninsula, as the moose previously had. They watched the humans with mild caution, big ears flicking back and forth.

"Eat up, boy," Dad said as he pushed the last shred of his jerky into his mouth. Pulling one of his work gloves onto his right hand, he took hold of the boiling pot of water and removed it from the coals. He turned back to Carl. "We've got a lot of trees to cut down over the next few days if we're to have a stable shelter in place by the time the snow begins to fly."

Carl nodded. He started to shove the rest of his breakfast into his mouth, but was stopped by Mom. "You know it's not good to eat that fast, so slow down."

"We can't afford to waste any time, Kel," Dad said with a smile that told Carl his father was kidding around. The way Mom squinted back at Dad seemed to insinuate that he was only *half* kidding.

"Well, you won't see snow for at least a month, and another five minutes for him to properly chew his food is going to benefit both of you in the long run." Mom shot Dad The Look, reminding Carl of Gram. "You don't want him getting sick out there."

Dad shook his head and waved his hands back and forth like he was fending off an attack. "No, ma'am. I reckon I don't."

"You getting smart with me?" she asked, her stern look dissolving into a teasing smile.

"I wouldn't *dream* of it," he replied, rising to his feet and pulling on his other glove. He gave Mom a wink and walked over to his backpack sitting beneath a cropping of large fir trees. Carl kept an eye on his dad and tried not to wolf down his food. Dad carefully unzipped the main pouch on his pack, making sure that the zipper didn't stick anywhere as he always did, and began to dig around. After a few seconds he held up a spool of gray twine.

"You going to try for more rabbit, Dad?" Zoey asked around a mouthful of jerky. She finished chewing and swallowed before pushing the last of her breakfast into her mouth.

Dad smiled. "I'll take whatever we get."

"Why not just shoot a deer?" Carl asked.

"In time," Dad. "For now we'll stick to small animals. No sense in wasting bullets on big game until we've got a proper place to store it. Plus, the smaller ones breed faster."

Carl nodded. He eyed the last of his rabbit jerky, and after a quick look at his mother to make sure that she wasn't going to voice any disapproval, shoved it into his mouth and climbed to his feet. He quickly grabbed his axe.

Across the pond, several deer lifted their heads and watched as Carl moved toward his father, axe in hand. They slowly resumed drinking as Carl followed his father back up the northbound trail.

Nineteen

Ma' Lee and what remained of her brood were able to make it through the forest fairly quickly. They had plenty of daylight, and they didn't have the added burden of carrying another human being inside of them.

Despite his fatigue, Brett couldn't keep his mind from drifting. Anyone else in their group would have overlooked the torn letter from Casey's sweatshirt, but not his mother. No, not Ma' Lee. If Brett had been in charge, they would've headed back along the road toward the last town. His powers of observation were nowhere near the level of his mother's. Though there was a very obvious madness to her, she had a sharply honed intelligence, and he supposed that was what had kept them all alive all those years dodging the militias.

Brett was snapped out of his thoughts as he reached a large cut in the earth. Beyond it, the grade turned downward, and the trees opened up just enough to reveal a vast, evergreen landscape peppered with oranges and yellows and reds. Rolling mountains stretched as far as the eye could see.

Bryar and Casey could be anywhere in all of that, he thought, not daring to pause as he and his brothers skittered and slid down the slope of the ravine. Brett quickly reached the other side and pulled himself up and out, using the exposed roots growing like boney fingers out of the earth. Ma' Lee's constant threats kept his brothers moving quickly behind him. He broke into a jog, wondering what Ma' Lee would do if one of them fell and hurt themselves. An impressive collection of slippery, brick-colored pine needles carpeted the forest floor, threatening to undermine his footing at any moment.

What if someone fell and was unable to walk? He shrugged the thought off and focused on his footing. If he or any of the others were injured, Ma' Lee was likely to keep them moving forward regardless of the severity.

"Double time it, or I'll cut off your little *peckers!*" Ma' Lee shouted as they reached the bottom of the hill and scrambled over a number of fallen trees before pushing forward into a thick tangle of ferns, bushes, and vines. The density of the undergrowth increased dramatically, making the going all that much harder. Brett was repeatedly slapped in the face by branches, and the grunts and whines behind him let him know his brothers were feeling his pain. He forced himself to keep moving without breaking pace. Being slapped by tree branches or scratched by brush was nothing compared to what their mother would do to them if they didn't keep up their speed. She chased after them like a demon at their heels, threatening to close in and eviscerate whoever failed to keep up.

Brett reached up and ran an arm across his brow, not too surprised to find the flesh of his forearm relatively dry. Given the severe dehydration that they were all experiencing, with the exception of their matriarch, the idea of consuming tainted water was mildly appealing. He had been in similar situations in the past where his mind luckily ended up prevailing over his base instincts, but he wasn't sure if he would be able to stop himself this time. *If* they came across water. He wasn't built for hours and hours of running over and around obstacles in the woods without a single stop.

Ma' Lee, on the other hand, was unstoppable when chasing down something she wanted. She could go for hours—he had seen it. One night years ago they had shared a dinner of dog meat (at least, that's what they'd *said* it was) with a band of fellow nomads outside of Portland. The group had taken off in the night after ransacking their things. Ma' had been off with Bryar, having her customary fun; the rest of them had been asleep. When she returned to the camp the next morning and found her last remaining bottle of whiskey gone, she'd driven Brett and the others up and down the coast for three days with little sleep.

When at last she gave up her search, she delivered a beating unlike anything they had ever endured.

"Gah!" Brett cried out as he leapt over a fallen tree, legs numb and mind dulled to everything except for the pace he was keeping. He broke through a wall of branches that slapped painfully at his arms and face into what looked at first to be a clearing. He lost his footing, tumbling into a ditch three feet below. He fell against the far embankment, his lower body rolling into mushy ground. Water filled his shoes and soaked his pants.

He rolled over onto his backpack, bracing himself as his brothers came into view above him. "Wade, stop! *Wade!*" he cried, raising his arms and bracing for the impact of his brother's body. He caught sight of the deep scratches Ma' Lee had left on his arms that morning. Thankfully the areas around them were dry and hadn't been exposed to the water.

Wade threw out his arms as he struggled to keep his balance on the treacherous edge. A deep groan escaped his lips and his face lit up in an expression of panic as he tumbled forward. Brett started to roll onto his side, but his younger brother crashed painfully down upon his left arm, pinning it to his chest and pushing his body deeper into the muck.

Brett glanced up in time to see Jack grab hold of two small trees and stop himself at the last minute. Suddenly his back arched and his hands lost their grip. Before Brett could warn Wade, Jack fell with a surprised cry on top of them both.

"Did I say anything about *stopping*?" Ma' Lee cried, standing above them in the spot where Jack had just been. She scowled down at them like a fierce predator ready to pounce. Brett struggled to move as his brothers pawed their way frantically over him. He kept his eye on Ma' Lee, relieved to see her attention shift to the open area around them. He stopped struggling for a moment and craned his neck, looking to see what had caught his mother's attention, but he was too far down in the ditch to see anything.

Biting down on his lower lip, Brett turned his attention back to Ma' Lee and resumed his attempt to extract himself from the ditch without getting too much wetter.

The scowl on Ma' Lee's face transformed into a look of careful calculation.

Brett heaved his struggling brothers off of him with his good right arm. He didn't care whether or not they ended up face down in the water. He pressed his lips tight as a spike of pain shot through his left arm. He squeezed his eyes shut and stretched the arm slowly out in front of him. There was a lingering pulse of pain, the nerve center of which seemed to be in his lower bicep, but he was able to work through it. He'd be in trouble if he found himself in need of both arms in order to work another person over, but fortunately nothing felt broken.

He rolled the rest of the way onto his stomach and crawled slowly out of the ditch, grimacing at the rank, spoiled onion smell of tainted water saturating his clothes. The sound of flapping leaves from the edge of the forest and boots slopping through the muck behind him created a sense of urgency. His mother was on the move. Planting both of his hands on the ground, Brett shuddered as a burst of fire shot through his left arm, then he pushed himself quickly to his feet just as Ma' Lee stepped onto the road beside him.

It *was* a road. Perhaps an old logging road. Two gravel ruts ran between a line of uninterrupted grass, heading off through the trees in both directions. The smell of gravel baking in the sun mixed with the hay-like smell of the dried grass, transporting him back to another time in his life, a time he could barely remember.

Brett turned to Wade and Jack, who'd quickly scrambled out of the ditch and stood side by side, waiting. Wade appeared to still be a bit frazzled, struggling feebly to get a grip on the situation.

"They came through here," Ma' Lee said, though not a single scrap of evidence was offered to support her observation. Brett didn't dare question his mother's instincts; they seldom led her astray. The only question that remained unanswered was: which way did they go?

He watched her stalk up and down the road, studying the grass as it waved and cocking her head in quick, jerky motions toward the ground every now and then, like a bird eying a worm. While she busied herself searching for clues, Brett pulled his sleeves down and removed his black wool jacket, wringing water out of it. The others followed suit almost immediately, removing their outer layers and twisting the wet clothing tight.

As Wade wrung out his red hooded sweatshirt with its golden PTK insignia on it, an acronym none of them understood, the reeking stench of unwashed skin wafted into the air from the stained white t-shirt he wore. The stench almost burned Brett's nose, and he backed away. The t-shirt was blotched with yellow sweat stains under Wade's arms and around his neck, with a lower ring that ran around his pronounced gut. Brett was all too familiar with Wade's years of neglected personal hygiene. In fact, as Brett thought about it, he couldn't recall when he had ever witnessed his younger brother bathing, not that any of them were often afforded such a luxury.

On the cleanliness scale, Jack wasn't too far above Wade. As he worked on his green thermal pullover, the tattered black t-shirt he wore saw the light of day for the first time in what must have been months. Though there were almost certainly a number of stains scattered throughout the dark fabric of the garment, the filth caked upon his arms in patchy, black streaks was enough to confirm that he paid no more attention to his hygiene than Wade.

"Jackson, Wade," Ma' Lee said.

The two looked up like a pair of thieves caught in the act, shook out their jackets, and jogged over to Ma' Lee. She stood twenty feet down the western side of the road.

"Here's what's gonna happen: the two of you are gonna go this way, walk until nightfall, and if you haven't come across them by then, you're to turn back and come meet up with us." She looked at Brett. "You and me are going to go the other way, same plan. If any of us find them, great, we bring them back the other direction until we meet back up again." She cracked her knuckles one at a time, working her thumbs along each finger. "Any questions?"

Even if they had questions, neither of his brothers would voice them. Brett wondered if it were possible for them to overtake his missing siblings before nightfall, but he wasn't about to bring this up and invite another beating. Instead he shook his head and walked over to join his mother.

"I'm hoping I don't have to remind you what'll happen if you mess this up," she said, eyes reduced to slits as she glared at Wade and Jack.

"W—we'll be good, Ma'," Wade said in a shaky voice. Ma' Lee slowly walked toward him, causing Wade to take a few steps backward, simultaneously cringing against Jack and grinning like a fool.

She stopped with her face just inches from Wade's. Her fingers curled up in fists. What Brett expected to be another severe beating, however, failed to escalate. Instead, she turned and looked at Jack.

"The only reason I'm letting him go off with you is 'cause I know he's useless on his own. You keep him in line and don't let him out of your sight. Understand?" she asked, her voice little more than a whispering hiss.

Jack nodded slowly, not once breaking eye contact. He cringed briefly as her hand came up slowly and her fingers splayed across his cheeks. She ran her hand gently down his face and over his patchy facial hair to his chin. Slowly, almost delicately, she twirled a bit of his short beard around her index finger, and in a flash she pulled her hand away, taking a clump of his beard with it.

Jack cried out in pain as Ma' Lee stepped away, looking over the coarse hair in her fingers before offering it to the breeze. Brett frowned as Wade turned around to eye the patch of blood running through his brother's dark beard. He smiled maniacally and began to jitter and bob, seeming to forget about his mother behind him until her hand came down upon the dome of his balding head in a loud *smack*. His body arched forward, shoulders lifting into the air as he cringed. Brett didn't need to see Wade's face to know that his smile had broadened.

"No more wasting time," Ma' Lee growled. "Get moving and double-time it!"

Jack took Wade by the wrist and began to lead him along the left rut, westbound down the old road. Neither of them looked back.

WITHOUT MA' LEE to act as slave driver, their pace slowed as Jack and Wade made their way along the old road. As the stress that came with knowing Ma' Lee's hand could fall upon him at any moment drifted away, Jack began to relax and acknowledge the fact that he was actually *away* from her for the first time in . . . well, as far back as he could remember.

It soon became obvious that Wade was not on the same page. In the two hours they had been on the march, his younger sibling had twice fallen into a state of panicked hysteria. Both times Wade had attempted desperately to turn back, only to find

Jack in front of him, trying to calm him down and explain the situation. In both cases, Jack was eventually able to refocus his frantic brother by reminding him that Ma' Lee had sent them to find Casey and Bryar, and that she would flay them alive if they turned back before fulfilling her instructions. The relief that came with Wade's eventual compliance left Jack extremely grateful that things hadn't gone the other way. At least he wouldn't have to haul his brother, kicking and screaming, down the road.

As time ticked along, Jack's stomach began to groan. The discomfort that came from digesting thirty-year-old beans grew until he almost couldn't stand it. He pushed himself to keep moving. Thirty minutes later, he grabbed his belly, trying to hold back what felt like an imminent explosion. The last thing he wanted to do was stop, though it was looking more and more like he wasn't going to have a choice in the matter—unless he wanted to push along with a wet load in his pants.

"Hold up, Wade," Jack said as he clenched his rear to avoid soiling himself. He glanced at the trees lining the road.

A few steps ahead of him, Wade stopped and turned slowly around. Jack watched his brother, hoping beyond hope that Wade wouldn't immediately notice Ma' Lee's absence and launch back into another fit. He forced his body's urgent plea for a pit stop out of his mind, and waited for the panic to fill Wade's face.

At first Wade's gaze ran down the old, grassy road lined by thin tamarack trees. A look of confusion spread over his face and the muscles in his cheeks twitched a bit. To Jack's relief, Wade's gaze quickly shifted over to him.

"What is it?" Wade asked.

"I gotta poo," Jack replied, watching in disgust and annoyance as Wade's face lit up in a buffoonish grin.

"Haha," Wade giggled, his body twitching and his hands shaking mildly. He made a series of flatulating noises with his mouth before losing himself in a fit of laughter.

Jack shook his head and sighed. He waited for his brother's hilarity to die down before saying, "Look, I'm going to go into the woods for a little bit. Just stay right there, okay? Can you do that for me, Wade?"

As if he had forgotten what he was laughing about in the first place, Wade stopped and his smile disappeared. He raised his eyebrows, as if asking exactly *why* he was going into the woods.

Again, Jack sighed. "Just stay here, okay?"

Wade nodded reluctantly, still obviously confused. He glanced back up the road and scratched his neck as if he were trying to remember exactly why they were out there in the first place. Jack couldn't care less at that moment, so long as Wade didn't get it in his head that they were unintentionally removed from Ma' Lee.

Confident as he could be that his brother would be okay, Jack headed into the woods, squeezing through some brush and a few saplings until he was far enough in to avoid having his privacy invaded. Turning back around, he noted that the road could be seen, but only barely, through the dense, dark vegetation around him. Though his body urged him to get on with it, he managed to hold off lowering his pants until he was certain that Wade wasn't coming in after him. When a minute went by without the goofy idiot bumbling his way into the forest, he took his jeans down and went about his business.

TWENTY

"C ANDY NECKLACES," BRYAR said with a smirk.

"What?" Casey exclaimed. "How did *that* work?"

"Well," he said, trying to think of how he might describe the candy in a way that she would understand. "You remember that stuff I gave you when we were coming out of Auburn? You know, the little round buttons that were hard and kind of sour, but they broke apart and got all sugary when you chewed them?"

Casey's face lit up and she nodded. "The ones with the clear wrapping that twisted open when you pulled on both ends, right?"

Bryar smiled, delighted to see her happy. "Yes, those," he said. "Think about a bunch of them, only with holes in the middle, strung around an elastic string—a *stretchy* string—so you could chew them off while wearing them around your neck."

She looked at him, then raised her eyebrows and shook her head. "And *that's* what you miss the most from the old days?"

He shrugged. "Well, you kind of caught me off guard with the question. I can't say as though I'd answer the same if I had more time to think about it, but that's the first thing that entered my head."

For a moment he considered asking her the same question. But Casey had been born into this world, not the old world, and asking might upset her, something neither of them needed.

"I thought you might talk about music or whatever that tee-vee thing is that Brett always yacks about." She laughed. "I didn't think you'd go with some weird—"

Bryar gently silenced her by pressing his index finger to her lips.

"Hub-a-bub-a-bub-a-bub-a-bub," came a very faint voice through the trees. A voice Casey and Bryar knew very well.

Bryar froze, his hand on Casey's arm. Though he had toyed with the idea that the others might somehow track them, the real possibility of that coming to pass seemed farfetched. Why would Ma' Lee think they'd run into the woods instead of heading back along the road?

Still, that blather could only come from Wade Perkins. He was still a good distance away, somewhere beyond the hook-like turn in the road some seventy-five feet behind them.

He glanced at Casey and saw his own fear mirrored in her face. Without a word, he took her hand, leading her off the road toward the forest. He pulled a section of red brush aside, using his foot to flatten the lower twigs and branches.

Casey waddled cautiously past him into the dense growth of pine, tamarack, and maple trees at the edge of the road. Bryar's instincts told him to rush her along, but somewhere in the back of his mind a logical voice insisted he allow her the time and care she needed. When she'd finally moved through the brush, he allowed the branches to fall back into place as quietly as he could, then followed her. Once they were safely through the thick vegetation that bordered the road, they pushed a good twenty feet deeper into the forest, then hunkered down behind a knot of trees surrounded by a large collection of yellowing ferns.

They waited.

"Bub-a-bub-a-bab-a-dab-a," Wade continued, spouting his happy gibberish as his voice grew louder and louder.

Bryar squatted down on the ground and motioned for Casey to do the same. He peered through breaks in the ferns, watching for shadows to pass along the sunlit road. The sound of his brother coming closer and closer shook Bryar to the bone. Wade's presence there was so wrong and so out of place that it took a moment for Bryar realize that Wade was alone.

The realization hit Bryar like a punch in the face. Wade's voice was the *only* voice disrupting the tranquility of the forest. The grating, raspy call of the demon mother herself, Ma' Lee, was completely missing.

Bryar thought hard. It could be a trick. Why would Wade be by himself? The only answer was that the group had split up. Ma' Lee had somehow known to follow them through the woods, but when she reached the road she wasn't sure which direction to take. Ma' Lee, clever wretch that she was, had sent Wade off one way and—

No, Ma' Lee would never have sent Wade off on his own. He must have wandered off.

Bryar slowly stopped shaking, and he rested his hand on the knife he had secured to his belt. Unfastening the leather strap that held the blade in place, he pulled it out and tightened his fingers around the handle. He was ready to use the weapon if he had to . . . or so he told himself.

"Hab-a-dab-a-doom-a-boom-a-tut-a-*butt*—" Wade burst into a loud fit of laughter. Though he was still out of sight, the closeness of his voice told Bryar his brother couldn't be any more than ten or twenty feet away.

"Butt," Wade said again, then burst into loud laughter. This carried on for at least a minute.

His laughter finally diminished and Wade quieted down, snapping his fingers rhythmically and making popping noises with his mouth. The sounds grew louder and louder until Bryar suddenly saw Wade's silhouette walking along the road between the dark shadows of the trees like a figure walking past windows in a well-lit house. Wade's body bobbed back and forth in its usual odd movement as he passed by—alone.

Where were the others?

"What are we going to do?" Casey whispered, her lips so close to Bryar's ear that the chapped flesh ran across his skin like sandpaper.

Bryar didn't answer. He watched as Wade finally disappeared down the road. Once his little brother was out of sight, he refocused his attention on Casey, and gave her question serious thought.

There was only one thing they could do.

"We need to get off the road and back to traveling in the woods," he replied. "But first I have to check something." Standing up, he slipped the knife back into its sheath and moved slowly back toward the tree line. He stopped and turned. "Wait here for me."

Cautiously, he worked his way back to the road, listening intently for any sounds that would indicate the others were nearby. The Perkins family did not travel quietly no matter how hard they tried.

JACK WANTED TO be done with his business and back on the road as quickly as he could, but his body wasn't willing to cooperate. It had been some time since he had been treated to a filling meal, and after two straight days spent packing his body with beans, he was now paying the price. He'd been patiently gathering leaves from the low-hanging branches above him, leaves which he held tightly in his hand and stared at almost longingly. All he wanted was to be done and get back to Wade before his younger sibling had an opportunity to get himself into trouble.

He gritted his teeth as another wave of pain rolled through his abdomen. While every natural impulse told him to stay until he was finished, he knew that finishing could take a very long time and he needed to get back. He cleaned himself as best he could, yanked up his pants, and worked his way toward his brother. It wasn't until he reached the edge of the forest and stepped back out onto the road that he found what he needed to take his mind off of the pain in his gut.

Wade was gone.

Jack turned and looked back in the direction they'd come. There was no sign of his brother on the road. Turning in the direction they'd been headed, he only saw more empty road.

Moving himself through the pain, he began to walk rapidly in the direction they'd been headed. As he found the willpower to break into a run, he was relieved to feel the pain in his stomach eventually ease. He broke into a sprint.

Bryar remained a good five feet behind the tree line as he studied the road. From what he could see through the trees, ferns, and brush, the road was clear. Wade had moved off, and his inane babbling could no longer be heard. The only voice that spoke now was the gentle song of the forest as the breeze played about in the leaves, causing them to rub gently together and sending several drifting to the ground.

It was now or never.

Bryar turned back to Casey, breathing deeply the scents of pine and freshly trodden grass. Casey's eyes remained fixed upon him as she waited for his signal to approach. With a silent gesture of his hand, he waved her over and watched as she waddled toward him, working her way carefully through the brush and over roots.

"Was it just him?" she whispered, her face creased in anxiety. She glanced at the tree line, then back at him.

"I can't be sure," he replied, "but I don't see anyone else."

"I thought you said we were going to stick to the woods."

He placed both hands on her shoulders and held her gaze. "We are, but we need to cross over to the other side. We'll head south for a while before turning back west. That way we can make sure we get farther away from them."

She nodded, and he turned back for one last look at the road. After a few seconds he took her hand and led her the remaining five feet to the forest's edge, slowly poking his head through the brush for one final look. In the eastbound direction, the hook-shaped corner that carved through the forest was clear. Westward, the road was also clear.

"As quickly as we can," he said softly, moving through the brush and then parting the branches for her. Casey stepped through with a bit more speed, though she was moving cautiously. They wasted no time crossing the overgrown road. Both sides were lined with the same thick, red brush, and he immediately went to work parting the branches so she could move into the shelter of the towering trees.

With one hand on her belly and the other held out for balance, Casey worked her way quickly through the brush as Bryar watched, prepared to catch his daughter if she stumbled. After a few seconds she was safely in, and he turned to follow.

That was when he caught a flicker of movement out of the corner of his eye.

For a moment Bryar thought about quickly following Casey, but it was already too late. He turned to face Jack as his brother slowed to a jog and then to a walk. As their gazes locked, the two of them separated by a mere forty feet, Jack stopped dead in his tracks. He pushed up the sleeves of his green thermal and panted as he struggled to catch his breath. His face was, for the time being, expressionless.

They stood there, staring at each other until Bryar lost track of time. He struggled against the anxiety that ripped like a spreading fissure through his chest, trying to get some kind of read on his brother, something that might clue him in to what was going to happen next.

It quickly became clear that Jack was just as shocked.

Jack's gaze briefly shifted over Bryar's shoulders, looking up the grassy road.

He was looking for Wade, Bryar suddenly realized. Their younger brother hadn't wandered off on his own. If Jack was this close, it was likely that they had been sent along together.

Bryar stood still and quiet as a statue as Jack looked him over. The apprehensive look on his face evolved into full-blown fear as his gaze fell on the knife in Bryar's hand.

Jack clutched at his gut and he hunched forward as if in pain.

"How far behind you is she?" Bryar asked, taking a few steps forward. He resisted the urge to look back at Casey, hoping she'd have the sense to stay put.

Jack stepped backward, hands still clinging to his stomach.

Bryar took another step toward his brother. "How far, Jack?"

Jack seemed transfixed by the knife. Bryar would have to use it soon. There was nothing else he could do. If he let Jack go, his brother would run back to Ma' Lee and tell her where they were.

Bryar waited.

At any second Jack would probably turn and try to make a run for it. But he had already been running full tilt for some time by the looks of it. It wouldn't take much for Bryar to close the gap between them.

Bryar felt a sharp stab of guilt and a rush of sorrow. All of his younger siblings had been too little to remember much of how life was before that final Christmas, how Ma' Lee was before the world around her became a place where she could blossom like a prickly cactus into the type of person she was destined to become. Brett had been seven years old; Jack and Wade were six and five. If they had any memories of how things were prior to their current life, those memories had been beaten out of them long ago.

They had been rendered little more than Ma' Lee's hopelessly obedient slaves. Perhaps that was why Ma' Lee only chose to take Bryar to bed with her. Because she saw the trace amounts of free will and individuality in him and that tiny bit of resistance somehow aroused her.

Bryar lifted his chin. She would have him no more.

He broke into a sprint toward his younger brother, catching Jack off guard. Jack stumbled and turned, running like a maniac, his hands flailing, his greasy, brown hair whipping about in clumps.

Closing the gap between them was even easier than Bryar had imagined. Though he stumbled a few times over the uneven ground, within seconds he was at his brother's heels.

"Wa—"

Before Jack could finish the word, Bryar leaped on his brother, carrying him to the ground like a wild predator taking down its prey. He spun Jack face up, straddled him, and pressed the knife to his scrawny throat.

Blood trickled from Jack's left eyebrow down into his eye, causing him to blink a few times to try to clear it before clenching it shut tight. Bryar's hand shook as he tried to keep the blade pressed firmly enough against Jack's flesh for him to feel the sharpness of its edge but not break the skin. Jack looked up at him, his expression again unreadable. He looked exhausted, his one eye staring up with barely a pilot light of energy lit behind it. Trickles of sweat had cut lines through the layer of filth on his face. He looked so pitiful and pathetic. Ma' Lee had been pushing them hard. Bryar wasn't surprised. She would run his brothers straight through Hell before she let him go.

She'd run them to death.

"Where is she, Jack?" Bryar asked again, his voice quivering. He glanced up and down the road to make sure that no one else was approaching, then looked back at the knife that he had pressed beneath his brother's Adams apple. He blinked hard against the burning in his eyes, staring in disbelief as he realized what he was about to do.

"Please, Bryar," Jack pleaded. His voice cracked as he spoke, his tone weak and pathetic, like that of a small child begging to sleep the night in his parents' room after waking from a terrible nightmare.

"I can't go back to her, Jack," Bryar said, speaking more to himself than his brother. Something wet dripped on Jack's face and Bryar realized it was his own tears.

"Please," Jack said again.

For a moment Bryar thought about taking Jack with them, but he knew that if Ma' Lee were ever to get close again, Jack would offer them up in an instant. And there was Casey to think about. Though Wade was the chief culprit when it came to the rapes she'd endured, not one of their brothers was innocent.

In the end, it all came back to Casey. He had to protect her…

… The infant's tiny cries eased Bryar awake. At first his daughter's tiny voice registered as a dream, something distant and almost otherworldly, but he had trained himself to decode such tricks of his mind for what they really were. Over the four months since Casey had come into the world he had learned to sleep lightly in order to move quickly and tend to her needs. It was important that he quiet her before the crying grew loud enough to disturb the other members of the house.

Ma' Lee specifically.

Bryar sat slowly up in bed and felt in the darkness until his hands closed around Casey's tiny body. Lifting her gently to his chest and cradling her in his left arm, he reached his free hand over to the nightstand that had stood beside his bed since he was a small child. It still held a small lamp, the stem of which was made from hollowed out baseballs, even though the house hadn't had electricity in more than half a decade. His hand ran along the edges of the small table, looking for the bottle he placed there every night in anticipation of Casey's midnight feedings. Because to knock it over would create additional noise, he had trained himself to do this very carefully despite the growing urgency of her cries.

The tips of his fingers brushed gently across the plastic bottle, and he took hold of it. Tipping the rubber nipple downward, he ran his pinky along Casey's little cheek to find her lips before delicately rubbing the nipple across them, inspiring her to latch on.

Her cries stopped immediately, replaced by tiny sucking sounds and little grunts. Little fingers moved up to his hand, seeming intent on grasping the bottle for themselves. They curled around and took hold of his thumb and pinky.

Never was his bond with her stronger than at feeding times. He could stay like this forever if the brutal world around him would allow it, but that would never be. *Could* never be. A seventeen-year-old boy and a four-month-old infant wouldn't last a week in the outside world. For starters, there was no way he'd be able to smuggle all of Casey's formula without it eventually being found and repurposed by the militias. More importantly, Ma' Lee would never allow them to leave. At least not together.

Over the months since Casey's birth, Bryar hadn't let his daughter out of his sight for even a second. Ma' Lee had recovered almost completely from the birth after about a month and had resumed bringing him to her bedroom. At first he had thought about locking Casey in his room during such events in order to keep her safely away from his brothers, but even a locked door didn't seem secure enough. Add to this his suspicion that Ma' Lee might have told Brett to dispose of the baby while Bryar was distracted, and his refusal to leave Casey alone solidified.

So he started bringing her into Ma' Lee's chamber with him. The first few times Ma' Lee had a screaming fit. Bryar felt the sting of her fingers across his face and the burn of her nails digging into his flesh, yet he did not back down. Eventually his mother's sick needs carried her past the point of caring, but only after Bryar outright refused to engage in such acts unless he could be certain that his daughter was safe.

There was nothing that pushed Ma' Lee into a blind fury faster than taking away even a small degree of her control. She had beaten Bryar to a bruised and bloodied pulp only to find that he still would not relent. In a fit of anger and lust, she took him like an animal those first few times until having the baby wrapped in Bryar's own comforter and placed at the opposite end of the bedroom became the norm.

Bryar took a deep breath and listened to the stillness of the house as his daughter drank and grunted in his arms. Outside, a gentle wind caught in the leaves of a massive, centuries-old chestnut tree that grew beside their house. Its fingerlike branches scraped eerily against the shingles above, as if some great beast was trying to claw its way in. Trace amounts of moonlight from the quarter moon cast milky light on the trunk through narrow, serrated leaves. The moonlight slipped through a lone window on the far wall, throwing a distorted rectangle on the floor in which shadows from the swaying branches danced.

Aside from the weather outside, the house was silent, and for this Bryar was thankful. On several occasions, Casey's crying had woken up his brothers. Wade in particular had an obsessive interest in the infant. Even at eleven years old, he was starting to show signs of what he was to become. Bryar had detected it almost immediately, studying Wade's face as he watched the baby crying for the first time. He studied her almost hungrily, like a predator sensing weakness in a herd of potential prey. After that he would occasionally show up at Bryar's door on nights when Casey's crying went on too long, whispering to his older brother to let him in.

Fortunately, it had been several weeks since Wade's last midnight visit, and Bryar had kept honing his ability to respond quickly to Casey's cries. Confident as he could be that nobody was up and about, he leaned his head back against his headboard and closed his eyes.

"Where have you been getting the stuff you feed her?" Ma' Lee whispered from the darkness of his open closet. It carried like the voice of a demon, gentle and restrained in appearance but ever ready to bite into him.

Bryar startled so violently he nearly dropped his daughter. He found the presence of mind to keep her cradled in his arms with the rubber nipple still in her mouth, but his head whipped to the right so hard a blast of pain shot down his neck. A bloom of anxiety rippled from his chest through the rest of his body like an electrical current through water.

He didn't respond. He *couldn't* respond.

Slowly, Ma' Lee stepped out of the shadows just enough for a tiny shred of moonlight to cast a streak of light down her face. It ran over her left eye and down across her nose at an angle. Her mouth could not be seen.

"The formula," she hissed, "where is it? I know you haven't been milking me—" she paused for a moment, and Bryar knew she was playing out the fantasy in her head. After a few seconds she continued. "Where is it?"

The whiskey on her breath was like a gas that pervaded the room. He hadn't detected it at first, but as she talked the stench flowed from her like a smokestack. Something was off. Ma' Lee, though recklessly impulsive and prone to certain addictive habits, very rarely drank to the point where she was drunk. Her whiskey was something she savored.

Suddenly Bryar began to wonder just how much danger he and his daughter were really in. Ma' Lee was unpredictable enough without a handle of whiskey to dull her limited inhibitions. What, exactly, was she planning to do?

"Ma'," Bryar started, his voice crackly and sleepy, "I don't know—"

"*Don't you lie to me!*" she cried, her voice loud enough to wake the entire house.

He needed to defuse her before she woke his brothers, assuming she hadn't already. Taking a quick look down at the bundle in his arms, he turned back to Ma' Lee and whispered, "Why don't we move into your room and see if your Anthony has any surprises for you tonight?"

No response came from her. It was obvious that she was thinking it over.

"I've got a better idea," she said at last, her voice once again a whisper. She took a few steps out of the closet and the moonlight slipped from her face, leaving her shrouded in blackness. "How about you give me that little wretch and I spill her guts all over your room?"

Bryar's anxiety quickly escalated to fear as the metallic edge of a knife suddenly caught the moonlight. His arms tightened protectively around Casey.

The knife disappeared back into the blackness, and all was silent except for the floorboards creaking as Ma' Lee approached. Closer and closer she came, prompting him to tighten his hold on the baby a little more with each creak.

"Ma', please—"

"You've had your little pet long enough. Now it's time to put her down," Ma' Lee said, her voice coming from just beside him. The floorboards creaked one last time, and then all went quiet.

"Ma', you can't do this. She's just a baby."

Her hands came gently down, her left hand on his shoulder and the right hand, the one with the knife, on his belly. She tapped the blade against the fabric of his t-shirt.

"That *thing*," she hissed, her lips less than an inch from his ear, "is not a baby. It is an animal, a *mongrel*. Just another mouth to feed and a reason for you to hide good food from those who truly need it. Now you give it here, or I'll stick it as you hold it."

Casey kept drinking and grunting, undisturbed. Bryar kept his attention on her as his eyes burned with unshed tears. The knife—one of the longer, eight-inch kitchen knives from downstairs—continued to tap against his gut. In his ear, the moisture from Ma' Lee's hot breath dampened his skin, and the stink of her whiskey breath surrounded him like a thick cloud.

Ma' Lee slowly ran the blade up his chest, the edge scraping against his shirt. Not once did Bryar look away from his daughter's tiny face, what little of it he could see in the moonlit darkness.

A tear slipped down his cheek as he shifted the bottle into his left hand. Casey's little fingers clung to his thumb and pinky. He blinked as his jaw began to quiver and a low moan escaped his throat.

"That's right," Ma' Lee growled. "Stop fighting and give in to your mother."

Her voice registered on some level, but in a way Bryar was deaf and blind to the world. All he could sense was Casey's little hands wrapped around his fingers. His breathing intensified, and he felt the knife move farther and farther up his body. Clenching his eyes tightly shut, focusing on the grip of his daughter's fingers, he took hold of Ma' Lee's knife-wielding hand.

She stopped, then started to push back against him. Despite his best efforts she wriggled out of his grip and lifted the knife into the air. He reached for it, determined to keep the blade from Casey's flesh.

"No!" Bryar said, his voice cracking. He didn't need the moonlight to know that his mother's face was twisted into a furious scowl. She jerked her arm and he missed, desperately raising his hand once more in an attempt to grab the knife.

He winced as the knife sliced into his hand.

"No?" Ma' Lee asked, her voice soft and distant. "No?"

Bryar clutched his hand to his stomach, feeling the warm blood soak through his t-shirt. He clung to the pain, using it to keep a tight hold on his will and determination. "No, Mother, I won't let you kill her."

"What did you just call me?" she asked, her voice tight with rage.

"I called you *Mother*, and you aren't going to hurt her."

"My name is Ma' Lee, and that is the only name you are to call me by!" she yelled, bending down so that her mouth was right next to his ear. "You give her here right *now*, Bryar!"

The baby coughed as the bottle fell from her lips. She immediately began to cry.

"No, I will not!" he screamed right back. The threat that would keep Casey alive into adulthood flashed into his mind.

"If you kill her, I swear you'll find me *dead* by morning. No more pleasure, no more sex, no more *Anthony*, you fucking *bitch*!"

He cringed in disbelief at what he had just said as Casey's cries escalated. It was as if they were standing together in defiant solidarity. Clenching his eyes tightly shut once again, Bryar prepared for another blow or perhaps a series of stabbings that would end his life, but instead he heard the knife clank against the hardwood floor. He opened his eyes, and saw Ma' Lee standing over him, still as a statue. The hands he'd expected to viciously rain blows down on him remained at her side.

"Ma'!" Brett called through the door. "Ma', you okay?" The door rattled and Bryar could hear his brothers arguing in the hallway. The baby's cries had reached their zenith in both urgency and intensity.

Bryar kept his eyes on Ma' Lee, who continued to stare down at him before whipping around without a word. She walked through the distorted rectangle of moonlight and yanked open the door, her fist colliding with the first of his brothers to come rushing in. Based on the sound of the voice and the pitch of the yelp, it was Wade.

She slammed the door behind her and went to work, taking her fury out on her other children. Pleas for her to stop were met with harder hits and the loud thudding of one of them falling down the stairs—Brett by the sound of it.

Then all went silent.

Bryar sprang to his feet, the baby still cradled in his arm, and locked the door. He returned to his bed and finished feeding Casey, laying her down on the bed just long enough for him to remove a sock from his dresser beside the closet and tie it around his hand. With the sock in place to stop the bleeding, he turned back to Casey.

Laying a towel over his shoulder—being vomited upon dozens of times had taught him this particular lesson—he moved back to the bed and went to work burping Casey. As he sat there gently patting her back and waiting for the gas to be expelled, he couldn't help wondering if he'd staved Ma' Lee off for good. Only time would tell, but of one thing he was certain: he had discovered a bit of nerve in himself, and with it the knowledge that he would do anything and everything in his power to keep Casey alive . . .

. . . "Please," Jack repeated. His jaw quivered and tears pooled in his good eye.

Bryar slowly reduced the amount of pressure on the knife, lifting it just enough for Jack to swallow. "I . . . *we* . . . can't go back to her, Jack. I'm sorry."

He turned the knife in his hand so the tip of the blade pointed down.

"I don't want to die, Bryar," Jack said. "Just let me go. I'll tell her we couldn't find you. I swear it." His lips curled downward in a frown of despair that Bryar had seen on numerous occasions, though it was never caused by his hand, and it was never this intense. That's when he realized that Jack was studying him, trying to figure out just what Bryar was going to do.

Bryar gazed at the scar on his right palm. He studied the decades-old wound, looking upon it like the old friend and reminder that it was; something that had been with him nearly as long as Casey. The scar represented a promise to himself and to his daughter.

He would never allow Ma' Lee to hurt them again.

Bryar's fingers tightened upon the knife handle once more, and he looked down at Jack. His little brother's body began to tremble as he struggled.

"Please, Bryar!" Jack pleaded, his voice louder than before.

"I'm sorry, Jack," Bryar whispered, plunging the blade into his brother's throat just above his collar bone.

Jack's eyes grew wide in horror, and a gargling sound escaped his throat, followed by a spray of blood as he coughed. Bryar turned away and closed his eyes as hot blood coated his hand. He heard someone crying, then realized the sound was coming from him. Working quickly, his mind struggling to place itself elsewhere, Bryar calmed himself as best he could.

His brother's body jerked weakly. His hands pawed at Bryar's arms and chest, urgently at first, then quickly diminishing to a light, rhythmic patter. Bryar stifled a wail, his gaze drawn back down as Jack's mouth fell slack and a syrupy trail of saliva joined the blood spilling down his jaw. This was it, Bryar suddenly realized. This was the price they would have to pay for their freedom.

After a few minutes Jack was completely still.

Bryar pulled the blade free. He couldn't look away from his brother, little Jack, with his face all busted up and his good eye staring absently at nothing. For a moment the world spun and vomit burned in his throat, but somehow he was able to keep it down.

He staggered drunkenly to his feet and struggled to stay upright as he stared at the bloody knife in his hand. He dropped the knife and stumbled backward, making it a few steps before tripping and falling to his hands and knees.

Bryar blinked, trying to bring the spinning world back into focus as a figure blocked the sunlight.

"Wade," Bryar mumbled, looking around for his knife.

"Shhhhh, it's okay, Dad," came Casey's soft voice. Bryar relaxed, the sound of his daughter's voice reminding him *why* he had killed Jack.

Bryar looked back, scanning the road for signs of Ma'Lee or Wade.

Casey came up and rested her hands on his shoulders as he took another long, careful look in each direction, trying to keep his attention from settling upon Jack. With a deep breath, he got carefully to his feet. They were not out of danger, not yet. Jack's death would be meaningless if they were caught now. He could deal with the emotional fallout of what he had done at a later time, a time when they were safe from Ma' Lee.

He turned to Casey. "We have to get him off the road and get out of here."

LOST AND
FOUND

TWENTY-ONE

BY LATE AFTERNOON Dad and Carl had piled close to two dozen medium-sized pine logs at the edge of the pond—logs that would eventually be used to build their cabin on the peninsula. Shirtless and sweaty, they dropped the last log onto the pile and set to work building a proper lean-to out of smaller sticks and branches at the edge of the forest. There was no sign of rain, but they weren't about to let Mother Nature catch them off guard.

As usual, Dad's instincts and reasoning were right on the money. The decision to build the lean-to just inside the tree line, but facing the pond, was his. The location would take advantage of the thick forest canopy, which would help to keep them dry. The structure was little more than an open shelter with a slanted roof that would be thatched with as many pine boughs as they could pile on top of it. After pounding two large branches into the ground, each forked at the top, they were able to run supporting branches both horizontally across and down at an angle to the ground, using twine to further secure each point where branches came together. After tying a number of smaller sticks to the angled branches, they started thatching.

A permanent fire pit was built close to the lean-to so that the thatched roof could reflect the heat. Carl had come up with the idea to build a large stack of rocks along the back of the pit to also reflect the warmth from the flames into the lean-to. For this he received praise from both Mom and Dad, though Zoey wasn't as enthusiastic. In fact, she had nothing at all to say on the matter.

After they finished with the shelter, the sun already starting to set over the western mountains, painting the sky in striking shades of orange and violet, Carl followed his father back into the forest to check the snares they had set earlier that morning. Even if the snares turned out to be as empty as his stomach felt, it had been a very productive day. Carl grinned down at Tripp trotting contentedly beside him.

They rounded the end of the pond and reached the small stream that they had followed in, making sure to avoid the bog. Carl shuddered as the memory of being trapped hovered over him like a black cloud on a sunny day. He focused on his father's back as they made their way upstream until they came across the first snare. Dad had attached a length of twine to a low-hanging branch and made a slip-knotted loop that hung just above the forest floor. Supporting the loop were two fork-shaped twigs driven into the ground. They'd set the snare in what Dad called a "rabbit run," a path heavily used by rabbits. The snare was supposed to snag a rabbit as it went about its daily routine.

The snare was empty.

Dad led the way towards the next snare without saying a word. The heavy scents of decaying leaves and evergreen needles surrounded them and Carl began to feel the cold. The drop in temperate wasn't dramatic, though weather in Maine had a way of surprising you. He knew it wouldn't be long before the soft soil hardened as winter came on. He was thankful that he had thought to wear his flannel shirt. Dad seemed perfectly comfortable in his thermal.

Tripp trotted ahead of them, busily sniffing both dirt and underbrush, as they continued along to the next two snares. Both snares were also empty. Each snare was left in place, something Carl found confusing until Dad explained that one day was not enough time to determine if the trap was truly a failure. His initial excitement and optimism dwindling, Carl followed his father to the final two snares as Tripp inspected the greenery and laid claim to his new territory.

At the second-to-last of their traps they found success. A black-and-brown rabbit struggled to free itself, the twine loop tightening more and more with each frantic leap. At the sight of the two men the rabbit staggered back as far as it could into the underbrush, eyes seeming to bulge in its sockets as the twine went taut. Watching the rabbit draw in breath after panicked breath made Carl wonder if it might just die of shock right there and then. Thinking back to the rabbits they had raised at the Rangeley House, he couldn't recall ever seeing them so terrified, though he was quick to remind himself that those had been domesticated animals.

"Looks like dinner to me," Dad said. He pulled his knife, bent down beside the frightened animal, and deftly cut its throat.

Carl expected his father to flip the rabbit onto its back and gut it. Instead, Dad stood up, removed the snare from the animal's neck, and reset the trap. Then he wiped his knife on the rabbit hide and slipped the knife back into its sheath.

"Aren't you going to gut it?" Carl asked.

Dad shook his head. "Not until we get back. We might be able to use the organs as bait."

Coyote bait? Dog meat wasn't particularly appetizing to Carl, but the idea of killing them for food wasn't likely the reason his father wanted to hunt the animals. The coyotes had shown very little fear until they'd heard the rifle. Looked like Dad wasn't going to count on that to deter the coyotes forever.

He followed Dad to the next snare where they found another rabbit. The only difference here was that the rabbit had already strangled itself in its efforts to break free.

Dad bent down and removed the rabbit from the snare. Tripp trotted over and sniffed at the carcass. Dad nudged him away with an elbow, and the dog wandered off. After resetting the snare, Dad handed Carl both rabbits. "Looks like we'll be eatin' good tonight, son."

Carl tried not to stagger as Dad clapped him hard on the shoulder before turning and heading back toward Ben Gile Pond.

When they arrived back at the lean-to, they found that Mom and Zoey had been busy as well. Both sides of the lean-to—which had been open when they left—were now filled with pine boughs. They were just finishing the north side when Carl and Dad walked up.

"Haha, now *that's* why I married you!" Dad said as he reached Mom. He pulled her into his arms and planted a gentle kiss on her lips.

Mom shook her head. "It wasn't my idea, it was Zoey's." She smiled at the rabbits in Carl's hands. "I see we're eating tonight."

"Yes, we are," Dad said with a wide grin. He let go of Mom and turned toward Zoey.

"Great idea, Zo!" Carl said. He walked over and wrapped his arm around her in a quick hug before walking over to the lean-to. The thick smell of pine from the recently chopped trees and branches was almost overpowering. He turned back just in time to catch Zoey rolling her eyes as she turned back to her father, her face lit up in an eager smile.

"Very good, Zo," Dad said, wrapping his arms around her and pulling her close. As he planted a gentle kiss on her head, Zoey's smile widened.

Daylight was quickly fading as Carl helped move their packs into the lean-to and Dad got a fire going in the new fire pit. Soon, Carl, Mom, and Zoey were sitting inside their new shelter, bathed in the warmth of a roaring fire as Dad tended to the rabbits a good hundred feet or so away from the camp, toward the access trail. For the first time since their last night in the Rangeley House, Carl was perfectly comfortable, but as his gaze settled upon his father, still not finished with the day's work, he decided to offer his services. A good part of this decision was also inspired by curiosity. Why was Dad butchering the rabbits so far from the camp?

Carl rose slowly to his feet and walked over to his father. He eyed the hole Dad was digging beside the carcasses. "Anything I can do to help?" he asked, a part of him hoping that Dad would give him a pass. His body was already starting to ache from all the hard work he'd done chopping and dragging logs.

"See if you can find a good-sized rock," Dad said. He held up his gloved hands, indicating the size of rock he was looking for.

With a nod, Carl walked back toward the southern edge of the pond where the stream flowed out, the one place he could remember seeing rocks the size his father indicated. All he could think about was getting back to the fire and giving his tired muscles a break. For a moment he cursed himself for getting up at all. Still, he wasn't about to complain.

He reached the edge of the pond and gazed across the still water at the jutting peninsula and the vacant western shore. He forgot all about how tired he was as he lost himself in the beauty of the place that would be their new home. The majesty of the surrounding mountains, the warm colors of the darkening sky mirrored in the water, the occasional jump of a fish. He smiled and drew in a deep, satisfying breath before turning toward the stream and searching the shallows for a rock large enough to meet his father's needs. It didn't take long for him to find one just at the edge of the water. Squatting down, he reached into the cool water, pursing his lips as the muscles in his arms and shoulders screamed in protest. He gritted his teeth against the pain and stood, rock dripping in his hands. The pain diminished a bit as he allowed the rock to hang in his hands.

Carl waddled back to his father and held the rock out. The rabbits had been gutted and decapitated and their innards and heads placed in the hole Dad had dug. Dad shoved dirt back into the hole, then reached up for the rock.

"Good pick," Dad said with a wink before pounding the rock down over the freshly covered hole and standing back up, headless carcasses in hand. "Nothing's going to keep animals from catching the scent, but at least this will keep the coyotes from easily getting at the guts until we're ready to use them."

They headed back to the fire where Carl watched his father skin both rabbits. When Dad was done he stood and headed into the woods, returning after a few minutes with a semi-straight branch and two sturdy, fork-shaped sticks to support it above the fire. Dad drove the forked branches into the ground on either side of the fire with the butt of the axe, leaving the forked ends up, then went to work stripping bark from the branch to be used as a spit.

Dad smiled at Carl as he whittled the edges of the stick to sharp points. Turning back to the rabbits, he used his knife to puncture a couple of tiny holes in their flesh before pushing them snuggly together on the stick like Gram threading a needle. Then he set the stick into position over the fire, nestling the ends in the forked sticks at either side of the fire, and walked down to the pond to wash his hands.

Mom took over, watching the meat carefully as it cooked and rotating the spit as needed. As the scent of roasting rabbit quickly began to fill the lean-to, Carl's stomach began to feel as though it would collapse upon itself in hunger. It was all he could do to keep from getting up and removing himself from such torture. Somehow he was able to soldier through.

By the time the stars were beginning to speckle the purple sky and the moon began to rise over the mountains, they were pulling the meat off the spit and filling their stomachs. Not once was the word *ration* mentioned, nor did Mom or Dad caution them about eating too much. They had an abundance of food and fresh water and as long as they managed the resources carefully, the area could sustain them for the rest of their lives. But that night wasn't about management, it was about celebration, and as the Richmond family laughed and dined and drank the sweetest-tasting water ever, Carl offered a quiet thanks, happy to think they were finally home.

~

MA' LEE AND BRETT had been backtracking west on the old logging road for close to three hours without a single sign of Wade or Jack. Going east was a bust. They had barely traveled five or six miles after leaving the others before coming to the end of the gravel road at a wall of encroaching maple, pine, and cedar. On the other side they discovered the crumbling remains of the mountain highway they had originally been following north. Brett had immediately braced against a storm of fists.

But Ma' Lee barely paused before spinning on her heel and pushing back through the trees, retracing their steps. Her pace escalated.

Not a single word passed between them as they moved quickly along. Ma' Lee was dead-focused on getting her hands on Bryar and Casey, while Brett's major concern was keeping himself from saying anything that might result in her fingers digging into his flesh.

As the sun went down and the light in the sky quickly began to surrender to the darkness, Brett realized that his mother had no intention of stopping. Already exhausted, his stomach sank as desolation washed over him. They probably wouldn't be stopping for quite some time—if at all. He wouldn't put it past his mother to keep marching without rest until the missing family members were back in her razor-sharp clutches. His legs burned as he forced himself after her, moving into an agonizing jog when the gap between them grew too large.

It was in these intense moments, his body pushed to the limit, that his anger with Bryar and Casey swelled and throbbed like an infected sore. He snorted like a bull, breathing deeply of the hay-like smells of grass crushed beneath his mother's boots as he allowed himself to slow behind her and catch his breath.

The majority of the time Brett found himself in an almost constant state of fear of his mother, but at times like these he found himself regarding her in awe. Over the years, he had managed to keep himself well enough fed. He was large and bulky and in pretty decent running shape, but he was *nothing* compared to Ma' Lee. She moved like a wild boar on the charge, tenacious and aggressive, without a single break or dip in her pace. While he panted and struggled to keep up, she plowed along, leaving him half-expecting to see steam billowing from her nose.

He wanted to stop. He *needed* to stop, but there was no force on Planet Earth capable of bringing him to ask for a breather. No matter how tired she was, she always seemed to have enough energy to beat the living daylights out of him.

He pushed himself along behind her even though his legs screamed and every footfall sent a bolt of pain up his injured left arm. He considered shedding the backpack jostling around on his shoulders, but logic always managed to remind him that there were several items in that pack he just couldn't live without.

As the moon rose, casting shadows in its dull light, they pushed around a hook-shaped corner and up a slight incline. The road appeared to stretch pretty much straight through the wilderness, rising up and going down over various hills along the way, much as it had been. Brett figured they could see close to a hundred feet thanks to the mostly full moon above, but it was hard to tell. In any event, there were no signs of movement.

"Faster!" Ma' Lee commanded, startling Brett as she moved into a jog. He fought back the frustration as he struggled to keep pace.

For a moment Brett wondered if she would still beat him if he passed out from exhaustion. It didn't take long for his logical side to reassure him that there wasn't a single scenario that would spare him her hand if she were angry enough. Given how focused and intent she was on reuniting with the others, any kind of delay, regardless of the reason, would almost certainly push her over the top.

There was nothing he could do.

After ten minutes of jogging, the burning in his legs turned to fire. After twenty minutes, he started to feel nothing at all, as if his legs had turned to rubber. He was barely aware of what his legs were doing and where his feet were landing. The only thing that he could feel was the pain in his arm.

Brett panted along behind his mother, putting one foot automatically in front of the other as they crested another hill. The world around him seemed hazy, almost as if he was dreaming—

"*Stop, you stupid fuck!*" Ma' Lee cried out.

Brett opened his eyes just before running into Wade.

Wade crumbled, forcing Brett head-first toward the ground as he tumbled over his brother. He thrust out both arms, trying to break his fall. His left hand hit the hard earth between the gravel ruts and a sickening *snap* echoed in his ears as pain stabbed through his left forearm. He rolled over onto his right side as far as his backpack would allow and cried out in horror, realizing that he no longer had any control over his left arm below his elbow.

"What the fuck is *wrong* with you?" Ma' Lee screamed. She stepped over to Brett and delivered a powerful kick to his gut. Then she turned to Wade. He was sitting in the gravel rut, legs bent and pulled to his chest.

"Where's Jack?" Ma' Lee asked, helping Wade back up and rolling her eyes as he began to cry. For all she knew he had already been an emotional wreck, considering his intense fear of the dark. Without anyone around to help him feel "protected" he was probably hysterical.

Not that she cared.

She had ways of dealing with hysteria. She reached out and gave Wade's right cheek a hard slap. "Where's your brother, you retard?"

Wade cried out, bringing his arms up to shield himself. She shoved his hands aside and slapped him again.

"Talk!" Ma' Lee commanded, her angry voice echoing off the surrounding mountains.

His lips trembled and he looked like he was trying to form words. She gave him a few more slaps, trying to jumpstart the wheels and gears spinning slowly in his head.

He uttered one word, whimpering like a small child. "Lost."

"What do you mean *lost*?" she growled, the volume of her voice coming down a bit. "He was supposed to look after you. How did you lose him?"

"He h—had t—t—t—to *poop*," Wade responded with an idiotic smile. Somehow he managed to bring himself back together, his lips moving as if he was going to say more, but nothing came. Instead, he took a deep breath and frowned pitifully.

Though it was a source of almost constant ire and frustration, Ma' Lee knew her youngest son lacked the mental faculties of her other children. There wasn't likely to be anything she could do to siphon more details out of him. On a certain level she appreciated this, but that didn't stop her from giving Wade an additional thrashing.

His screams rose into the air and carried across the landscape as her fists and nails worked him over.

Frustration temporarily vented, Ma' Lee gazed back in the direction she and Brett had come. She squinted, trying to see better in the cold moonlight, but it didn't work. She bit down hard on her lower lip and tasted blood as she ran over a number of scenarios in her mind. The most logical conclusion was that Jack was truly lost. Maybe he'd wandered too far into the woods and couldn't find his way back to the road. It was far-fetched, but a lot more believable than the alternative she kept coming back to.

Jack couldn't be dead. Bryar didn't have that kind of balls.

Yeah, he had pressed himself between her and Casey on a number of occasions, even to the point where Ma' Lee found herself experiencing odd moments of admiration, but he had never gotten physical, never threatened to take another life. No, Bryar was more the type who would use his wits—what little he had—to get what he wanted.

"Jack's lost somewhere in the woods," Ma' Lee grumbled. She walked over to Brett and looked down at him like a hawk ruminating over a potential meal. She took hold of his left arm by the wrist and jiggled it a bit. Brett cried out, his face twisted in agony.

Ma' Lee shook her head in disgust and took a deep breath before releasing the arm. Brett cried out as his arm flopped to the ground.

Lifting her head, Ma' Lee screamed in frustration. Wade covered both ears with his hands and Brett clenched his eyes tightly shut.

Ma' Lee reveled in their fear, knowing her sons had no real understanding what she was capable of. She towered over them, her arms outstretched and her fingers splayed like ten individual shivs, absolutely livid and absolutely insane. Someone was going to pay for her frustration and she knew exactly who that someone was.

~

THE SCREAMS WERE so faint that he nearly dismissed them as tricks played by the wind, but the very last shriek that shattered the stillness of the night was unmistakable.

"Ma' Lee," Bryar whispered, feeling Casey shiver beside him. She was already pressed tight against his body, his arm slung around her shoulder in an effort to keep the both of them warm as they sat concealed in the middle of a thick cropping of brush beneath a large maple, the earthy smells of dry leaves and bark hanging in the air around them. She pressed closer even though there wasn't a single inch separating them.

"Shhhhhh," Bryar whispered, as she rubbed her head on his shoulder, "they're still a good ways away."

Judging by the relative hollowness of the scream they were miles away. A part of him argued that was just wishful thinking, but for once the logical side of his mind prevailed, assuring him that they had easily trekked at least two miles south into the forest and away from the road.

"Do you think they found Jack?" Casey asked, her voice muffled as she spoke into his sweatshirt.

"It's dark," Bryar said. "I doubt it. I'm thinking she caught up with Wade."

He took a deep breath, feeling Casey move with his chest. Though he was doing all he could to keep her comforted, he himself was a bit unsettled by the distant sound of their mother's voice. The thought that they were within earshot almost seemed to place Ma' Lee right beside them in his mind. After decades under her iron fist, learning to adapt and predict her behavior, the idea of coming back into her fold at this point . . . he would rather die.

"We have to go. We have to get away," Casey said in a voice that told him how close she was to crying. Her emotions were quickly escalating, leaving Bryar wondering if she'd felt some of his own fear.

"It's okay," he assured her, attempting to calm himself as well. He rubbed his right hand over her arm. "They're nowhere near us, and they aren't going to find us in the dark like this. If we don't rest, we won't make it very far tomorrow." He expected her to continue protesting, but was pleasantly surprised when her breathing slowed.

"Are you sure?" she asked, wrapping her arms around his belly.

Bryar wrapped his other arm around her. "Yes. They won't be going too much farther tonight, and if they do, they'll keep to the road."

Casey sniffed again and then went silent. Though he expected her to be up all night worrying, he was surprised to feel her body slowly relax. He smiled and leaned down, planting a kiss on her head. It was nice to feel loved and needed, but it was another thing entirely to know that he was capable of making his daughter feel secure. He absently traced the scar running across his right palm with the fingers on that same hand.

As his daughter slumbered, Bryar rested his head on hers and closed his eyes . . . only to find the face of Jack Perkins staring up at him. Not the reserved and often neutral *living* face of his younger brother, but the cold, lifeless face that he'd seen immediately after pulling the knife from Jack's throat. That lone eye, staring off into the forest as if he wished for his last vision in life to be anything other than his older brother murdering him.

Please, Bryar, Jack's voice echoed in his mind. *Just let me go. I'll tell her we couldn't find you. I swear it.*

Would Jack have told Ma' Lee if they had permitted him to escape? There was no way to know for certain, but Bryar's instincts told him that Ma' Lee would have beaten the truth out of Jack.

Killing Jack was the only option, and Bryar knew that he had acted appropriately. So why couldn't he shake the guilt? Would the ghost of his brother stay with him for the rest of his life?

I don't want to die, Bryar.

"I'm sorry, Jack," he whispered, keeping his voice soft so he wouldn't wake Casey. "I'm so sorry."

He blinked and a hot tear spilled down his cheek. Given his state of dehydration, he wondered how it was possible that he even had tears to shed. He thought about the bean can in his backpack. He would have to build a fire and boil some water tomorrow. He couldn't put it off any longer. They both needed to drink.

Exhausted from the physical demand placed upon his body that day, and overwhelmed by the emotional impact of everything he had done to keep himself and his daughter alive, Bryar finally succumbed to sleep. His rest was plagued by nightmares during which he drove the knife into Jack's throat over and over again as Jack continued to plead for his life . . .

I don't want to die, Bryar.

I don't want to die, Bryar.

I don't want to die, Bryar.

Twenty-Two

J AMES SAT BY the fire, watching the other side of the pond as the coyotes' eyes reflected the firelight. The animals had emerged shortly after his wife and children had fallen asleep beside him in the lean-to with Tripp snuggled between them.

He peered through the darkness in the direction of the rock under which the innards of the rabbits were buried.

Tomorrow, he thought. *We'll set out with the bait at first light, try to find their den, and see if we can't pick off a few members of the pack.* They could erect some kind of smoking rack and preserve the meat. While he wasn't all that thrilled about eating coyote meat, there was no way he was going to waste a kill.

It was a good plan. No harm in making sure that their base needs were met before moving on to bigger things.

"No harm at all," he whispered to himself with a smile. Just as he finished speaking, a faint noise carried over the mountains behind their shelter. It sounded like the screech of some kind of wildcat. Beside him, Tripp snapped awake. His head lifted and he stared at the back of the lean-to as if he could somehow see through it. His nose shifted subtly and the hairs on his shoulders and rump stood up.

Across the pond, the coyotes' eyes disappeared. Probably trying to sniff out the source of the noise just like Tripp. James half-expected to hear them yapping, but the coyotes remained silent.

Fisher cats, he thought. Add that to the list of predators.

He kept his attention on the opposite side of the pond and eventually the coyotes' eyes returned. "We'll see if we can't arrange a much more personal meeting tomorrow," he whispered to the pack.

MUCH TO HIS own surprise, Carl was up and moving before everyone else the next morning. He stepped out of the lean-to just as the first light of day cast a tinge of auburn over the bosom of the surrounding mountains. His father had fallen asleep in an upright position, hunched forward at the edge of the fire with his rifle laid across his legs. Carl stood next to the smoldering coals for a moment before adding a couple of logs and walking around to the pot of water that had been sitting next to the fire all night. Crouching down, he lowered his hands into the still-warm water and cupped them together. With a smile he brought his hands up to his face and sucked the sweet liquid greedily into his mouth before reaching back down for more.

Carl stood and watched transfixed as tiny ripples from jumping fish spread across the still surface of the pond. The ripples caught the odd shadows of the early morning light, rendering them into black circles that expanded slowly across the water. There were no other signs of wildlife just yet, but he was certain the deer and moose would be by for a morning drink fairly soon.

The air around him was still and humid. So much so that he swore he could smell the water in the air. Not even a light breeze moved over the mountains and through the trees. The eerie silence would have felt ominous and foreboding had Carl been anywhere else. After nearly two days at Ben Gile Pond, he was so much in awe of the place that he refused to harbor any negative thoughts.

With a deep breath followed by a long yawn, Carl stretched both of his arms over his head and turned back to the lean-to where everyone continued to sleep. He hunched beneath the covering of pine boughs and carefully stepped around his mother and sister to where his backpack lay. With his free left hand, he felt beneath the top flap of the rucksack until he found his gloves. Then he inched his way clear of the shelter and walked over to the right side and took hold of the axe. Laying it over his shoulder, he straightened, studying the game trail that ran beside the pond.

How about an early start to the day's work? Carl grinned, proud of his newfound ambition. He repressed the urge to whistle as he made his way up the trail into the woods. He'd fell and crop at least two pines to add to the collection for their new cabin, hopefully all before his father woke for the day.

He walked through the forest, following the trail gouged into the earth by thousands of hooves and paws before him. He shoved branches and limbs out of his way, thinking about the logs he and Dad had hauled down the path the previous day.

How long had his father stayed up last night? He must have been more exhausted than Carl after all that work. They'd been at the pond for two nights now and, as far as Carl knew, Dad had spent both nights on guard, watching out for marauding predators. If he had to guess, Dad had probably stayed awake until just before the sun started to rise before allowing his fatigue to overcome him. Come to think of it, his father probably hadn't had all that much sleep since they left the Rangeley House.

Tonight I'm going to stay up so he can sleep, Carl thought, nodding to himself. He pictured himself sitting beside the fire in the darkness with the rifle laid across his lap while the rest of the family slept peacefully behind him. He smiled. He'd never really been called upon to protect the family. It made him feel more like a man than he ever had before.

He reached the small clearing he and Dad had made the previous day. The once thick group of pine trees was now a number of splintery stumps. At the far edge of the clearing, just across from the area where he'd entered, was a tree they had started cutting, but had abandoned because Dad wanted to get back to the camp and erect their shelter before evening fell. The tree was tall and lean, the trunk devoid of lower branches. Carl approached the tree, his axe at the ready.

The smell of fresh-cut pine still hung strongly in the air, mixed with the deep scents of soil and sap. Carl drew it all in as deeply as he could before letting out a long, satisfied exhale. Though a part of him longed for another unseasonably warm day like the one they had experienced during the trek into the woods, the crisp mountain air didn't bother him that much.

Carl spread his legs and positioned himself at axe-length from the tree before raising the axe head over his right shoulder and swinging it forcefully. Woodchips flew from the gaping wound in the tree's long, slender body, and the sound of the axe cracking against the wood rang through the forest. With renewed energy and fervor, he chopped at the tree again and again until the gash in the trunk was so deep that it could no longer support its own weight. The tree cracked and groaned as the pine toppled forward into the clearing, prompting Carl to step quickly out of the way. He watched his footing as he moved, making sure that he didn't trip over any of the stumps.

The pine tree crashed to the ground, sending dust and leaves billowing into the air. He quickly moved to the treetop and went to work chopping off the smaller branches. They would be stacked and dried for firewood while the trunk would be added to the logs they had collected the previous day and used to build their permanent shelter.

Carl tried to picture the cabin Dad had described while they'd taken turns hacking away at the trees. It would be built from whole logs, cut at the ends so that they could fit into each other. The cracks between the logs would be filled with mud or clay. The finer points of the image still remained to be fully visualized in his head, but what he could picture of it brought a smile to his face as he finished limbing the tree.

Carl slowly lowered the head of the axe to the ground and let it rest against his leg. He used the sleeve of his black-and-green checkered jacket to wipe the sweat from his brow, then took a deep breath and peeled the jacket off, dropping it on one of the stumps before pushing the sleeves of his red thermal shirt up to his elbows and once again taking hold of the axe.

Leaves rustled and he turned just as Tripp trotted into the clearing.

Tripp looked at him as if somewhat surprised to see Carl there. He sniffed the air, his black-and-white whiskers curling slightly forward as his nose shifted from side to side.

"What is it?" Carl asked. Something had Tripp disturbed, but Carl had no idea what it could be. He scanned the tree line, half expecting Dad or Zoey to emerge.

Suddenly, Tripp's ears folded back, and the fur on his back stood up. The white tip of his tail stuck straight out behind him. Carl felt the hair on the back of his neck rise.

"Tripp," Carl said, his voice growing stern, "you *stay!*"

He lowered the axe to the ground and leaned its wooden handle against the fallen tree. He took a few steps toward the dog, noting the wildness in Tripp's deep, brown eyes.

"You *stay*," he repeated in a soft, commanding voice. Tripp's lips began to curl as he kept his gaze focused unwaveringly on the opposite end of the clearing.

Carl tried to see what Tripp was seeing, squinting his eyes and searching for signs of what had the dog so perturbed, but all he saw were trees and underbrush. He slowly began to inch his way toward Tripp, ready to grab him at the first sign of movement.

A low growl emerged from the dog's throat as his gaze remained locked on the far end of the clearing. Carl inched closer and closer until he was only a few feet from Tripp. He lowered himself into a squatting position and reached for Tripp just as Zoey crashed through the trees.

"No!" Carl cried as the dog bolted across the clearing into the woods.

"Carl?" Zoey growled. "What are you *doing* out here?"

"Tripp!" Carl yelled, scrambling to his feet. He ignored his sister—this wasn't the time to put up with her baseless reprimands—and dashed across the clearing into the forest. There was no sign of Tripp.

He turned back to Zoey. "Something has him freaked out. Any idea what it is?" Carl asked.

Zoey shook her head. "I don't know." She frowned. "He heard something and just took off." She glanced at the tree Carl had just cut, and for a moment he expected her to launch into an attack on him for cutting it down in the first place. Instead, she turned back and shook her head again, offering a shrug of her shoulders for good measure.

Carl glanced back at the forest, searching for signs of movement but finding none. Tripp was gone.

"Are Mom and Dad up?"

Zoey nodded.

"Go back and tell them what's happened. I'll go after him. Hopefully the little jerk isn't on the trail of anything with bigger *teeth* than his." He watched his sister, waiting for her to mount some kind of protest, but her concern for Tripp seemed to supersede her typical lack of respect for her younger brother. She nodded again and jogged back in the direction she had come.

Carl turned back toward the logging road and headed after Tripp.

~

BRYAR AND CASEY reached the top the mountain they had been climbing for an hour now, still pushing west through the forest. The first light of day was slowly brightening the deep violet sky. The trees thinned out a bit as the ground began to level, then quickly turned downward. Dead ahead, they were given a slightly obstructed view of the expansive forest blanketing the side of the mountain. At its base sat what looked like a pond.

At first he didn't recognize the pond for what it was, but as color began to build behind the mountains like a dim blue aura, the light reflected off of the water as if it were a sheet of glass. The pond was square-shaped, nestled at the foot of three pine-covered mountains, including the peak they currently stood on. An endless sea of trees extended for what looked like miles in every direction without a single sign of civilization—at least the kind of civilization they were used to dealing with.

"If that isn't the most beautiful sight I've ever seen," Casey said as she leaned against a tree. She winced and stretched her back. As much as it broke Bryar's heart to keep her marching, she'd be far worse off if they fell into the clutches of their mother and brothers.

"Glad we have that bean can," Bryar said, shoving aside his concern for the time being. They needed a rest, given the hours that they had been hiking through the forest, mostly uphill. They hadn't heard anything more from Ma' Lee and the others before falling asleep the night before. He figured that one of two scenarios had played out, each of which benefitted him and Casey: either Ma' Lee and their brothers had pushed on farther into the woods, putting more distance between them; or they had stayed where they were and spent the night, leaving Casey and Bryar to widen the gap with their own early morning start.

Mentioning the bean can represented a breach in an agreement they had established during their first night on the run. While the food had remained somewhat preserved over the decades it had spent in the logging museum, the beans had inspired some of the worst diarrhea either of them had ever experienced. And that said a lot given the sketchy things they had been forced to eat over the years. The embarrassment that accompanied their extreme distress prompted them to agree never to mention the beans—or the can—again.

Bryar raised his eyebrows in a silent gesture of apology. Casey squinted at him with a look of mock irritation before giving him a grin. "First and only warning."

"How kind of you," he said, his smile widening for a moment before he turned back to the pond. "I say we make our way down and get a fire going before it gets *too* light out. Boil up some water and drink as much as we can before moving on."

It was as good a plan as any. It looked to be no more than 400 feet or so to the bottom. They could cover that ground quickly. They would just have to make sure that when they got to the pond they went to work as fast as possible and kept their fire small.

"Sounds good," Casey said with a nod. She pushed herself away from the tree and started to make her way carefully down the needle-blanketed slope.

"Wait," Bryar said, moving in front of her as she stopped. He took her hand. "Let me go in front in case you trip."

"Pfft," she snorted. "If I trip, something tells me we're *both* going down."

They resumed walking with him in the lead. The trees thickened as they moved along, leaving them with no shortage of objects to hold onto, though the care necessary to maintain their careful descent slowed their progress a bit. Still, they moved along at a steady pace.

Once or twice Bryar thought he smelled smoke, but finally decided he was imagining it. They finally reached level ground and pushed out of the trees, emerging onto the grassy shore of the pond.

Twenty-Three

KELLY SLAPPED HER hands over her mouth to avoid screaming as the two strangers stepped out of the woods. James spun and jogged toward the lean-to. He grabbed the .308 and held it with the stock beneath his armpit and barrel pointed toward the ground.

Was this what Tripp had been upset about? Kelly wondered. The dog had taken off into the woods and Zoey had chased after him.

Where was Zoey, then? And where was Tripp?

Carl had been gone when they'd woken, but James had told her not to worry. The axe was gone, so he was somewhere busy chopping wood—

"How many of you are there?" James asked, interrupting her thoughts. Kelly tried not to hold her breath as he inched his way toward the pair, keeping the rifle lowered.

The strangers glanced over their shoulders at the forest as if they might retreat like frightened animals, but then both seemed to come to a decision almost simultaneously. First the man, then the woman gradually lifted their arms into the air. They looked at each other, then back at James.

Kelly came up behind her husband and studied the pregnant woman's bruised face, then her protruding belly. From the way the woman was carrying, she was due to give birth any day. She looked so emaciated and pitiful that it was a wonder she had carried her baby to term.

"There's just us," the man said as James took a few careful steps toward him. The man's gaze flashed nervously out over the water and along the opposite shore before returning to James. "But there are others after us. Please, mister, we mean you no harm."

I mean you no hahm, William Dewoh's voice echoed in Kelly's mind, sending shivers down her spine.

"We're just trying to get away from some really bad people," the man finished. He remained still with his hands raised and eyes shifting nervously from her to James and back again. "Please," he said once more.

"Where are these others, and how many of them are there?" James asked. He stopped and waited.

The man and woman looked at each other once more. They were either lying or they had no idea where their pursuers were, assuming the pursuers even existed.

"Answer my question," James said, shifting the weight of the rifle into his left hand beneath the barrel. He carefully moved his right hand toward the bolt handle, preparing to chamber a round.

The man and woman watched.

"When we last came across them, they were traveling west down an old road that ran through the woods," the man said, his voice slightly shaky. "There are three of them—our brothers, Brett and Wade, and our mother . . . Ma' Lee."

Kelly watched the man closely. The fearful tone of his voice took on a deeper quality.

"Do they have any guns?" James asked. Then, "Do *you* have any guns?"

The man and woman both shook their heads.

"I have just this knife," the man said, slowly reaching down to a sheath on his belt. With his free hand still raised, he carefully removed the weapon and tossed it a few feet into the grass.

"What about those who're after you?" James asked.

"My mother and brother each have small knives."

The woman stepped slowly forward and spoke as the man gently took hold of her hand and tried to pull her back. It was impossible for Kelly to deny the passionate look of concern in his face. His love and fierce worry were as plain as the daylight now flooding over the mountains.

"Please," she said, her voice low and meek. "You look like good people."

It wasn't made specifically clear if she was pleading for their release or for protection, and Kelly imagined that it might have been a bit of both.

Kelly looked at the woman's belly. The worn pink sweatshirt with the word GUNQUIT across the front didn't quite cover all of her. The woman unconsciously stroked her belly with her left hand while her right remained in the hand of the man Kelly assumed was her husband.

"Did you do that to her?" James asked, nodding at the woman's scarred face.

Kelly waited, trying not to form an opinion of the man just yet.

"No, sir," the man said, seeming to take great offense to the implication. "I would *never*—Ma' Lee was the one."

James nodded. Kelly imagined him to be equally as conflicted as she was with regard to what they should do next. On the one hand, there was Carl and Zoey to think of. On the other . . . Kelly looked the woman over again, analyzing her defeated, demoralized face. Her words . . . her pleading . . . the entire scenario was very familiar to Kelly Richmond.

Too familiar . . .

. . . Kelly huddled on the couch, struggling to make sense of what was happening. She'd been dragged out of bed and told to "get ready." Her father was yelling at her mom, which was normal. But the stack of china plates in her mother's hands wasn't.

"Fuck that shit, Lauren, we gotta get the fuck out of here *now!*" Kelly's father cried, knocking the plates out of her mother's hands. Her mom cringed away, raising her hands to protect her face. Fortunately for Mom, he was too busy rounding up the weed, coke, and prescription painkillers to smack her around like he usually would.

He edged his way past her mother without knocking her to the floor, and moved through the open living room into the kitchen as the building shook and bright orange light flared outside. Kelly watched as he swiped knick-knacks off the top of the fridge, sending them crashing to the floor. He ran a hand over his bald head before reaching into the cupboard and pulling out an old cookie jar shaped like a white dog. He fumbled the jar, dropping it on the floor. The jar shattered, but her father didn't seem to care. He reached down and pulled a wrinkled paper bag free of the pieces.

Kelly rubbed the sleep from her eyes. She was old enough to understand that what her father kept in the bag was bad. Drug programs at school had taught her to be on the lookout for such things and to stay away if she could, even though some kids in her class already claimed to have smoked pot and said it was no big deal.

Her mother sobbed, trying to pick up the shattered china plates. These were plates Kelly had been instructed to keep away from, as if to touch them would somehow cause her hand to melt right off. It was a curious sight to see them now in pieces just like the old cookie jar in the kitchen.

A small plastic Christmas tree stood on a table at the edge of the couch she sat upon. Beneath it were the few presents her parents could afford, of which she knew five were for her. She had looked them over several times already.

An explosion shook the ten-story apartment building, and suddenly she realized why her father was so frantic. The building swayed and she cried out, jumping to her feet. She could hear others in the hallway outside their apartment door.

She wrapped her arms around her waist wondering what they were going to do. Her father went about the apartment, opening containers and sifting through drawers until the remainder of his stash was added to whatever else was in the paper bag. He headed to the front door, grabbing hold of her mom's arm and yanking her to her feet.

"C'mon, we don't have time for this!" he yelled, shoving her toward the door. "Put your fucking shoes on! Kelly—"

Kelly cringed as her father turned toward her.

"Get your damned shoes on now!" he shouted, taking a few steps toward her.

She knew how this would end if she remained standing where she was. Kelly pushed herself toward the door and went to work pulling her fuzzy winter boots onto her feet. As she worked, she glanced back at the presents beneath the Christmas tree.

Did she have time to take just the one? The one that looked small enough to contain the new smartphone she had placed at the top of her gift list?

She studied her father, who was busy pulling on his tan work boots, paper bag tucked snugly beneath his left arm. She shoved her foot into her last boot and dashed toward the small tree.

"No you don't!" her father yelled, grabbing her hair. "We don't have time for that shit! Don't be stupid, Kelly!"

She reached up to her burning scalp and tried to push herself through the pain. It was stupid for her father to be pointing out what they did and did not have time for. He hadn't even taken any food or family pictures. He'd gone straight for his drugs, cursing the two of them the whole time. Just as he always did.

Still, Kelly hadn't survived as long as she had without learning to abandon many of her hopes and dreams. With one last mournful look at what would likely have been her very own smartphone, she turned back toward the door as her father pulled it open and went out into the hallway.

"C'mon, little girl," her mother urged, her bloodshot eyes blinking rapidly. She took Kelly by the hand and pulled her down the hallway after her father, who didn't even glance back to make sure they were still with him. The corridor lights flickered on and off with the trembling of the building. As they moved forward, other doors slammed open and shut, the other occupants rushing into the hallway carrying as much stuff as they could. Silver picture frames, jewelry, DVDs, and various electronic devices were dropped on the worn, green carpeting and crushed underfoot as people shoved each other, desperate to get out of the building.

Kelly screamed as her mother pulled her past an elderly man on the floor in a white undershirt and striped pajama pants. His face was bloodied and his body convulsing as people stepped over and on him. He clutched an old military cap he must have stopped to pick up before he was trampled by his neighbors.

"Mom, *stop*! Mr. Welks is hurt!" Kelly screamed. She pulled hard on her mother's hand.

"We *can't*, baby!" her mother cried, "We don't have time!"

"Fucking move your asses!" her father's voice roared farther down the hallway.

Kelly sobbed as she allowed herself to be pulled along, struggling to catch up. Her father reached the end of the hallway and paused beside the elevator, then headed to the stairwell.

Kelly was shocked to feel herself lifted into her mother's arms and carried through the doorway into the stairwell. She was twelve now and hadn't been carried by her mother for years. "Mom . . ."

They were surrounded by a violently shifting sea of people. Her mom stumbled as someone shoved them aside and suddenly Kelly could picture her mother and her being trampled on the floor like poor Mr. Welks.

"Just put me down, Mom," Kelly pleaded. "I can make it."

Her mother paused, and Kelly could see the sweat dripping down her forehead. People teemed around them and Kelly's mom stumbled again. Her mother planted a quick kiss on her cheek and allowed her to slide down her body. As her feet touched down, Kelly felt her mother's hand tighten around hers, and she was pulled forward through the panic that continued to erupt around her.

About halfway down the last staircase, Kelly was able to get a look at the landing below. She focused on her father's bald head as she was jostled back and forth by her neighbors. Mom must have caught sight of him, too. She pulled Kelly along even faster, yanking her through tightly pressed bodies in her struggle to get out. Kelly felt like she was going to pass out, but somehow they managed to weave their way through the sea of confused people until they reached the bottom floor and rushed out through the front entrance.

Outside it was snowing and the people shoving their way through the small doorway looked like a swarm of angry bees exiting a hive. They rushed in every direction as the city of Portland burned around them. The sky was lit with orange and yellow as explosion after explosion pounded against Kelly's ears and echoed throughout the buildings.

Kelly stopped abruptly as a car raced toward them, sliding on the slippery pavement and nearly clipping the two of them as they moved into the street. She glanced at her mother, struggling to calm herself, trying not to shiver in the frigid night air. Her father was already on the other side of the street, unlocking their small, red sedan. All around them the lights from the city buildings and the streetlamps flickered as the ground quaked.

"C'mon, fucking *now!*" her father yelled, pounding his fist on the roof of the car. He ducked down into the car and slammed the door shut, and Kelly wondered if he might leave without them. The ignition turned and the headlights pulsed as the car struggled to life.

They reached the car and her mother threw open the back door, shoving her inside. As the door slammed shut, she kept her eyes on her mother as she ran around the back of the car and jumped into the passenger seat.

Her father threw the car into gear and took off in a wide turn, scraping the SUV in front of them. As the car moved out into the street, they were narrowly missed by a speeding police cruiser, lights flashing through the falling snow. Her father jammed on the breaks as the cruiser passed and they were immediately surrounded by a surging crowd of people, some of whom Kelly recognized from their apartment building. The people banged on the hood and windows, pleading for her father to take them as well. Kelly buckled her seatbelt and gazed out at the terrified faces—adults and children of all ages.

"Fuck off!" her father screamed as the car lurched forward.

Kelly gasped in horror as a young woman and her daughter fell in front of the car. The front of the car bumped as it rolled over them, followed by a second bump as the back tires followed. Kelly swallowed hard, struggling not to think of what had just happened as the car raced down the street, swerving back and forth.

"Matt, you're gonna to get us *killed!*" her mother cried, her voice shrill and piercing.

"Shut the fuck up!" he yelled. Kelly shivered in fear as her mother cringed.

The car reached the end of the street and they took a hard right. The tires screeched and for a minute Kelly thought the car was going to flip over. The car straightened and sped forward in the direction of the I-295 signs. Kelly leaned down and put her face in her hands, unable to keep watching.

"Where are we going?" Mom asked in a weak, hesitant voice.

"North," Dad said. The car lurched again as they took another turn.

They rode in silence for a few minutes.

"Fuck, look at the jetport," her father groaned. Kelly straightened and peered out the window.

The Portland Jetport was doused in flames so high Kelly half-expected the *clouds* to catch fire. The red runway lights that extended over the I-295 highway and out on wooden platforms over the bay flickered and went out completely as they passed. She gazed back over the city of Portland, horrified to find that it, too, was covered in flames. Bright balls streaked through the sky like shooting stars, turning the falling snow into tiny black silhouettes as the balls rained down upon the city and exploded in plumes of orange flame.

Kelly buried her face in her hands again, though the bright auras of the explosions erupting around their car penetrated easily.

"Who do you think it is?" her mother asked.

"Fuck if I know. Fucking Republicans and their wars," her father said.

"Oh, my God. They blew up Juvie. All those kids . . ." her mother said. Kelly didn't need to look up to know what she was talking about. Her parents talked about the juvenile detention center every time they passed it. She pictured the buildings that stood on the hillside overlooking the water. Something told her that the flames in her mind weren't nearly as bad as what her mother was seeing.

Her father chuckled. "Good."

She felt the vehicle begin to slow and lifted her head, peering around the driver's seat. Ahead of them was mess of red tail lights. Horns blared and someone shouted. They were in some kind of traffic jam. In the distance were the tolls and I-95 onramp.

"Son of a fucking *bitch*," her father sighed, bringing the car to a stop. Kelly heard the paper bag rattle and realized he'd had it on his lap the entire trip. She didn't need to see what her father was doing to know that he had found a bottle of pills. It rattled around in his hand as he fiddled with the safety cap, popped it off, and shook a couple of them into his mouth.

"Do you think I could have—" her mother's words were cut off as a deafening roar filled the air. Something flashed over them and struck the ground. The night blossomed with blinding white light and the windshield cracked into a spider's web of fractured glass. Kelly covered her face with her hands, huddling back against her seat as the windshield shattered and the car flew into the air.

Kelly screamed and then realized her parents were screaming too. The world spun and she realized she was about to die. Tiny shards of glass pelted her from all sides, and she screamed again in terror as everything went haywire. Her seatbelt cut into her chest and her body felt pulled in all directions. She struggled to find something to focus on as everything around her seemed to move in slow motion. She caught a glimpse of another car that seemed to be flying backward through the air beside her, then it was gone and their car landed upside down. The roof crumpled above her head, but did not collapse entirely. The seatbelt felt like it was cutting through her chest.

As their car screeched to a grating stop, it slowly leaned sideways, rolling onto the passenger side. It stayed that way, propped in place by the car it had landed on. Other cars smashed to the ground around her, and she covered her ears until the grinding of metal and shattering of glass finally stopped.

For a moment all was still, save for the shadows cast by burning flames in the distance.

Reluctantly, Kelly opened her eyes and gazed around. She was half-lying on her side, the seatbelt keeping her from falling onto the passenger door. The seatbelt cut painfully into her right hip and lower belly as she straightened as much as she could. Her parents were crumpled together in the front of the car; spilled drugs and other paraphernalia from the paper bag were scattered everywhere.

She moaned, the cold night air biting at her skin as snowflakes drifted through the shattered windows and melted upon her mother's face. She stared at her mother's wide, lifeless eyes peering out at nothing from beneath her father's arm.

"Mom?" Kelly screamed, struggling to free herself. "Mom!" She wrestled with the seatbelt, her eyes focused on her mother. "Help! Someone please *help*!" she screamed, kicking her legs as her fingers fumbled with the release button.

She slowly became aware of sounds outside the car. Other screams and people calling for help. In the distance something flickered. Kelly clamped her lips shut tight and focused on getting the seatbelt free.

The sky lit up again and she flinched as another rocket whooshed over the car. The sound was louder than anything she had ever heard. It hit nearby, the aftershock from the explosion rocking the car. She screamed for help once again.

But no help came.

Certain that the next blast would hit the car, Kelly took a deep breath and bent her knees so that she could place her feet on the inside of the passenger seat. She shoved her body upward as hard as she could while pushing down on the seatbelt release button. The belt slackened, and she gritted her teeth, pushing down harder on the release. Finally, the belt snicked free and she fell against the rear passenger door.

She took another breath, ignoring the pain in her side, and gathered her feet beneath her. Then she stood, grabbing hold of the headrest on the driver's seat to steady herself. Trying to get the back doors open was impossible. The car was laying on one of the doors and the other one was over her head. Not only would she have to push the thing open and hold it while she tried to crawl through, she was barely tall enough to reach it.

There was only one way out. Over her parents' broken bodies.

Snow fell harder, coming through the shattered windshield in a white flurry. Kelly kept hold of the headrest as she carefully stepped one foot over her lifeless parents, stretching until she felt her foot come to rest on the metal edge of the windshield. Pushing herself forward so that the majority of her weight was on that foot, she shifted her grip and shifted her weight into the front so she was half sitting on her father's shoulder. Trying not to think about what she was doing, she grabbed hold of the top edge of the windshield with her free hand, bent her lower knee, and shoved herself upward. For a moment her back foot caught on her father's arm, then she scrambled free, dragging herself through and into a crouching position on the hood of the car they'd ended up on.

She made herself look at her parents. They were dead. There was no denying it, but a small part of her refused to believe that they could have died while she herself survived. It felt like someone had punched her in the gut. She glanced around wildly, wondering how she would survive on her own.

More missiles lit up the sky. Kelly watched as they punched through dark clouds before diving toward earth and exploding miles away.

She scooted off the hood and slid down onto the snowy pavement. Shivering, she studied the other people climbing out of their cars and starting to walk. A big SUV crawled along the grassy patches of earth that ran alongside I-295, heading toward the burning tollbooth.

She slid her way between cars—some toppled, some twisted, some simply abandoned—and made her way toward the shoulder. The majority of the people walking alongside the highway were headed toward the main strip of Route 1 where a number of buildings, including the Maine Mall, were currently burning.

She didn't want to go that way.

Tears trickled down her cheeks as Kelly walked toward the burning tollbooth and the I-95 highway. A man and a woman leading a boy who looked to be her age rushed by and she quickly caught up with them. "Please, help me. My parents are dead and I—"

The man spun around and shoved a snub-nosed revolver in her face. "Back away!" he commanded. "You stay away now!"

Kelly froze, tears once again flowing down her cheeks. Her chin quivered as she watched the man turn back and herd his family toward the highway. For a time she just stared. Then she drew a long breath and exhaled until her lungs were empty. She waited a moment to allow some space between her and the family before continuing along the shoulder, past the flaming booth and torn-off EZ-Pass signs.

As she reached the bridge that ran over I-95 and connected with a circular onramp, she followed the family ahead of her, picking her way carefully down through the snow blanketing a steep hill overlooking the highway. She used the path they had already created, though she was careful to keep her distance. About halfway down, she spotted the man with the gun on the highway below and stopped.

Cars sped by and the man seemed determined to get his family a ride. He walked out on the highway with one arm outstretched and his gun pointed at the next oncoming vehicle. His wife and son waited at the edge of the road.

"Stop, damn you, *STOP!*" the man cried out. His voice was powerful enough to carry over the din of traffic and explosions in the distance, though Kelly knew there was no way the driver of an approaching car was going to be able to hear him.

At first there were just the brightening lights of a car's headlamps shining beneath the bridge. Then an SUV shot out from under the span. The high beams of the SUV glared across the man with the gun. There was a loud smack, a thump, and the sound of glass breaking.

The gun went off and the SUV swerved for a second before the driver recovered and continued north.

Kelly stared for a moment at the body pieces strewn down the road. Blood smeared across the pavement where he'd been standing. Both wife and son still stood on the shoulder and suddenly Kelly realized they were covered with blood and gore. She watched in frightened disbelief as they burst into screams and raced into the woods at the edge of the highway.

"Wait!" she cried, running as fast as she could through the snow and out onto the shoulder of the highway. "Please, take me with you!"

But they either couldn't hear her or were too crazed to care. She slowed, realizing the pair was headed in the same direction as the majority of the people she had seen earlier—toward the burning restaurants and stores of Route 1.

Kelly fell to her knees and covered her face with her hands. What was she going to do? What hope of survival did she have in a place where a man would turn a gun on someone like her? Who would take care of her when people were driving their cars into other human beings and sending their body parts flying all over the highway just so they didn't have to stop?

Lights from other cars flashed by as she sat, the cold of late December nibbling at her skin. She rubbed at her arms, shivering, and closed her eyes against the glare of the passing vehicles, feeling like the weight of the world was sitting on her shoulders. This was where she would die. She would just sit there and wait for it. There was no hope for anything else.

She lifted her head as the low hum of tires hitting the rumble strip reached her ears. She jumped to her feet and backed up a few steps as a vehicle came to a stop in front of her and the passenger door opened. A skinny woman with shoulder-length hair emerged, her figure silhouetted in the lights of oncoming traffic, snow swirling around her. She moved quickly around the open door as a man yelled to her from inside the car. The words were inaudible, though Kelly wouldn't have paid much attention to them anyway—her eyes were fixed upon the woman.

"Are you all right?" the woman asked, her voice rising over the hum of the engine. She stopped a few feet from Kelly. "Where are your mother and father?"

Kelly burst into tears. "H . . . help me, p . . . p . . . please."

The woman walked over and wrapped her arms around Kelly's shoulders. Smelling of perfume and Christmas tree, she pulled Kelly close.

"We'll take care of you, baby," the woman whispered, her voice soft and her breath warm on Kelly's ear. "Will you come with us? We'll take care of you until all of this blows over."

Kelly nodded and wrapped her arms around the woman.

"C'mon, little hitchhiker," the woman said tenderly, "let's get you warmed up and away from this mess . . ."

. . . "James," Kelly said, finally speaking up. She stepped up beside him and reached across his chest, gently running her hand down his left arm and resting her hand on his.

He looked down at her and their gazes locked. With every bit of willpower she could conjure, Kelly projected all of her caring and compassion into a silent plea. The corners of her husband's lips rose in an affectionate smile and she warmed at the love in his eyes.

James let the rifle drop and slung it back over his shoulder. He nodded at the man and woman. "James Richmond," he said. He wrapped an arm around Kelly's shoulder, pulling her toward him. "This is my wife, Kelly."

The strangers glanced at each other for a moment before relieved smiles spread across both their faces.

"I'm Bryar Perkins," the man said, "and this is my daughter, Casey."

Casey stepped forward, right hand outstretched. Kelly took the girl's dirt-encrusted hand, giving it a slow, delicate shake. She could tell by the pungent scent that they had been on the move for quite some time. Casey offered her hand to James who shook the girl's hand as if afraid she might break. Bryar walked slowly around his daughter and offered his hand to Kelly as well.

"These *bad people* who're after you," James said, getting right back to business as Bryar shook Kelly's hand. "They're dangerous to us, I take it?"

"I'm afraid so," Bryar said.

"But they have no firearms," James said.

"They don't."

"And you said they were following an old road through the forest?"

Bryar nodded, looking down at his knife. He looked back at James, and Kelly got the feeling Bryar would wait for James to give his knife back to him.

"If it's the same road we used to get in here, it'll bring them pretty close to us," James said, glancing at the trail, then down at the fire. He began to kick dirt onto the burning coals, shoving what was left of the logs off to the side.

Kelly stomach clenched as a realization swept over her.

"Oh, no," she gasped. "*Tripp!*"

Bryar froze in place as the man's expression turned hard.

"Stay right here," James commanded, nodding at the women. He looked at Bryar. "Come with me."

The stern look in the man's eyes made Bryar's insides feel like jelly. Bryar wasn't about to say no, not that he had any real reason to anyway. He started forward—

"Your knife," James said.

Bryar glanced down at the blade before bending over and picking it up. He pushed the blade into its sheath and looked up to find James was already well down the trail. Though his muscles still hurt from all the traveling they had done over the last few days, he forced himself to sprint to catch up with him.

"Where are we going?" Bryar asked, watching as James pulled aside some branches and plunged into a curtain of trees.

Bryar held up his hands, shielding his face as the fir branches snapped backward. Forcing the prickly branches out of his way, he pushed his way through.

"My dog," James said. "He took off after something just before you arrived. Not sure if it's just an animal or what, but my daughter chased after him."

"Animals?" Bryar asked.

"Yes," James replied. "I'll explain later."

Bryar thought about pushing for further information, but decided this probably wasn't the time. He followed as quietly as he could, wondering what kind of animals James could be talking about.

Before long they broke into a small clearing with an old fire pit, their speed increasing as they entered the open area. James broke into a run and they raced toward the other side. About three quarters of the way across, they were both startled as a young woman burst through the trees and nearly collided with them.

She skidded to a halt, gaze fixed on Bryar, and planted her feet in a defensive position, ready to react. "Dad, who is this?"

"Where's Tripp?" James asked, stepping in front of Bryar. It wasn't difficult to sense her anxiety. It hung around her like a throbbing aura.

The girl's eyes flickered like a flint spark for a moment and Bryar wondered if she was going to give her father a hard time. Her shoulders sagged just a bit. "He ran farther into the woods. Carl went after him." She opened her mouth as if wanting to say more, but hesitated.

"Which way?" James asked.

"He ran north from the clearing where you two were chopping down trees yesterday."

James closed the gap between himself and his daughter. He shot a quick glance back over his shoulder, presumably to make sure that Bryar wasn't approaching, knife drawn, now that his back was turned. Though Bryar couldn't help taking mild offense, he also couldn't fault the man for being cautious.

"You go back to the pond right away and stay there with your mother. I'll be back as soon as I have your brother."

"But, who—"

"Right now!" he commanded, taking his daughter by the shoulders and turning her in the direction they'd just come. The power in the man's voice was so strong Bryar found himself shuddering.

The girl glared at Bryar over her father's shoulders, then took off, making sure to give Bryar a wide berth. He watched as she went, trying his best to be non-threatening. This did nothing to wipe the distrustful look from her face as she entered the forest and disappeared.

"Would these other family members of yours hurt my son if they came across him?" James asked.

"My mother is unpredictable," Bryar said. "I've seen her kill without much of a reason before. I think it all depends on whether or not she thinks she can use your boy to get to me and Casey."

"Then we need to move faster." James took off in the direction of the road.

"Can you protect us from them?" Bryar asked, then flushed, suddenly aware of how out of place such a request was.

James stopped and spun around. He stared at Bryar, his face as still and expressionless as a sand-blasted statue. It almost felt as though the man's eyes were gazing right through him, as if the man was using Bryar's own eyes as windows to his soul and was sizing him up.

"You're going to help me avoid the mess you brought along with you," James said. Nothing in his tone conveyed anger or resentment as Bryar would have expected, but there was no overlooking the gravity in his voice. "Once I have those I love and care about in the same place, and once I am certain that they are safe, we'll talk about what I can do for you. Okay?"

Bryar shuddered. "I can't face Ma' Lee again. Not unless I know I won't be going back with her."

"I don't know anything about that, but I want to make sure you understand one thing: until we get my son back neither of you will get *anything* from me. Now c'mon," James said, heading back into the trees.

TWENTY-FOUR

"FASTER, DAMN YOU, *faster!*" Ma' Lee shrieked, her voice splitting the mountain air like a sharp axe. She ran behind the two of them, her body hunched forward like an animal on the hunt and her bony fingers curled into claws.

They had been on the road for at least an hour, running through the darkness, Brett's heart in his mouth until the sky started to brighten and daylight brought the world back into focus. It hadn't been an easy run through the darkness, but fortunately there were no further accidents.

He rounded a corner lined with birch trees with Wade keeping pace beside him. Sweat rained down his face, and he found himself immediately disheartened at the sight of another uphill climb, this one much steeper than those that had come before. The road ran like a reverse mohawk through the trees and up the mountain ahead, curling at about the halfway point as if those who had originally laid the road decades earlier had at first tried to run straight up and over the mountain only to change their minds.

To say he was tired was a dramatic understatement. He had only been allowed a few hours of sleep. Ma' Lee probably wouldn't have stopped at all had he not fallen over Wade and broken his left arm. The arm was strapped across his chest, supported by a sling made from one of his shirts and secured with duct tape. This held the arm stationary, but didn't help the pain.

Brett gritted his teeth and began to accelerate up the hill. Despite the pain in his arm, his anguish had been lessened a bit when he'd shed his backpack at the spot where they had found Wade. Ma' Lee had permitted him to leave it behind, not saying a word as she watched him remove his valuables and stow them in his pockets. Perhaps she reasoned as he did, that they would be coming back in that direction once they had Casey and Bryar, but something told Brett that his mother was thinking with less and less clarity by the minute. As her time without Bryar now stretched into days, she was beginning to lose it.

Brett had left behind what was essentially a bag of dirty laundry. There was no way he was going to carry that entire load with his arm in a sling. After removing his knife, the only one of his meager possessions with any practical value given the current circumstances, he placed it in his pocket and was back on the road at Ma' Lee's command, running along like a man who had just shed thirty pounds of body fat overnight. Beside him, Wade shot frequent glances back at Ma' Lee, probably making sure that she was still with them and that he stayed out of striking range.

Brett found himself doing the same.

Ma' Lee's hair stuck up in all directions. Though she kept Brett and Wade moving at speeds they were having trouble maintaining, she herself didn't seem to be the least bit fatigued. As far as Brett could tell, she hadn't even broken a sweat.

She was focused on the hunt, set on reclaiming those audacious enough to believe that they might enjoy a life outside of her control. Brett could only hope they found his brother quickly. His body couldn't handle much more.

"Faster!" she cried. Brett glanced back and saw her eyes settle on his duct tape sling and his heart lurched.

"Can't believe I raised such a stupid fuck as you!" she snarled. "If you were a horse, we'd have had to put you down in the grass where you fell!"

That thought had occurred to him. He had been relatively certain that Ma' Lee wouldn't kill him off before she had Bryar back. Injury or no injury, she needed him. Still, just before he'd drifted into pain-riddled sleep, he'd found himself wondering if she wouldn't kill or abandon him. Somehow the idea both delighted and horrified him.

As they reached the top of the incline and the road began to level out and curl around the mountain, Brett was relieved to feel the burning in his legs subside a bit. Though Ma' Lee would not allow a break in pace, he was able to catch his breath. They circled the mountain, Wade at his side, until the road turned downward at almost the same grade as the hill they'd just climbed. While Brett had shared very few moments of comradery with Wade over the years, he couldn't help giving him a brief smile at the sight of such a lengthy downhill.

"Double-time it, you miserable—" Ma' Lee began, but was cut off as a herd of spooked animals dashed across the road twenty feet ahead of them in a series of leaps and bounds.

Brett stopped, off guard and confused. He had seen deer before in books and on old posters in hunting shops they'd looted, but this was the first time he'd seen them in the flesh. He broke into a ragged trot, fearing Ma' Lee's wrath more than the sight of the fleeing deer. Slowly he realized both Ma' Lee and Wade were no longer moving and gradually came to a stop.

Struggling to catch his breath, Brett slumped over for a moment, wincing as pain lanced through his left arm. He straightened, cradling the injured limb with his good arm. He turned back and looked at his mother and younger sibling. Wade had an almost lustful look upon his typically dull and vacuous face, while Ma' Lee appeared genuinely frightened. Just the sight of her displaying such vulnerability turned Brett's stomach and made him feel as though he might vomit. He couldn't figure out *why* she was so tweaked, except that she had become so comfortable in what the world had become that seeing evidence a part of the old world had survived did not sit well with her.

The last of the herd disappeared into the trees and brush at the side of the road, and the rushing of large bodies through the leaves dulled to almost nothing. The rustling moved deeper, fading until the herd was out of earshot, and once again the forest was quiet.

Wade stared after the deer, a look of deep longing and loss spread across his face. Behind him, Ma' Lee's fright quickly boiled into rage. Sensing how close she was to losing her temper, Brett whirled around and began to run downhill once again.

"Move your worthless *ass!*" Ma' Lee's voice rose behind him over the sound of air rushing past his ears. Wade shrieked, probably snapped out of his trance by her hand.

A quick look backward confirmed that they were all back on track and moving downhill together, Ma' Lee driving them from behind with Wade just ahead of her, face lit with a beaming smile as he rubbed at his cheek.

After fifteen minutes of painful running, during which Ma' Lee struck Wade several more times for not moving fast enough, they reached the bottom of the hill and rounded a corner. Brett jolted to a stop as a small, black-and-white dog barreled toward them, barking ferociously. Though none of them found themselves terribly intimidated by something so small, they kept their distance. The dog continued to bark and snap around them until all at once Wade launched himself forward and snatched it up in his arms.

CARL STUMBLED OUT of the woods onto the gravel of the road, nearly tripping over an unearthed root and falling flat on his face. He recovered his balance and stopped to catch his breath.

"Stupid mutt, you're gonna get it *good* when I catch up with you," Carl grumbled. He cupped his hands around his mouth, took a deep breath, and prepared to call the little mongrel's name. He froze as a faint sound carried through the forest.

An excited, *human* cry.

"Tripp!" Carl gasped, breaking into a run. His feet flew so fast that he barely acknowledged that they were touching the ground as he sprinted along, listening for other sounds while panic welled in his gut. If he didn't find Tripp before he was spotted by whoever made that cry, his family would likely never see Tripp again.

Turn back. Go and get Dad, you idiot! a voice screamed in his mind. *It's just a dog. Is that worth your life? What if they see you?*

He skidded to a stop, his mind racing like a bullet fired from his father's rifle. What if they saw him, whoever they were? Then they would know there were others nearby and they might find the pond. The last thing the Richmond family needed was to have their new home, a place capable of sustaining them comfortably for the rest of their lives, snatched away by intruders. As much as it hurt him to admit it, Tripp was expendable when weighed against the survival of his family.

Carl listened for sounds of approaching strangers before turning reluctantly in the direction of the pond. He had to get back to Dad, let him know there were other people . . .

Tripp barked and a series of yelps carried through the still mountain air.

Don't even think about it! Zoey's voice thundered in his head. *Don't be an idiot, Carl! Keep going! Get Dad!*

But he couldn't. The sounds of his dog crying out in pain were too much to ignore.

He turned slowly back around and gazed down the winding road. Suddenly he wished that he had thought to bring the axe along with him.

These are obviously bad people, Zoey's voice insisted. *What do you think you're going to do?*

He started after Tripp, his slow walk turning into a cautious jog as yelps of discomfort and fright continued to reach his ears. Soon the yelps were joined by human voices.

"No tags, but this isn't any wild dog," came the hoarse voice of a woman.

Carl kept moving, shifting course so he was no longer following the road, but was headed straight into the brush at the road's edge. His pace was slow and deliberate, and he made sure to watch his footing very carefully to avoid stepping on anything that might generate noise. Reaching down with his gloved hands, he gently eased slender red branches out of his way. As he slipped further into the trees, he listened carefully as the strangers continued their conversation.

"Maybe we're near a homestead," a man's voice suggested.

Tripp yelped again.

"Quit holding him like that, you feeble-minded shit," the woman commanded, sending shivers down Carl's body. He moved deeper into the woods, closer to where the road picked back up on the other side. Through slits between trees and the surrounding brush, he began to see little flashes of movement, though it wasn't enough for him to get a clear look.

"Give him to me," the man ordered.

"No, I wanna hold him," a new voice pleaded. It was dopey and almost oafish, like that of a small child, though it was clearly another man speaking. Carl continued forward, picking his way cautiously through the mud, sticks, and leaves. With every step, his concern for Tripp intensified as a knot twisted in his stomach. He felt so disturbed that he began to worry he might lose whatever was left of last night's dinner.

"Neither one of you is gonna hold him, damn it!" the woman cried, and Carl saw a flash of motion through the trees. "Brett, you get your knife out so we can bleed him out and cook him up later."

Tripp yapped, and Carl moved faster, the discomfort in his stomach building to a full-blown anxiety attack that seemed to shoot through his chest like splintering glass. He was about twenty feet away from the group, but still could see very little of them.

"No, Ma', please. I wanna—" the oafish man was silenced by a loud smack. The man began to cry like a baby, his loud voice filling the forest around them.

Tripp yelped again, the urgency in his voice escalating.

"I said give him up, you stupid *shit*. You *give him up!*" the woman screamed.

Carl stopped as the dense foliage thinned out just enough for him to get a look at the strangers. The one holding Tripp sat in the tall grass between the ruts. He was balding with strands of hair flowing out from his head in odd places and thin patches of facial hair. Tripp struggled in his arms, trying to get away from both his captor and the stick-thin woman who struggled to pull him away. Behind them, a burly man, one arm wrapped with duct tape, watched nervously. He held what looked to be a four-inch folding knife in his good hand.

"Give him to Ma'," the burly man shouted.

Carl watched in disbelief as the woman balled her hands into fists and began to brutally pummel the bald man. A flurry of hits landed in rapid succession, eliciting ear-splitting shrieks from the man, but he would not release the dog. The woman went to work on him with her boots. She kicked him in the lower back time after time, causing the man to keel over, his arms still tightly wrapped around Tripp.

Just bite him, Tripp! Carl thought as he watched the man's fingers dig into Tripp's fur. With every kick his fingers tightened around the folds of flesh on Tripp's body, mostly near the neck, to the point where the skin around the dog's frantic eyes was pulled back. Tripp yelped and Carl's heart felt like it was torn to pieces.

After all the fantastic things that had come to them over the past few days, he couldn't believe that everything could be turning bad so quickly. He frowned, and his jaw trembled as he watched the newcomers, feeling totally helpless.

The woman delivered one last, brutal kick to the man's lower back and staggered backward. The man screamed, a blood-curdling sound that felt like it went right through Carl. The woman looked furious and bewildered, evidently not accustomed to disobedience or rebellion. Strands of hair hung over her eyes and dangled around her mouth. Carl stared in fascination as several strands sucked into her mouth when she took a deep breath, staring hatefully down at the man, who lay curled on his side, still cradling poor Tripp in his arms.

"You stupid *fuck!*" the woman screamed. "What is it you plan to do with it? Take it apart bit by bit? Make sure it suffers enough for your needs before discarding it in the woods? That's a fuck-ing *meal*, you miserable *shit!*"

"I got it, Ma'," the burly one said, shifting the knife in his good hand and walking toward Baldy. He crouched down on his haunches. It was obvious that his injured arm had a nega-tive effect on his balance. Carl could probably push the man over without really trying . . .

Carl bit his lip to keep from gasping as the burly man low-ered one knee onto the side of the bald man's head, pinning him down. The bald man squirmed, as did Tripp.

"N—n—*no*—, Brett! Na—na—*no!*" the bald man pleaded, but the burly man wasn't listening.

"SHUT YOUR HOLE," Brett ordered, leaning harder on his broth-er's head and delighting in Wade's screams. If it hadn't been for Wade, he'd have the use of both his arms. He jerked his knee, grinding Wade's face farther into the grass and gravel, then di-rected his attention to the dog. Doing the job one-handed was not going to be easy, but he would try just the same.

Brett juggled the blade in his hand until the sharp edge faced toward him. He stared at the dog, seeing the fear and panic in the little animal's face and feeling absolutely no sympathy for it.

Perhaps in another life, before the world had changed, he might have regarded such creatures as cute and innocent, but that wasn't the case anymore.

"*Please!*" Wade cried.

"Don't you learn?" Brett yelled, baffled by his brother's insubordination. There was no point in delaying things any further. It was time to get this over with and move on before they attracted someone's attention. Ma' Lee had completely lost it. If there was anyone else around, they would've heard the commotion.

He swallowed hard and adjusted his balance again. His left arm moved involuntarily, sending a fresh jolt of pain through his body. He took a deep breath and moved the blade slowly beneath the struggling dog's chin.

The dog yelped again, louder than before. Wade let go of the animal just as it buried its teeth in the black wool of Brett's jacket, into the skin of his lower arm. Fury burned in the dog's eyes. It growled, an intense, guttural sound.

Brett squawked, dropping the knife and shaking his arm to free it from the dog's mouth. He lost his balance just as the dog's teeth came free. The dog took off like a shot back down the road in a flash of black and white that wove through the grass like a fish through water. Before any of them had a chance to react, the dog had disappeared around a turn in the road.

Brett flailed with his good arm, trying hard to keep his balance and hoping to find something to keep him from going down, but it was of no use. He landed hard on his left side, sending a burst of unbearable pain through the broken arm. He screamed in agony, the sound echoing through the trees.

"Can't I count on you for *anything*?" Ma' Lee screamed. "Get after him!"

But Brett wasn't getting up. Not yet. Even the fear of what would happen when he failed to obey Ma' Lee's commands wasn't enough to get him on the move. He was down for the count.

PERHAPS IT WAS the lack of sleep over the last twenty four hours, or perhaps it was the fatigue from being made to run full-tilt down the gravel road for hours on end without a break, but Ma' Lee was furious that neither of her sons scrambled frantically to their feet as they should have. It didn't click in her head that Brett was in such intense pain that no force on the planet could coerce him to his feet, nor did she understand that the beating she had just given Wade had left him unable to stand. Her calculated beat-down approach had been skewed, and her focus lost as Wade's stubborn refusal sent her into a raging frenzy.

Ma' Lee glared at her sons. Her mouth curled into a snarl, and she gritted her teeth as she fought the urge to deliver a second beating. She glanced at the trees where the dog had disappeared.

An animalistic growl escaped through her clenched teeth as she broke into a sprint down the grassy road. She'd catch up to her sons later. As she charged around the corner, arms and legs pumping like a well-oiled machine, she found herself staring down an "S" shaped series of curves in the road.

She came to a gradual halt at the sight of the dog cradled in the arms of a middle-aged man of medium build with long, black hair. The man held the dog firmly in one arm while his free hand ran over its body, presumably inspecting it for wounds. A rifle was slung over his shoulder, and on his belt he wore a hunting knife in a sheath.

But it was the man standing beside the stranger Ma' Lee was the most interested in.

Bryar.

CHILDHOOD'S
END

TWENTY-FIVE

B RYAR FROZE IN place, his body as rigid as a corpse floating beneath a frozen lake. He held his breath as he watched Ma' Lee slow to a stop. His heart pounded as anxiety flared.

Their eyes locked.

"Where's my son?" James asked. Bryar looked away from his mother at the man who had led him back toward her. James was watching Ma' Lee very carefully. Slowly, he shifted the dog into his left hand and moved his right up the strap securing the .308 to his back. Bryar's warnings had definitely struck home.

But Bryar knew that Ma' Lee didn't care about the man or the dog. As Bryar looked reluctantly back at his mother, he found her eyes fastened on him. Though she remained still as a statue, she seemed poised to spring at any moment, as if somewhere in her mind she imagined she could clear a twenty-foot gap in a single bound.

Suddenly Bryar found himself wondering if they were standing at a safe enough distance.

"I said: where's my *son*?" James growled, his waning patience obvious.

Bryar started to step behind James.

"Stay where you are," James said to Bryar, not at all concerned with lowering his voice. Bryar looked at the man, hoping for some showing of confidence in his eyes, something that might reassure him that things weren't about to go horribly wrong, but James kept his attention focused squarely on Ma' Lee.

She suddenly looked at James, her stare so piercing and hateful Bryar shivered. James remained cold, emotionless, not twitching a muscle.

"Where's the bitch?" she asked, her voice low and seemingly calm despite the fact that Bryar knew a storm was brewing within.

"You answer my question first," James said.

She cocked her head toward him. It was a tic Bryar knew all too well. The expression on her face did not change.

"I don't know you," she hissed. She moved slowly forward at a pace Bryar recognized, a pace intended to intimidate, a pace that promised violence if she didn't get her way. Bryar couldn't help wondering how she intended to get around the fact that James was packing iron. "I don't have to answer to you," she hissed, "but you'll soon find out what happens to those who don't answer to *me*. Now where's the bitch?"

In what seemed like one move, James set Tripp down, pulled the .308 off of his shoulder, and chambered a round. Then he brought the rifle tightly into his right shoulder and pointed the barrel at her face.

"Tripp, *hush!*" he commanded. The dog stopped barking, though he continued to growl. "Last chance," James said, raising his voice once again, "where is my—"

"Dad," came a voice from the woods to their right.

Startled, Bryar glanced at the tangle of ferns and branches along the side of the road. A young man stepped through the brush. The young man stared at the dog with a look of elated relief. His attention drifted to Ma' Lee, but didn't linger there for long.

With a nod from James, the young man moved behind him, eyeing Bryar suspiciously as he picked up the dog.

James hadn't turned his attention from Ma' Lee, keeping his head cocked to the side as he sighted down the rifle. Ma' Lee appeared to be sizing the man up. Her body language told Bryar she wasn't intimidated.

"Where's the bitch?" Ma' Lee hissed as her eyes narrowed into slits.

James took a few steps forward. He stopped after exactly five steps, leaving only ten feet and some change between them.

Bryar's chest tightened. Just the sight of the man standing so close to his mother, seemingly without a shred of fear, was simultaneously one of the most inspiring and the most harrowing sights of his life.

"I don't know what you're talking about," James said. His voice was low and emotionless.

The anger and hatred on Ma' Lee's face intensified, pulling the wrinkles on her skin taut. A few gold and auburn leaves drifted lazily toward the ground. The air was still, and there was no sound in the forest.

"I've no reason to shoot you," James said, though he made no move to lower the rifle. "You just turn around and walk away. Leave us in peace, and we'll be through with all this."

Again, Ma' Lee cocked her head, causing the wispy strands of her hair to flutter about her head before settling. Her lips pursed together. She was exercising a great deal of patience, though Bryar knew that patience was not really a measure of her self-control. No, what held his mother at bay was the rifle in her face.

"What do you say?" James asked.

Bryar's eyes were drawn to movement behind Ma' Lee as Brett walked slowly around the corner. The skin on his cheeks and forehead was a deep red, and his face was twisted in what Bryar realized was pain as he lumbered toward them, wincing every now and then. As soon as he saw the rifle, he held the knife he carried out to his side non-threateningly, though he did not drop it.

Ma' Lee's gaze did not leave the man standing in front of Bryar. "I say you hand over those who rightfully belong with me, and I'll offer the same deal. Leave you in peace."

All at once, Bryar found it difficult to breathe.

JAMES THOUGHT OF the pond as the woman made her offer. She and her muscle-bound son with the injured arm did not know about Ben Gile and its fresh water. If he turned Bryar and Casey over to her, it might mean the preservation of their new way of life. Never before had he been so aware of the stranger behind him.

But he had seen the bruising on Casey's face, bruises inflicted by the hands of the woman who stood before him like a demon that had crawled out of its den in search of human sustenance.

Don't any of you forget who you are while you're out there, Bampy's voice echoed in his head. It boomed through his mind like the voice of a mighty giant through a massive cavern. There was no choice; he knew exactly what he must do.

"You want me to hand them over so that you can go back to beating on a pregnant woman and toying with the mind of this poor man?" he asked, his voice rising in spite of his attempt to stay calm. "I don't think so. I've learned enough about people like you to know when the answer has to be *no*, regardless of the cost. This is the last time I'm going to tell you to turn around and go back where you came from. You won't lay a finger on them again."

"I know what kind of person you are too, tough man," Ma' Lee responded without hesitation. Her voice was a raspy hiss, low and venomous. "You act all tough, as if you have what it takes to pull that trigger and take the life of another, but I know better. I've been stepping over people like you for thirty years now, and I'll be doing it for years to come." She began to close the gap between them, moving with the confidence of an expert gambler. "It's not often I give a person a way out, let alone a second chance, so I suggest you take it and hand them over *now*."

James flicked his finger, disengaging the safety on the rifle. He took another couple of steps toward her. "Not another step," he said, his voice low and commanding.

"Dad—" Carl said.

"Stay where you are, Carl," James ordered, not taking his eyes off Ma' Lee. She came to a stop, close enough she could reach out and touch the barrel of his rifle if she were so inclined. The look of cold, menacing confidence on her face shifted for just a moment as the edges of her eyes began to twitch ever so slightly.

James didn't need to know the woman to recognize the anger building in her.

Her hands moved down to her hips and her long, boney fingers dug into the material of her tan, hooded sweatshirt. "So what is it you think we should do here? I'm not going anywhere without my beloved children."

The woman's use of the word *beloved* would have been amusing had it not sounded so horribly raped coming off of her lips. It was all he could do to keep from losing his composure. James settled his cheek against the gunstock, keeping himself focused.

"They're not your *children* anymore," he said, thinking briefly about the middle-aged man quivering behind him. "Go," he commanded, aiming the rifle at her left thigh. Any doubt in her mind as to whether or not he was a killer was inconsequential. He could maim her and send her off without a death on his conscience.

Ma' Lee's lips puckered so tightly that what little red remained in them was quickly chased away by white. Her nostrils flared, and behind her eyes a fire burned unlike anything James had ever seen before. He braced himself.

Without a word, Ma' Lee spun dramatically around and marched off in the opposite direction. She stopped as she reached the large man who had come to join her and punched his wounded arm. The man cried out and fell to his knees as she moved swiftly past him and disappeared around the bend.

James remained where he was until the man struggled awkwardly back to his feet and stumbled after his mother.

For a long moment not one of them spoke. Finally, Carl stole the words right out of James' mouth.

"What kind of trouble are we in?"

AS THEY WALKED along, James quietly explaining things to his son, Bryar noticed the man glancing back at the trail just as often as he did. Even then Bryar wasn't sure they hadn't been followed.

When James reached the end of his story, Bryar added a few more details.

"She's always had a tight hold over us," he said, "my brothers more so than me. They were too young when everything around us turned to what it is now. They have very few memories of what life was like back then."

"Why does she want you back so bad?" Carl asked as he shifted Tripp into his left arm. He took hold of a branch and held it back as James walked past.

Bryar tried to figure out how he might explain his relationship with his mother. Though Carl was hardly a small child, it still didn't feel right to talk about his life as his mother's sex slave. In the end, he decided to keep it vague. There was no reason why he needed to divulge everything—it would probably do more harm than good.

"Control," Bryar said after a brief silence. "We're all she has in this world to dominate, and she needs to have that power—especially over me. Plus people think twice about messing with a woman surrounded by a posse of men."

"She's not right in the head," James said very bluntly, his voice so low that they barely heard him.

"No, she isn't," Bryar said. "Never has been. She was able to hide it better before the last Christmas—"

"You mean Black Christmas?" Carl interrupted, his voice excited for reasons Bryar didn't understand.

"I've never heard it called that, but we're probably thinking of the same thing," Bryar said. "She was able to hide it better before the world turned. When everything went dark and the water was tainted, I suppose she saw no reason to hold back anymore."

"She won't give you up," James said matter-of-factly. And he was right. "She'll come for you again, and we need to figure out how we're going to handle it."

Bryar didn't respond, retreating into his head to think things over. They reached the grown-over campsite and paused as Carl told them about the axe he'd left behind when he'd gone after Tripp. James nodded toward the right side of the clearing, and the men pushed into the woods in the direction of the work site. It wasn't long before they emerged into a clearing littered with spiked stumps and hacked branches. Carl recovered the axe and turned to his father with a nod.

James led them back through the woods toward the pond trail. Bryar kept looking back over his shoulder until he was satisfied that they weren't leaving evidence of having come this way. They returned to the overgrown game trail and minutes later broke out of the trees onto the grassy shore of the pond.

"Is it just me, or does the water not have a smell here?" Bryar asked, curious to find both James and Carl slowly turn around to face him.

Father and son looked briefly at one another.

"The water here is fresh," James said after a moment.

At first Bryar thought James was pulling his leg. He glanced at Carl but the young man was just as serious as his father.

"No," Bryar said, his voice a shuddering whisper as he gazed across the pond. On the opposite shore a large, brown animal and what he imagined to be her baby stood chest deep in the water drinking. His mouth fell open. "This isn't . . . *possible*," he said, suddenly having trouble forming words. His tired legs wobbled a bit, and he clutched at a nearby cedar tree.

"That's a moose," Carl said. "We didn't believe what we were seeing at first either, but it's true. There's fresh water here and whole herds of other animals."

Bryar stared at the large creatures, entranced. He had never seen a moose before, and for the first time in his adult life, the sight of an animal did not immediately register as a potential source of food.

"DAD, CARL!"

Carl turned to face his sister as she raced up and took Tripp out of his arms. She gasped and parted the bloodied white fur on his neck.

"What *happened* to him?" she cried, giving Carl a suspicious look as if he had assaulted the dog himself.

"The people who're after Bryar and Casey got him," Carl said. "They went to slit his throat, and the wimp decided to turn into a tough dog." He decided to downplay the situation, swallowing hard against the sudden lump in his throat as he thought about how the sight of that knife held to Tripp's throat had driven him to tears.

Zoey glanced down the trail. "Where are they now?" Her quivering voice told Carl that Casey had filled both Zoey and Mom in on the situation.

"Gone for now," Dad said, placing his hand on Bryar's shoulder. He tipped his head toward the lean-to. "But they'll be back," he added after a brief pause.

Bryar nodded, and they all followed Dad along the edge of the water to the shelter. Bryar immediately got down on his knees beside his daughter, who was leaning back against the backpacks and a few blankets. She smiled up at him.

"She's out there, Casey," Bryar said. "We drove them back, but I know she'll come eventually."

"Sooner rather than later," Casey said, her voice tight. She frowned, her eyes glistening with unshed tears. "Why can't she just leave us alone?"

"I'm sorry," Bryar said, "I didn't want to tell you, but we're better off than we ever have been, thanks to these caring people." He looked around and Carl tried to see his family through the man's eyes.

Mom stood with her arms around Dad as he whispered in her ear, no doubt catching her up on the events on the road. Zoey looked lost in thought and Tripp stared almost absent-mindedly over the top of the lean-to.

"No," Casey wiped at her eyes, leaving a dirty streak behind. She stared blankly down at her belly. "I'm glad you told me." For a moment she was silent. "What are we going to do?"

Carl knew exactly what had to be done, though he was reluctant to come out and say it. He watched the newcomers as the two of them sat close together in the lean-to. Casey reached out and took her father's hand. Mom and Dad kept staring at each other, their expressions echoing what Carl felt inside.

Don't any of you forget who you are while you're out there, Bampy's voice echoed in Carl's mind.

They hadn't forgotten, and they wouldn't forget. Though Bampy's words cautioned against losing themselves in order to survive the new world, they were writing their own rules at this point. They had taken in a father and his pregnant daughter. They had protected them from the so-called *bad people* that the world had created. Because of this, their humanity remained intact. But they had to preserve their own lives now.

It was a matter of self-defense.

"We kill her," Dad said, at last breaking the silence.

TWENTY-SIX

MA' LEE HAD BEEN gone for what felt like an hour already. Though Brett had spent the entirety of the welcome break attempting to calm Wade—who flopped about in the grass at the edge of the road, unable to get to his feet—it still felt like a vacation. But it was not to last.

Ma' Lee emerged from the forest like a wraith exiting a tomb. Her face was emotionless, though Brett thought he actually saw a tinge of sadness mixed with the rage. He didn't devote too much thought to the odd sadness, though a part of him wondered for just a moment if perhaps the crumbling of his mother's dominion was inspiring a different coping mechanism than her usual blind rage. Sorrow and depression was not her.

Brett turned back to his younger brother, using more of the same useless verbal threats of what Ma' Lee might do to him if he didn't move. Only now he spoke in a whisper, attempting one final time to coax Wade to his feet before their mother came within earshot.

"They have a camp next to a pond," she said somberly, though it was obvious she was trying her best to hide her emotions. The power and rage she generally exuded seemed to have disappeared. Still, her voice wasn't lacking in rancor. "Bryar and that little shit were talking so loud there was no way they would have noticed me tailing them."

"That's good, Ma'," Brett said, not sure what else to add as he worked to reposition Wade against a tree. Wade struggled against him, his wild eyes returning constantly to Ma' Lee as his hands pawed at Brett. Restricted to only one good arm, Brett quickly gave up and turned back toward his mother.

She looked at Wade as he panted heavily, his legs splayed out in front of him. "What's the matter with the retard?" she asked, moving past them down the road.

Brett shook his head, his eyes never leaving his brother's face. He'd never seen Wade look so scared. For a moment Brett struggled with what he could say that wouldn't make her lash out at him. In the end, he found himself blurting out the facts before she flew off the handle as a result of his delayed reply.

"It's been mostly his usual gibberish, but somewhere in there he said he can't feel his legs," Brett whispered just loud enough to reach his mother's ears. Wade's eyes darted wildly around and finally locked on his as they shared a collective dread for what was almost certain to come. Wade's typical goofy smile was nowhere to be found. The only question was: which one of them would she beat first?

Ma' Lee turned slowly around, hands on her hips, fingers digging into her sides. Without a word she stalked toward them, and Brett wondered if he'd imagined the sadness he'd seen on her face earlier. She pulled her switchblade from her pocket and snapped the blade into its open position. She waved it slowly back and forth, rotating it so that the blade stuck out from the bottom part of her hand.

Wade stared, wide eyed, at the knife in his mother's hand. His jaw began to quiver and a garble of inaudible words spewed from his mouth.

Brett wanted to stay with him, but the fear driven into him by his mother's slow approach had him up on his feet and moving away before he even knew what was happening. He glanced down and locked gazes with Wade as his younger brother silently pleaded.

I'm sorry, Brett mouthed, moving back onto the road and out of the splatter zone. He watched in horror as Ma' Lee reached Wade's side and squatted by his knees. Though Wade's upper body trembled violently, it was obvious that his legs were not moving.

"This is your only chance, Wade," Ma' Lee growled. "Stop faking and get to your feet."

Wade uttered another torrent of gibberish, faster and with greater urgency. As if such things made a difference with Ma' Lee. Even if he had been able to plead for his life, she wouldn't have backed down.

"You feeble-minded *prick*," she said, voice soft as the mew of a kitten. She drove the knife down into Wade's right leg, just above the kneecap.

"Aaaaaaargh" Wade cried out, closing his eyes in a tight grimace. It was evident to Brett that the screams were screams of fear, not of pain. They weren't loud enough, and after a few seconds, Wade's voice diminished to a low wail, and he opened his eyes. He stared at the blade, buried to its hilt in his leg.

Ma' Lee twisted the blade, watching for signs of a reaction. Wade gave her that dopey look that even now was saturated with adoration. She slowly pulled the blade free and gazed down at the blood flowing steadily from the wound.

In her rage she had allowed herself to go too far, and the tip of her boot had broken Wade's back. Brett had been aware of the possibility almost since the moment it had happened. His mother sniffed and moved quickly to her feet, backing away from Wade, whose eyes followed her, his jaw trembling and tears cascading down his cheeks. His shoulders and chest heaved up and down dramatically, yet he showed no signs of hatred or blame for what she had done. His expression held only fear and love.

Ma' Lee turned her back to them once more. For a few minutes she remained where she was while Brett tried to figure out what she would do next. All at once, she broke the silence, her voice distant and dreamy, as if she had removed herself from the situation entirely. "Well, I guess if you aren't going to get up and walk, we'll just have to leave you right where you are."

Brett gasped. Wade began to shake violently. "N—n—n—na —no!"

"Now, now," Ma' Lee said softly. "You know what you have to do if you want to come with us." She started walking, her long strides taking her swiftly down the grassy road and around the bend.

Brett watched in disbelief as she disappeared, looking back and forth from his mother to his baby brother. He watched with pity and dismay as Wade pushed himself up, only to fall face first into the grass.

"*Ma'!*" Wade cried, grasping at clumps of grass and struggling to pull himself after her. "*Ma', Ma' n—n—no!*" he screamed, dragging his dead legs behind him for a few feet before giving up and collapsing.

Trying his best to keep it together, Brett walked in a large circle around Wade, and made his way after Ma' Lee. He blinked as his eyes burned, and his breathing grew heavier with each step. While he'd never experienced remorse for the beatings he'd unleashed on his brothers over the years, beatings he gave mainly to win Ma' Lee's approval, deep down he loved his brothers. It wasn't until he walked into Wade's field of vision, however, that the tears started and he had to pause for a moment to contain himself.

"Brett! No, Brett, *no!*" Wade yelled after him. He cried the words out over and over as if they were the only ones he was capable of forming, the fear and anxiety in his voice almost impossible to ignore. It shook Brett to the bone, leading him to wonder if the same fate awaited him one day.

"I'm so sorry," Brett whispered, fearful that any further delay would warrant punishment from Ma' Lee. Not willing to roll the dice on her mood any longer, he turned his back on his brother and followed the woman who guided their destinies like a drunk driver behind the wheel of a speeding car, soon to crash and burn.

Twenty-Seven

ARL STUDIED THE strangers resting side by side against the backpacks. He could tell that they were absolutely wiped out. Casey's face would occasionally contort in obvious discomfort and she'd move around, her hands shifting from her belly to her lower back until she finally settled into another position.

"You've been wandering the state for almost twenty years?" he blurted. "What was it like out there? How did you survive?" He stared at them in amazement, and belatedly realized his mouth was hanging open. Mom, Dad, and Zoey sat in front of the newcomers, listening closely. Dad's attention drifted constantly out to the tree line beyond the lean-to. They sat with their backs to the cold, ash-strewn fire pit.

"We weren't wandering the whole time," Bryar said, spreading a quilted blanket over Casey's belly. "There were a number of years where we were trapped in the territories of the militias that sprang up after your Black Christmas. As for how we survived . . ." He trailed off, having obvious issues translating memories into words. His gaze locked with Casey's as the two of them seemed to share memories that were not so pleasant. "Some things are best left in the past, my friend," Bryar finally said.

"Back to what we were talking about," Dad said, giving Carl a warning look. "How long do you think we've got before she comes?"

Both Bryar and Casey shrugged. "There's no way to be sure," Bryar said. "She's usually pretty quick with things like this. When her temper goes off, she doesn't usually cool down until she's seen blood."

Dad nodded. "I got that impression."

"There's only one absolute truth I can tell you about Ma' Lee," Bryar said, his tone grave and sincere. "She's as sharp as a tack. Just because you have a rifle doesn't mean that she's in any way given up coming after us. It'll probably be at night. She'll hope to catch us while we're sleeping."

The group fell quiet as Dad thought this over.

"We need to think of how we're going to do it," Dad said, at last bringing an end to the silence. "The obvious choice is the rifle, but I'm not entirely certain I'll be able to pull the trigger when the time comes. To take a human life . . ." He turned away and stared out across the water, his back to them with the rifle draped across his lap.

Carl thought immediately of Bampy and his parting words.

Mom inched closer and draped her right arm over Dad's shoulders. She leaned her head on his shoulder without saying a word.

"I'll do it," Zoey said, standing up proudly like a soldier who'd just bravely volunteered for some kind of suicide mission. Carl stared up at her, slightly in awe of his sister's gumption.

"No," Dad said, still facing the water.

"I agree with your father," Bryar said. "We can't ask you to do this for us. There has to be another way."

Carl watched as Casey looked at her father.

Zoey didn't argue, much to Carl's surprise, but she didn't completely back down either. She turned to Bryar. "Why don't *you* do it?"

What a bitch, Carl couldn't help himself thinking. He glanced at Mom for a moment as if she was somehow able to read his thoughts and would get after him for even thinking such a word. His mother didn't move.

"I can barely look at the woman," Bryar said, "let alone shoot her."

Zoey looked down at him with her hands on her hips. Though Bryar wasn't privy to the Zoey that the rest of them all knew and tolerated, he didn't seem the least bit intimidated or offended.

"Your father was big enough to admit that he might not be capable of doing it," Bryar continued. "Like him, I don't want to form a plan built upon a lie. We need something solid."

As bad-tempered and irrational as Zoey often was, she still backed down. They were once again left in silence, interrupted only by the light breeze that had picked up, carrying gold and red leaves from the trees out across the water.

A scream rose through the trees, tearing the silence in half. After a few seconds the sound faded, and everything was quiet again.

"I think that was Wade," Bryar said.

Casey nodded.

"One of your brothers?" Dad asked.

"Yes," Bryar said, looking as though he had more to say, but not elaborating.

"He sounds like he's in pain," Mom said, gazing over the trees in the direction of the voice.

Bryar drew in a deep breath and sighed. "He probably is. My mother likes to take out her frustrations on the weakest of us. Normally that would be Casey, but without her around . . . well, Wade's next in line."

More screams echoed through the trees, fainter this time and not limited to one long burst. The cries continued as Carl thought long and hard about how they might dispatch Ma' Lee. He studied the trail of logs spread across the bog to the place where he had nearly lost his own life, suddenly realizing there was one course of action that could spare them all from having blood upon their hands.

"I know what we have to do," Carl said, distracting them from the cries that continued to echo through the wilderness.

By THE TIME they finished discussing their plan, Casey and Mom seated beneath the lean-to while the rest sat around the cold fire pit, the sun had reached its zenith and begun its slow descent. Even as they committed to their plan of action, now easily an hour since Carl had laid it out for them, the distant cries continued, leaving the group to wonder exactly what had happened. The screaming didn't sound like a man in pain, more like this Wade—or whoever it was—was screaming in terror.

As the sun touched the tips of the western mountains, the cries finally faded. Had the man given up or had he died? Carl shivered. There was no way to know for certain.

"Should we check the snares?" he asked his father, who was crouched in silent reflection across from him. His stomach grumbled so loud everyone looked at him. Heat flushed his cheeks as he looked around the group. Zoey sat next to him, gently stroking Tripp who lay in her lap sound asleep. Behind their father, Mom helped Casey drink from the previous day's pot of boiled water. Though the water was fresh, Dad insisted that they couldn't be too careful and still took precautions to boil whatever water they consumed. Casey finished and thanked Mom with a smile, followed by an unexpected burp, which brought a look of shy embarrassment to her face. Mom smiled back and patted her on the shoulder before passing the pot along to Bryar, who sat on the other side of his daughter. Like Dad, he also seemed lost in his own head, staring almost absent-mindedly into the cold mound of black coals in the fire pit.

Dad stood without a word and walked to the water's edge, rifle in his hand. He gazed out across the water. Carl didn't need to be a mind reader to know that his father was looking for signs of movement. "No," he finally said. "We stay together until this is done."

Carl watched as his father took a deep breath and exhaled slowly. It was the only time he had ever seen the man so uneasy. Turning to the Perkins, he watched as Bryar looked into the pot.

"Is it okay if I finish this?" Bryar said.

With a warm smile, Mom said, "You go right ahead." She nodded at the still waters of the pond. The only movements were the ripples cast by the occasional falling leaf and jumping fish. "We have plenty more where that came from."

"Thank you," Bryar said before tipping the pot up and swallowing so loud Carl could hear him. When he finished, he handed the pot back to Mom with a smile and turned back to Casey. "How are you feeling?"

"Hungry," she said with a smile, "but it's great to have water in me again. I've never tasted water so sweet."

"Me neither," Bryar said in a low voice that somehow managed to sound excited.

Casey's smile disappeared. "Do you think we'll make it? Do you think it'll work?" she asked, glancing at Dad, then back at Bryar.

"You know her as well as I do," Bryar said with a sigh.

The knotty feeling in Carl's stomach tightened.

"I have no way of knowing how it'll go," Bryar continued. "I'll do my best to make sure that my part is done, but beyond that, I . . ."

"What if this doesn't work?" Zoey asked, startling them all. "What if your little *plan* doesn't—"

"Enough, Zo." Carl glared at his sister. "Do you really think that helps right now? You know, we could all be *dead* by morning, and here you are, critical and negative as ever, right up until the very end."

"That's enough," Dad ordered.

"I'm sorry I've never been as tough as you," Carl continued, ignoring his father's words, "or as careful, or as *smart*, but I'm your brother, damn it! I love you and I *respect* you, yet all I get in return is your constant bullying and judgment!" He jumped to his feet, feeling the eyes of every member of their group staring at him. He drew in a deep breath and closed his eyes, tilting his head back so far his neck popped. As he inhaled, the spicy scents of decomposing leaves from the forest mixed with the rich odor of mud from the edge of the water. The stillness and quiet of the campsite left him very much aware that all attention was on him even though he could see nothing.

He exhaled and lowered his chin. He took another deep breath and opened his eyes, feeling the weight of everyone's gaze. Even Tripp regarded him with a cocked head and confused expression.

Perhaps the stress had finally gotten to him. Perhaps it was just that he'd taken Zoey's abuse for sixteen years without a break and this moment just happened to have been the last straw. Carl didn't understand exactly why he'd blown up at her, but now that his head was clearing, he regretted his outburst.

He looked at Zoey, who looked away almost as soon as their gazes met, making him feel even worse. He knelt in front of her and whispered, "I'm sorry, Zo."

He sensed Dad walking quietly over from the edge of the water. The sound of rocks and gravel crunching under his feet was unmistakable in the silence.

For once, Zoey seemed to have nothing to say. She continued to look away, her eyes glistening.

"I didn't mean all that," Carl said, even though a part of him knew it might be best to just leave it alone and give her some space. As he struggled to understand how someone so unbreakably strong could suddenly be so submissive, he realized that all of his sister's toughness, her abrasive personality, was just a front for the insecurity she felt. It was all just a defense mechanism.

He got to his feet and started to walk around the lean-to, intent on disappearing into the forest for some time alone, only to find himself stopped by his father who took him gently by the shoulders.

"We stay together," Dad said, turning Carl around and looking him in the eye. It was not a threatening look, nor was it one of judgement or condemnation. Dad would leave Carl and Zoey to sort this out on their own. He startled Carl by pulling him into his arms and holding him tightly. Dad's stubbly cheek felt like sandpaper against Carl's face.

"You know I was much older than you when I first found my backbone," Dad whispered. "You're already so far ahead of me. You'll be twice the man I am."

Carl clenched his eyes tight, fighting the tears threatening to spill down his cheeks. He breathed deep his father's scent, the natural smell of sawdust and soil.

They were all afraid, Carl realized. And rightfully so. Death could be coming for dinner or breakfast.

"I'm sorry to interrupt." Bryar's voice cut through the cloud of emotion like a horn through fog. "Mrs. Richmond, could you help me please?"

Carl spun to find Mom had started toward him and Dad. She turned back toward the lean-to and gasped.

Casey leaned against the backpacks that had been laid out for her, chest rising and falling as she panted. Her face was twisted in a grimace of pain, and her hands were wrapped around her stomach with Bryar's on top of them.

"Oh, no," Mom said, rushing back to the lean-to. Wetness stained the crotch of Casey's blue jeans. "I think the baby is coming."

JAMES HAD NO choice but to build a fire. As each contraction hit, what started as a series of uncomfortable groans turned into agonized wails that echoed across the waters of Ben Gile Pond and reverberated off the surrounding mountains. He shook his head and sighed. Ma' Lee was likely to have found them on her own anyway.

"It's okay," Bryar said, kneeling on Casey's far side. He glanced at Kelly as if confirming that he was doing things properly, then helped Casey focus on her breathing. "Watch me," he said, "breathe like me." He began to breathe in and out. It was obvious that Bryar knew little about what he was doing, most likely drawing from a foggy memory of a similar event on television, but Kelly would keep things under control.

Carl and Zoey moved away from the lean-to and stood over James as he broke twigs into kindling and arranged them in a skeletal, boxlike structure around puffs of dry moss. The setting sun rendered the clouds into purple balls of cotton suspended in a sea of murky violet. Soon their safest bet would be to huddle together and listen for the sounds of anyone approaching.

"You okay?" Carl asked Zoey. The apprehension in his voice was unmistakable.

Zoey was quiet, distant. "I'm fine," she finally said in a voice so soft James could barely hear her. He struck a flurry of sparks into the dried moss and bent down to blow gently on the smoldering heap. As a flame gradually grew, he added more kindling. Then he sat back on his heels and studied the shoreline for signs of movement.

Nothing. Not even a single forest creature visiting for an evening drink.

He stood, turning to face his children. Judging by the way Zoey fidgeted and her reluctance to make eye contact with Carl, she definitely was not fine. How could she possibly be? The only person in the world she held any power over had finally called her bluff. She was left with authority over no one. Add to this the very real danger that could descend on them at any moment, and you had a recipe for something that was everything *but* fine.

"I really am sorry," Carl said.

"Just leave it alone," Zoey grumbled. She glanced at James, then over at Casey.

James followed her gaze, his heart warmed by the care and compassion that Kelly showed the woman.

"I can't leave it alone, Zo," Carl said, his voice deep with emotion. James watched, curious. "If we're going to die out here tonight or tomorrow or *whenever*, I don't want us to be angry with each other.

"This isn't how Bampy would have wanted us to treat each other," Carl continued. "He and Gram and Mom and Dad . . . they didn't raise us to hold grudges or feel negative thoughts about each other. They raised us to love each other."

Zoey shoved a few stray locks of hair out of her face, tucking them behind her ear. She nodded her head slowly and James felt himself relax just a bit. Carl's argument was strong, but even the most persuasive argument wasn't enough to bring Zoey around full-circle when her emotions had gotten the best of her. Still, it seemed to at least inspire a moment of care and compassion.

"Come here, you idiot," she growled, wrapping her arms around her brother and pulling him in tightly. Their foreheads came together and they stayed as they were without saying another word.

James nodded to himself, satisfied with his children's resolution.

After a time, the two separated and turned their attention back to the pond.

James rose and moved away from the fire, adjusting the rifle on his shoulder. He tucked his flint back into his pocket and started to make his way down to the shore, but paused briefly and turned his attention to Bryar.

"Join me for a few minutes, would you, Bryar?" he asked.

"Go ahead," Kelly urged, "she's just fine with me."

"But I should—"

"It'll only be for a moment," James said, noting that Carl and Zoey were also on their way toward the water.

He was relieved when Bryar moved slowly to his feet, stooping like an old man until he walked out from under the pine boughs that covered the lean-to. With a last look at his daughter, he stepped around the fire. James headed over to Carl and Zoey.

"See anything?" James asked. He studied the pond and the wilderness surrounding it.

"Nothing yet," Carl answered, looking at Zoey.

"Not a single sign of them," Zoey added.

"Don't you doubt for a second that they're out there," James said. They stood in a line, the still waters of Ben Gile Pond mere inches from their booted feet. He glanced back periodically, keeping an eye on the lean-to. Something told him that Ma' Lee wouldn't hesitate to make a move on the women if she found them with their backs turned. "I know we've been over this already, but I just wanted to make sure that we're all on the same page. Bryar, you're sure that she'll go after you?"

Bryar shot a look back toward the lean-to. "I'm the one she wants. She'll come after me, most likely with Brett, and once I'm beaten to the point where she can tie me up or do . . . whatever else she has planned, she'll go after Casey. I've made threats over the years that have kept her from trying to kill my daughter, but I'm not sure that'll be enough now. I've never seen Ma' Lee so out of her mind."

"We're counting that as an advantage," James said. "You just make sure to lead her away from Casey and Kelly, and we'll take care of whatever else comes at us."

"Even if that means killing someone?" Bryar asked.

"We'll do what we have to do," Zoey said, speaking for all of them. James could tell that she was trying her best to sound strong and confident, to reclaim some of her former hardiness, and for the most part it landed. Some reservations remained, hanging in the air like low-floating clouds around their heads, but bringing those reservations into the open served no practical purpose. Things were what they were, and they would have to make do with the tools at their disposal.

"I don't know just *how* things will play out, but I promise you that I won't let them harm your daughter," James said, looking back to reassure himself that the women were okay. "But I need to know that you're going to be able to do your part when they strike. If you find yourself unable to leave Casey, you'll throw our entire plan in the trash." He placed his hand on Bryar's shoulder. As their eyes locked, James said, "Are you going to be able to do this?"

Casey's voice rose again as she moaned in agony. Bryar nodded. "We'll never be safe until Ma' Lee is dead. I'll do whatever I have to do. It's the only way."

"Good," James said. "Now go back to your daughter."

NIGHT FELL, CHASING Carl, Dad, and Zoey back to the lean-to where they sat with their backs to the fire, each facing a different direction. Carl held his father's hunting knife clenched tight in his hand. Zoey had Bryar's knife. He had made it clear that he was incapable of using the weapon against his mother anyway. Zoey held the knife in her right hand and Tripp's leash in her left while the dog slept peacefully.

Casey's pain and contractions grew worse as the night went along. Her water had already broken, prompting the removal of her denim pants. As the moon poked over the mountains and slowly traversed the sky, seconds becoming minutes and minutes becoming hours, still without a single sighting of Ma' Lee, Brett or Wade, Carl began to wonder if she was going to come for them at all that night.

Mom stayed by Casey, never leaving her side. In between moments when his attention was drawn by shuffling leaves or flapping branches, Carl found himself wondering how Casey would have gone through her labor had she and Bryar not encountered the Richmond family.

Carl watched, trying to keep his eyes from Casey's woman parts as Mom pulled the quilted blanket back over Casey's bare legs and hips. Casey moaned as another contraction hit, harder than before. She shook so hard the quilt slipped off again. Bryar sat on his knees beside Casey, working to keep her focused on her breathing while Mom dabbed the sweat from Casey's head and neck. She kept pulling the quilt back in place and peeking beneath to see if the baby was crowning.

"Is . . . it . . . *coming* yet?" Casey asked, speaking between short breaths.

"Not yet, sweetie," Kelly said, lifting the quilt up for umpteenth time and taking another look. Luckily for Casey the firepit was in a good spot for Mom to use the fire's glow to see. She lowered the quilt gently back down and pulled it over Casey's belly. "But you're ready for it. Just a matter of when he or she feels like coming out."

"You're doing great, Casey," Bryar said. He stroked her hair with his right hand while she held his left.

Carl turned away and looked at Dad who sat with the .308 laid across his lap, finger on the trigger. The agonized moans that came from the lean-to made Carl's stomach churn.

"When this is all over," Carl said, rubbing his left hand on his jeans. "I say we shoot us a buck and have a huge feast. You know, to celebrate."

At first there was no response and Carl's mind started to wander. Would they all still be alive after it was over? Would they really be in any condition to celebrate?

"You got it, kid," Dad finally said.

"It's coming!" Mom said, excitement in her voice. Carl turned, watching as his mother shifted to her knees before Casey's splayed legs.

"Breathe, baby," Mom said as Bryar wiped a cloth across Casey's forehead. "Breathe and push."

Carl craned his neck, mildly disturbed by a sense of guilt that swept over him. He frowned at himself. There was nothing wrong with wanting to watch the birth. He'd seen plenty of rabbits being born, after all, but never a human. Who knew if or when he'd get another chance?

Casey's face contorted and she started grunting. Her lips puckered and her chest heaved.

"Looking good!" Mom exclaimed. She reached back and pulled another blanket from her backpack. The blanket was small and had once been red, but had faded to pink over the years. Gram used to wrap that blanket around Carl after his bath—when he was young.

"Keep pushing," Mom said. "It's almost over."

"That's right, bitch, it's almost over!" a voice shrieked.

Carl's heart leaped into his throat as Ma' Lee sprang around the lean-to, emerging from the darkness like a nocturnal predator descending upon its prey. Tripp sprang to his feet, barking ferociously as Ma' Lee grabbed Mom's hair and yanked her backward onto the ground. Switchblade already in hand, Ma' Lee pulled back on Mom's hair, lifted her chin up, and brought the blade to her throat.

"Don't any of you move or I'll slit this cunt's throat and spill her juices down her belly!" Ma' Lee cried, pressing the edge of the knife to Mom's skin.

TWENTY-EIGHT

JAMES ROSE TO his feet, pulled the rifle to his shoulder, and aimed. He glanced at Bryar cringing behind Casey. Casey's breathing sounded erratic and offbeat. After all of their careful planning and all the reassurances that he wouldn't choke under pressure, Bryar looked to have shut down completely. It was like watching a child cowering beneath his blanket at the sight of some imaginary boogey man. James was hit with an odd mixture of pity and contempt.

Time seemed to freeze. James could feel sweat beading on his skin. Fear, anxiety, and adrenaline threatened to overpower him, though he worked hard to keep himself as sharp as possible. If he was going to find an opportunity to flip things in their favor, he would have to be quick and was likely to only have one opportunity.

Even if it meant taking this horrid woman's life, he was ready to do it to keep her from spilling the blood of others. Even Bampy would be with him on that.

"Lay your weapons down," Ma' Lee commanded, her voice low and malevolent, but still loud enough to rise above the barking dog. Her eyes reflected the dancing flames of the fire as they flicked from person to person. Kelly sat still as a statue. Though the expression on her face conveyed the fear she was feeling, she did not make a sound and did not struggle. James knew his wife—she understood that her only chance of survival rested in the hands of the others.

Making sure that he didn't move too quickly, James eased the rifle away from his shoulder and angled the barrel upward before lowering it slowly to the ground beside the fire. Carl and Zoey followed his lead and placed their knives in the dirt. Zoey reeled Tripp slowly in and took him into her arms, where he continued to growl, but ceased barking.

For a moment all was still and quiet save for the constant moans from Casey and the small, motor-like growl of the dog.

All eyes were on Ma' Lee.

"Brett," Ma' Lee said with a toothy grin. Her voice pervaded the darkness around them like the call of a screech owl. "Take the gun."

From behind the other side of the lean-to, closest to Bryar, the man called Brett emerged from the shadows and walked carefully over to where the rifle lay at James' feet. His gaze remained mostly on James as he approached, though he glanced at each of them. It was obvious that the man didn't consider the others to be as much of a threat.

As Brett reached the rifle, he lowered his good hand to the ground and slowly picked it up without looking away. He took his time standing back up, not once breaking eye contact with James.

"Shoot the bitch," Ma' Lee commanded. James wondered just how Brett was supposed to fire the rifle with only one good arm. The toothy grin she had been wearing returned as she stared at them over Kelly's shoulder. She moved her head forward so that she was cheek-to-cheek with Kelly. "Put a bullet right in her snatch. Two birds with one stone."

James looked at Casey, watching as her eyes widened with fear. Panic threatened to overwhelm him as he found himself powerless to act. Casey looked desperately over her shoulder at Bryar as Brett turned away from James and moved obediently in her direction, his face painted with cruel indifference. He balanced the .308 awkwardly in his hand, leaning slightly to the right as if compensating for the weight of the firearm.

Carl and Zoey watched, their eyes wide with the kind of horror they had never known prior to William Dewoh's upheaval of their lives—the event that had set in action everything that led up to this moment. Never in his life had James felt so crushed, yet still he struggled, using every ounce of self-control to stay collected so he could figure out a way to act against Ma' Lee and Brett without deadly consequences for the members of his family.

"BRETT!" BRYAR YELLED. His voice wavered like that of a small child. "Please! You don't want to do this!" He moved in front of Casey.

"Get out of the way you miserable shit!" Ma' Lee cried. "I'll be dealing with *you* in a second."

Bryar tried to get a brief look at his mother, but all he was able to see was Kelly's frightened face and the knife held to her neck. He focused on Brett. "I'm not going anywhere. If you want to hurt her, you're going to have to kill me first."

"No!" Casey cried. Her cry turned into a screech and her face wrinkled with pain.

Bryar tightened his lips, fighting the urge to comfort his daughter. He locked gazes with his younger brother, studying Brett's face. Brett stared back, his expression indifferent as he waited for direction from their mother.

An abhorrent scowl spread across Ma' Lee's face. She glanced around the fire at the others, all standing as still as statues, then shot them a demonic grin before planting a long, wet kiss on Kelly Richmond's cheek. "He moves, or I set her to bleed right here, right now."

Bryar looked at James. Their gazes locked for a brief moment and suddenly Bryar knew what he had to do. They needed to carry out their original plan. It was a gamble for sure, especially given how out of control things had spun, but it was now or never.

Time to roll the dice.

Bryar studied Brett for a long moment. Then he lifted his hands into the air as though he was surrendering. A slight sense of relief ran through him as Brett seemed to relax a bit, though his face remained just as emotionless. Bryar shivered in fear as his mother's hateful eyes stared up at him through wisps of Kelly's hair, still holding her tightly, cheek-to-cheek, with the knife pressed to her throat. Though the sight of Ma' Lee alone threatened to derail him entirely, Bryar somehow found the strength and willpower to push himself forward.

He slowly turned until his back was to Brett. He blinked back tears as he silently mouthed the words *I love you* to Casey.

Then he spun, darting between Brett and Ma' Lee. His vision adjusted to the moonlight as he sprinted down the shore toward the path of logs and branches running out into the bog. As he fled into the darkness with no way of knowing if Ma' Lee had sliced Kelly's throat open or not, he kept himself focused on the fact that he had not yet heard the crack of the rifle. Casey was still alive.

"Get him!" Ma' Lee cried, her voice echoing through the darkness. A shot split the air and he skidded to a stop just as he was about to set foot upon the large tree leading to the bog. His heart almost exploded in his chest as he whirled around to see what had happened. Brett was in the process of picking up the rifle, which had obviously been kicked out of his grip as he fired it one-handed. As he stood Ma' Lee jumped on him in a fit of rage.

"What the *fuck* is wrong with you?" Ma' Lee screamed, knocking Brett backward into the fire. Tripp barked ferociously. "You would shoot my *Anthony*, you stupid *fuck*?" Ma' Lee's voice was so high-pitched and doused with fury that it was almost inaudible.

"Get me out, get me *out!*" Brett wailed. Ma' Lee straddled him like a jockey on a horse, keeping him pinned in the fire. His screams intensified, but Bryar wasn't worried about his brother.

"Casey? *Casey!*" he yelled, grief stealing the breath from his chest. He started back toward the campsite, then stopped at the sound of Casey's voice.

"I'm okay!" Casey yelled. "Run, Bryar . . . *run!*"

Feeling sweet relief spread over him, Bryar spun back around and began to traverse the trunk that led to the other logs laid out across the bog. With as much care and patience as he could muster, he inched his way across the remaining logs on his way toward the area where Carl had gotten stuck.

Twenty-Nine

James watched in almost joyful disbelief as Ma' Lee pummeled Brett repeatedly with her fists, causing him to scream even louder. The air filled with the stench of burning flannel and something else James didn't want to think about.

"*Please*, Ma'!" Brett screamed, his voice loud and high-pitched.

James glanced at Kelly. She was already back with Casey, not hesitating to go where she was needed. Despite the ghastly events taking place around them, he couldn't help loving her even more. It filled him with a sense of pride to know that she would shrug off everything she had just been through in order to get back to a person in need.

Somewhere, Bampy was proud of them.

A flash caught his eye. Ma' Lee had lifted her switchblade in the air, holding it high in both hands. The moonlight reflected brightly off the metal as the firelight died beneath Brett's body.

"You would shoot my *Anthony*?" she hissed, her voice cutting through his screams.

"Ma'!" Brett cried. "Do you know what you're saying? Do you—"

"You—would—shoot—my—An—tho—ny!" she screamed, swinging the blade down into Brett's throat, pulling the blade free, and swinging it down again.

Brett lifted his good hand to try to deflect the knife and she pierced the flesh of his arm and hand, spraying blood all over his face. Within moments his body went limp, and his protests ceased.

"He went *that* way!" James yelled loud enough to catch Ma' Lee's attention. Her head snapped up, sending her wild hair flying as her gaze darted around the campsite. The crazed malevolence in her eyes seemed to burn right through him. "That way," he repeated, pointing in Bryar's direction. "Your *Anthony* went that way."

She moved slowly to her feet, the smell of Brett's burning flesh following her. The switchblade shifted ever so slightly back and forth in her blood-drenched hand, and for a moment, James wondered if she might make a move on him. He tensed, preparing to defend himself, but her eyes squinted and she turned to look in the direction he pointed.

"*Anthony!*" she yelled, sprinting off into the darkness. James quickly moved to the fire, falling to his knees and shoving Brett off of the burning coals with a grunt.

Zoey released Tripp and the dog rushed over to Brett's unmoving body, sniffing him over from head to toe. Zoey and Carl went immediately to their mother.

"Mom, are you okay?" Carl asked, his voice filled with panic.

"Did she cut you?" Zoey asked.

James watched as they knelt and peered at Kelly's neck, then gave her a hug. She quickly hugged them back, insisting she was just fine and shooing them away. A moment later, Carl joined James. Together they watched Ma' Lee chase Bryar into the bog.

"Do you think it's going to work?" Carl asked. Ma' Lee was making her way over the logs. She moved so quickly it was a wonder she hadn't already missed her footing and fallen into the muck.

James shook his head. "I don't know. If the coyotes were out and about, that gunshot was sure to have scared them off." If the coyotes didn't show up to dispatch Ma' Lee, they'd be left once again with the grim task of doing it themselves.

C'mon, Dad, James thought, appealing directly to Bampy. *Help us out just a little.*

"What are we going to do?" Zoey asked. Tripp trotted over and sat at her feet, looking up at the three of them.

James didn't say anything. He watched as Bryar came to a stop on the last of the logs spread out across the bog and waited for his mother to catch up. This was it. Would Bryar be able to do what needed to be done?

James bent down, picked up his rifle, and handed it to Zoey. "If the other one of her boys shows up, you do what you can to hold him back." He put his hand on Zoey's shoulder. "Don't you pull that trigger unless you absolutely *have* to."

She nodded ferociously.

"Come on, son," James said. He picked up his hunting knife, slid the blade into its sheath, and headed toward the bog.

BRYAR WATCHED AS Ma' Lee seemed to fly across the logs and branches as she traversed the muck. Though he couldn't see her eyes in the milky light cast by the slightly waxing moon, he knew his mother well enough to know that her progress across the makeshift bridge was governed by an immense amount of luck. There was no doubt in his mind that her attention was directed toward him more often than down at her footing. Still she moved toward him almost at a sprint, calling him by his sex name all the way.

He took a wide stance on the last log and struggled to maintain his balance. Ma' Lee didn't slow as she continued toward him. Moonlight glinted off the knife in her hand and he wondered if she even realized she was still holding the blade. About ten feet away she came to an abrupt stop and adjusted her footing so she stood balanced on two logs with both of her steel-toed boots facing forward.

"You stopped," she said. Though she sounded calm, Bryar knew better. A fire burned intensely within her, even when she was at her most pacified.

"I stopped, Ma'," Bryar confirmed, not sure where he should lead the conversation. He could see James and Carl slowly approaching and struggled not to focus on them.

"Does this mean you're done running?" she asked, her voice uncharacteristically soft and meek, as if she had forgotten about everything that had transpired on the shore. As if she had forgotten Casey even existed.

Bryar took a deep breath and held it for a moment. As he released the air from his lungs, he thought about his daughter giving birth beneath a canopy of pine boughs, aided by a woman who had been a complete stranger not twenty-four hours earlier. How much pain and suffering had been visited upon them by his sociopathic family?

He straightened his shoulders. It was time to stand up to Ma' Lee once and for all.

"No, you *bitch*, it doesn't mean I'm done running," he said, noting the look of confusion that spread across her face. Then her mouth tightened in fury.

"You don't like it when I speak to you that way, do you, Molly?" He clapped his hand over his mouth. "Oh, no. Did I just call you *Molly*? You hate that name, don't you? I know one that you hate even more. How about *Mother*? As in, I'll run circles around this planet for the rest of my life if it means that I'll never have to see you again . . . *Mother*."

Ma' Lee's lips pressed together. Her eyes grew wide and her nostrils flared. Her fingers curled tight around the switchblade.

From the back of her throat came a low, guttural growl. She spoke, her voice deep and coarse, like that of a dark demon recently awakened from a thousand-year slumber. "How *dare* you speak to me that way. After all I've done for you, *Anthony*. I ought to kill you where you stand, but you're coming with me whether you like it or—"

"No," Bryar said, "this ends right here. Turn and leave—and *never* come back—or you die, right now."

"You . . . wretched . . . little . . ." she lunged forward like a cheetah chasing its prey. Only Bryar wasn't running, and he had no intention of doing so. He watched as she crossed two, three, four more logs. He ducked as she hurled herself forward, intent on driving him to the ground, and felt her fly over him.

He struggled to keep himself together as his right hand missed the log in front of him and sank into the mud. Fortunately he caught the log with his left, keeping him steady enough to turn around just as one of Ma' Lee's steel-toed boots clocked him in the head. The kick didn't diminish her momentum or alter her trajectory, and she dove face first into the muck.

Her voice went silent, muffled by the bog. She'd sunk all the way to her waist. Her legs kicked wildly, reminding Bryar of a feral animal pinned against its will.

Bryar watched with conflicted emotions as his mother continued to fight. Ma' Lee kicked violently, her thrashing slowly calming. Finally, after a minute or so, her steel-toed boots came down upon the mud with one final *splash*, and she was still.

As Molly "Ma' Lee" Perkins' wretched, horrible life force was forever sponged from the face of the new world, the sound of a new life reached their ears.

James helped Bryar to his feet, and they both turned with Carl to face the lean-to as the cries of Casey's baby carried across Ben Gile Pond.

EPILOGUE

AD CHAMBERED A round and pulled the rifle in tightly to his shoulder, lifting the tip of the barrel through the green ferns and fiery-colored leaves at the edge of the woods. Carl was sitting on his haunches a few yards behind him, watching as Dad sighted in on one of the young bucks drinking from the pond a hundred or so feet down the shoreline. Holding the rifle in place with his left hand, Dad moved his right hand up to his mouth, took the middle finger of his glove in his teeth, and pulled the glove free, dropping it from his mouth before taking hold of the rifle again. Carl marveled at the way his father's attention stayed focused on the buck. He watched his father watch the buck and let his mind wander.

It had been three days since they buried Brett, first chopping at the ground with the axe to loosen the soil, then digging the rest with their hands. They collected rocks of varying sizes and laid them over the unmarked grave to keep scavengers from digging the corpse up and feeding on it.

Ma' Lee's body turned out to be more of a challenge than any of them had expected. It had taken all three men, positioned atop widely dispersed collections of twigs and branches, to pull her out of the mud hole. The fury that had apparently driven her most of her life was still frozen on her mud-caked face. Bryar had looked like he was going to be sick and Carl couldn't blame him—she was an absolutely horrific sight.

They'd carried her carefully back across the log bridge with Bryar in the lead holding onto her by the ankles. Dad and Carl had created something of a stretcher with their interlinked arms, supporting her upper body well enough that neither of them really felt fatigued by the time they reached Brett's burial site and went to work digging her grave.

It felt good not to be constantly looking over his shoulder every few minutes, jumping at the snap of a twig in the woods, and Carl was sure Bryar and Casey were relieved, too. Casey had taken to motherhood like a duckling to water—according to Mom—though Carl wasn't sure why she hadn't named the baby yet. It made him want to laugh every time she nursed the tiny infant. For some reason, Casey would start throwing out names to "see if they'd stick." Evidently, none of them had, not yet, anyway.

Dad's chin rose and Carl tensed.

"You see where his front leg meets his shoulder?" Dad whispered.

"Yes," Carl whispered.

"Just to the right of that is his heart. If you hit him there, he'll die almost instantly without much pain. If you can't get that clean of a shot, go for the neck."

He could see Dad's finger slowly tighten on the trigger as he let out a long exhale. The buck remained perfectly still, complete-ly unaware that his life was about to end. *Thank you, my friend,* he thought, mimicking the thought he knew was in his father's mind. Bampy and Dad both had always paid their respects to the animal whose meat would sustain the family.

The crack of the rifle echoed across the pond, and Carl jumped even though he'd expected the shot. He followed Dad out of the woods and was startled again when Mom and Zoey began to clap as they worked their way to the waters' edge. The rest of the herd had bolted, disappearing into the forest in a flash.

Carl waved back and grinned, his fist pumping up and down in the air.

"C'mon," Dad said, clapping Carl on the back, "let's go prepare a feast."

THE BUCK HAD been gutted and skinned and butchered. What was left of one leg still roasted over the fire, sending the tantalizing aroma of cooked meat spiraling into the air. They'd fed until they were stuffed after most of the meat had been cut into thin fillets, laid on smoking racks, and set to cure over a small fire fed with green pine needles. On the far side of the fire, Carl lazed back against his backpack with his legs crossed and a greasy hunk of venison in his hand.

James smiled at the sight of his son's gut bulging out and stretching the fabric of his thermal shirt. He should be sitting back and relaxing too, but there was one more thing he had to do.

"I wish you'd reconsider," James said, laying another log on the campfire.

"I thought we were done talking about this," Bryar said. "We went through it about as thoroughly as possible last night. After everything we've put your family through, there's no way we could make a life here together. You may think you see something in us that's similar to you, but the fact of the matter is that we've seen and done things that are unforgivable. I'm sure that Casey, the baby, and I will be able to make a life somewhere, but not here. You already have four mouths to feed. We'd be just another burden to you. This place is yours."

Dad shook his head, "We could make it work. I don't care about who you were before all this. You've shown me who you are now."

"James," Bryar said, shooting him a serious look, "I'm not going to change my mind. I understand why you keep pushing.

You're a good man, but this is what Casey and I have to do. You have to let us go."

Suddenly, James felt himself slipping backward in time, hearing those same words from another man's lips.

You have to let us go. You have to let us go. You have to let go . . .

. . . "You have to let go, boy," Bampy said, walking over to the boarded-up front door where James stood with his face pressed to the wood and his eyes perfectly lined up between the slits. Trace amounts of sunlight found their way into the house as the sun slowly disappeared over the mountains across Dodge Pond, and even though the light shined directly into his eyes, leaving his visions speckled with orange and purple dots, he kept his gaze focused on the hole in the deck.

The hole through which his mother had fallen to her death just twenty-four hours earlier.

Silence filled the Rangeley House, something that none of them were used to, but on this particular day, it seemed proper. Kelly sat on the couch, Carl and Zoey sleeping on either side of her, their arms wrapped around her neck like a human necklace. James almost jumped when Bampy's hand came down gently on his shoulder.

"I know you blame yourself," Bampy said, his voice uncharacteristically soft. "And you're an *idiot* for that. We should have declared that old deck off limits years ago." The fingers on James' shoulder tightened and he felt Bampy's breath against his ear.

"For years I've seen you get all bent out of shape for things that are out of your control. You're all about looking backwards, as if you possess some special ability to see where things went wrong and how you could have fixed them. Well, I've got news for you: we've all got that ability. Now I know you've listened to me over the years for the most part because you've grown into a better man than I could have possibly hoped for, but you've missed the most important lesson of all."

Anger flooded over James. He turned to his father, their noses millimeters apart. "This day isn't about *you*, Dad. You've made a career out of giving me *shit* all my life, and that's just fine. I'm used to it. Today, however, is about Mom. She hasn't even been in the ground for an hour and you're telling me that I need to let it go . . . that I need to move on? Why won't you let me grieve in my own way?"

"Is everything I'm saying going over your head?" Bampy shook his head and sighed. "I love your mother. There's a part of me buried out there right now that I'll *never* get back, but I'm not going to sit here and sulk about it because that's not what *she* would have wanted. Same as you taking on all the weight and responsibility for her death—it's not what she would have wanted." He paused for a moment before adding, "And what you're doing isn't *grieving* . . . it's obsessing. You're obsessing about something you couldn't possibly have prevented."

James opened his mouth, but just as he was about to speak, he glanced at his wife and children sitting on the couch. Kelly stared back at him, her eyes glistening and full of love, but behind those eyes was a silent plea for him to back away from the door and be with his family.

He took a deep breath, reprocessing his father's words as his boiling blood cooled. Bampy was right, as he often was, but it was difficult for James to acknowledge that fact. He walked over to the couch, lifted Carl into his arms, and sat down as close as he could to Kelly. He took another deep breath—and let the tears flow.

"I love you, James," Kelly said, kissing the top of his head. She put her arm around his shoulders. "You know it's not your fault."

The couch shifted as Bampy sat down on the other side of him, shocking James with a gentle touch.

"I'm sorry, Dad," James whispered, his voice cracking.

"No need to be," Bampy said. "This, like everything, is just another part of life that is out of your control. Out of all of our control. It's just the way of the world, son. You've grown into a strong, level-headed person, but there's one thing that even the strongest of us struggle against. You have to learn to let go. Do not forget, but let go. Move forward with your children, looking to the future and only glancing backward for reminders of the lessons you've learned."

They sat in silence for a long moment.

"Your mother was very proud of you," Bampy finally said. "Of *both* of you, though I'll admit that her image of you, Kelly, turned a bit at the end."

"What?" Kelly asked, her voice confused and filled with grief. "How? What did I do?"

Bampy chuckled. "She found out you slipped me some extra vodka."

James watched as Kelly studied the old man for a moment, looking totally confused. All at once her face lit up and she laughed so loud both Carl and Zoey lifted their heads. They looked around groggily and then went back to sleep.

"You wicked old man!" Kelly hissed. "What were you thinking, saying something like that?"

"It's my revenge for you pushing your bad influences on me." Bampy laughed. "My mother always said never pick up hitchhikers and look where it's gotten me."

"I'd say it was *me* who got the bad end of the deal," she said. She winked at James and he felt the dark burden he'd been carrying lighten. Looking back at Bampy, she said, "But my life's turned out better than I ever could have hoped." She smiled warmly for a moment, then her expression turned into a glare. "Don't you think I'm going to go out of my way to make you any more personal bottles, though. I don't care how much *arthritis* you've got!"

Bampy grinned and shot her a wink before standing up and walking toward the kitchen. "I'll drink to that, girlie," he said . . .

. . . James glanced back at Bryar as the half-moon poked its blemished face over the tip of the eastern mountains. The moon's reflection was caught by the still water, shimmering alongside glimmering stars. The only sound that cut through the calm night air was the sound of popping coals as fatty juices dripped down from what was left of the deer leg, causing tiny, fiery eruptions from the dying embers.

He looked over his shoulder. Kelly, Zoey, and Casey slept soundly beneath the lean-to with Tripp. Beside the lean-to, the remainder of the butchered deer was in the process of being smoked inside a shroud of pine boughs built over a makeshift shelf. Beneath the shelf smoldered a fire just large enough to send a constant plume of smoke billowing around the curing meat.

Casey let out a soft yawn and shifted a bit beneath her blankets. A soft mewling came from the newborn tucked beneath the folds. Casey murmured something James could barely hear and both mother and baby were still.

"It's going to be tomorrow, isn't it?" James asked, turning back and staring into the dancing flames. He glanced at the pile of logs stacked at the edge of the woods. There were more than enough logs now to build the shelter that would protect them through the winter. It wouldn't be much work to add space enough for two more . . . "I can tell just by the way you're acting that you're ready to go," he said without looking at Bryar.

Carl sat up as if he finally understood what they'd been talking about. "You're leaving?"

"Are we going to go through this again?" Bryar asked, taking a deep breath and releasing a dramatic sigh.

"I'll only make my case one last time," Dad said as Bampy's voice bounced around in the back of his mind, "after that I'll leave you to do what you need to do. Okay?"

Bryar nodded reluctantly, his eyes never leaving the fire. "Okay."

Dad took a deep breath and glanced at Carl before focusing his attention back on Bryar.

"You won't survive a week out there alone," James said, seeing no reason why he shouldn't get right to the point. "You say that you want to follow the river, and that's all well and good, but how do we know it stays fresh? What if there's something in the soil here that . . ." he trailed off, searching in his mind for the right word. "That *purifies* it?"

"We have a can for boiling," Bryar said.

"Okay," James said, pulling his legs back and folding them in front of him. He leaned forward. "But what about food?"

"We can set traps as far as the water stays fresh," Bryar said. "All I ask is that you send us along with some of your twine. I'll gladly trade you something for it. Beyond that, we'll find a way. We know how to survive, James."

"What about the militias? You ran north to escape them. What makes you think you won't run into another group?"

Bryar finally looked up and their gazes locked. Bryar's expression fell into a look of immense sorrow, though the stubborn line of his jaw didn't soften. He picked up the charred stick lying close to the fire and poked at the coals. "I don't want to have to deal with militias again, James. I don't want to have to deal with any part of that world anymore. If I have it my way, we'll find a place just like this somewhere up north. A place of our own."

"That makes no sense," James said, trying his best to hide his frustration. "We have all this space here—"

"Why do you *care*?" Bryar demanded, giving the coals a vicious shove that sent sparks crackling into the star-lit sky. "Why won't you just let us go?"

"Partly, because there's no need, and mostly because it's not who we are," James said, feeling like grabbing the stick from Bryar's hand and smacking him in the head with it.

"You deserve this place," Bryar said, lowering his voice. "I won't stay here as a constant reminder of how you nearly had to compromise your personal integrity. You deserve a life of peace and solace . . . alone."

For a moment, nothing could be heard but the popping of coals and the sputtering of fat hitting the fire.

"You're a good man, Bryar," James finally said, reaching up and rotating the spit so what was left of the meat didn't burn. He studied Bryar, his anger fading until nothing remained but the despair burning in his chest. Nothing he could say would change this stubborn man's mind. "You really should give yourself more credit."

Bryar shook his head. "You've no idea the things I've done." He glanced Carl, then back at the fire. "And I'll not get into them here."

Carl looked as if he were about to voice an argument of his own, but he closed his mouth and sank back down against his backpack. He whistled and Tripp's ears lifted. He saw the meat in Carl's hand, trotted over and took the venison gently in his teeth, then turned around and trotted back to his bed.

"You'll at least let me send you along with some supplies," James said, breaking the silence after a few minutes. "I don't need anything in return."

"Thank you," Bryar said. "Just some twine. We'll do just fine with that."

"Load up with as much of that meat as you can carry," James said, gesturing at the makeshift smokehouse.

"Thanks again," Bryar said.

James rose to his feet and walked over to his backpack beside the lean-to. Unzipping the top flap, he dug around inside and found the twine. He immediately began to wind it around his hand, making dozens and dozens of passes before stopping and severing the line with his knife. Walking back over to Bryar, he slid the twine over his palm and fingers and held it out. Bryar reached up and took hold, but James didn't let go.

"At least promise me that you'll turn back if you don't find a place," he said, his voice almost a whisper. He let go of the twine, but didn't break eye contact.

Bryar nodded, stuffed the twine into his backpack, and turned his attention back to the fire.

James studied the man's hunched shoulders and partly bowed head, then did as his father had taught him.

He let go.

CARL WAS STARTLED awake, looking around wildly for the ferocious coyote he'd just seen stalking him. His hands tightened on the rifle as he tried to catch his breath and get a hold on reality.

There was no coyote. Just darkness and the smoldering remains of the fire that he had been tasked with maintaining.

You dozed off, you idiot, he thought, *and here you were supposed to be on watch.*

He stood, tossed another log on the campfire, and walked back to the curing fire that had been built beneath the racks of deer meat. He slung the rifle over his shoulder as he reached the makeshift smoker and used both hands to lift some of the pine branches away. The smoking process had been going on for more than sixteen hours, and as he reached out and pinched the nearest cut between his thumb and index fingers, he nodded happily to himself at the rubbery texture and consistency.

It was nearly done—as far as he could tell.

He replaced the pine boughs, moved sideways to the next set of shelves, lifted a few pine boughs and checked the meat. He repeated the procedure, finding all of the groups at about the same state of readiness—with the exception of the final bunch. It wasn't that the meat wasn't ready. All of the meat on the last set of shelves was missing.

Carl pulled the rifle from his shoulder and spun around. Maybe that coyote hadn't been a dream, after all. The moon had set hours ago and he peered into the darkness surrounding their camp, struggling to see by the weak light of the stars.

If the coyotes had been here, they were long gone.

Carl lowered the rifle. Something was missing. Something besides the meat. He squinted at the lean-to, picking out the slumbering forms of Dad and Mom, Dad on his back, Mom's head resting on his chest. Beside them, Zoey lay curled up with Tripp, who lay on his back, all four paws sticking up into the air.

Carl's heart sank.

Bryar and Casey were gone.

A sense of loss hit him in the stomach as he gazed along the edge of the water to where the grass ended at the forest trail, enshrouded in blackness. The breeze blew lightly through the trees, gently tousling the leaves and needles and suddenly making the world seem even emptier.

They must have been worried that Dad would try to talk them out of it, he thought. Either that or they didn't want to suffer through a teary goodbye.

Carl swallowed the lump in his throat, surprised at how tight a bond they had formed with the pair. They had been together for less than a week, yet he felt as though he'd known them for a lifetime. Perhaps it was the debunking of the idea that all outsiders were inherently evil, completely devoid of decent human values. Perhaps it was the fact that Carl had identified with their plight in a way. He struggled to come to some kind of conclusion and failed, deciding that he would more than likely just have to let it go.

He thought for a moment about waking Dad, but quickly decided against it. There was nothing that could be done about the Perkins' disappearance. Not now, not in the morning, not ever. A part of him clung to the hope that they might return, that they wouldn't find any suitable sources of food or shelter as they moved along the river. He gazed at the still water of Ben Gile Pond. The night-black water reflected the sparkling heavens so magnificently he was afraid—for a moment—that he might be dreaming, that it all might disappear just like the coyote.

That's when he realized that all any of them could do was hope. Hope for their survival during the long winter ahead. Hope that their new life at Ben Gile Pond would go unnoticed by outsiders during the coming years. Hope that their health and their love for one another would keep them strong no matter what the future held. After all, hope had delivered them to their new home and hope had carried them through their ordeal with Ma' Lee and Brett Perkins.

Carl moved back to the fire and seated himself once again. He grabbed a log as long his arm and twice as thick from the stack beside the fire and placed it on the smoldering coals. Before long the dried wood caught fire and he let the warmth soak into his bones. He sighed and thought about Bryar and Casey and the new baby—still unnamed as far as he knew—as he gazed back out at the mirror that was Ben Gile Pond. He stared at the small peninsula where they were going to build their cabin, then studied the patch of soil to the left of the peninsula where the southern part of the stream flowed off through the forest. Mom would make her garden there the following spring, a garden that would grow green beans and tomatoes and all kinds of other vegetables.

Finally, he turned and gazed back at his family, at those who mattered most to him, who had made him the man he was and would continue to give him strength as he moved further into adulthood.

Though his thoughts would return to Bryar and Casey over the coming days and weeks, in that moment he was able to focus himself exclusively on the people who had been the only constant in his life and would stay as such for decades to come. Smiling, he picked up the empty pot sitting beside the fire and rose to his feet, then stepped around the crackling flames and walked quietly down to the edge of Ben Gile Pond. There, he scooped up a potful of fresh water, sending ripples that trembled the stars across the pond's surface.

ACKNOWLEDGEMENTS

As always, I must first thank my wife, Dina. Nobody in this world is a bigger cheerleader for my work. When I'm composing, she takes ten pages at a time and burns through them, giving me insightful feedback every step of the way. During the research phase of this novel we hiked out to the very real Ben Gile Pond, guided by my brother, Ryan, and entered through a bog on the north side. Dina almost lost a shoe in that muck as she struggled to get out. I gained certain ideas.

Second I must thank my aforementioned brother, Ryan. He's my best friend in the world and the only guy woodsy enough to help me pull this novel off. He was the leader of our research expedition, and even though he unintentionally subjected us to that harrowing bog experience, he taught me all kinds of things about the woods of Maine, including the edible nature of cattail roots. I love you, brother!

Sam Dunbar was also instrumental in this book's evolution. Always the first person to read and give a light edit when I produce a second draft, his eyes were the third pair to see *Fresh Water from Ben Gile Pond* and his pencil was the first one other than my own to mark it up. In addition to catching the typos I missed, he joined Dina in providing the feedback that would complete the manuscript for my editor.

And, speaking of my editor, I must give a huge thank you to Louisa Swann. This was our first project together, and certainly will not be our last. She wasn't afraid to slather me up in red in order to make this book as perfect as possible. Her professionalism and meticulous attention to detail make her an asset to Lucky Bat Books and a treasure to the literary world.

Glennis, Jock, and Bly from Two Sons Automotive must also be mentioned here. A lot of this novel was composed in their waiting room while I waited for oil changes every month (I drive a lot). We enjoy much more than a client/customer relationship, though. Glennis is always sending me clippings from newspapers of local literary events and chatting me up on the like while I'm waiting for my car. They've supported my writing since I released my first ebook, and I can't thank them enough!

Lastly, I want to thank my parents Melanie and Raney Tromblee. They took draft two of this book with them on vacation and both read it in seven days. Feedback was all positive—as it usually is from parents—even though they had to spend their vacation reading about beatings and incest. Among the handful of people who read my work prior to its release, they are easily two of the most faithful. I love you guys and can't thank you enough for all of the things you do for me.

There are too many more to count, but here are the ones who stand out: Cedric Wilford, Dick & Sheila Yorke, Virginia Yorke, Jeff & Cheryl Greenfield, Jeff Wilford, Kristen Gustavsen, Brittany Tromblee, Emma Sinden, Morgan Tromblee, Vickie Wacek, Erin, Tim & Cecelia Sullivan, Brenda Lewis, Jed Power, Joe Foster, Paul & Nancy Mann, Rosaleen Moore, Tina Leikam, Tripp the Lawnmower, Commander Black, Cynthia Luckadoo, Meredith Griswold, Nate Dufresne, Dave & Erika Vargas, Daniel Fernando David, Brad Goodale, Zach & Bevin Smith, Justin & Lauren Cummings, Gary Rooney, Lorri Gagnon, Cindy Chase, Jim Smith, Monica Blake, Jeremiah Johnson, all the Yorkes and Wilfords and Bonillas and Portillos and Sullivans and Dufresnes and Gustavsens and Beals and Goodales and Valenzuelas and Valemblays in my life, everyone at Lucky Bat Books, and everyone at Red Door Title (just for the hell of it).

. . . oh, and Stephen King. You messed me up properly, sir.

ABOUT THE AUTHOR

Earl Yorke is a Novelist and Network Analyst to over 80 companies in Maine and New Hampshire. His hobbies include reading and running. His obsessions include his cat, Commander Black, the rock group The Dandy Warhols, and collecting rare vinyl. He also enjoys exploring the delightfully tasty world of craft beer. He currently lives in Eliot, Maine with his wife, Dina and son, Cedric.